Kelven's Riddle

Kelven's Riddle

The Mountain At The Middle Of The World

Daniel T Hylton

2007

Kelven's Riddle

For my parents,

And for my little buddy, James

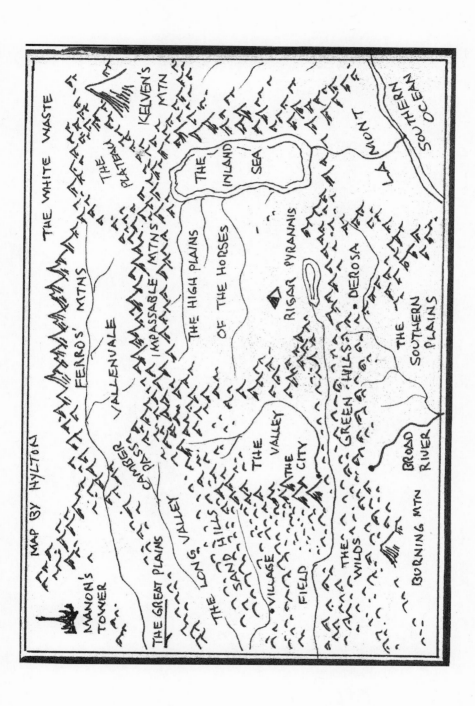

He comes from the west and arises in the east,
Tall and strong, fierce as a storm upon the plain.
He ascends the height to put his hand among the stars
And wield the sword of heaven.
Master of wolves, Friend of horses,
He is a Prince of men and a walking flame.

-Kelven's Riddle, an ancient saying among the horses, though they ascribe its origin to an older, and higher, source.

I

The column of dust appeared in the north, moving above the flat, cold horizon an hour after sunrise. It grew steadily larger throughout the morning as the instrument of its creation advanced southward along the road. Aram was at work in his assigned field west of the village and saw it come. He knew whose dust it was. It could be no one else, for only they were allowed use of the roads—though usually they came to his village at the end of summer, not in winter. The last time they'd come in winter, people he cared about had died.

By midmorning the cloud of dust had grown into a massive gray stain against the pale blue of the winter sky. Clearly, it was the product of a long and ponderous caravan. As it approached the village just before midday, Aram ceased working and stood still, watching it overspread the sky. Trouble surely came with it; the only thing to be determined was the extent of that trouble and whether it would touch him directly.

In the next field over, Aram's friend Decius had spent the morning clearing willow shoots from an irrigation channel and watching the ominous cloud expand out of the north with growing alarm. He, too, knew who it was that came down the road beneath it, and the possibilities suggested by their coming filled him with dread. Finally, as the dust and its attendant travelers neared the village, he could stand it no more. He dropped his shovel, hopped the drainage ditch, and sprinted across the frozen field to be near Aram.

Decius was a year younger than Aram, short and stout, and possessed an uneasy round face framed by hair so faintly yellow it appeared white in the crisp light of the winter sun. He had a compact pug nose, and a rounded chin. In fact, for someone who'd never known the simple expedient of a proper diet, Decius was remarkably round and solid. His eyes, as blue as the sky above him, were open windows to his inner state. On this day those small circular apertures were filled with apprehension.

In contrast to his friend, Aram was tall and lean, and the features of his face were sharply defined, almost severe. Green eyes with flecks of gray at their edges, like bits of granite showing through a growth of moss, were set under straight, black brows and maintained a serious expression in their depths even on those rare occasions when he smiled. His hair was dark like the rich earth under his boots. Against that hair, his face, though tanned by a life lived entirely outdoors, looked pale as steel.

Decius nodded anxiously toward the massive blotch defiling the cool blue of the winter sky. "Who do you suppose that is, then?"

"You know who it is, Decius." Aram answered shortly and he scowled at the blotted atmosphere as he leaned on the handle of the hoe he'd been using to separate willow roots from their tenacious grip in the frozen earth. "Overseers. Who else would it be?"

"But why would they come at this time of year?" Decius' blue eyes were rounder than usual and there was a current of raw fear in his voice that sounded as if it might easily dissolve into terror.

Aram reached out and briefly put a hand on the younger man's shoulder. He spoke more gently. "Courage, my friend. It likely has nothing to do with us. They're probably just here to sort through the new crop of girls." His eyes narrowed and grew hard, his features stiffened, and the gentleness left his voice. "They've done that before, you know."

Normally, the overseers came to the village once a year, in autumn, to collect the harvest. Seldom—almost never—did they visit in the waning days of winter. The people of Aram's village knew from experience that their masters' purposes, never benign, could be particularly malicious when they came at odd times.

The caravan halted on the road beyond the village just as the winter sun reached its apex. The two men gazed across the frozen fields in silence, unmoving, waiting for some sign of the overseers' intentions. Probably, as Aram suspected, they had come merely to look over the young women. They did that from time to time, like dogs scrounging for scraps far from their master's table. If that were the reason for their appearance, it could not touch him. There was no woman in the village now—of any age—that mattered especially to him.

It had not always been so.

Five years before, in the winter when he turned eighteen, the overseers had come and had decided to take his younger sister, Maelee, who was slender and pretty, with hair that shone like gold in the sun. Aram resisted them and they beat him to the edge of death. But since he was young and strong with years of labor in his muscle and sinew, they did not kill him. As punishment for his rebellion, they slew his aged parents instead.

As he'd recovered from the beating, and mourned the loss of his parents and younger sister, the rebellion in his heart took root, grew and hardened. Over time, it had developed into an iron determination to escape the chains of his servitude and find freedom somewhere out in the world beyond the fields. In fact, it was his intention to put that determination into action at the end of this very winter.

Remnants of the dust cloud were still drifting in the air above the village when the bell tolled in the square, summoning the workers in from the fields. Aram straightened his back and treated his friend to a grim smile.

"Looks like they've come for something more than a few morsels of flesh." He said. He swung his hoe in a high, sweeping arc and drove the metal bit into the soil. "Come on, Decius, we'd better go see what our beloved masters want of us."

Decius looked up at his friend sharply. Aram often said things like that, in a proud and sarcastic tone, words of contempt for those that ruled them. He was different from other men and seemed to Decius to have little capacity for fear. With his high forehead, clear green eyes and straight nose, Aram looked more like a nobleman—albeit a ragged one—than the slave, and son of slaves, that he really was.

Decius, of course, had no idea what nobility would look like. Humanity had not been allowed to produce such a thing for thousands of years, since the coming of the tyranny of Manon Carnarven, the great and grim lord of the world. There were stories that told of the ancient times, before Manon, when men and women of greatness and power walked the earth and were recognized as such. But those days, if indeed they ever existed, had passed long ago into the dim realm of myth. Still, tales of those times persisted, related with grave insistence by old men and women in the solemn quiet of evening.

Manon had managed to oppress almost everything that was good and decent and significant out of the race of men, but not the old legends. Though vulgarized by time, they had survived in the way such things always do—passed from fathers to sons, and mothers to daughters, across the centuries for countless generations, time out of mind. Aram seldom exhibited much interest in them but Decius loved hearing stories of the old world and he often thought that his tall, fierce friend looked like a remnant of those ancient days.

The incident with Aram's sister and parents had been deliberately played out for the benefit of the entire village, an object lesson in the futility of resistance. Decius, however, had taken a lesson from it different than the one intended. No one had ever stood up to the overseers before—until Aram. He'd done it and though severely beaten, had survived a direct confrontation with his masters. So when he spoke of them with contempt, it frightened Decius but it gave him a secret thrill as well.

They left their tools in the field and headed northeast toward the village. The sun was at its late winter zenith, low in the southern arc of the sky, halfway between the vast, level horizons, east and west. As he strode across the fields, Aram's tall shadow pointed due north toward the distant dwelling place of the lord of the world, in whose interests the overseers acted.

As the world went away in all directions from these fields, it was flat. And except for staccato bursts of red willow along the drainage ditches and the clump of drab huts that defined the village, it was also featureless. Somewhere out beyond the cold fields there was more to the world than endless plots of level farmland, but it was all very far away and Aram had never seen it.

Few of the people of his village had seen much of the world beyond the fields. Most, like him, had seen none of it. Their lives were entailed to the soil, bound to small plots of earth by the chains of servitude. Travel beyond the limited and prescribed paths of their existence was forbidden and was punishable by death. The people of Aram's village, like those of all the villages of the plains, were forced to expend their labor and their lives in submission to the grim lord of the earth and in ignorance of the broader world.

But knowledge, like groundwater, tends to seep and get collected, and moves from place to place by whatever means it will. And even if that knowledge is corrupted by the passage of distance and time, it still has value to anyone who will listen to it and sort it out. Aram was such a man. Whenever anyone that might have knowledge of the world beyond the fields—however limited—spoke of such things, he sat silent and paid attention.

Far away to the north, it was said, in a broad valley set between restless, smoking mountains, there was a great tower. It was the seat of government for him who was named Manon Carnarven, who ruled the world. He'd come down from the stars in fury long ago, in an age lost in the deeps of time, bringing death and chains and darkness of soul and mind. With

4

him came his terrible lieutenants, the lashers, vile and monstrous creatures that affected the reach of his power throughout all the land.

Eastward, far beyond the plains, were mountains, some of them tall enough to pierce the firmament, with rugged peaks silvered by ice and snow. To the south was a broad, deep ocean verged with cities of trade. And to the west lay a vast marsh, dank and endless, which only a few had entered and none had traversed, for out of it came the rumor of things more terrible even than the lashers, the rumor of things ancient and foul. The water in the ditch at Aram's feet would eventually find its way there where it would remain until the clouds picked it up and brought it back as rain.

But Aram had seen none of these marvels in his twenty-three years. He was a field-tender, the lowest of slaves, and the son of slaves for generations. His life, thus far, had been a relative thing, short in years and long on misery. The field in which he labored was the farthest distance he'd ever been from the hut where he was born.

Except for the overseers who came once a year to collect the crops, the few hundred inhabitants of his village were the only people he'd ever seen. They were all of them like him, born of slaves into slavery, never knowing or having known anything else, wretched segments in an endless, miserable chain.

But Aram was different from his fellows in one essential way; he would not wear his shackles meekly nor did he intend to wear them forever. In fact, in just a few weeks, with the coming of spring, he meant to be free.

As he stepped across the culvert onto the path he looked down to his left at the tangle of willow roots edging the ice-encrusted water. There was something hidden there that he had placed. For weeks now, ever since he'd made his decision to escape, he had saved a portion of each morning's measure of milcush, rolling the small damp grains into a ball and slipping it inside his shirt.

Once in the field, he transferred the ball of meal to a leather sack he kept hidden in the willow roots near the culvert. There it froze and was preserved. When spring came and the nighttime temperatures rose above freezing, he meant to take the cache of food and escape to the west, into the Great Marsh. He meant to be something of which he had no real concept—a free man.

Decius saw his glance and stopped him with a tug on his sleeve. "Aram, I've seen you put that food there. Why do you do that? Are you thinking about running away?" He cast furtive eyes toward the village and then stared up into Aram's somber face. "Can it be done?"

Aram pulled his arm free. "No. No one can escape. No one ever has. You know that, Decius, don't be a fool." But his eyes lifted and narrowed and looked for a moment into the west.

Decius caught that look as well and sucked in a sharp breath. "You're going into the Great Marsh, aren't you? Yes, I know you are. My God, Aram, you're crazy." But then he stopped and looked toward the village and listened for a moment to the tolling of their masters' summons. Fear convulsed across his face and he clutched again at the sleeve of Aram's coat. "When you go, please, let me go with you."

Aram frowned and turned away and continued on toward the ringing bell. "Don't be silly, Decius. The marsh would kill you—it would probably kill me. Nobody's going to try to escape. It's folly. Don't ever talk of such things—not even to me."

With a rough hand, he reached back and grabbed Decius and pushed him along the path before him. "Let's not be the last ones there—there's no point in getting a beating today."

Little was known of the Great Western Marsh except for the thing that interested Aram most; the fact that few went in and none came out. It was a region of such dread that its entrances were not guarded. The rumors generated about it—and of its monstrous inhabitants—were enough to keep the slaves upon its eastern borders out of its swamps and in their chains. A place so desolate, wild, and mysterious that it wrought fear in the hearts of all others was a perfect destination for a man willing to risk much, including life if necessary, to be free. Aram was willing.

Besides, it was the only direction that made logistical sense to his intent. The mountains to the east, according to common knowledge, were hundreds of leagues away, as was the ocean to the south, both too far.

And he could not go north. That way lay the capitol city of the lord of the earth. Lashers slaughtered wayward humans with officially sanctioned impunity, and they patrolled all the roads in that direction. An escape into the marsh was his only real option.

Despite what he'd said to Decius, he turned his head as he walked along the path toward town and gazed back into the west. The marsh was not visible to him at this time of day or from this location, but it was there, a couple of days' journey beyond his sight. From the top of the ladder on the granary in the village square he'd gazed upon it dozens of times. On clear days, at midmorning, it could be easily seen, a dark band of lush green, edging the horizon.

He turned his attention eastward toward town and as he walked, pondered what the overseers' visit might mean for his plans to escape. Maybe, hopefully, nothing. Perhaps they'd come to deliver new farming implements or to change the nature of the crop to be grown in the fields in the coming season. It had occurred before. If that were the case, he would simply have to keep his head meekly down, endure a day or two of instruction, and then the overseers would leave. His plan to escape in the spring would be unaffected.

But then he saw Decius, who was a few steps ahead of him, stop dead at the corner of the granary and begin to visibly tremble. Aram stepped past his friend around the edge of the granary wall and found himself immobilized in fear and wonder at the sight of something he'd never before seen.

There was a lasher in command of the village.

The monster stood motionless on the northern side of the square, a mal-formed and frighteningly large presence of evil intent, like a hideous horned horror from the underearth's deepest, most shadowed chamber. Only its eyes moved, slowly, as it surveyed the ragged cluster of humans that gathered and trembled before it in the small patch of open ground at the center of the village.

Aram stared at the beast with a bizarre mixture of terror, awe, and curiosity. Because he lived in a relatively unimportant part of the world, he had never looked upon one of Manon's lieutenants. In every story he'd ever heard they were described as large, vicious, and hideous, but nothing in his imagination could have envisioned the thing he now saw.

The lasher was huge, larger than he had imagined, and tall, nine or ten feet tall, at least. Its upper body was massive, with leathery skin and a cape of short, matted dark hair. Large ribbed horns, black and burnished, grew out of the top of its head and curved down to either side of its face before turning upward again and ending in razor points, thin and flat like the blades of scythes.

The lasher's enormous hands and feet were gnarled and clawed with dangerous looking talons and its arms and legs were knotted with muscle, but it was in the character of the face that its cruel nature was revealed.

Wide, slatted black eyes stared unblinking from deep hollows in the broad head. The nose was long and hooked like a beak and when it opened its mouth, sharp discolored teeth were exposed. The chin was pointed and was as bald as the top of its head. In one hand it held the multi-thronged whip that gave the species its common name and in the other it held a short straight sword. Aram felt his insides contract and grow cold at the fierce aspect of this terrible servant of the lord of the world.

There were several overseers with the lasher and one of these, an obscenely fat man with sagging eyes and jowls, stepped out and spoke to the assembled villagers.

"Every able-bodied male, aged eighteen to thirty will form up here," he said, and with a wave of his arm he indicated a line running across the front of the square. "All others will move back. *Now.*"

The overseer's sharp command, weighted by the awful presence of the lasher, stimulated immediate obedience. The men of the prescribed ages lined up quickly in front of the group of overseers, Aram and Decius among them. When they had formed up, the lasher went around behind them and moved slowly down the line of men. He stopped behind the fourth man and there was a moment of intense, uncertain silence.

Then, abruptly and with savage force, the lasher kicked the man forward onto his face. Immediately, an overseer was upon the fallen man, tying his hands behind him. The lasher moved on, stopped again and another man went down, like the first, then another, and so the process continued. Every so often, he would stop to consider a man and, less often, dislodge that man viciously from the line. Aram suddenly realized that it was an act of conscription, a drafting of able-bodied men for some unknown purpose.

He felt tepid, foul breath wash down over the back of his head as the lasher stopped behind him. Please, God, no, he thought. In just a week or two, maybe less, the wind would come from the south, bringing the smell of salt air and temperatures warm enough that a fleeing man could sleep outdoors on the open ground. Aram desperately wanted to be that man.

He most certainly did not want to go wherever these conscripts were to be sent. The thing he feared most, right now, was the foiling of his plan to escape. Even if he ultimately lost his life in the marsh, he wanted to make the attempt, to try and live life on his own terms. He wanted to be free.

As the lasher considered him, there was a long terrible moment when time seemed to stop, a moment of awful certainty in which Aram felt his hopes for escape begin to turn to dust and drift away across the heedless earth. He ceased to breathe and inside the tense silence of his head he heard the distant rhythmic thump of his heart.

And then, with sudden, sharp force the breath was slammed from his body and he was impelled to the ground. Before he could regain his breath and get to his feet, his hands were bound behind him and his face was pushed into the dirt. As he gasped against the fierce pain in his upper body, he realized with sickening, utter certainty that he would never recover his cache of food from its place in the willow roots by the culvert and escape across the plains into the marsh. There were other plans made for him.

He looked up but a boot forced his head back to the ground.

"Stay down if you want to keep your brains inside your skull." The fat overseer warned him.

The process of conscription went on, punctuated by grunts of pain as other young men of the village were picked from the lot and kicked to the earth. Then, finally, it was over and there was a long silence followed by the clank of chains. Aram couldn't see what was happening but he knew instinctively what came next. Moments later, his wrists and ankles were locked into shackles and he was yanked to his feet.

There were twelve men, all of them young and strong like Aram, the cream of the village, bound together in two groups of six. Without any further explanation or communication of any kind, they were moved through the town to wagons drawn up on the road outside the village. Hitched to each wagon was a pair of oxen. There were eight wagons in all and the rear doors of two of them were open.

The wagons were shaped like inverted triangles with broad tops and slanted sides that angled inward to a narrow floor that consisted of a single walk board running along the bottom from back to front. The sloping walls were made of thick planks with gaps between them. Six of the gaps, three on each side, were quite wide. There was a pipe running along the top of the wagon's interior with six secondary conduits extending from it, three off to one side of the wagon and three to the other.

Before the men were loaded, an overseer went around with a long knife and cut the clothing from their bodies, stripping each man of everything but his boots. Though the day had warmed a bit with the promise of spring, the air was still vicious on Aram's exposed flesh. It happened that he was the last man loaded into the first of the wagons and he was chained opposite Decius.

Decius met Aram's eyes with a look of sheer terror and opened his mouth to speak, but Aram silenced him with a shake of his head. It would not be wise to gain the lasher's special attention or incur its wrath. The door was closed and a bolt was thrown. Outside, an eerie quiet fell over the village. No one spoke and the villagers stood motionless as the process of loading the men into the other wagon was accomplished.

The reason for the six wide gaps between the planked sides of the wagons became immediately apparent. Each man was chained to the side in such a way that his legs straddled one of the gaps in the planks. Over the course of a long journey the gaps would allow the men to take care of necessary personal business without the overseers having to loose their prisoners and remove them from the wagons. It was an efficient, if degrading, system.

When the door was shut, even though it was a bright morning, the wagon's interior fell into gloom. The angled sides were slatted, but the broad tops were solid and the net result was that no light found its way directly inside. Views of the outside were limited to narrow vertical strips in the planking between the bodies of the men chained opposite.

Aram stared out though the narrow slats at the only place in his life he'd known as home. Everything had happened so quickly, there had been no time to have any reaction to the turn of events. Now, helpless, being carted away to an unknown destination for unknown reasons, he wished that he'd taken his chances and run for the marsh when he first saw the dust appear over the horizon that morning. Considering that thought at length, however, he knew it to be utterly foolish. As soon as his absence was discovered, the lasher would have run him down with ease and slain him without mercy.

He would have to endure the unfolding of events and when his destiny was made plain, consider starting over again under new circumstances. Perhaps, and this was likely, they were being transported to another village where there was a need for more workers. It would take time to build up his cache again but maybe, in the new place, there would be a better chance for escape. With luck, it might even be nearer the marsh.

There was the snapping of whips and shouts from the drivers and with a jolt, the wagon began to move. But not toward the west and the marsh. Instead, they went east. The sun had slid past noontime and was angling westward. The wagons turned away from the declining sun and went toward the place of its rising. As they rolled away, the sounds of sorrow and loss erupted from the village and a single woman's voice lifted in a mournful wail above the rest. Aram wondered who it was that realized she'd just seen the last of her husband, her brother, or perhaps her son.

His feet were shackled into stirrups connected to an angled standing board and for a while he was grateful because this allowed him to push with his legs and take some of the stress off his naked upper body. But the constant jouncing of the wagon on the rutted road soon began to bruise his heels and arches even through the thick soles of his boots. He was obliged to alternately rest his feet while his torso was banged against the planks, then shift as much of the punishment as he could to his legs. This routine would soon become an exercise in agony that would last for more than six weeks and extend across eight hundred miles.

He looked across at Decius. The shorter man was responding to the grim pounding in the same manner. He met Aram's gaze and gasped.

"Where are they taking us, Aram?"

Aram shifted his weight again and answered through gritted teeth. "How would I know? To the east, at least for the moment. They're probably in need of workers somewhere."

The man to Decius' right, in the middle, a lean, hook-nosed man with large ears who was called Flinneran, looked at Aram with frightened eyes. "Maybe they're going to kill us."

"No." Aram said shortly. "They would have done that at the village. They need us for something else. Now both of you leave me alone."

All through the rest of that miserable first day the wagons went east. Through the slats, Aram watched the shadows cast by the wagon change on the ground as the sun fell away behind them. About an hour before sundown, without warning, a stream of water suddenly poured from the conduit in front of his face. It was shockingly cold and before he deduced that it was meant for him to drink, the flow stopped. He'd missed his ration. Fortunately, the day had remained cool, and he didn't suffer much from the loss of the water.

But he was hungry. The men were given no food throughout the whole of that afternoon, however, nor was there any indication of when that particular need would be addressed. As the day waned away, and Aram tried vainly to find a way to dilute the punishment to his body, the wagons continued trundling relentlessly eastward.

Just after sundown while it was still twilight, they stopped on the road. The door at the rear opened and an overseer stepped up onto the walk board. He lengthened the chain on one hand of every man so as to give some freedom of movement and then shoved a small wooden bowl and spoon into the other.

"Eat it all, boys," he said. "That's all you get 'til tomorrow night. Drop your bowl through the slat when you're done. Try not to piss on it afterward. And no talking."

The stuff in the bowl was salty, cold, and chewy, and tasted of something pungent and raw that Aram had never encountered. It was awful, but since it would keep him alive, he managed to get it down. As soon as the last man's bowl dropped, the utensils were collected, a short stream of cold water spewed from the pipe and they heard the steps of the overseer walking away. Aram was ready for the water this time. Though his muscles were rigid with cold, he was thirsty, especially after the salty gruel.

The day was now completely gone and it was clear that the wagons had stopped for the night and that the men would remain chained inside. Realizing this, Aram leaned his head back against the side of the wagon, closed his eyes, and tried to relax.

The bruising inflicted on his body during the day allowed for nothing but intermittent, fitful sleep, and the bitter chill of the night gnawed at his fingers and toes like a sharp-toothed, hungry dog. Some of the men began to moan in sleepless agony and Aram found it difficult to refrain from joining in the miserable chorus. After a few hours, he was alarmed to realize his fingers and toes were growing numb from the cold. To ward off that danger, he began a regimen of moving all parts of his body throughout the night. As badly as he needed sleep, the insidious cold was a greater danger to his welfare, so he forgot about sleep and concentrated on keeping the most vulnerable parts of his body alive.

At dawn, the wagons began moving again and again that day they went east. As the sun ascended, the day grew substantially warmer and Aram was ready for the spurt of water from the pipe long before it came. About mid-afternoon, the wagons stopped for a while and there was the sound of activity. When they eventually moved on, once again there arose the mournful cries of loss and anguish. Other wagons had been filled with human cargo. More men had been conscripted for whatever lay ahead.

Several days went by with more stops at other villages, and all the time the wagons trended generally eastward. In the midst of his increasing misery, which now included daily bouts with thirst because of the warming temperatures, Aram knew that his plan of escaping into the marsh was utterly lost. At least a hundred miles or more of open farmland had been put between him and the Great Marsh. It would be far too great a distance for any escape attempt.

Partly to distract himself from his agony, he turned his thoughts to the mountains, which in every tale lay to the east. Would their final destination, he wondered, be near enough to the mountains to render those highlands a viable goal for an escape attempt? Or were they only going further out onto the plains where his dream of a flight to freedom would be destroyed by the presence of endless level ground in all directions?

Fortunately, they weren't going north toward the capitol where there would be no possibility of escaping into a wild place. But Aram's relief at that thought was necessarily tempered by the fact that he had no real idea of the true geography of the world. For all he knew they might be heading straight into Manon's stronghold. Only time would tell whether the stories he'd heard of the world's cartography bore any resemblance to reality. In the meantime, the wagon train rolled purposefully on with its load of increasingly miserable cargo.

The days grew warmer, but the nights were still very cold and sickness eventually set in. The insidious mixture of constant exposure to the nighttime chill, the forced immobility, and scant rations of food served in filthy dishes began to take its toll. Every man endured fits of fever, diarrhea, and vomiting. The close air inside the wagon became sickeningly pungent and those that weren't already ill were induced into that state by the pervasive smell. At suppertime, the overseer kept his face covered with a cloth when he brought in the bowls.

Decius began to sleep for increasingly long periods of time, hanging unconscious in his chains while his body was beaten mercilessly by the jouncing of the wagon. Ignoring the proscription on talking, Aram would periodically wake him and keep him engaged for as long as possible in pointless conversation. Inevitably, however, Decius would drift off again and as Aram's own condition worsened, his ability to worry over Decius waned as well.

The man two places to Aram's left, at the front of the wagon, seemed to suffer more than the rest. He moaned continuously, and kept few of his meals down. Most mornings found him covered in the regurgitated contents of his stomach. The time came when he was too weak to hold his evening bowl or feed himself. For a time, the overseer tried to feed him, but the terrible conditions persisting inside the wagon forced him to give up the effort.

One day about the middle of the sixth week after the wagon train left his village, the wagons began to ascend a slight incline and Aram could see through the slats that the ground had become uneven. There were mounds of grassy earth with protrusions of rock, and small hills blotched with patches of brush. Later that day, he began to see scattered trees, and even rougher, rockier ground that angled upward and obscured the sky.

With a sudden thrill that momentarily neutralized his pain, he realized that they were entering the region of mountains. They gained altitude all that day and the road became rougher as it wound through the corrugations in the hills. When they stopped for the night the wind came down the slopes and it was colder than it had been down on the plains, but the overseers gathered wood and started fires near the wagons to keep the men warm.

The next morning, before it was fully light, the wagons began to move up the bumpy grade. The sun was still behind the mountains to the east and the air was chill. Aram's body was stiff from the cold and the unending abuse inflicted by being bounced around in his shackles and against the hard planking. But there was more abuse to come as the oxen strained to pull the wagons up the steep, rutted, rocky road. In the morning twilight, he could hear the drivers cursing their oxen, and the animals grunting and wheezing with exertion. By grinding his teeth and tensing all his muscles against the horrible jolting, Aram barely managed to keep from groaning in pain like some of the other men. Finally, after about an hour of rugged, painful travel, the track leveled out and they rolled in a nearly straight line along a smoother course.

When it grew light enough to see through the slats, Aram gazed out upon rolling hills covered in long grass cut by ravines full of trees. Here and there were outcroppings of gray rock. And there were animals. Birds fluttered above the thicketed trees and small furry beasts scurried in the grasses. He could see little from his slatted viewpoint, but the landscape visible through those slats was the most interesting thing he'd seen in his life.

If there could be any pleasure found in being chained naked to the inside of a stinking wagon and transported to an unknown destination, then the next few days revealed it. For the better part of a week the wagon train traveled over relatively smooth roads through increasingly pleasant country. The days were warm, though the nights were still cold enough to be something of a torment. But there was a marked improvement in the quality of their food. Supper now consisted of ground meal soaked in a kind of sweet milky sauce. If Aram had not been shackled inside the foul, cramped hell of the wagon he would have been delighted by this novel treat.

His wounds and contusions, imparted to him by the thick planks of the wagon, began to grow callused as the level of abuse slackened and the toughening of his body assuaged some of the misery he'd endured for the last several weeks. He began to feel well enough to ponder the reason for his transport. Judging by the generally unimproved nature of the roads they traveled, they were not getting nearer to any major cities; indeed they seemed to be entering into a wild region. Aram didn't know what this meant but it planted in him the seeds of hope. Perhaps the long miserable transportation he'd endured would, in the end, be a blessing on his efforts to escape his bonds.

He was chained on the left or north side of the wagon as it went eastward which meant that his view through the slats was to the south. In that direction the ground rose away from the road in a long slope, punctuated by dry, sandy watercourses. The watercourses appeared to run under the road, which probably meant that there was a sort of valley behind him but he couldn't turn his head around far enough to verify if such was the case.

For four days more they went along the slopes of the hills although the direction of travel had changed slightly. The sun, which had usually come up over the front of the wagon, was now coming up obliquely opposite Aram. This meant that the tangent of their travel was aligned somewhat to the north of due east. The daily regimen of water twice and food once at evening had not been altered, except for the marked change in the quality of the food. It was by far the best he'd ever eaten. This puzzled him but there was nothing within his limited horizons to explain the reasons for it. He settled for being grateful.

About mid-afternoon on the fourth day of the seventh week, the caravan crossed a narrow bridge, turned to the southeast and went up along the north side of a steep-walled canyon through which ran a substantial stream. Out the slats, Aram could see tumbling water verged by tall slim trees with needle-like leaves and branches that swept downward close to their trunks. Later he would learn that these trees were conifers, pine, fir and spruce. When he caught a glimpse of the stream, it was clean and clear, frothing its way among smooth boulders to settle occasionally in deep pools. Cool breezes filled the canyon with a sweetly pungent scent.

After a couple of hours, the caravan came out of the narrow canyon into a small circular valley surrounded by rumpled hills with conifers clustered in the hollows of the slopes. Growing out on the open hillsides were intermittent large patches of blue-gray brush. The floor of the small valley was level and open except for stands of tall broadleaf trees over against the hills. The wagon train made a wide loop around the valley before stopping near a grove of these trees.

When all the wagons were halted, the overseer, who'd not spoken since the first day's instructions, and had forbidden the men to speak to each other, appeared at the door to pass out the evening's meal.

"What do you think, boys?" he said, and his face bore a tired, sinister grin that exposed stained, gapped teeth. "Here's your new home, and now that you're here, I can go back to my old one. Good luck with your new friends."

Aram was overjoyed that at last they'd be getting out of the dark and filthy interior of the wagon, but the overseer made no move to release them.

"You know what to do with the bowls," he said. "It's been anything but a pleasure dragging your sorry asses to this godforsaken place." With that he locked them in for the night.

In the morning, it was a lasher that flung the door open and then a foul-looking, bald and skinny overseer with a pinched nose and small, dark, flinty eyes entered and unshackled the men from the wagon's interior. When the overseer finished turning the locks, the lasher grabbed the chain and jerked the men roughly from the wagon.

Because of their extended imprisonment, and the damage done to their feet, none could stand easily. Aram, however, instinctively knew that to remain on the ground was to invite punishment. He got to his feet quickly, standing as tall as his cramped muscles would allow, and yanked Decius upward as well. His instincts proved to be correct. The skinny overseer set about kicking any man who remained prone.

It was discovered then that the man who'd been at the front of the wagon on Aram's side was near death. The overseer examined him while the lasher looked on. When the overseer stood and shook his head, the horned monster drew his sword, pushed the point into the man's neck and sawed his head from his body. It was a sudden, stunning reminder of the men's true status.

Aram was horrified by the casualness with which the deed was done but there was worse to come. The man from his wagon wasn't the only casualty. Of the forty-two men in the other wagons, two were in such bad condition that they were killed as well, in the same cavalier manner, and three had already died somewhere en route, their rotting bodies hauled along without regard to decency or the welfare of their fellow travelers.

And there was another ominous surprise. Somewhere during the trip, two more lashers had joined the caravan. After the slaughter of the weak and diseased, the three monsters moved off to one side and watched disinterestedly as the overseers disposed of the bodies and set about organizing the surviving slaves. Aram was one of the first to be positioned in line and was left alone while the others were being sorted, so he took the opportunity to survey his surroundings. To him, a man who'd never seen anything but flat ground, it was astonishing.

The wagons had been drawn up in a circle on the eastern side of the small valley near some tall trees with broad, pale green leaves. Surrounding the valley were high hills broken here and there by rocky outcroppings and indented with wooded hollows. Besides the mouth of the canyon, which was behind him on his right, the line of hills was broken in two places, once in the northeast, which was to his left and in another place on his right to the south.

There was the sound of water from behind him and though he did not dare turn and look, Aram gathered that the stream that tumbled westward down the canyon was there and issued from the gap in the hills to the northeast. A dirt road led through the gap in the hills to the south beyond which there was a glimpse of more open country, larger than this valley, and at some distance beyond that, more hills.

At the eastern extremity of the valley, over against the base of the hills, there was a long, low structure made of stone. Its outer wall was punctuated every few feet by rectangular doorways, fifty or more, more than enough to accommodate all the men in the transport. Aram realized that he was looking at his new home.

II

After being numbered, the men were unchained and directed toward the long, low building set against the hills. As they stumbled along, Aram looked through the gap to the south and saw that beyond there was indeed a large, wide-open area bounded in the distance by more hills, higher and rockier. Because the valley where the wagon train had stopped was quite small, barely more than thirty or forty acres, it occurred to him that the road leading southward through the gap probably lead to the new fields of his labor.

Between the wagons and the low building, four newly set posts marked the corners of a rectangular assembling area. On the eastern edge of the assembling area, next to the building with all the doors, a water tank stood on stilts with showers protruding from beneath it. The men were marched through the cascading water four abreast and were allowed to stand in the stream for a few minutes and scrub their bodies clean of the grime of nearly seven weeks' transport.

After all had passed through the showers, they were led toward to their new housing. Once there, they were ordered to stand facing the assembling ground while each man was assigned to housing and then they were fed. Afterwards, clothing was brought, roughly sized to each man, and two sets each were distributed. They were allowed to dress and every man was given a bag of wheat-meal and a small pot containing the sweet sauce, which they were allowed to put away inside their huts.

These were no more than individual cells, six or seven feet wide by eight feet deep with no windows, the only point of ingress and egress being the narrow door opening onto the assembling area. The single item of furniture consisted of a sleeping mat placed on the floor at the rear of each hut. When they had finished dressing into their new clothes the men were again ordered to line up and the wiry overseer addressed them. He held a short whip similar to that used by the lashers and he flicked it against his leg as he spoke.

"You have been brought here, to the very edge of the civilized world, to open up new ground and make it produce for the glory of His Magnificence, Manon the Great, lord of the world, and for the benefit of his loyal subjects everywhere. His choosing of you for this task should be a cause for pride. You will take your instructions from me, but you will be governed by your masters who will be ever present." Here, the overseer glanced briefly down and his small, narrow eyes slid in the direction of the massive lashers standing a little to his left behind him. "If you do well, you will not only be allowed to live, but will, in time, be given women to help share your beds and your burdens. If you do not do well, you will most certainly die. And it will not be a quick or pleasant death."

As he was speaking the wagons out in the valley turned and began to move away down the canyon. The drivers put the whip to the teams of oxen in obvious desire to quit the lonely outpost among the hills. The men watched them leave with a variety of emotions. Aram was certain that his feelings were quite different from all those around him. The overseer's words "edge of the civilized world" reverberated through the secret chambers of his mind like the ringing of a clear bell of hope, promising a chance at liberty.

With a snap of his whip, the scowling overseer regained their attention.

"You will find that I will not be ignored. Slaves you are and slaves you will always be. Only the strength in your arms and legs gives you any value. I'm sure this has been satisfactorily demonstrated by the fate of those men who could not properly endure the journey to this place. Remember that lesson always. Your masters," again his eyes darted down and to the left, "have graciously decided that you will not go to the fields today. I suggest you go into your huts and rest, for tomorrow you *will* work."

Aram was grateful for the respite. It was now just early afternoon and would be several hours before the sun dropped below the hills to the west, allowing for a long, much-needed rest. Feeling a curious pang of emotion, he stopped for a moment in the doorway and looked to the west.

Beyond those hills, far away, a thousand leagues or more across the plains, milcush was no doubt sprouting in the sodden fields of his youth and his cache of food had long since rotted. Very likely, he would never see those fields again in the course of his life. He went into the hut and without undressing laid his battered body down on the woven mat on the floor. Despite everything, he was asleep in minutes.

The ringing of a gong awoke him early in the morning. He went outside and found the stump of an old tree to one side of his doorway. Sitting on it he ate his first breakfast in more than a month while across the canyon to the west and north the hillsides began to color with the sunrise. The huge bodies of the lashers moved about in the morning gloom, shadowy and sinister.

A half-hour after the ringing of the gong, the overseer lined the men up and they marched along the road through the gap in the hills to the south. It was a cool morning and Aram's muscles were stiff but he was anxious to get to the fields and survey his new surroundings for the possibility of escape. This new place was wilder and perhaps more dangerous, but it might also allow for a better opportunity to flee. Throughout the long miserable transport from the plains, Aram had firmly decided one thing; within the year he would either be a free man or a dead one but he would no longer be a slave.

They marched south out of the dim canyon into the northern fringe of a long, broad valley that sloped gently from east to west, encircled by hills. To the east, on their left, beyond a long upward slope that ended, far away, in a mottled jumble of black foothills, the massive ramparts of a dark mountain blocked the body of the rising sun. Before them, to the south, the valley sloped gently away toward a line of rocky, steep-sided hills, and there was the sound of rushing water in that direction. On their right, towards the west, a half-mile or so from where the road entered into it, the valley floor merged with low, grassy uplands tufted with scattered stands of brush.

Across the valley, in the pale light of early morning, Aram could see the white froth of tumbling water. There was a river, or at least a fair-sized stream on the valley's southern border, scouring the base of the steep ridge of hills as it rushed westward toward the convergence of that rocky spine with the gentler hills on the west.

The ridge on the north that separated the field from their sleeping quarters ran generally east and west. As this ridge ran to the west, its steep contours broke and crumbled gradually into rounded and rumpled hills and merged with the grass and brush covered uplands. As it ran the other way, eastward, it became rather more sharply defined, almost like a dike, driving into and eventually being swallowed up by the broad rocky slope that rose toward the massive bulk of the distant mountain.

That broad eastern slope fanned out as it rose toward the foothills below the mountain and was strewn with rock and patches of brush. It gained height gradually and must have spanned a distance of twenty or thirty miles before it touched the distant foothills. The river flowing along the southern edge of the valley issued from somewhere in the region to the south of that slope.

The valley that the men would turn into fields was about twice as long, east to west, as it was wide, north to south. Tall grass, rooted in rich black soil, covered the valley floor. All the arable ground in the valley, three or four hundred acres more or less, was marked into square sections by stakes driven into the ground and connected by lengths of twine. Each square looked to be about an acre or so in size.

Shovels were stacked neatly at the end of the road and these were handed out. Each man was directed to a plot of earth containing several squares marked by the stakes and instructed to begin turning the soil. Aram was given a plot at the far southeastern corner of the valley near the river where the grasses were intermingled with low brush at the base of the eastern slope.

Because he was assigned to the extreme southeastern part of the field, Aram found himself laboring under the cold black eyes of a lasher. The three enormous lords had positioned themselves at the corners of the valley, one at the corner where Aram worked, one over on the northeast at the juncture of the separating ridge and the eastern slope, and the other at the gap where the stream exited to the southwest. The skinny overseer was stationed at the northwest, near where the road entered the valley.

It seemed evident that escape, something that was not considered a possibility for slaves out on the plains, had been considered here. But as the morning lengthened and the work got organized, Aram noticed that the lasher spent most of its time watching the ground out beyond the perimeter. It soon became apparent to Aram that its efforts were directed more toward preventing something coming in out of the wild than stopping the slaves from escaping into it. He wondered what could be present in the countryside round about that required the size and strength and ferocity of a lasher to prevent its killing or capturing the slaves or otherwise hindering the work in the fields. And he wondered what that might mean for his plans to escape into the wild.

He was glad that his body was strong and had remained in reasonably good condition during the long transport from the plains. He'd regained a good bit of his health during the last week of the journey. And now, after just one night sleeping on a normal bed, his strength was remarkably improved. By the end of the first day's work, he'd made serious in-roads into his plot of ground and the lasher had taken more interest in his neighboring workers than in him. Until he knew a bit more about his new surroundings and had a solid plan for escaping, he intended to exhibit meekness and to mind his work.

Decius had been assigned to a group of plots just behind him and slightly further into the field. Over the course of the next week, as Aram worked that way, he intruded as far as he dared into the smaller man's area in an effort to help him keep the pace and avoid punishment. Decius had suffered terribly during the transport from the plains, but with Aram's surreptitious help gradually began to recover his strength.

As the days passed firmly into spring, Aram finished turning one plot after another. He kept his head down at all times when he was in the field, but often his eyes were turned outward toward the surrounding landscape. Whenever he was faced away from the lasher, he studied the countryside as he worked, especially to the east, south, and west. To the north was the low rocky ridge through which the road led back to the sleeping quarters. Aram rarely saw much of the country to the north of the small valley where they slept because it was usually dark when the workers left the assembly area in the morning and always fully dark when they returned at night. As a consequence he took no interest in the region to the north.

To the west the northern ridge converged with the gentle grass and brush covered hills that rose slightly higher as they trailed away. In that direction, far to the west, Aram knew that those hills eventually submerged themselves in the flat soil of the great plains. He soon lost interest in that direction as well, as it led back to more populated areas.

On the southern border of the field there was the river, wearing away at the base of the rocky spine of hills. On most days, it was a gentle gurgle of sound, a pleasant aural backdrop to the backbreaking work of the day. After a hard rain, however, it would roar and then, if he looked in that direction, Aram could see a roiling muddy current. The river would be impossible to cross during any of its flood stages, but even when it wasn't flooded it was an impressive stream and would be a formidable barrier. So it was to the east that his hopes lay, and it was in that direction that Aram looked the most.

The broad valley that he was helping to transform into rich farm-land rose gently toward the east until it became lost in the broad slope that supported, here and there, patches of stubby gray brush. As the slope rose away toward the jumbled foothills at the base of the distant black mountain, it grew gradually rougher and rockier and there were areas of piled rock where nothing grew. These outcroppings were odd; it was as if rock had poured directly out of holes in the ground like a liquid and then hardened into rough globules. To Aram it looked rather like a giant had probed the ground with a huge pike, grubbing randomly in the earth as he crisscrossed the area.

Further east as the slope gained height toward the foothills; it was punctured here and there by tall spires of jagged stone, like the magnificent ruins of abandoned towers. Eventually, the slope merged with the distant foothills which were themselves but minor precursors to the great broad-topped mountain rising beyond. Aram could not begin to guess the distance up the ramparts of the mountain to its summit regions, but it was vast; the many black and broken peaks seemed to plumb the very depths of the sky.

The immense bulk of the mountain fascinated him. Whenever he could raise his eyes without drawing the attention of the watchful lasher, he gazed at it. At its southern extremity, the mountain broke off rather sharply and fell away out of his view. Aram wondered if the same stream that marked the southern border of his valley flowed out of the regions beneath that broken edge of the mountain.

Back the other way the mountain rose ever higher as it ran to the north until its black massiveness was lost behind the eastern heights of the rocky ridge that separated the field from the sleeping quarters. Day after day, Aram stared out at the vast expanse of country between his field and that distant mountain, trying to spot the places where a running man might quickly get out of view of anyone in the valley.

Problems between the lashers and some of the men soon developed. Those men that had not borne the rigors of the transport well began to lag behind in the amount of work they produced. Stronger men like Aram were able to turn the soil quickly, but as planting time approached, one of the lashers, the one that guarded the northeast corner, began to abuse the slower workers in his area. At first it was just a rude kick or shove from a clawed hand that put a man in the dirt, but as the plowing of the field neared completion, the abuse grew more severe, and the lasher would occasionally use his whip. One day, in a fit of irritation, he swung his sword and slew a man.

This action brought the other lashers charging to the scene of the slaughter. The skinny overseer came running as well, his face red with anger and his dagger drawn. It was his neck that was at risk if the new field did not produce its expected quota. The three lashers came together in an explosion of fierce sounds, cursing ferociously and gesturing angrily with their whips though there was no actual physical contact. Work ceased as everyone in the field stopped to watch the tableau unfold.

As the argument raged, the lasher who'd killed the worker suddenly spun and swung his sword at the overseer. Fortunately for the little man, he'd stopped just beyond the reach of his overlords. But the action intensified the conflict between the lashers. Swords came out, threatening deadly force against the one who'd done the killing and as if he knew he'd crossed a line that should not be crossed; he retreated, dark and sullen.

Aram knew nothing of the seniority that governed the ranks of the overlords. One of them was larger but he couldn't tell if that attribute imparted any real sense of superiority. But from the incident there sprang the seed of an idea. If lasher society was not monolithic and serious disagreements could occur within their ranks, then this incident would probably not be the last. Here, beyond the outskirts of civilization, there would very likely be more—and perhaps more serious—incidents. Aram would lie low, do his work, stay out of the line of fire, and plan anew. And he would make the southeastern corner of the field his own plot of earth. There he would work every day until the opportunity came.

Since, at the first, he'd been assigned to the far southeastern corner of the field he thought it should appear a natural thing for him to work that area as his rightful place. Every day, head down, he went to that corner and worked the ground there where the river issued from the wilderness and ran along the south side of the valley. When it came time to plant, he planted there; when weeds sprouted and the natural grass tried to re-assert itself among the wheat, he took his hoe and fought the necessary vigorous battles in that part of the valley. Working hard and diligently, he slowly but surely enlarged his area of responsibility until he was virtually alone in that part of the field. Eventually, he was generally ignored and the lasher that guarded that corner of the valley spent most of his time walking the perimeter and gazing out at the eastern slope.

Because of the constant presence of the overlord, Aram realized that starting a cache of food as he'd done before was impossible. Besides, there was really no good place to store a cache. There were ample rocks and brush in the virgin ground just beyond the edges of the field but that area was separated from the field by a strip of no-man's-land. From the first they'd been instructed to leave a wide swath of bare ground around the whole of the field into which no one but the lashers could go. A lasher was always within sprinting distance of Aram's corner and any excursion beyond the prescribed borders would result in an instant death.

He contented himself with studying the lay of the ground beyond the fields while he worked. The river that ran along the southern border did not come straight out of the eastern slope. A few hundred yards beyond the extreme southeastern corner of the field there was a break between the ridge on the south and the broad slope where the stream rushed into the valley at a nearly right angle from south to north. Colliding with the last rocky vestiges of the slope, it was then forced back to the west where it ran between the new field and the base of the ridge as it flowed westward.

If an opportunity was presented and Aram could dart across that section of ground between the field's corner and the opening of the canyon from whence the stream came, it was possible that he could get into the canyon and be out of sight of the field within minutes. Whenever he could, he studied that ground, trying to get to know every outcropping of rock, every clump of brush between him and the near bank of the stream where it turned the corner. The ridge to the south was effectively ended at that point and the long slope formed the eastern bank of the river as it went out of sight. Whatever lay beyond that point he would have to deal with as it came, if he ever got the chance to run.

One day, when he lifted his eyes to study the ground beyond the field, he froze in astonishment. Standing in plain view among the brush and rocks just beyond the eastern edge of the field was a tall figure dressed in dark clothing, looking directly at him. A deep, black hood hid the figure's face, but there was no doubt—he was staring at Aram.

While he gazed at this apparition in wonder, forgetting his work, he found his view suddenly blocked by the enormous bulk of the lasher. Startled, he looked up into the cold black discs of the monster's eyes and the hideous, massive face framed by sharp, shiny horns. The flat black discs gazed down at him without expression.

"Why do you come to this part of the field everyday, little man?" The lasher's voice was cold and harsh and rumbled like low thunder.

Aram averted his eyes downward and stood very still as he stared at the bright green blades of new wheat pushing through the earth. Deep in his chest he felt the thrumming of the increased tempo of his heart. He swallowed and gave his answer. "Because this is where I was sent on the first day."

With vicious suddenness, Aram was seized by his neck and lifted from the earth. Instantly, he was in agony. His breath was cut off and he could feel his heart straining to pump blood to his head. The pain was intense and grew at an alarming rate. He dropped his hoe and tried desperately to insert his fingers between the great clawed hand and his throat in an attempt to regain his breath and lessen the horrible sudden weight that his body was exerting on his neck. The lasher pulled Aram close to his face and loosened his grip slightly. Aram gasped for air and inhaled hot putrid breath. The leathery skin of the lasher's face contracted in a malevolent grin.

"Do you think perhaps you will escape into the hills, little man? Let me tell you, you should try. There are wolves in this country, fierce servants of my great master. If they catch you they will tear your flesh to ribbons. They will feast on your bones while you yet live."

Aram recoiled at both the content and the delivery of this statement but managed to suck in enough air to croak out a respectful answer. "I was sent to work here at the first. If my lord wishes me to labor elsewhere he need but send me."

There was a halo of red growing at the edges of his vision and he felt the deep well of unconsciousness opening below him. His plunge into that darkness was imminent. Then, with a snort of disgust, the lasher dropped him and moved off to patrol the perimeter. Aram lay recovering his strength for as long as he dared and then, careful not to look around, he got to his feet, raised his hoe with shaking hands and quivering arms and went back to work.

When he dared, he glanced back out at the edge of the slope but the strange figure was gone and no one else seemed to have noticed him, not the other workers or the lashers. Perplexed, he wondered if he'd hallucinated. But that didn't seem reasonable—he had not been sick recently and it wasn't a particularly hot day. There was nothing to explain the vision and the mysterious figure never reappeared. But at least the lasher had not ordered him to another part of the field.

As the wheat grew taller and the days longer, Aram grew increasingly impatient. He'd grown strong from the amount of work he'd forced himself to do. He was a model slave and as a consequence, except for the one incident, he was left pretty much alone. But the lasher, though he'd shown no further interest in Aram, was always patrolling the perimeter nearby. The one that had precipitated the earlier incident in the northeast corner of the field now guarded the southwest corner where the river left the valley. Aram suffered the anguish of guilt for wishing that someone in that area would lag in his duties enough to precipitate another distracting incident.

He never talked to Decius of his desire to escape for fear that the younger man would want to come with him. It would be difficult enough to manage an unseen exit from the field without having a second person to worry about. Further, escape into and survival in the surrounding wilderness would be dangerous enough for a man as strong as Aram, let alone someone less hardy. And there was the very real likelihood that such an attempt would fail anyway, that the lashers would catch them, and Aram did not want to be responsible for Decius' death.

The wheat grew taller, spring began to warm toward summer, and Aram's desire to escape devolved into anxiety as the year slipped away and week after week went by without opportunity. Finally, in a spasm of frustration, he decided to consider the option of making a bold daylight run and began to surreptitiously watch the lasher's movements for signs of a pattern he could exploit. But nothing came of it. The lasher was always nearby, and always alert.

Then, one afternoon in late spring, a terrible thunderstorm arose in the foothills to the east, piling its dark masses high and obscuring the mountain. It rumbled and flashed as it overspread the whole breadth of the eastern slope. Suddenly, like a beast loosed from its leash, it crashed down the slope and roared across the valley. Lightning sizzled on the ridges round about as thunder rolled back and forth. The dark clouds opened up and rain poured down in a flood. The deep loam of the valley floor quickly became unworkable. Aram looked up to see the lasher striding his way, motioning for him and the other workers to quit the field and make for the road.

Just then a bolt of white-hot power exploded into the earth a few yards away, blinding Aram and knocking him to the ground. When he found his feet again, the lasher was standing over him, bellowing at him to get back to the road; then the overlord strode away to the north to empty the other workers from the field. In moments he was lost in the driving torrent of rain.

Aram stood gazing after him only a moment before the years of pent-up yearning erupted inside him. Without further thought, he turned and sprinted out of the field toward the southeast. In a few strides he was among the brush and rocks. Then, though he was nearly blinded by the downpour, he started to run as fast as his legs would move, for with the action he'd just taken there came a sudden rush of great fear. Now that he'd actually turned his fiercest desire into action, he felt his guts recoil inside him in a paroxysm of sheer terror.

If the lasher had seen him bolt, he would be dead shortly. If the rain lessened before he could round the corner out of sight or if it stopped so that his flight was seen, he would certainly be caught and killed. But he'd cast the die and there was nothing to do but run. He was already well out of the field and if he went back; if he was discovered coming in out of the brush, there would be no questions asked of him. He would be slain.

But the rain did not stop. If anything, it came down more heavily. Aram was running blind and grew so afraid of losing his direction in the sodden gloom that he angled to the right and made for the river. In the terrific downpour, he almost ran into the churning water, sliding to a scrambling halt just in time. Finding the river and avoiding a plunge into its current, he had his bearings, so he turned upstream and ran alongside it. Navigating the rocky slope and brush-covered ground was more difficult than he'd anticipated. Any misstep and he might twist an ankle and ruin the progress of his flight. Then suddenly the stream angled sharply to the right. He'd reached the corner and was into the canyon. And he was still alive.

There was smooth, bare rock at the river's edge where the current dug into the flank of the slope and scoured away the soil whenever the level of the water was high. With the amount of rain falling from the sky, the river would likely be over this rock in a few minutes, so he made the most of it, pushing the muscles in his legs to the limit. But even as he ran he could see the water level rising. Finally, he was forced off the smooth rock by the growing flood and back out among the grass and brush of the slope. And still the rain pelted down. He was thoroughly soaked by this time, his clothes weighed on him and his boots had become large clumps of muddy hindrance.

Then the river angled sharply back to the left, toward the east, and the wall of the canyon grew steeper, with slag heaps of rough and tumbled rock between its base and the river's edge. The going became extremely difficult. It was at this point, as he paused for a moment to examine the ground to his front, that he heard the thunk of heavy feet and the sound of hoarse grunts coming from behind him. He swung around in stark fear, expecting to face the fury of a lasher's whip and sword. Instead, he saw a sodden shock of yellow-white hair and the frightened round face of Decius pop up over a boulder.

Somehow, the little man had seen Aram's exit from the field, discerned its meaning, and followed him. In a brief moment of time, Aram's emotions ran the gauntlet from fright to anger to disappointment and finally to acceptance. There was no time for recrimination, and now that Decius was here, he couldn't send him away. Quickly, he ran back to the boulder and yanked the smaller man up and over it.

"Stay with me, Decius, and don't look back, whatever happens. Follow as close as you can because I won't stop. Understand?"

Decius blinked his round eyes and nodded breathlessly. Aram glanced down the canyon but saw no sign of pursuit through the driving rain. He clapped Decius on the shoulder and hurried on.

As the river roared along the bottom of the canyon, it tumbled over massive boulders, the detritus of eons of erosion from the canyon walls. The two men were forced to scramble over and around enormous piles of jumbled rocks, among which grew masses of willows with exposed roots that caught at their feet and tripped them again and again. If they hadn't been running for fear of their very lives, Aram would have abandoned this tangent of flight and backtracked, maybe to negotiate the broad slope to the east of the field where running would be easier. But that tack would take them back out into full view of the field. So, instead, he kept doggedly on, though he knew that over such terrain as they now traveled any lasher chasing them would have a marked advantage.

After an exhausting hour of stumbling forward with all the speed he could muster, slowing now and then to help the shorter Decius over particularly rough spots, the rain began to slacken and he could see the way ahead more clearly. It would get no easier. Not only was the canyon becoming rougher, its walls were growing ever higher as it cut its way eastward into the broad slope below the foothills of the great mountain. And the waning of the storm meant that they could be more easily seen by anyone following them.

If their absence was discovered and they were accurately tracked, they would be caught, of that Aram was certain. His only hope was that they'd gone far enough to the east to get past the worst of the storm but that it was still raging over the valley behind them. Certainly there would be some confusion as the overseer sorted the men and counted them. If they were lucky, it would be some time before it was discovered that two of the workers were missing and the trajectory of their flight discerned.

The river was now a roaring flood and Aram and Decius were forced higher up the flank of the canyon into even rougher ground where for centuries the rock had broken from the walls and piled onto the slopes. As he scraped and clawed his way forward, a tiny voice in the back of Aram's mind kept screaming at him to run, but he could not obey. The way forward was barely navigable. It was all he could do to just keep moving. He did his best to ignore the terrified gasping of Decius and the screaming in his own skull and concentrate on making progress up the tangled canyon. Eventually, looking for any advantage, he made his way up the slope to the very base of the sheer walls and found that the rocks piled there were small enough to facilitate somewhat better progress.

Gradually the storm shredded itself into jagged gray clouds and began to die away to the west. The evening sun angled into the canyon through rents in the cloud cover. Aram judged that there were less than two hours until sunset. If they could keep moving and get into the darkness of night without discovery, they could remain high on the slope at the base of the cliff and feel their way forward throughout the night. Aram knew that they needed to put as much distance as they could between themselves and the lashers. Saturated and chilled as they were, with nothing but rock around and no decent-sized patch of level ground, sleep would be impossible anyway.

Freedom was somewhere ahead; if they avoided capture and lived until nightfall, Aram intended to keep them moving toward that goal.

The storm finally dissipated completely and the lowering sun shone in a clear sky. Now Aram suffered the agony of anxiety. If they were being followed, and by now that was probably the case, they could be clearly seen against the backdrop of the canyon wall, scrambling over the loose, jumbled rock at its base. Without looking back, Aram tried to listen for sounds of pursuit behind them in the canyon but heard nothing. He steadfastly resisted the urge to turn and look. To do so would detract from their progress but more importantly, if he looked back and saw lashers on their track, stark fear would derail him.

If by now the lashers were on the hunt, they could certainly make better progress through the ruin of the canyon with their longer and stronger legs, but if the two men had not yet been seen they just needed to stay ahead of the pursuit until dark. Aram knew nothing of a lasher's ability to see at night, but he felt that given the cover of darkness, he could think of some way to avoid capture, even if it meant plunging into the flooded stream and trying to float past their pursuers in the dark water.

The sun sank lower and the canyon began to fall into shadow. And still, he heard nothing behind them. Then quite suddenly, they came out into a narrow valley where the canyon walls curved away on both sides of the river. There were large stands of trees at the base of the slopes that encircled a long, flat, grassy meadow. The river had spilled over its banks to flood most of the valley floor. At the edges of the meadow, mingled with the groves of fir and pine, there were small clusters of slender trees with pale green leaves and white bark. Followed by Decius, Aram descended to the edge of the water and found the going much easier.

At the far end of the valley, the canyon wall on their side of the river closed abruptly inward and the way forward became completely impassable at the scene of an amazing thing. The river had curved against the canyon on that side and ran turbulent and deep along the base of a perpendicular cliff. At the base of this cliff, at the level of the river, there was a wide fissure running back into the rock.

Out of the fissure poured a vast amount of water, equal at least to half the volume of the river with which it mingled in violent fashion. They stared for a moment, astounded by this sight, but Aram knew that they had no time to waste on marvels. For several frantic minutes he explored the cliff for a way ahead or up and over but it was hopeless. The route was blocked and they must either backtrack or find a way across the swollen river.

On the other side of the flooded river, the canyon wall had become less steep and had broadened out into a series of corrugated ridges punctuated here and there by tall spires of rock and ravines filled with trees. Aram peered eastward in the failing light of the day and it looked as if the other side of the canyon was accessible for as far ahead as he could see. In order to keep going eastward, they would have to find a place to cross the swollen river, before dark if possible. Fortunately, the river had spread out over the narrow floor of the valley and as a result, the vigor of the floodwaters was somewhat reduced.

Aram looked at Decius. "Can you swim?"

Decius stared back, breathing heavily with his mouth hanging open, and slowly shook his head.

"Well, that's what we have to do," Aram said bluntly. "We can't stay here and we can't go any further on this side. We must get across. Follow me and do the best you can. If you get into trouble, I probably won't be able to help you but I'll do what I can. Come on."

He'd never swam in the whole course of his existence, but his life and liberty were now at stake, so he plunged into the water and waded toward the far shore. The water was not deep at first, rising to about his knees and he instinctively stayed on a line that would keep him at the upstream end of the valley. As he waded out into the water he glanced down at the far end of the valley, afraid and half-expecting to see lashers making great easy strides toward him, swords at the ready to sever his life. But there was nothing moving against the flat light of the setting sun, and except for the distant call of a hawk, and Decius' hoarse breathing, the evening was silent.

Suddenly Aram's feet slipped off an underwater ledge into nothing and the current had him. He went momentarily under and came up gasping for air and flailing at the water. Frantically, he pulled at the water with his hands and kicked at the flood with his booted feet and was surprised to find that he was making progress despite the weight of his sodden clothing. The current was rapidly washing him toward the lower end of the valley but by thrusting one arm forward and then the other and cupping his hands as he dragged at the water, he drew the other side of the river ever nearer.

Within moments he was through the swiftest part of the current. Then his feet touched bottom and once more he was wading in the thigh-deep water of the flooded meadow. He turned to check on Decius and found that the stocky young man had done almost as well and was chugging determinedly through waist deep water just a few yards downstream.

Jubilantly, they made for dry land and when they'd cleared the water, Aram looked once more down the canyon to the west, then motioned for Decius to follow, turned back to the east and ran on.

Even in the fading light the topography of the south side of the canyon made for good progress. The slope was even less steep than it had appeared and there were wide grassy alluvial fans nearly devoid of rocks. Crossing the ravines was tricky, especially in the gathering darkness, and when he came to one he invariably slowed to help Decius, but his heart was lightened by the fact that at no time did he see or hear evidence of pursuit.

A short way to the east of the flooded narrow valley where they'd crossed the river, Aram angled up the slope in search of a better way across one of the wooded ravines and came across a dim trail leading up the canyon. There was nothing to indicate whether it had been made by humans or by animals but since it made movement easier and more certain in the twilight, he took to the path and he and Decius went on as hard as they could. In less than an hour, however, it was dark, too dark to see and Aram was reduced to feeling for the relative smoothness of the path with his boots.

Throughout the first part of the night he kept going, probing the ground ahead with his feet to determine the course of the path, and whistling low every so often to keep Decius in tow. Eventually, however, he strayed in the darkness and they found themselves in a steep area in a tangle of trees. By this time both men were exhausted. Utterly out of energy and encouraged by the apparent lack of pursuit, they felt around under the trees until each of them found a reasonably level spot blanketed with fallen leaves. Then they dropped wearily to the ground and slept.

III

Aram awoke in the morning stiff from the exertions of the previous day, cold and hungry. The sun had not yet cleared the heights of the mountains to the east and there was mist in the canyon. Decius was asleep. The morning was still with not a breath of wind and he sat quietly for several minutes and listened. There was no sound of anything as large as a lasher moving around anywhere in the dim canyon. Except for one lone eagle tracing wide circles in the air high above the canyon rim to the north, nothing moved in all the world. He got to his feet, rubbing his aching legs, and looked around.

They'd spent the night in a tiny grove of the slim, white-barked trees that grew on a kind of shelf about halfway up the slope. When he could move without cramping, he extricated himself from the growth of trees and eased down the incline. He found the trail they'd been following the previous evening and was surprised at its quality.

It did not appear to have been engineered by human hands, in that no rocks had been moved or any earth disturbed in order to improve it, which suggested that it was made by the frequent use of some kind of animal. It was narrow and worn pretty deep in some spots. There were small hoof prints here and there in the mud and he wondered if it was used by animals similar to the deer he had seen now and again in the fields of his youth. But Aram had little time to examine the matter further; he could only congratulate himself on finding the trail and then put it to use.

He climbed back up to the grove of trees and found Decius sitting up and staring about himself groggily.

"Where are we, Aram?"

"I don't know," Aram answered, and he reached down to help the shorter man to his feet. "But we're certainly not anywhere near where we need to be. The field is only a few miles behind us. We need to get moving, Decius."

With a groan, Decius took the proffered hand and pulled himself up. "I'm hungry," he said.

"Me, too," agreed Aram. "But that will have to wait. They know we're gone by now and they'll be coming. We have to put as much ground as we can behind us. A lasher could easily cover the distance from the field to where we are now in much less time than it took us to get here."

They worked their way back down the slope to the trail and turned east, striding determinedly, but this morning they did not run. They were both still weary from the previous day's exertions and from the lack of food. Sustenance, Aram realized; something he hadn't considered at all on the previous day was going to become a serious problem as they went forward.

Still, they moved along briskly once back on the path. Anxiety over pursuit was still very strong but as the morning wore away, hunger gradually replaced it on Aram's list of priorities. They'd expended massive amounts of energy the day before and somehow would have to replenish it. Food would give them strength and strength would mean more distance.

As they progressed eastward up the canyon and the day brightened, Aram began to study the trees and brush for signs of fruits or berries but had no luck. It was still too early in the year for anything to be bearing fruit but it had advanced too far for there to be any nuts or fruits left from the previous fall. By the time the sun topped the hills to his front and shone on his face he was growing worried. Somehow, he would have to answer their need for food.

The sun seemed to impart a measure of strength to the men's wearied muscles, so for the moment, they pressed resolutely ahead. Every step took them farther from danger and nearer the hope of freedom. The slope of the south side of the canyon across which the path ran gradually moderated and lost some of its rockiness. Plants of all kinds, grasses and brush, grew upon the ridges, and thickening groves of trees filled the ravines. The path became ever easier to navigate. Before another hour passed, they were running again. Aram decided that if this day passed without signs of pursuit, he would devote a good portion of the evening to searching for food. In such a green land as they now passed through they could surely find something that was edible.

Every so often, they stopped to quench their thirst at one of the tiny streams tumbling down the slope toward the river, but they did not rest. Aram was determined to put another day's progress between himself and his former masters. The whole canyon had opened up and was now in fact no longer really a canyon but rather a steep-sided valley through which the river wound in sweeping curves. The flood of the day before had subsided and the river was back within its banks. Across the valley to the northeast the black mass of the great mountain was coming closer, running off to the north at an ever-sharper angle.

That day they progressed several miles up the valley toward the east. The trail wound higher and higher up the hillside until finally they were walking on the very top of the ridge. To the south lay a wide region of grassy ridges and hills and wooded hollows that seemed to go on without end. It was a green country, blessed with trees and plenty of water. Streams gurgled at the bottoms of all the draws, verged by abundant willows. As they went forward throughout that day, Aram often let his gaze wander out over the maze of hills and hollows and several times considered leaving the trail and plunging southward. But he did not. His instincts drove him east.

That afternoon, they found the deer whose kind had made and used the trail. Walking around a bend in the path where it passed out of a stand of evergreens, the men surprised a group of the animals feeding just below the brow of the hill. With short, sharp cries, the deer bounded down through the hollow and disappeared into a thicket of willows.

They were very like the deer Aram had seen once or twice as a boy but larger, and one of them was antlered. He'd heard once that overseers were allowed to kill and eat deer and he wondered how such an animal was to be caught. He'd never hunted or killed, but the growing emptiness in his stomach made him wish desperately that these were skills that he possessed.

About mid-afternoon, they came to a place where the trail quit the ridge entirely and wound away to the south down a hollow that was substantially wooded and had a sizeable stream flowing at its bottom. Aram sat down on a rock and spent several undecided minutes resting on the ridge top pondering the decision whether to turn southward and follow the trail or continue eastward up the valley. Decius collapsed on the grass beside him and lay back, covering his eyes with his hand, his breathing raspy and labored.

Aram glanced down at him. "Are you alright, Decius?"

Decius didn't uncover his eyes and he answered between gasping breaths. "No, Aram. I'm ungodly tired and hungry as hell. I really don't know how much farther I can go."

Aram scowled at his friend. "You're going to have to go a lot farther if you stay with me. I promise we'll find something to eat tonight, even if we have to graze on grass like oxen. But you can rest a few minutes while I decide what to do here."

At that, Decius sat up, resting his stout upper body on his hands. "What do you mean? Decide what?"

"I'm trying to decide what to do about that." He indicated the trail angling away down the hollow toward the south. "The trail turns off here and I'm not sure whether we should follow it or keep going up the canyon."

Decius stared out over the green, timbered country to the south for awhile and then his gaze came back to rest on the trail. "What's to decide? The trail makes for easier walking so we can go a lot farther in less time."

Aram nodded but said nothing and turned his face to look up the long valley to the east. It was true that the trail made for easy walking and carried him quickly away from his old life, but he'd grown fond of the valley as if it were a friend that had been kind to him. Besides, though it was rougher and perhaps harsher than the wooded hollows to the south, it carried him more directly away from his enemies.

Looking backward once more along the way they'd come, he eye fell upon something that decided him. In the dirt of the trail that had been softened by the previous day's rainstorm, there were clear and distinct tracks left by their boots. If there were pursuers behind them, they would need only to discover this trail and they could track him and Decius easily. If they left the trail and went cross-country the task of tracking them would be rendered more difficult.

Aram stood up and pointed up the valley. "We're going that way, Decius."

"Why?" Decius got to his feet and stared at his friend in consternation. "I thought we'd agreed—"

"Look at the mud in the trail, Decius, and tell me what you see."

Decius spun around and stared and he also saw the telltale tracks. His shoulders slumped as understanding came and he turned to follow Aram. "You said that at least we'd get to eat tonight?"

Aram started across the ridge top to the east. "I promise we'll find something."

By late afternoon he felt a measure of confidence that they were winning their freedom with every step they took through this wild country.

Several times throughout that day he gazed carefully back along the valley as they rested. Not once was there any sign of pursuit. He found this fact as curious as it was heartening. Why were they not being followed?

Certainly by last evening their absence had been discovered. Perhaps the severity of the storm had caused some confusion as to what had happened to them. Maybe the lashers had decided that the missing workers had gotten caught in the flood somehow and been washed down the river to the west. Aram liked that thought, he liked the idea that his enemies might think he was dead and that his body lay in the other direction. Whatever the reason, for the whole of that day there was no movement anywhere back along their track.

The lessening of his anxiety about pursuit only sharpened his need for food. Decius was suffering severely from the lack of sustenance and mentioned it every time they stopped to rest. Finally, as the sun began to settle near the horizon, Aram sat down in the grass and decided to consider their options logically. First, he considered their clothing, whether any part of it might be consumable. Finding that to be an utterly impractical consideration, he turned his attention to the grass and plants growing about him on the slope.

There was one type of bunched grass that resembled wheat or milcush, although this early in the year it had not yet made a head, but if it was in the same family then its leaves might contain a measure of nutrition. He pulled a handful of it and carefully chewed. It had a bitter taste, but was full of moisture and it eased some of the agony in his belly. It was, however, very unsatisfying and he doubted it would do much to defray their need for serious nutrition.

He glanced over at Decius. The stout young man was lying flat on his back with his head up the slope and his hand over his eyes. He looked completely spent. Aram studied the hillside and then got to his feet.

"I'll be back in a minute. Stay here, Decius."

Since it was near sunset and they needed to find a place to pass the night anyway, he went into a grove of woods in a hollow of the hillside and examined the trees and the plants that grew there. And then he got lucky. Growing beneath the trees he discovered a small plant with broad leaves and a center stalk of flowers that had a large bulbous root. He dug it out and as he had no means of stewing or heating it simply bit into it like a fruit.

To his surprise and delight, it was fairly tender and had a mild, sweet flavor. He ate it all and then hunted the ground under the trees until he found another, which he carried back to Decius. After they'd supped, they went down into the darkening ravine below the copse of trees and drank from the spring there. Then they went back among the trees, scraped out hollows in the bed of leaves and lay down. Before the stars were bright in the heavens, both men were asleep.

For the next three days they journeyed eastward along the course of the river. On the south side of the stream where they walked the landscape was nearly unchanging, an endless series of undulating hills covered with grass and brush and copses of trees where they often found patches of the plant with the sweet root. Whenever they walked along the very top of the ridge, Aram could see the same green country as always rolling seemingly without end into the south, a pleasant aspect. Often as he gazed southward over the lush hills and hollows, he considered finding a small valley with a clear spring and enough trees to construct a dwelling and settling down to cultivate the root plants that had kept them alive.

In the end—somewhere ahead—they might do exactly that, but for now the anxiety of possible capture remained with him even though there was no evidence that they were being chased. Aram was determined to put a large mass of the wild country between him and his old life so he kept them going resolutely toward the east.

Across the river to the north, the land grew increasingly wild. The crumbled walls of the canyon on that side grew higher and the region above the canyon rim began to angle severely toward the north. They had progressed far enough to the east to be beyond the influence of the long gentle slope he had gazed upon so many times from the confines of the field and had passed the region of jumbled foothills that had once seemed so far away. The huge black mass of the mountain was now almost due north. Wherever the river touched the slopes on its northern bank it tended to carve great amphitheaters out of the steep walls, exposing black rock streaked with shades of deep red.

There were long dark ravines that cut back into the lower flanks of the mountain and these were full of evergreens, tightly packed. The upper ramparts of the mountain were so high and so far away that his eye could resolve very little of their rocky detail. One day when the sun was near its zenith, they rested for a while on a large flat rock and ate some of the sweet root. The great mountain was exactly opposite their position and Aram gazed up at the immense spires of rock and the deep, dark canyons that cut into its sides. It looked like a giant black pyramid with vicious wounds in its flanks. Forests of trees blanketed its lower regions, so thick and dark that they seemed to swallow the sunlight that fell on them, holding its power hostage.

Decius was watching him. "Surely you don't want to go over there?"

Aram laughed. "Why not, it looks wild enough. I'll bet you that if we could get into those deep forests we'd be hard to find. Probably find someplace defensible, too, where we could construct a fortress." Then he looked away toward the east and got to his feet. "But no, I think we'll keep going straight ahead up the canyon."

Over the next two days the mountain fell behind them to the west and vistas of a wide country began to open up beyond it. On the eastern side of the dark mountain, north of the river, there was a broad open land, green and gentle with stands of trees beyond which, at a great distance, rose the gray, snow-covered peaks of more high mountains.

In Aram there grew a desire to enter this region, to put the bulk of the great mountain firmly between him and the world of his former existence. But that meant that they would have to cross the river and at the moment this appeared to be a difficult prospect. The canyon wall on the other side was rough and steep with sharp outcroppings of rock. The river seemed to prefer to run near that far bank, grinding away at the ancient rock while it spared the gentler country on its southern shore.

But the southern country where Aram and Decius walked was becoming rougher as well, and higher. The gentle rolling hills were giving way to steeper, rockier terrain. Most of the trees now were conifers, pine and fir; there were few broad-leafed trees, and the rooted plant that had been their mainstay was becoming scarcer. They often found it necessary to ration their supplies of the root. With the lessening of their anxiety about capture, Decius often grumbled about having bypassed the green southern hills for this rough wilderness.

Several times Aram also considered returning along his steps and finding his way into the rolling hill country to the south but could not bring himself to do so. The wide land to the north was calling him like a siren. Despite the rising frequency and volume of Decius' complaints, he continued resolutely eastward along the south bank of the river but he moved down the slope and traveled near the water for he was actively seeking a way across now.

The great mountain had begun to recede to the west. From the depths of the canyon, its lower slopes were hidden by the heights of the cliffs on the far side but he could still look up and see its highest ramparts towering into the sky. Aram could not help but think that its enormous, rocky mass would make a fine, formidable barrier between the life he'd been born into and the new life of freedom he intended to forge in the wilderness.

Toward evening of the ninth day since their escape, they found a large patch of the plant Decius had named sweetroot and they filled all their pockets. Aram decided to try and discover a flat spot to pass the night. They would continue searching for a place to cross the river on the morrow. He wound up and down the steep rocky slopes and finally came upon an overhanging rock that formed a wide and fairly deep cave, with a flat dirt floor.

He was about to enter and find a place away from the mouth where they could spend the night when the sickening odor of rotted flesh rolled out of the cave and overwhelmed him. It was then that he saw the bones, hundreds of them, scattered about on the floor inside the cave. Some of the bones still had bits of flesh attached but they had all been thoroughly gnawed by sharp teeth. In his shocked mind he saw an image of wild, savage lashers, killing men and consuming them like rats. He was horrified by the imagery and terrified by the reality of the gnawed bones, and he stumbled backward into Decius, nearly causing both of them to fall down the slope into the river.

"What lives in there?" Decius gasped, stupefied with fear as he stared into the darkness with rounded eyes.

Aram spun and grabbed him by the shoulders and pushed him away down the slope. "It doesn't matter, Decius, we've got to get away from here."

Whatever foul thing or things lived in the cave, it was no place for two tired and unarmed men. Quickly he moved down the slope toward the water, intending now to cross the river before night even if they had to swim. But it was a plan that was not only desperate but was impossible to execute. The river was narrow but deep and running very fast, and the other bank was made of perpendicular rock that rose straight out of the river with no purchase for their hands and feet. Even if they were able to get across the quick water and extract themselves from the current they could go nowhere.

For as far as Aram could see in either direction, the opposing canyon walls were vertical for a hundred feet or more above the level of the water. He stared upstream in the failing light for signs of something better but saw nothing. But he knew that they had to get away from the cave. Whatever used it was absent for the moment but would undoubtedly return, the fresh nature of some of the bones signified as much. Aram intended to be as far away from the cave as possible when that occurred.

As long as the light held, they followed the river upstream, hoping to find a passage across. Finally, when it was almost fully dark Aram realized that they had to give up the quest or risk an accidental plunge into the dark, dangerous current. He moved away from the river's edge and searched the ground above for a suitable place to rest and, if possible, to hide. He found an overhanging rock a little way up a watercourse and the two men curled up beneath it. But neither of them could sleep.

Decius was gazing out into the suddenly menacing darkness. "W-what do you think lives in that cave up there, Aram?"

Aram's mind was full of images of monsters, killing and tearing at the flesh of their victims. He slowly realized that the denizens of the cave up the hill were probably not lashers but that realization brought with it its own brand of terror. What other loathsome beasts inhabited these hills?

He knew that Decius needed an answer of some kind or his terror might spiral out of control, endangering them both. "All I know is that it's something we don't want to tangle with, Decius. Don't worry, it's not there now and we'll get away from it across the river first thing in the morning—put the water between it and us. Now, try to rest, my friend."

He thought he knew now why the deer trail had turned south so far back down the ridge. The more he thought about it the more he believed that the bones inside the cave were those of deer. But something big enough to slay a deer could also kill a man, especially an unarmed man. As the night closed in, he prayed that he and Decius would remain undiscovered until they could put the power of the river's current between them and whatever it was that lived in the cave and prowled these hills.

They spent a fitful, frightening night and Aram was pleased when toward morning it began to rain. It was not a downpour like that from a severe storm, but it was steady. It would grant them some cover as they looked for a place to cross the river and enter the country beyond. As soon as there was enough light to enable them to see the far bank, the men went back to the river's edge and continued looking for a way across.

The steady rain continued all morning and as the search for a crossing remained fruitless, added a new dimension to their worries. If it continued to rain and if the storm was widespread over the region drained by the river, they would once again have to deal with a river in flood and that might prevent them from crossing even if they found a place where crossing was possible. Aram moved upstream as quickly as he dared across the slick rock, anxious to find a place to put the river between them and the things that used the cave.

Then they had a bit of luck. There was a place where the canyon widened a bit and a substantial stream bounded down from the southern heights to join its strength to the river. The river curved away just a little from the far shore and flattened out into a series of shallow rapids as it crossed a gravel bar at the bottom of a long pool. The water level was higher than normal due to the constant rain but it appeared manageable nonetheless.

Aram studied the wall of the canyon opposite. There was a flume in that sheer wall where the rock had crumbled away under the influence of a small stream and it looked as if they might be able to climb up through it and access the top of the ridge beyond. He was seized suddenly by the firm conviction that this was their chance—and that it had to be taken. The rain was still coming down steadily so there was no time to lose.

Aram grasped Decius by the forearm and waded into the water. "Stay right with me, Decius, on the upstream side and lean into the current. If it doesn't get too deep and we hang together, we can use our combined strength to keep from being washed away. Hold strong onto my arm."

Decius, who'd been in a state of mute terror since finding the cave, didn't answer but simply grabbed onto Aram's arm and followed him into the water.

The force of the river was strong but the water level rose only to Aram's shins for the first several feet. He took care to remain slightly on the upstream side of the gravel bar. Thankfully the bar was broad and firm. Only at the very center of the river where the current rose up to about the middle of Aram's thigh did they have to struggle, both men leaning hard into the current and for a while it was a doubtful thing.

Thirty or forty feet downstream below the gravel bar, the river narrowed into a series of more powerful rapids and then plunged into a deep hole at the base of the canyon wall. If they lost the fight against the current and were swept into those rapids it would result in a struggle for life and it would be a struggle that they probably could not win.

But then they were through the deepest, swiftest part, and in another ten minutes were wading ashore on the far bank. Immediately Aram made for the cliff in order to find a way to the heights.

The north side of the canyon was almost perpendicular and the flume turned out to be so nearly vertical and so slick from the rain that it was impassable. Distressed, Aram turned upstream. There was about a quarter-mile of canyon wall between the place where they'd crossed and the point upstream where the river curved back. They had to find a way up to the ridge top somewhere along that short strip of sheer rock. If they were unsuccessful, they would have to fight their way back across the current and continue up the eastern side. Aram dreaded that possibility; he feared both the rising strength of the river and the presence of unknown predators on the south shore. But then, at last, he thought he saw a way up.

In one place a little further along; there was a fluted chimney in the canyon wall leading up toward the top. It was narrow and water splashed and tumbled down through it, but the sides were rough and broken with natural hand and foot holds. It would require skills they might not possess to climb up through the chimney but they had to try. Aram stepped into the semi-circular indentation in the cliff and began to examine the walls for the best route upward. Just then there was a strange noise behind them. Decius turned to look and let out a small sound of raw fear. Glancing back toward the river, Aram felt his blood freeze.

The predators had tracked them.

There was a flurry of movement on the far bank where they'd stood just a few minutes before. Huge rangy beasts with straggly black hair and enormous heads with mouths that flashed sharp, yellow-white teeth were sniffing around in the grass at the water's edge. Though he'd never seen their kind before, Aram knew instinctively what they were.

Wolves. Nine or ten of them.

Into his mind rang the words of the lasher—*they will gnaw on your bones while you yet live.* One of the beasts snapped at another that got too near and Aram had a terrifyingly clear glimpse of the long sharp teeth.

Fear gripped him and he grabbed Decius and tried to force him up into the chimney. It was a mistake. In his hurry he dislodged chunks of stone that clamored down the side of the rock and made the wolves look up. They saw the two men. Howling and snapping they plunged into the deeper, slower water above the rapids and began swimming toward them.

With an effort driven by terror, Aram pushed Decius up the rough side of the chimney but Decius, panic-stricken, fought away from him and turned to flee up the bank of the river. Aram grabbed at his shirt.

"No, Decius! We have to climb—you can't outrun them. We have to go up."

Wild-eyed, Decius turned on him and drove his fist into Aram's face, dislodging the hold Aram had on his shirt and knocking him to the ground. Howling in terror, the stocky little man took off running along the riverbank away from the wolves.

Aram leapt to his feet, intent on giving chase to his fear-crazed friend but the eager yelps from the wolves made him hesitate and look toward them. The lead wolf was almost across and its eyes were fixed hungrily on Aram. If he went after Decius, they would both die. Probably, he suddenly realized, they were both going to die anyway.

He turned and jumped into the chimney and scrambled recklessly up the rough passage, trying desperately to get above the reach of the wolves. He climbed like a madman and when he was no more than twenty feet off the ground, he heard snarling and the snapping of teeth immediately below. He glanced down. A wolf was climbing the rock.

Gripping the protrusions in the sides of the chimney with long sharp claws, the wolf was climbing at least as fast as he was. With stark fear crashing over him in waves, Aram willed his arms and legs to even greater effort as he pulled himself toward the top, tearing his flesh as he scrabbled at the rough stone.

Suddenly, from down on the river, there came a long, terrible scream that rose to a sickening pitch and then, just as suddenly, was cut off. The rest of the pack had caught Decius.

Aram felt instant, violent nausea at the thought of what had happened to his friend, but he had no time to grieve. He knew that he had to put all his effort into climbing or the next scream that echoed in the dark canyon would be ripped with vicious teeth from his own throat.

Finally, his hands found the end of the chimney and he reached out and pulled himself up onto the top of the ridge. But there a new and frightening apparition confronted him. Standing before him was the cloaked and hooded figure of a very tall man, his right arm extended, pointing firmly to Aram's left back down the river. A voice exploded inside Aram's head, potent and commanding.

Run. That way.

No sound was uttered by the figure; the voice seemed to come from the depths of Aram's own mind. As he stood dumbfounded, the voice came again, sharp and urgent.

They will kill you. Run. That way.

The figure's arm pointed resolutely to Aram's left, back to the west along the ridge he'd just climbed. Numb with fear, unable to think for himself, he complied. As he ran he glanced to his left toward the river crossing and saw that the entire wolf pack was climbing the cliff. One by one they were bounding into the rough hollow of the rock chimney. Those waiting to ascend howled at him and showed their glistening teeth. Stark fear took him and drove him on.

He saw nothing of the surrounding countryside he'd so longed to explore. He was, in fact, still separated from the broad land that lay to the east of the mountain by yet another deep canyon running parallel to the one out of which he'd just climbed. He ran with desperate speed back to the west, down the narrow top of the ridge, frantically scanning the ground ahead for whatever refuge the unnatural, ghostly figure had directed him toward. He saw nothing to his front but the ridge top growing narrower and narrower and the black mass of the mountainside growing nearer.

On his right, at the bottom of the parallel northern canyon was another fast-moving river, also running to the west. There was now water on either side of him. To his left as he ran westward was the river he'd followed for days and had just crossed. On his right ran another larger river in the same direction. The rain was falling harder and both rivers were flooding. And the path of his flight along the top of the ridge was growing ever narrower even as the mountainside came nearer. Now he could hear the wolves behind him; they'd reached the top of the ridge and were giving chase.

And it appeared as if he was running out of room. A narrow spine of rock, steep and as sharp as the blade of a massive sword, began to rise out of the ridge on his left, slicing upward into the flank of the great mountain, forcing him to the right onto a tiny ledge. He could no longer see the river to his left and he was in imminent danger of falling into the chasm on his right. The snarls and grunts of the wolves grew louder as they strained to catch him.

A horrible suspicion began to grow in his mind that the hooded figure had directed him into a trap. Probably, he thought, the wolves were the minions of the sinister figure and he was being given to them as a prize. As he considered that thought, his fear began to be replaced by rage. Reaching deep inside himself, he put on a desperate burst of speed. They had not caught him yet. The mountainside was close and he could see stands of tall conifers. If the narrow ledge lasted and he made the trees ahead of the wolves, he could shinny up the slick trunks and perhaps put himself out of their reach. If it came to it, and he ran out of time—if the wolves came too near—he would simply hurl himself off the cliff and into the river.

And then, suddenly, any choice he had in the matter was abruptly taken away. The narrow ledge, slick with rain, ended, and he ran straight off into space. As he tumbled through the air, the rain pelted him from all sides, and the growling and the snarls of the wolves on the cliff above were overwhelmed by the approaching sound of the furious floodwaters below. The only thing he could clearly see as he tumbled end over end through the air, getting closer and closer, was a roiling mass of churning river.

IV

There was a moment of very odd silence when he smashed into the water and went under. He felt curiously weightless even as he was pulled down into a muted, distant roaring that completely enveloped him. The air had been knocked from his body and his lungs burned, but he instinctively kept his mouth shut. Wrapped in liquid gloom, he didn't know exactly which way was up. Knowing of nothing else to do, he flailed about with his arms and kicked mightily with his legs. Finally his head broke the surface and he gulped in air and found that he was a bobbing cork in a writhing cauldron.

Looking about to find the bank so that he could make for it, he was stunned to discover that in nearly every direction there were sheer rock walls. The water was churning and spouting in miniature geysers and was carrying him around in a circle. On every side except the narrow defile where the river entered the maelstrom there were slick, sheer walls of smooth rock. He was in a gigantic whirlpool and he was being pulled toward its center.

He fought frantically against the current but there was nowhere to flee even if his efforts were successful, and they were not. The roiling current pulled him to the center of the vortex where the water surged downward in a furious spiral. He felt himself going under and with a last desperate effort filled his lungs with air. Then he went down into a churning, roaring darkness full of things that banged into him and jostled by in a mad rush. There was a moment when he felt almost weightless again and then there was the sudden sensation of intense speed. The flood was carrying him under the earth in rapid fashion.

He was caught in a siphon and it was taking him into the bowels of the earth. In a flash of memory, he recalled the peculiar spring spewing into the river from the fissure in the canyon wall far to the west. If this was the current that was going there, he was doomed. He would never survive such a distance unless there were cavities underground where he could replenish his air. And he knew so little of such things that he had no reason to hope.

There were other bits of flotsam, large and small, that collided with his head and body in the surging water. He was at the mercy of the flood and in constant danger of being brained or having the breath knocked from his body. In order to extend the value of the air in his lungs, he could not risk an energy-consuming struggle with the current but was forced to let the river take him. There was no point in struggling, anyway, in such a torrent. He was probably going to drown, but he was determined to hang onto life as long as possible and hope for a miracle.

Once, he opened his eyes and peered about into the water, a dangerous maneuver in the muddy maelstrom and it availed nothing. It was utterly dark and he could not make out even the simplest of shapes. Every so often his head and body banged against something slick and unyielding. It finally occurred to him that it was the side or perhaps the top of the rock tube through which the siphon flowed.

On and on he went, helpless in the power of the water, until his lungs burned so fiercely that he realized that the end of his struggle was imminent. There was no more virtue in the air contained in his lungs but even so he was loath to let it go. He felt that if he did so, he would yield to the temptation to gasp for more and fill his lungs with water. A sense of detachment slowly began to creep into his consciousness and he knew that the end was near.

As he began to slip into blackness, a thought occurred to him that, oddly enough, pleased him. During the journey across the plains in the wagon he had vowed to himself that before the end of the year he would either be a free man or a dead slave. It now appeared that he would, in fact, die. But he had not been a slave now for more than a week. He would die a free man.

Then a voice broke in upon his thoughts and he recognized it as the voice of the cloaked and hooded figure he'd seen up on the ridge.

Hang on, it said, *you're almost there.*

Suddenly, as in a dream, he felt his head break through the surface of the water into free air. He was certain that it was illusion brought on by the nearness of death, but he was so utterly fatigued that he welcomed it and relinquished the dead air in his lungs and breathed.

He was stunned to discover that instead of the warm shroud of death, he suddenly felt colder and clearer headed. His lungs burned as if they were on fire, but he was breathing real air. He was still charging along at the mercy of the flood but was evidently out of the siphon. As he breathed in good air, his head cleared and he looked around. He was in utter blackness; either that or he had been knocked blind by the many collisions with the rock walls of the siphon.

It gradually occurred to him that not only was his head above water but that the pace of the current was slowing until he was floating along rather gently, as if the stream had opened out and lost a good deal of its impetus. He could feel movement in the air but couldn't be certain whether it was an independent breeze or if the rushing of the water had caused it. He moved his arms and was able to make progress against the slowed current, but which way to go?

All around him was complete and utter darkness. His eyes, for whatever reason, were useless to him. While he moved his arms and kicked his feet, looking around in the blackness for any clue, his feet touched the malleable surface of an underwater gravel bar.

The underwater bar seemed to slope up to his right so he swam in that direction and after a few moments found the water shallow enough that he could stand. He waded carefully about in the dark until he was sure of which way the water grew shallower. Then he moved cautiously in that direction.

While he was still in knee-deep water, he came to a place where the water was suddenly deeper to his front and the gravel bar sloped away sharply. As he stood wondering what to do, he realized that the sound of the rushing water came mostly from behind him and to his right. The main current of the river, then, was to his rear, flowing from the right to the left behind him, which meant that he was moving away from the strength of the underground siphon that had carried him inside the earth and was probably facing a shore somewhere to his front.

The deeper water in front of him was probably a backwater but to be safe, he eased along the top of the bar to his right, feeling his way with his feet, without plunging ahead. The bar angled obliquely to the right for a short distance and then curved slowly back to the left. He waded carefully along it, one step at a time, as the water grew gradually shallower.

Abruptly, he came to the end. His feet were still in about a foot of water when he came up against the face of a vertical rock wall. He reached out and felt for the extent of the wall in all directions. It extended farther than he could reach, up and to either side. He would have to go either to the left or to the right, blindly, completely embraced in darkness.

He eased a bit to his right, but the sound, the deepening water, and the movement in the water confirmed what he'd already suspected—that that way led him back into the river's current. He started back to the left, feeling his way along the wall as the water deepened and the soft mud and gravel sloughed beneath his boots with each step. The water grew deeper as he eased along the smooth face of the rock wall but remained relatively calm. Finally, he was in over his shoulders. But just when he thought he might have to swim, his feet touched a smooth bottom that was hard and level. With just his head above the water he continued to work his way carefully to the left.

The sound of the rushing river ebbed slowly away behind him as he moved cautiously through the deep, still water at the base of the wall. Then his foot came up firmly against something solid as if there was an inside corner in the rock wall. He felt out to the left with his hand but the smooth face of the wall went straight on into the darkness. There was no corner in the wall above the surface of the water. Gingerly he raised his foot up and it came to the top of the underwater impediment.

There was a stepped place in the smooth floor. He stepped up onto it and immediately his probing foot came up against another obstruction. Above that was another. Amazingly, there was a series of underwater steps rising out of the river and they did not feel as if they were a natural occurrence but rather the result of deliberate construction. Although it was difficult to be certain through the thick, sodden leather of his boot, they seemed to be too smooth and too even to be the result of natural forces.

He rotated his body to the left and keeping his right hand firmly on the vertical wall of rock, carefully climbed the underwater steps. Slowly but surely, he walked up out of the water. In the complete darkness, he knelt down and crawled up the evenly cut steps on his hands and knees, careful to stay near the wall. A blind, but careful examination of the surfaces with his hands told him that the steps were not natural but that, in fact, someone had made them. Finally, after twenty or thirty steps which brought him several feet above and away from the river, he came to a smooth level place.

Exhausted from his exertions in the siphon and the mad charge along the ridge, he lay on his back on the smooth rock and rested. His heart was pounding in his chest and it seemed to him that the sound of it was booming out and echoing in the darkness.

Lying there, enjoying his first respite in several terrible hours, he grieved for Decius and found that he blamed himself. Decius had not been forced or even encouraged to come along but even so, the decisions Aram had made had helped bring about the horrible end of his friend. He suffered the pangs of terrible guilt for being thankful that the intensity of the day's events and the sudden, bizarre change from rainy afternoon to utter, subterranean night made Decius' death seem distant and unreal.

Remembering the voice he'd heard while he was under the water, he sat up and looked around. In all directions, it was impenetrably black. If the tall man were present he would not be able to see him anyway. He stood up and stepped back to lean against the wall and faced the darkness.

"Hello," he said aloud and waited. All he heard, several seconds later, was his own voice bouncing back to him off distant unseen surfaces. Judging by the time that it took the echo to return, he surmised that he was standing in a very large chamber.

"Hello." He said again and again there was nothing but the echo of his own voice. If the strange person from the ridge had somehow accompanied him underground, that person was not responding. After thinking about it for awhile, Aram decided that he had imagined it. Almost certainly, he'd imagined the underwater voice and owing to the extreme duress he'd been under, probably the cloaked figure on the top of the ridge as well.

Unable to see anything, and finding balance a difficult thing to maintain in utter darkness, he went back down upon his hands and knees and made several forays away from the rock wall across the level platform and returned. The platform seemed to be large and broad, and the steps went away from the wall farther than he cared to explore without the advantage of sight.

Staying by the vertical wall and keeping one hand upon it, he got to his feet and moved away from the sound of the stream across the broad floor of smooth rock. After several minutes, he came to a corner in the stone. Another vertical wall went away from the one he'd been following at a ninety-degree angle to the left. Cautiously, he moved along this new wall, negotiating the unseen floor with careful steps.

He came to another corner a little way along but this one turned inward to the right. Easing around the corner, Aram discovered that there were more steps leading upward along this wall. He was uncertain as to what to do. He wasn't sure that he wanted to abandon the river just yet.

Following it to its egress from the mountain might be his only certain escape from the depths of the earth.

Before deciding whether to climb up or go back down, he eased across the steps in the dark and about ten feet away came to another wall of vertical stone, this one angling upward exactly opposite the other. So there were steps leading upward between two vertical walls of stone. Uncertain of what he should do and unnerved by the lack of sight, he sat down on the bottom step and gazed into the darkness in blind indecision. *Where was he?*

What if he was not underground at all? Perhaps he'd been blinded by one of the many blows to his head he'd suffered in the maelstrom and he was even now sitting out in the open, exposed to other's eyes even as he was helpless. But he rejected that thought—it *felt* like he was underground. The cool, damp air and the complete lack of environmental sounds other than that of the stream as well as the absence of outdoor sensations—like wind or rain—convinced him that he was under the earth.

And that deepened the mystery. Who had built stone steps and platforms here inside the darkness of the mountain? Was it his mysterious hooded friend? If the spectral figure was real and not just a figment of Aram's imagination, where was he and why didn't he show himself?

Then, staring into the utter gloom around him, he finally saw something—just a small thing—that brought him great relief. He was certain that he was not, in fact, blind. For if he looked toward the river and gazed slightly left toward the loudest part, he could see a faint, tiny glow, clearly shimmering with the movement of water. The siphon had seemed hideously long when he was caught in its power but evidently it was no so long as to completely exclude all light from the world outside.

He was obviously in some kind of underground cavity where there was evidence of intelligent construction. The river had siphoned him into the guts of the mountain. And though the steps cut into the rock seemed to be proportioned for a man's foot, he couldn't help but wonder what thing lived here under the earth in the dark. What kind of danger was he in now, and how could he know when that danger was near?

Pondering that question, he felt his insides tighten in fear. If he were attacked, especially if the attack was launched in silence, he would be utterly defenseless. He stood up. Action was much better than inaction and doing something would help to defray his anxiety.

As much as he hated to abandon the familiar landmark of the river, the risks inherent in negotiating its deep current or even finding his way along its banks in the subterranean blackness made him decide that he must. Besides, if this was the stream that he and Decius had seen erupting from the rock into the river to the west—and he felt certain that it was—that point of outflow was three or four days away at least when moving above ground in the daylight. In the darkness beneath the earth, it would be an impossible distance.

There seemed to be no other intelligent choice but to climb up the steps into the regions above, wherever that led. Certainly the sun and the open sky were somewhere above him so it made sense, since he had steps cut into the stone to guide him, to go up.

Returning to the wall at the right side of the steps, he ascended them one by one carefully. Eventually, his hand discovered the top of the wall as he climbed and in a few more steps he'd left it behind. With nothing to support him vertically, he dropped to his hands and knees and negotiated a few more steps until he came to another level place. Remaining on his hands and knees, he eased out across the open space.

Shrouded in darkness he did not know if he should, or even could, go straight, but there was nothing else to do. If there were any light ahead of him, or a way out of the mountain, he believed that it would be above him, so he would keep going up if he could discover more steps, or lacking that, sideways to the right. Since he'd come in from that direction, it made sense that the edge of the mountain would be nearest there.

After what seemed a long time he bumped up against another vertical wall of stone. He hoped rather than knew that he'd gone straight. He eased along the wall to the right and came to a right angle turning back to the right. This he didn't want because it would force him to backtrack and by listening carefully he could still hear the river running below him in that direction. He went back to the left and after a while found another stairway of stone indenting this wall and leading up. So after checking the width of the passage and finding it delineated by a wall on the other side as well, he went up.

This stairway was narrower than the one that had brought him to this level, only about eight feet wide. Again as he climbed he stayed near the right hand wall. When this wall abruptly fell away from him he assumed that he'd come to another level open area. But as he eased his foot that way it came into contact with nothing. Kneeling down, he felt along the edge of the step. The wall of stone had gone and he felt only rough rock angling away from the stairway. The steps along this part seemed to have been carved from a natural slope of rock that was pitted with holes. He would have to be careful to remain on the steps and not stray.

For several hours he worked his way up the stone stairway on his hands and knees. As his amazement at the novelty of his situation ebbed, and his fear eased as he remained unmolested in the sinister darkness, he began to be hungry. His knees were sore and he was tired. The sweetroot in his pockets had been turned to mush by his ordeal in the siphon, but he decided that he should consume whatever nutrition the soggy mess still contained before it became completely inedible. Sitting on the stairway in the dark he ate all but a small piece of the mushy pulp and after a bit felt revived. Then, once again turning to face the unseen stairway, he went on.

On and on, up through the darkness, wearing his knees away on the stone, he crawled for hours. Finally, as he was nearing exhaustion, he came upon another level place in the cavern. This space was small and square and surrounded by a short wall of rock. Exploring ahead in the dark, Aram discovered that the stairway ascended again after a few feet. He'd come to a kind of way station, about a hundred feet square. At the back there was a corner in the wall and he lay down there. Despite the pain in his knees, the totality of the darkness and the coolness of the air, exhaustion took him and he slept.

When he awoke his joints and muscles were stiff and he was very cold. The absolute lack of light was disconcerting even after he remembered where he was. He ate the bit of food he'd saved from the day before and then stood up gingerly and massaged his sore muscles. He wasn't very thirsty because of the humid, cool conditions underground but his need for water and nutrition were problems that would eventually have to be addressed.

After loosening his aching muscles, he felt around until he found the stairway leading up and continued his climb. This time he did not crawl, but stepped carefully up; his knees would not take much more punishment and still function. Again there were no walls and the steps seemed to wind back and forth as they climbed upward across the rising rock. It was a difficult task negotiating the steps in complete darkness. Every so often, he found it necessary to lean forward and rest for a few moments with his hands on the steps in order to regain his sense of balance.

Compounding the fatigue wrought of the unending physical strain, the utter darkness also began to wear on him psychologically. It was frustrating to have only two dependable senses of direction—up and down—at his disposal, and to have no real sense of his surroundings or his progress. At least he seemed to be alone under the earth. If there were an enemy about, surely that enemy would have attacked him as he slept.

He came upon several more of the way stations throughout that day as the stairway ascended up into the subterranean night. The reason for the staircase's existence puzzled him. Who lived in this dark place and had gone to such trouble to gain access down through the earth to the river? Where were they now? The vast underground cavern seemed deserted. At no time did he hear anything out in the darkness to suggest that he was not alone. Whenever he stumbled and banged his boot or slapped his hand against the stone, the echo of that sound was all that the darkness returned.

He realized, however, that if he were threatened at any time, there would probably be little warning so there was no point in worrying about the possibility of assault. Besides, he'd been through so much already, the fact that he was still alive made him feel as if he were charmed. The one concern that grew in him was the lack of food and the onset of thirst. He needed desperately to get out onto the surface of the world where the gift of vision would be returned to him and he could attend to those needs.

There was no way of telling time's passage or whether it was day or night, so he trusted his body. When he was awake he climbed the seemingly endless stairway; when he grew tired, he went to the next way station and slept. After two more sleep periods, the long stair ended and he came out into a wide level avenue.

By carefully exploring in the dark, he learned that on one side, the side where he'd ascended, a low intricate wall of stone marked the extent of the avenue. On the other side was a vertical wall of indeterminate height. The avenue was about thirty feet across but there was no way of determining in the darkness how far it extended in either direction.

He decided to follow the wall to his right, because he still believed that he was just inside the confines of the mountain in that direction. He did not go very far along the wall until he discovered a doorway leading to his left into the rock. On a whim he decided to explore the tunnel beyond. The hallway led back into solid rock and continued for a good distance in a straight line. Every few yards along the corridor his hand touched extrusions from the wall. He surmised that, once upon a time, they had been used to hold some kind of light source. Once, to the left, he found a small square room with nothing in it, so after walking the perimeter he went back out and continued along the corridor. His energy for that cycle wore out before he found an end to the tunnel, so, thirsty and very hungry, he curled into a ball along the wall and slept.

In his sleep there was a curious distant sound that grew no nearer as he slept yet remained constant. He dreamed of wind and storms. When he woke and lay groggily against the wall, rubbing his aching joints, he slowly realized that the sound that had haunted his sleep was perceptible to his waking ear. It was a curious sound. He couldn't decide whether it was a kind of hissing or a gurgling. It emanated from along the corridor to his front so he eased cautiously along the wall in that direction. As he did, the sound grew clearer. Finally he knew what it was. It was the sound of running water, a tiny stream.

A short way further along the corridor he found a circular indention in the wall on the right hand side. Feeling with his hands along the rounded back wall of the indentation, he discovered a pipe that extruded a few inches from the wall from which a stream of water poured into a drain at the floor. Thirsty enough to care nothing about the quality of the stream of water, Aram put his face into it and drank deeply and long. The water was sweet and cold and seemed to pour its refreshing strength straight into his muscle and sinew. He wondered how many more outlets he would find and decided to believe that in the level of the subterranean structure where he now was, they might be a regular thing. If that proved true, his only remaining problem, beside the continuing blindness, was the lack of food.

The corridor went on for two or three hour's worth of walking, even though he was moving faster now. He came upon another water station and again drank his fill. A few steps beyond the water station, he came out into a large open space. The corridor ended and the walls went straight away from him at right angles to the corridor in both directions. He decided to step cautiously out into the open space. Almost immediately, he ran into another wall. He'd come to an intersection. This new corridor ran at right angles to the one that he'd just exited. Again, after consideration, he decided to go to the right, toward what he hoped eventually would be an outlet from the mountain.

This time, in order to inject some kind of routine into his journey through the dark, he went along the left wall as he groped his way forward. That way, if he came to another intersection, he would have an idea of its relationship to the progress he'd already made and he could continue on in an orderly manner. Again, there were extrusions in the walls and every so often, there were more of the water spigots though many were evidently plugged and did not flow. Hunger began to exert its influence, making him weak, and his forward progress became slower.

After a short distance, he found another intersection and again he was forced to choose between going right or left. Going right would take him back toward the way he'd come so again he decided to go to the left. Blinded by the absolute lack of light, there was no way for him to know whether his decisions were good or bad, so he decided to ignore any attempt at logistics and just be methodical.

This corridor was like both the earlier ones. There were extrusions along the walls, small rooms containing nothing, and periodic water supplies. Aram stopped exploring the occasional small rooms. It was a waste of both time and precious effort.

The corridor was not as long as the previous two had been, and he came to the end of it quickly. He was nearly exhausted and debilitated by hunger, so he stepped across the open space toward what he expected would be another wall. But there was nothing. Exploratory trips to either side found only more empty space. He took several cautious steps out into the open and finally touched stone with his outstretched hand. But it wasn't a smooth, straight wall. It turned out to be a rounded structure. He walked slowly around it, letting his hand brush along the surface, and discovered that it seemed to be almost perfectly circular, perhaps six feet or so in diameter.

In the dark, he couldn't be exactly sure of when he'd made a full circuit of the rounded structure, and he wasn't certain of the way back to the wall containing the corridor. He made a calculation and with his hand outstretched, moved in the direction he thought was right. In three steps his leg pushed against something that caught his leg just above the knee.

Reaching down, he felt a wide flat stone surface like that of a table, covered with something that felt like soot or dust to his probing fingertips. It was about four feet wide and stretched away from him further than he could reach. His strength was completely spent by this time, so he lay down next to the table-like object on the floor and tried to sleep. The endless night had wearied him, body and soul; had sapped his strength, drained his courage, and depressed his spirit. He was exhausted by the cloying darkness and weakened by a desperate need for food.

That night, he dreamed of finding a large patch of sweetroot on a bright sunny day. Birds sang in branches overhead and sunlight filtered down through the leaves. When he awoke, he thought that he was still lost in the dream.

He could see.

Just a little, but he could see.

There was faint light all around him, just enough that he could make out dim shapes in the gloom. It was still too dark to determine the extent of the chamber, but he was undoubtedly in an extremely large room. The object next to him was in fact a table, about four feet wide and ten feet long with benches to either side. The large round object he'd circumnavigated earlier was an enormous column of stone, rising up and disappearing into the gloom overhead.

He could not locate the source of the light. Indeed, it was so dim it seemed to be not much more than a lessening of the dark. But even as he sat rubbing his sore muscles and massaging his empty stomach, the light grew. In a few minutes he could see to the far side of the great hall in which he sat. A few minutes more and yellow light streamed in from a point high in the ceiling to his right, flooding the room.

It was the morning sun, somehow finding its way inside through secret passages in the upper reaches of the chamber.

And a magnificent chamber it was. It was more than fifty feet across at least and three or four times as long. It was oriented so that the light from the sun streaming from the east lit it fully from end to end. Six feet or so out from the walls on each side were rows of enormous columns extending from the floor to the ceiling. Beginning at a point a few feet above his head, the columns were intricately carved with leafy vines laden with fruit. At the top, where they touched the ceiling, the columns spread out like the canopies of trees.

The center of the chamber was filled with rows of tables. There were four rows with a wide aisle between the center two rows. At the far end of the hall, away from the sun, there was a raised dais with another long table turned crossways. Some of the tables and benches were broken down and over everything lay the deep, thick grime of centuries. Dusty and silent, the great hall had the appearance and the feel of utter abandonment. Aram had leapt to his feet when the sunlight had revealed his remarkable surroundings, fearing discovery, but now, looking around, he knew instinctively that the builders of this great hall, whoever they were, were gone.

The most magnificent aspect of the great hall was revealed when Aram walked out into the center aisle and gazed around. Adorning the walls high up off the floor and running all the way around the chamber were beautiful frescoes. In magnificent color, they portrayed tall, magnificently dressed men and women engaged in various activities. The majority of the frescoes were of men, clad in armor, performing feats of warfare. Though the color in all of the frescoes was slightly dulled by a covering of the dust of countless ages, and some were streaked with vertical water stains, they were nonetheless vivid and beautiful.

Beneath the frescoes there were symbols, cursive, linear, and sweeping—writing, Aram assumed; he knew of such things though he had never learned to read—that ran around the walls in a long, broken line. The written language of whoever it was that built this hall, it no doubt described the magnificent achievements of those men and women depicted in the frescoes.

Aram slowly walked the length of the hall, gazing around himself in awe. One fresco in particular, at the very front of the hall where the table was turned crossways on the dais, intrigued him. It depicted a tall man with tanned skin, vividly green eyes, and long black hair, dressed in silver armor, sitting astride a magnificent black beast. It was not a depiction of a clumsy, stout ox; this animal was tall and well proportioned with long legs and a proud arching neck.

The animal was also protected by armor and the man upon his back held a bright sword aloft as if in victory. Near him stood a beautiful, dark-haired woman dressed in white, looking down the length of the hall. She had one hand on the neck of the beast, in the other she held the end of a rainbow that arced upward and disappeared into a field of stars in a black sky.

Aram climbed the dais and looked down through the hall toward the light source high in the ceiling. It was a magnificent great hall, worthy of a mighty king, but it was obvious from the deep layers of dust and heavily mildewed water stains on the walls that none of the people depicted in the frescoes had sat in it for a very long time.

At the far end of the hall from whence came the light, there was a broad arch that led beyond to another, brighter room. Aram made his way between the tables through the hall and out through the arch. He found himself in a large brightly-lit foyer that stretched away in both directions into other large halls. Over his head the rays of sunlight came in through open arches high in the stone wall. Straight ahead, out through another set of arches was a broad area of sunlit stone pavement and beyond that he saw a wide and fair green land bounded in the distance by forested hills and tall mountains over which burst the morning sun. He'd come out of the mountain into a magical place.

V

Aram went out through the arches onto the broad paved area that was bordered on the far side by a pillared stone railing overlooking a wide green valley posited with groves of trees. The paved court was at least a thousand feet broad and stretched for a mile or more away from him in both directions along the front of the mountain. Looking back, he saw that the stone in the face of the mountain fronting the court had been magnificently worked to create a tall, imposing façade the color of a pale rose.

The facade was broken at regular intervals by several series of arches leading back into the mountain. It appeared to Aram that an enormous mansion had been carved into the stone face of the mountain. He walked out across the pavement a ways toward the distant railing and turned to look back again. The sight he beheld nearly dropped him to his knees.

It was not merely a mansion; it was a city of mansions, some of which were veritable palaces, carved from the living rock, rising in seemingly endless splendor up the side of the mountain, and bathed in the glorious light of the morning sun.

The sight of it was stunning; especially to a man who'd seen nothing more substantial than wooden sheds and stone huts in the whole of his life. Tall arches, windows, verandas, and magnificent facades were stacked above him to a dizzying height. Mansion upon mansion upon mansion. Here and there, where before the making of the city there had been ridges between the furrows in the ancient mountainside, stood tall towers of solid stone, anchored in the living rock of the mountain itself.

The rock from which the city had been carved was cast in varying shades of tan, dark red, and pale rose; in places there were streaks of white that dazzled the eye. And there were patches of green vegetation everywhere, trees that reared their heads above the tops of stone walls, and flowering shrubs that peered out of hidden courtyards.

The city appeared to be about three or four miles square as it rose up the side of the mountain. On either side the city was bounded by the rough flanks of the vast sloping rock and behind it the mountain became black as iron as it rose up to a great height where, far away, snow gleamed on the northern sides of towering ramparts. Set in the midst of this black fastness, the city gleamed like a multi-colored jewel. It was astonishing to Aram that such a thing could be created or that having been created could be abandoned.

But such was evidently the case. There was no movement or sound except the wind sighing through empty windows and porticos. Whatever magnificent race of beings had made this place, they were gone, claimed by some unknown calamity in a distant age long past. He turned away and went to the rail to examine the valley below.

Before him spread a very broad and very green land. Between the city and the distant forested mountains lay a rumpled valley of meandering streams, lush meadows, and knotted, dense clumps of trees. Out in the valley, four or five miles distant, he saw the glint of sunlight on water. A dark green coiling line of trees marked it as a river. Judging from the lay of the ground, the river flowed from north to south, from his left to his right.

Several miles to the north, on his left, the valley tumbled up into a tangled jumble of grassy foothills spotted with trees. Beyond them were higher, timbered hills and behind them there rose the fierce gray stone of high, wild mountains marching out of view into the north. There were a few craggy peaks rising above the forested mountains to the east as well but they were a bit gentler in aspect than those to the north.

Southward, the valley broadened and was eventually swallowed up in distant rounded hills. Somewhere down there, Aram believed, was the ridge he'd climbed to escape the wolves and where he'd been plunged into the depths of the mountain, probably by the river flowing through the valley before him.

Immediately before him, twenty or thirty feet out from the railing where he stood and separated by a deep, narrow, paved alleyway running along the front of the great veranda, there rose a defensive wall of worked stone. The wall was about a dozen feet thick and was buttressed at regular intervals. Above each buttress, the wall was capped by square towers, many of which had crumbled. The top of the wall was accessed by arched bridges that extended out from the great porch and spanned the emptiness in ten or twelve places, though, like the towers atop the wall, most of these had crumbled as well and had fallen into the alleyway below.

One of the bridges, however, larger than the rest and situated in the very center of the great veranda, was still intact. At the point where it accessed the defensive wall, there was a rectangular raised area atop the wall and a railed dais that extended a few feet beyond the far edge of the wall, providing an unobstructed view of the valley. Aram eased across the bridge and went to the dais. There was a platform in the center where it extended from the wall and he stepped up onto it and looked out over the valley.

Below the wall lay a broad, paved parade ground from which a grand avenue led out from the city through the broken ruins of ancient buildings. These buildings, like the defensive wall, were not carved from living rock but had once been stoutly constructed of worked stone as was the retaining wall of the grand porch behind him that fell away to the alley below.

The four or five square miles of the valley immediately before the city, outside the area of ruins that lined the great avenue, was mostly open and fairly level, though covered in several disconnected places by tangled groves of trees. It appeared that at one time there had probably been extensive farming activities conducted on this land that had included the maintenance of fruit orchards.

Aram turned and looked along the defensive wall in both directions. It was anchored on each end, a half-mile away to the north and to the south, by strong, high towers with crenellated turrets that had once been connected to the city by substantial, walled bridges spanning the narrow alleyway. The southern bridge was still mostly intact, though damaged, but the northern bridge had completely collapsed; the ruins of it were piled in the dark alley below.

There was, in fact, extensive damage to the defensive wall, to the towers, and even in some places, to the beautiful façade of the city behind him. At each end of the alleyway between the ramparts of the city and the defensive wall was a jumble of broken stone where at one time there had been retaining walls or gates. It appeared as if sometime in the distant past, the city had been besieged and at least partially breached.

There were two unusual apertures in the railing on the valley side of the dais. The railing at this point was nearly chest high on Aram as he stood on the stone platform. The apertures, each about six inches in diameter, rather than being mere gaps in the railing, appeared to be the openings of, or access into, two fluted, metallic tube-like structures attached to the exterior wall. Curving down the outside of the stone and angling slightly away from one another, each metallic flute ended about seven or eight feet below the dais in a larger aperture of a foot or more. Aram could discern nothing of their possible purpose and after gazing out over the valley a few moments longer went back across the bridge and onto the great porch.

Luxuriating in the wonderful sunshine, he explored the length of the grand porch. A few hundred feet either side of the bridge to the dais, wide stairs were cut into the level expanse of pavement, indenting the porch a dozen feet back toward the mountain. Each stairway dropped straight down the front of the retaining wall to the alleyway below. The steps at the north end were so badly damaged as to be unusable but the steps on the south end were sound and would allow him access to the valley.

What had happened, he wondered, to make people abandon such a beautiful and livable place? What calamity had befallen them that had taken them all away? War, he thought, by the look of things.

He would have liked to investigate the depths of the city but it was time to turn to the problem of food. Making his way back to the southern stairway, he went down the steps to the alleyway, climbed over the pile of jumbled stone under the turreted tower and made his way out among the trees. In just a short time, he found sweetroot growing in abundance. He sat on the grass and ate his fill and it seemed that the fibrous goodness went straight to his nutrition-starved muscles.

There was water flowing out from culverts beneath the retaining wall of the grand porch; sparkling streams that meandered toward the distant river. The retaining wall beneath the porch was thirty or forty feet high and solid; there were no openings except for the small culverts that gave egress to the streams of water. He wondered if it was hollow beneath the porch or solid.

The grand porch extended beyond the high towers that were at the limits of the defensive wall to the north and to the south for perhaps a thousand feet in each direction whereupon it turned back at right angles into the living rock of the mountain at the limits of the city.

There were many interesting plants growing in wild profusion in the rich soil, including one grassy patch that resembled new wheat. And there were young vine plants that looked as if they might produce fruit of some kind, some just now putting out their first blooms, growing among the weeds.

Too hungry and exhausted for the moment to explore the area below the walls, he gathered several tubers of sweetroot and went back toward the city. As he approached the south stairs he froze as his nose caught a familiar and dangerous odor. He'd smelled it once before at the entrance to the cave down in the canyon. It was the scent of rotting meat and in his limited experience meant but one thing.

Wolves.

Easing toward the stairs, his weary nerves twitching and twanging with fright, he examined the area around the tower. To the left of the stairs where the gate to the alleyway had tumbled into ruin, there was a place where the stone had collapsed in such a way that it created a cave under the piled rock. On the ground in front of the opening to this grotto, scattered about on the green grass, were deer bones. For several moments he stood frozen in abject fear that the wolves would usher forth and slay him. But there was no movement or sound in the darkness back under the rocks. They were evidently off hunting somewhere out in the countryside.

Aram ran for the stairs and fled deep into the city. He charged up streets and occasional wide avenues that were lined with marvelous two and three-storied apartments, beautifully hewn from the lustrous stone, but he dared not take time to pause and admire. Overwhelmed with the need to put distance and altitude between himself and the denizens of the grotto, he sought streets and alleyways that led up.

The city was diffused with light throughout all its upper levels though, here and there, there were doorways and passages leading down into the darkness under the mountain. There were occasional patches of small wilderness that no doubt had once been parks or private gardens. As he ran through one of these patches of overgrown trees and shrubs, he frightened a covey of quail that thundered into the air around him. Startled, he tripped on an exposed root and fell headlong.

For several minutes he lay there, gasping for breath and tried to listen for sounds of pursuit over the wild thumping of his heart. His strength was far too debilitated for him to exert such effort. His chest ached and there was a roaring in his head. He shouldn't just run mindlessly anyway, he knew that. But he also knew that he must take steps to secure his safety.

After recovering his breath and a measure of his strength, he sat on the grass of the small park, listening for telltale growls and yelps in the city below, and considered his situation logically. He hadn't explored but a tiny portion of the city, but it appeared to be his alone, for there was no evidence of anyone else living in it. By all appearances, it had been abandoned for centuries. Consequently, he now had but three basic concerns: food, water, and defense against wild beasts.

Water was abundant in the valley and even flowed through the city in several locations. There appeared to be ample sources of food out in the valley. He only needed to provide for defense against wolves. He needed to locate a secure area where he could stay and, if possible, find some sort of weapon.

He spent the rest of the morning getting his bearings and exploring the city. There were many beautiful apartments with superb views of the valley but none of them were defensible if he were attacked. Every so often, Aram would stand quietly and listen for evidence of the wolves below. He had no way of knowing their habits or how often they frequented the cave beneath the rubble but he believed, based on his one-time experience with their kind, that they would make noise when they discovered his scent.

He began to search the deeper regions of the city, looking for a place he could turn into a stronghold. A result of this search was that his explorations began to give him a rudimentary idea of the layout of the city. The great frescoed hall into which he'd entered at the first lay at the very heart of the city's lowest section, bounded on both sides by smaller halls and anterooms. Just to the north of the great hall was an immense square room without windows that appeared as if it could be used for storing food. Aram decided to call it the granary. Beyond the granary, from the next street all the way to the northern edge of the city were large, beautiful halls and courtyards.

Above that, there was a layer of what had once been magnificent mansions. These buildings, comprised entirely of carved stone, were very beautiful, but there were no furnishings and some had evidently had roofs of wood, which were long gone. Most of the subterranean passages on this level led into what appeared to be small storage rooms for food or other goods. Some of them were obviously sewers and access tubes into deeper regions of the mountain.

He finally found a broad stairway behind the walls of the great hall that led sharply up and into an alley beyond which was a wide, square courtyard surrounded by tall walls of worked stone. At the far end of the courtyard, another stairway led up to a landing below the sheer face of a wall of rock in the center of which there was a heavy door of solid stone that hung slightly ajar on massive iron hinges. He went up onto the landing and tried the door to see if he could move it. It moved.

Pushing it open with an effort, Aram entered the room beyond and then heaved on the heavy door until it was nearly closed. He looked around. He found himself in a kind of large anteroom with doors leading off from it on three sides, to the left, right, and rear into other interior rooms. There was no outside access other than the heavy door at the front and two windows high in the wall above it. He nodded to himself, satisfied. Here was the place, then. If he had to defend this door, he felt certain that he could.

All he needed now was a weapon of some kind. Probably, he would have to go out into one of the overgrown gardens and acquire a long pole, then devise a means of sharpening it to a point, creating a crude sort of spear. First, though, he decided to examine the room he'd chosen as his fortress and the rooms that lay beyond. As he turned to do so, he was stopped by the sight of something that, until this moment, had escaped his notice.

On the back wall of the anteroom, just above the interior door, there was a faded fresco of a man pulling back on a curving piece of slender wood which he held extended away from him with his left hand. The man's right hand, positioned on the cheek under his right ear, held the end of a projectile with a pointed end that crossed the curved wood horizontally. The projectile was put under strain by virtue of a cord or wire that was attached to the ends of the curved wood. Aram had seen a bow just once in his life in the possession of an overseer but that weapon had been much smaller than the one depicted in the fresco. This bow was nearly as long as the man who wielded it.

And there was more. Above the door on the left was another fresco; this one, also badly faded and water stained but still legible, depicted a man with a spear drawn back ready to throw. Across from it, above the door on the opposite wall, there was a man holding a sword at the ready. Beneath each fresco, over each doorway, written in the same flowing symbols used below the frescoes in the great hall, there were words that Aram could not read, but his heart leapt in sudden understanding and excitement.

He was in what once had been an armory. Perhaps the ancient warriors that had defended this city so long ago had left something behind that could aid him in his current hour of need.

Trying the interior doors one by one, he was finally was able to move the one on the left. Beyond was a vast rectangular room running deep into the mountain. Along the walls, there were wide stalls that had once been sealed by massive wooden doors. These had rotted completely away, leaving only the great hinges, but there were hundreds of bits and pieces of dangerous-looking metal in the heaps of dust that carpeted the floors of the stalls.

Upon closer inspection, these turned out to be sharp spear points of various widths and lengths that were still good and sharp and shone when he cleaned them. The wooden shafts, of course, had long since turned to dust. How a man would use and handle a spear was made obvious in the fresco but Aram didn't need anyone to tell him what could be done with a sharp piece of hard steel. If he could cut and shape a length of wood and figure out a way to attach a spear point, he would have a weapon.

A row of windows high in the exterior wall gave plenty of light to the room and Aram carefully went through the stalls one by one. There were hundreds, perhaps thousands of usable spear points littering the floors. They were all of the same basic shape—a sharp, flattened oblong blade with flared barbs to either side of the conical base—but there were three distinctly different sizes, as if they had once been attached to different lengths of wooden shafts. At the rear of the long room there was another door and after going back out into the anteroom and making the exterior opening secure against wolves, he returned and went through this door.

The room behind was also quite long, but narrower, windowless and dark, so he pushed the door wide to let in some light. There were hundreds of long metal boxes stacked six and seven high and two deep along the walls. Pulling the lid off one of the boxes, he found more spear points and, surprisingly, bits and pieces of wooden shafts. Evidently, the spears in these boxes had once been stored in a kind of protective oil or wax, but over the centuries this had degenerated into fine, black dust and occasional hard, dried bits like tar, but shiny as flint. Two of the spears at the bottom of the box looked to be in surprisingly good shape, but when Aram tried to lift them out, the wooden shafts crumbled in his fingers.

Nonetheless, it gave him a measure of hope. There was the possibility that in one of these containers, perhaps in the deepest part of the room, a spear or two had survived. If such were the case, he would be instantly armed. He began methodically on the left-hand wall and went through the stacks of containers one by one. Near the bottom of the first stack he actually found a crate in which the oil or waxy substance still had a bit of integrity, but only in disparate places along the shafts of the row of spears at the bottom and rot had gotten in and destroyed most of the wood. There was enough of a shaft still protruding from the point of one spear, perhaps six or eight inches of reasonably sound wood, that it might be useful in close combat but it would be an unwieldy and cumbersome weapon.

Doggedly for the next several hours, he went through the crates, and then, finally, fortune smiled on him. Near the end of the wall at the back of the room, in the crate next to the bottom, at the center of the stacked remains of spears, there were six that were still slimy with the waxy oil. Covering them were bits of what must once have been a wrapping of rough cloth. Miraculously, the spear shafts were sound. Joy rose in his heart at the sight and the feel of them. He was armed. He had weapons.

He spent the afternoon going through more crates, occasionally uncovering more miracles and at the end of it all, as the room darkened with the waning of the day, he had a dozen usable spears. Besides that, he had thousands of spear points for which, eventually, he could create his own shafts. He had not only escaped slavery and survived to become a free man but now he also had shelter, food, and weaponry.

He went back out into the main room and cautiously slid the main door back. Thankfully, there was no sign or sound of the wolves. He sat at the table in the main room of the armory for a while and ate some sweet-root, then addressed the doors he couldn't open earlier. The door below the fresco of the man with a sword particularly interested him. He knew what a sword was and how it was used. Retrieving the spear with the short shaft from the spear room, he forced the wide sharp blade into the slot between the door and its frame and pried outward. The shaft broke under the strain.

Using one of the whole spears he tried again. This time the door moved just a little. Gently he inserted the metal point deeper into the gap and carefully exerted pressure until the door swung open. Beyond, in a deep, narrow room similar to the one opposite, were more crates like to those in the spear room but smaller, and many were filled with swords, stacked neatly blade to hilt. He gazed upon this treasure with unbounded joy, upon stack after stack of clean, hard, deadly metal, more precious than gold. The swords were made of fine, hardened steel and except for the fact that the leather had rotted off the grips; all were in excellent shape. He found one that suited his hand particularly well and carried it with him.

There was no such luck in the bow room. Everything in that room had been reduced by the centuries to dust. It was a bitter disappointment. The idea of sending a projectile toward his enemies from a distance appealed to him greatly. He dug through the dross of eons of decay but though he found odd bits of curved wood, there was nothing resembling a bow. There were, however, thousands of metal arrowheads everywhere in the debris. If he could master the engineering of a bow and the making of arrows he would not lack for tips.

Going back into the foyer of the armory, he cleared the table of debris, collected the good spears and several of the swords and sorted his cache of weaponry. He had all the swords he could use and he found several beside the first one that fit his hand nicely. There were no scabbards to be found, of course, but he felt certain he could devise something that would serve for that purpose. He had twelve usable spears besides countless spear points and arrowheads. Arming himself with two of the best spears and two swords, he went back down through the shadowed city toward the great hall at the front. His spirits and his confidence had risen dramatically with the miraculous discovery of weapons. As he negotiated the ancient streets, armed with the ancient steel, he felt almost like a warrior.

The city had been laid out amazingly well. Beside every street and alley ran gutters for shedding excess rain after it had been captured and distributed throughout the city's system of conduits. During the day the light from the sun was diffused brilliantly throughout all the levels of the city and yet the deep, narrow streets were shaded from the full force of its might. At the moment, the sun had slipped behind the great mountain and evening filled the city.

As he approached the great porch, Aram moved carefully, easing along walls and peering around corners and out through the arches at the valley beyond. If at all possible, he was never going to be caught off guard again. Standing in the main hall at the front of the city, he practiced some thrusting and parrying movements with one of the swords and then did the same with a spear. Hopefully, the wolves would not return to the cave in the rubble today, but if they did, he wanted to be reasonably ready to defend himself.

As evening deepened toward twilight, he eased out across the pavement of the great porch and across the bridge to the pillared railing at the center of the defensive wall where he could look out over the valley. A pair of hawks wheeled in the sky and smaller birds twittered in the trees as they began to settle in for the night. As he stood gazing across the broad, darkening expanse of meadows and trees and streams, his eye caught a movement out on the main avenue leading through the ruined gardens.

Black objects came purposefully toward the city. The objects came rapidly onward until they were close enough that he recognized their shapes. Wolves. They were trotting single file up the cobbled road toward their lair under the south steps. As they reached the point where Aram had dug the roots earlier in the day, the first wolf, a great shaggy beast, suddenly veered off into the grass beside the avenue and began eagerly sniffing the ground, emitting urgent yelps and short, deep, growling barks. The others joined him and together they began to track Aram's scent toward the south steps.

There were five wolves in all, two of them substantially larger than the others. It was not a large pack, but seeing them at such close range, Aram realized he was not ready to take them on in the open. Having found his scent, they would undoubtedly track him into the city and hunt him. He needed to quickly find a means of preventing them from cornering him inside.

He had only a few minutes before they tracked him into the city, and the slipping of the sun over the edge of the world beyond the mountain had cast the vaulted streets and byways into deep shadow. He thought about defending the narrow steps to the dais in the great hall or making a stand at the entrance to the armory, but neither of those options gave him the ability to flee if things went badly. Besides, the possession of quality weaponry had altered his thinking in a fundamental way. No longer did he just want to defend himself; he wanted to drive the evil beasts from the city he'd discovered and adopted as his own.

Then, like an unexpected flash of lightning out of a clear sky, the answer came to him. He needed to kill the biggest wolf, the head of the pack.

If such a deed could be accomplished, it would demoralize the others or at least make them less inclined to take him on in a straightforward assault. To turn this inspiration into execution, however, he would have to find a way to ambush them and draw first blood in a surprise attack.

As he moved quickly deeper into the city, he inspected all the narrow alleyways running crossways to the main streets. He decided that if he could find just the right spot, he would leave his fresh scent going straight into the city along a narrow street and then swing around and launch an attack from a side alley as the wolves went past. But it needed to be a position from which he could make a tactical retreat as well, if necessary.

Two-thirds of the way up the street that ran beside the granary, he found a spot that would serve his intended purpose. There was a narrow, guttered alley that ran behind the granary at right angles from the street on the south that went toward the armory to the wider avenue on the north that ran straight back into the city between the granary and the first row of magnificent mansions.

Immediately he put his plan into motion. He could already hear the excited yelps of the wolves as they ascended the south steps. He ran up the street between the mansions and the granary making sure to leave his scent on the left side so it would draw his prey right by the entrance to the narrow alley. Then he doubled back by the armory and into the alley that connected the two streets. He'd had no time to practice hurling a spear but now he practiced the motion over and over until it felt right. He crept along the guttered alleyway until he came to within a step of the opening to the street. The street was dark but the alley was darker—he believed that they would not see him until it was too late. He leaned his left side against the wall and practiced thrusting the point of the spear toward the gap.

Finally, he heard the wolves baying as they caught his fresh scent and came rushing up through the city. His heart was in his throat, and his whole body quivered in grim anticipation of the conflict to come but he didn't for a moment consider running away. He was determined not to give up control of the city to merciless beasts like the ones who'd killed his friend. He'd spent the last two or three weeks fleeing a deadly variety of threats and dangers. Now, he was through running.

A few minutes later he heard the thrumming of padded feet in the street and the eager yelping drew nearer. His muscles taut with apprehension, he eased closer to the exit from the alley and cocked his arm. He intended to be close enough to thrust the spear directly into flesh rather than to simply throw it. If he could impale one of the wolves, preferably the largest one, at the gap leading into the alley, he would have time to escape to the armory and shut the door, leaving the rest of the pack to ponder the lethal nature of the enemy they were facing.

The passage of the front wolf caught him off guard as it went rushing up the street at an incredible speed. Fearing to let any more get past him, he leapt forward and thrust the spear out through the gap with all his might, plunging it deep into the neck of the wolf behind. What occurred next stunned and shocked him. In an instant of the wolf's anguished howl of pain, the other four, ignoring the spear and leaving off pursuit of Aram's scent, fell upon the fallen animal and began tearing its flesh as it died. Aram stood for a moment, watching in astonished immobility. He'd assumed that the wolves were intelligent hunters—deadly predators who hunted with common purpose—now he saw sudden and shocking evidence that they were nothing more than mindless, vicious carnivores. Not one of them looked at him, so busy were they consuming their compatriot, as he backed carefully away.

Regaining the street below the armory he began sprinting in that direction, but then slowed. Something about the affair troubled him. In the midst of success, he suddenly felt that his victory was incomplete and he wanted more. He stopped at the steps to the armory and considered the situation. The killing of the wolf had not been exceptionally difficult. The spear had penetrated deep into the wolf's body with surprising ease. Thinking about it, he suddenly felt superior, not like the cornered quarry defending itself but more like the predator, able to inflict death at his own volition. And then something else occurred to him; he needed to retrieve the spear that he'd used to slay the wolf. Until he learned to make more, each of those weapons was precious.

Holding his sword at the ready in one hand and the second spear in the other, he eased back down the street in the deepening twilight, listening to the sounds of savagery emanating from the scene of the kill. If they would willfully cannibalize one of their own without giving thought as to why it bled and died, they were the most mindless of all beasts and deserved annihilation. The darkness increased as he drew nearer and the noise from the barbaric feast was dying down. Before he made it all the way back to the alley, silence had fallen. He moved cautiously forward with the sword in his left hand and the spear cocked in his right, but nothing moved in the shadowed streets.

When he came to the entrance to the alley, he peered cautiously around the corner before entering, but he could see no movement at the other end. He crept along it until he gained the street where he'd killed the wolf. The remains of the animal lay heaped in a steaming, stinking mass of hair and bone and entrails. Its compatriots had engorged themselves and left. They were nowhere in sight. Still, Aram was anxious to make sure they'd left the city completely. And if the twilight held a bit longer he actually wanted to kill more of them if an opportunity was presented. They had trespassed and committed an unfathomable atrocity in what he now considered his city.

Moving carefully east, street by street, down through the city, he finally reached the great porch. The last remnant of the setting sun was coloring the tips of the highest peaks that rose above the forested hills to the east and the valley was plunged into the deep shadow cast by the mountain behind him. Slipping across the pavement to the railing, he crouched and listened. From the area down near the rubble by the south steps, he heard the wolves sporting amongst themselves in the quiet of the evening. He dared not attack them in the open, especially in darkness, so he decided to sleep in the armory where he would be safe and plan a new course of action on the morrow.

He slipped back up through the dark streets, entered the armory, shut the door, and stacked crates filled with swords before it. Then, suddenly spent from the exertion and despite the excitement that still crackled along his nerve endings, he stretched out on the stone table in the anteroom and fell asleep.

When dawn came, he opened the armory door carefully and heard in the distance the snarling of the remaining wolves fighting over the carcass of their fallen companion. Suppressing a shudder at the thought of such vile behavior, he decided he would try to kill another. He picked up four spears, including the one he'd retrieved the night before and eased out into the city. Reaching the guttered alleyway, he saw that the largest wolf had dragged some of the carcass back into the narrow defile and was gnawing on the bones and flesh of its former companion with its back to him.

All right then, Aram thought, *you might as well be next.* Crouching low and moving with extreme caution, he slipped carefully up behind the shaggy black monster and drew back the spear. Just as he was about to release it, one of the smaller wolves looked into the alley and saw him.

The smaller wolf howled and the large one turned its head toward Aram. Instantly the wolf leapt to its feet, snarling, but the alley was too narrow for it to turn its body, so Aram quickly thrust the spear with all his might into its back. The point entered the wolf's body just in front of its rear haunches and hobbled it. Nonetheless, the beast was able to exit the alley and turn to face its attacker, snarling and slobbering in its fury. But Aram's blood was up and he hurled another spear into the wolf's face. This one went straight into the beast's open mouth and through the soft tissue at the back of its throat and Aram saw the light of life go out of its eyes as the steel pierced the base of its brain.

That was enough for the three smaller wolves. Howling in fear, they sprang away down the street out of the city. Aram leapt over the twitching body of his latest kill and pursued them but, run as he might, he could not catch them. Again he found himself longing for a bow and arrow.

When they had cleared the city and descended the steps, the three wolves made for the lair in the rubble. After sniffing around there for a few moments with small whines of uncertainty, and seeing Aram charging down upon them with the dreaded steel, they ran out onto the broad avenue and made for the open valley beyond. Aram sat down on the rubble and watched them go.

Only then did it occur to him that the wolves had been a family unit and by a stroke of luck, he'd been able to kill both parents. He thought about the four of them consuming with ravenous savagery an animal that had been both a mate and a parent and shuddered. What vile beasts behaved in such a manner? Somehow, he thought, the malignant hand of a great evil must have touched their species and reduced them. No normal beast would act in such a despicable way. Sitting there in the expanding light and warmth of the morning, having regained his city, he vowed to be an enemy of wolves forever.

VI

After a while, he went out into the valley below the walls and ate a breakfast of sweetroot. Now that hunger was no longer a pressing issue, he found that the root—though he was still grateful for its plentiful existence in the valley—was becoming substantially less desirable as a daily fare. He decided that after removing the dead carcasses of the wolves from the city, he would spend his time trying to improve his diet.

For several days following the slaying of the wolves, Aram made a methodical and careful survey of the grand avenue, the courtyard and the ruined gardens, and the surrounding fields and groves of trees. It was obvious that at one time in the remote past this had all been rich and carefully tended ground. The trees were now not much more than stands of thicketed brush and having grown untended for countless years were full of dead branches and unproductive growth. Some species were in bloom and others were already forming small green fruit. With care, they would no doubt someday produce in abundance.

Sweetroot grew in thick patches beneath the trees. There were vine plants in bloom and Aram decided to weed around them and see what sort of fruit was produced. He also found scattered clumps of grass that resembled wheat. He decided to cultivate it and see whether or not it produced heads of grain. If it did, he would turn over an open area of earth and sow it in larger patches the next year. He enjoyed the novel feeling of proprietorship he was beginning to have over this land. For it was his land. Not once did he discover any signs of another human presence.

As he explored further afield, he carried two spears and a sword, in case he encountered wolves or other threats. Often, during his forays out into the valley, he came across the ruins of buildings tucked into folds of the hills or situated on high points above running water. No doubt they had once been productive farms and again he wondered about the nature of the disaster that had emptied this rich land of its people.

On the level plain before the great city, there was a major thoroughfare of stone that extended from the walls of the city straight out for about two miles where it intersected another main road running north and south. On each corner of the intersection stood a pyramid, each about a hundred feet square and sixty or so feet high. He examined them closely on several occasions but could find no entrance into them. Their significance remained obscure.

The valley between the city and the forested hills to the east was rolling and green, cut by many streams from the springs that issued forth from the mountain and fed into the river. The river wound gently through this broad land and it was obvious to Aram from the many stone walls and ruined structures scattered about the long, broad valley near to the city that it had once been full of prosperous farms. Now, it was all a gentle but overgrown wilderness.

He estimated the distance from the city to the eastern hills as being about ten or twelve miles. It was about five or six miles south to the river that entered the mountain in the siphon and the spiny ridge that separated the valley from the rolling hills to the south. Northward, the valley stretched away for perhaps twenty miles or more, growing gradually narrower and rougher until it mingled with rocky, timbered foothills that increased in size as they rose toward distant snowcapped gray peaks.

On the west, the valley was bounded by the great mountain that had appeared black as coal when he had viewed it from even further to the west in the fields of his enslavement. Seen from this side where the city had been carved from its living rock, its basic elements were the color of gold and rose, especially in the morning sun, and only took on a blacker aspect as it rose up to the heights.

He occasionally saw deer but not nearly as many as he thought there should be in a valley so filled with natural feed. He attributed this fact to the number of wolf tracks that he encountered. Wolves were obviously the major predators in the valley. As he roamed farther away from the city, he encountered tracks that were much larger than those left by the three young wolves that had escaped him. As a consequence, he took his weaponry regimen seriously, using an old dead tree just to the south of the city steps for his training, hacking it into kindling with thrusts and blows from his sword.

He spent his days expanding the perimeters of his knowledge of the countryside and his evenings sorting through the various deadly bits of steel in the armory. He now had seventeen good spears, thousands of arrow points and countless steel swords. One day, while sorting through crates in the back of the sword room he found something that filled him with joy. It was a box of knives and daggers. All the handles were missing their wood or leather elements and had been reduced to raw steel, but other than that they were in excellent shape. Now he possessed ancillary weapons that he could slip through his belt for use in extremity or as tools.

The swords that came into his possession were of various lengths and he preferred one of medium size. He practiced striking and thrusting at the old tree, and though he knew nothing of the formal use of a blade, he soon felt sure that he could kill as easily with a blade as with a spear.

On stormy or rainy days, he explored the city. The making of it had been a magnificent achievement, and he constantly wondered what catastrophic event had occurred to drive its makers from it. It had, he believed, probably been war because of the damage to the defensive structures along the city's front. But if it had been war, why hadn't the victors stayed and enjoyed the spoils of their conquest?

There were magnificent grand halls and mansions throughout the lower reaches of the city, but the upper levels contained living quarters of every size and quality. One day, while exploring the topmost levels of the city, he found a small room cut into the rock out of which, leading further into the mountain, there ran a narrow passage that accessed a winding staircase. The staircase went up and around just inside the flank of the mountain. As it ascended, there were windows providing light and air cut through the decreasing thickness of the rock to the world outside. Eventually, the structure broke free of the mountain and there were windows on all sides. A hundred feet or so above that and the staircase ended in an observation tower with a view of the entire valley.

A large bowed window nearly encircled the rounded room, supported every few feet by steel rods set into the rock. In the center of the room there was a thick glass set in a bronze metal frame and mounted on a bronze tripod. On the opposing sides of the metal frame there were handles by which the glass could be turned in any direction. When he looked through the glass, faraway parts of the valley were magically brought close. His respect and admiration for the genius of the city's ancient inhabitants grew exponentially with this discovery and deepened even further the mystery of their absence.

Over time, Aram developed a habit of examining the countryside with the glass and he often saw wolves roving the valley in packs. Consequently, as he grew more confident in his fighting abilities and roamed further from the walls of the city, he became ever more certain that contact with one or more of the packs was inevitable.

For the time being he lived and slept in the armory or in the high tower but he was always looking for a suitable residence toward the middle section of the city. It was in this region of the city, as he was exploring it one day, that he discovered the infirmary. Set back from one of the small parks there was a squat building with tall windows on either side of a central door. The structure was fully detached from those around it.

Inside, Aram found a bright room with walls covered in colorful frescoes. On the back wall above a stone table in front of a doorway that led into an interior room, there was a fresco of a man and woman administering to a prone and obviously distressed child. All around the other walls were the depictions of dozens of leafy and spiny plants. It took him only a glance to discern that the plants were medicinal in nature and that the man and woman treating the child were healers. Below the depiction of each plant, written in the ancient script, there were words, no doubt giving the name of each plant, or perhaps a description of its uses. He determined to find and identify most of these plants, assuming that they grew in the valley and the surrounding hills, and learn their medicinal value.

He found a great treasure in the interior room. Lined up along the back wall of this room was a row of large stone urns. Most were filled to various levels with different colors of dust but one contained salt. Exposed to air and moisture, it had hardened into a solid chunk but when Aram chipped it with his knife and gingerly tasted it, he smiled to himself with satisfaction. He had found one more vital necessity of life.

And there was more. While sifting through a heap of trash in a corner, he dug out a variety of small tools from the rotted mess, including steel needles of various sizes and several small knives. They had rusted together over the eons and most were ruined but he was able to save a few of each. The needles would help him make badly needed clothing—if he could somehow acquire leather—while the knives would be useful for many different tasks. Among the trash there were also wedge-shaped pieces of flint of various sizes and round ironstones—tools for making fire. For a man born into the utter poverty of slavery, Aram was now wealthy beyond his wildest imaginings.

One morning, as he was pruning the tangled fruit trees, he heard a fierce commotion out on the main thoroughfare that went toward the pyramids. Grabbing his sword and two spears, he sprinted toward the sound. A half-mile from the city he came upon four wolves fighting over the carcass of a dead deer and anger surged inside him. Charging forward, he raised a spear and when he was close enough, hurled it into the nearest beast. The metal point caught the wolf just in front of its rear haunches and with a shriek of pain it went down.

Instantly, the other wolves attacked the fallen one in a mindless frenzy and consequently did not see Aram. He switched the other spear to his throwing hand and ran close enough to thrust it into the neck of another. At that the remaining two wolves turned to attack him. In his fury, Aram ran straight at them, driving his sword right down the throat of the nearest wolf and using its body to shield him from the other's teeth while he extracted the blade.

Then the fight was between him and one wolf, a large, dangerous-looking beast. They circled each other for a few moments until the wolf, overwhelmed by the smell of the blood of its dead companions and sensing mortal danger, turned to run. Aram's fighting spirit was running hot and he would have none of it.

He knew he couldn't run down the fleet wolf so he jerked the spear out of the body of one of those he'd just killed and hurled it after the fleeing wolf with all his might. He missed. Cursing in anger, he retrieved the spear and turned back to examine the three wolves he'd dropped. One, a large male with steel gray fur, was still living, so he dispatched it with the blade of his sword.

It was only after the heat of battle had dissipated that he had time to be surprised by his feelings. He was amazed to discover that he was no longer afraid of the savage beasts. He would always be wary of wolves of course, because of the danger and the threat they represented, but he would never again fall prey to witless fear.

He went over to examine the carcass of the slain deer. It had been torn severely, but it had been freshly killed and some of the meat was still untouched, and there were some fairly large pieces of usable hide. He used the sword to cut away the portions the wolves had shredded and carried the rest with him back into the city. He knew nothing of cooking meat but he had learned to make fire as a boy and now he had obtained a serious source of nourishment quite by accident.

Carrying the meat into the city he went to the infirmary and laying it out on the stone table, skinned the hide away and rubbed the meat all over with salt. Then he went to the fire pit in the great hall and started a fire. Piercing a piece of the meat on the tip of a narrow sword he held it over the flame and roasted it. It turned out to be wonderfully satisfying. He realized that if he could get the deer populations to increase in the valley, meat could become a major part of his sustenance until such time as he could consistently grow and harvest crops.

First, though, he would have to drive out the wolves. This he set about to do. It had become clear to him that the beasts had no real sense of tactics or strategy and were susceptible to hard, sharp steel that was guided by a focused mind. For his sake and that of the deer populations, he made a conscious decision to go to war and rid the valley of the scourge of wolves.

Before going on the offensive, however, he needed to limit access to the city. He collected stones from the ruin of the northern staircase and carried them to the southern staircase. At the top of the stairs he built a defensive wall, eight feet high, anchored every three or four feet by buttresses. He left a narrow opening along the side nearest to the city for him to enter and exit. Wolves could enter there too, but only one at a time, and Aram was perfectly willing to kill them one at a time.

After completing the wall he grew even more serious in his practice with the weaponry. He found a grassy levee that the ancient people had built and practiced throwing spears into the soft earth from various distances, standing, crouching, and while on the run. For sword practice he abandoned the large dead tree that he had nearly severed and instead used the stump of an apple tree that lightning had killed. He did this daily without fail. He soon grew very comfortable with the sword and learned to control the trajectory of his spears so that they entered the target at a downward angle and had greater impact.

One day, while exploring the depths of the city, he found a room that had evidently once been the private armory of some very important men. Lying in heaps below the remains of pegs in the wall were components of metal armor of various shapes and sizes. The armor was covered with the grime of ages but when he wiped it with his hand, the shining black metal came clean. Like the swords and the spear points, it was made of a type of metal that didn't rust. And he found a helmet that fit him, black, with short bronze horns that extended upward on either side of the crown. The helmet had a slatted visor that opened and closed over his eyes.

He dug through the heaps until he found pieces of armor that fit his chest and upper legs and arms. The leather ties were long gone but he was certain that he could find a way to use deer's hide to bind the pieces of armor to one another and to his body. And there was an even more important discovery. Lying flat in an alcove in the back of the room was a sword of such lightness that even though it was longer than the one he was used to, it seemed to almost wield itself. It felt as light as a stick of wood in his hand.

He took it outside and swung at a branch of the dead tree he had been using and to his amazement the blade slipped through the old hard wood as if it were butter. This, then, became his sword. But he still longed for a bow, and as the spring turned into summer, he studied the fresco of the man with the bow and began to experiment with construction. It was a hit and miss proposition for he only had the one fresco of a man with a bow fully drawn. It was some time before he figured out that the bow itself was either straight or curved slightly in one direction and that it was the drawing of the wood against its natural strength that launched the missile.

In the meantime, he went hunting and he found wolves. Usually they traveled in packs of three to five and he began to attack them in an ever-widening circle out from the city. At the first, he had good luck, destroying pack after pack but as the summer waned, the wolves learned that the man with the steel was to be avoided. It became increasingly difficult to ambush them. Even when in the midst of a feast, they were wary and watched for him.

Still, he reduced their number in the immediate vicinity of the city and the deer populations began to come back. This provided him not only with an occasional source of fresh meat—when he was lucky enough to take one by stealth, a difficult, painstaking process—but provided him with hides to tan as well, a procedure that, once he'd conceived of it, he learned through dogged trial and error. The tanned deer hides gave him ample supplies of leather straps and simple clothing and he created a proper scabbard for his sword, leaving his hands free as he wandered.

As he traveled throughout the valley all that summer, one by one, with a few exceptions, he found and identified the plants depicted on the walls of the infirmary. Discovering their relevant uses was a tricky thing but he was able to identify one plant in particular that, when crushed and bound next to a wound caused by a knife blade or a rock scrape, caused the blood to clot and cease its exit from the injury. Also, upon use, it appeared to prevent infection. He developed a habit of always carrying a supply.

One day he made it all the way to the river in his search for wolves. The river was peaceful here in the center of the valley, dropping from pool to pool through gentle riffles. It was seldom more than twenty yards across and was only very deep through the middles of the pools. Fish moved in abundance in its clear depths.

Aram was moving cautiously through a stand of tall, thin saplings that bordered the stream when he pushed one of the saplings aside and it snapped back sharply, striking him in the head and nearly dropping him. Rubbing his forehead, he examined the sapling more closely. The saplings were tall, slim, and straight with tiny leaves and they were very strong. Drawing his sword he cut one and tried to break it over his knee. It was impossible. Quietly, he rejoiced; perhaps, he thought, he'd found the material to make a bow.

He cut several of the saplings and took them back to the city. With his knife he cut one to about a five-foot length and began to work it. He left it stout in the center and tapered it toward the ends. He cut a notch to nock the arrows just below the halfway mark and shaped the ends so that they would hold a braided thong of some kind.

When he was finished his creation resembled the bow held by the man in the fresco except that he had no string and no arrows. There was an obvious solution to the lack of arrows. He simply used some of the smaller, straighter saplings and cut them to an approximate length. Then he forced points on the ends and cut notches in the other. But he had no idea of how to attach feathers for fletching the missile like those on the arrow in the fresco.

After completing his rudimentary bow and an even more rudimentary arrow, he stripped bark from various trees and species of brush and tried to weave a bowstring but nothing worked. Everything he tried snapped when pressure was exerted. It was while he was making himself clothing from deer hides that he had an idea that addressed the problem. While he was cutting the finished hide into strips so that he could make ties to fasten his armor it occurred to him that by cutting it into very thin strips and weaving them together he could make a rough bowstring that might handle the strain.

This, then, he did, and though his finished product looked only vaguely like the bow in the fresco, when he nocked an arrow and let it fly, the arrow sailed far out over the courtyard, though its flight was erratic. There was still the problem of controlling the trajectory of the missile but he'd made a weapon. As he watched the arrow thunk firmly into the ground about forty yards out from the wall, he felt like shouting for joy.

Now, he had only to acquire some feathers, shape them properly, and devise a way to attach them to the arrows so he could properly direct their flight. Until he found a way to solve that problem, however, he would have to hunt wolves with sword and spear, and over the next several weeks, that proved sufficient.

The wolf packs were growing wary of him and began to avoid the twenty or thirty square miles or so immediately surrounding the city. The deer became more plentiful in that area while the wolves nibbled at them from around the edges. They knew his scent and had learned to stay clear of him.

For a time, Aram was content with the sort of truce that existed, which no one had agreed upon but just happened. He spent most days tending and improving the area near the south stairway; pruning the trees and weeding everything from the ground that either wasn't familiar or looked like a weed.

As summer wore away and autumn approached, there came to be a kind of perimeter fixed that extended from the hill on the left to a broad upland on the right or south and from the city to the river. Inside this twenty-five square mile area the wolves did not come and Aram rarely ventured outside it. There were even a few late fawns born inside it and a small herd of a thirty or so deer fell under Aram's protection.

He labored inside the city as well. He decided to move into the small apartment below the tower, and he wove a bed of willow bark and constructed crude shutters for the windows. As the year waned and nights grew cooler, he brought up wood and used the fire pit on a regular basis. His old life as a slave was fading into the past with amazing rapidity.

By the middle of autumn, things were pretty well in hand. He harvested the few apples and plums the scraggly trees produced as they ripened and stored them for the winter. Some of the vine plants he had tended so carefully proved to be squash and the sweetroot he'd separated and cultivated had grown to a substantial size. The grass he'd suspected was a type of grain turned out to be so. But it didn't produce enough to eat. He allowed the heads to mature and then stored the grains in a dry willow basket in one of the basement rooms. When the next spring came, he intended to open a plot of earth and seed it properly.

He became adept enough with a spear to bring down a couple of deer for his winter's meat. It was an arduous task because he had to get close in order to make a clean kill and the methods he employed to hunt wolves did not work on deer. Wolves were predators themselves, more used to hunting than being hunted, so the only real advantage on either side of the issue was found in Aram's skill and steel.

Deer, on the other hand, possessed the highly developed senses of prey animals and were accustomed to being wary. Their senses of hearing and of sight were acute and when startled they ran like the wind. Aram was forced to develop new strategies of stealth and silence and he learned to stay downwind when stalking them. Ultimately, however, he was successful and took a young buck and an older doe.

Though not actively hunting wolves, he continued to practice with the long, light sword. And he finally perfected the art of tanning hide and utilized the deerskin for not just clothing but bedding as well. He also made for himself a pair of high-topped moccasins for daily use as his old boots were approaching the end of their serviceability.

The informal truce with the wolves held until late fall.

One day as he was scouting outside his protected area along the sinking river to the south, he surprised six wolves at their feast. He watched them from a hill as they snarled at him but held their ground. He was about to move on when he looked more closely at their partially consumed quarry.

Sudden recognition of the savaged forms made him ill enough to vomit.

They were eating two humans. Even at that distance, he could see the distinctive lines of human bones and skeletons. In sudden rage he charged off the hill into the midst of them. He carried only his sword but he made it sing, killing two with his first strokes and wounding a third. But these wolves were used to humans as prey so they attacked. Aram backed up against a wall of rock and let them come straight at him, dispatching them one at a time.

He drove his sword deep into the throat of the first wolf that attacked and then slid to the side using its body as a shield. A second wolf bounded over the body of the first and with a slash, Aram severed both its forelegs, but he also went down and the third wolf leaped. Aram rolled toward it, sliding under the trajectory of its attack, and shoved his blade deep into its belly. When he got to his feet, three wolves were dead and the others wounded. He killed them all.

Then he examined the remains of the humans. The bodies were so badly torn that he couldn't tell whether they were men or women. At first he had the thought that other slaves had escaped from the colony down river, but the clothing that was strewn about belied that notion. These men or women had been dressed in leather, and had both been armed with short daggers. Every slave he'd ever known had worn simple cloth and none had ever been armed. These people had come from someplace else.

The thought troubled him. There had been times over the summer when he missed the companionship of other people and often had wished that Decius had survived. But he had also gotten used to the idea that the valley was his and his alone. Where had these two come from? They weren't overseers; that much was certain—they'd have never been allowed to travel alone into this wild country. A lasher would have been with them and he would have slain the wolves.

Aram walked to the top of the ridge and looked down into the canyon. Below him, sweeping around to his right in a wide curve was the stream that had carried him away and plunged him into the mountain. He walked downstream far enough to observe the whirlpool but on this day the water was low and the river simply ran directly into a cleft in the vertical rock.

He went back and dug trenches with the men's daggers and put what remained of them into the ground. He decided to salvage what he could of their leather clothing. He was in constant need of leather goods and these men would have no further use of them. As he stood quietly for a moment over their makeshift graves, he wondered again where these men had come from and what they'd been doing here on the fringes of his valley.

What if, he wondered, and this thought was amazing, they were free men like him? He had never known of any people but slaves and overseers and the thought that there might be others like him who were free of Manon's tyranny was compelling. One thing, he decided, the entire valley must be rid of wolves. No more truce. He was going back to war.

VII

Fall waned toward winter and he harvested the last of his crops. Worms had ruined many of the late apples and in the end he was able to fill only seven of the willow baskets he'd made. There was plenty of sweet-root, which he stored in an underground shelter he dug out near the south stairway. Some of the squash had made, though the fruits were small and few. These he stored in a subterranean room below the granary in the lower part of the city where they would remain cool without freezing.

The last of the wheat was necessarily scattered and he filled barely half of another basket. Bread, at least for the coming winter, would remain an unmet desire, but he had higher hopes for the coming year. He decided that before going to war with the wolves, he needed to kill one more deer and cure the meat. Once again, he wished for a bow that worked. He preferred to kill the animals from a distance. He did not want them to fear him and he enjoyed their peculiar and graceful beauty.

Lacking a bow and arrow, he was forced to take the deer with his spear. After the meat was cured and the hide tanned for future use, he made certain all his food stuffs were safely stored against the coming winter and then he armed himself, filled a pack with supplies and went out to hunt wolves.

He decided to scour the countryside methodically from north to south, beginning on the long ridge to the north of the city that angled northwest into the foothills. It was from here that one of the larger streams that fed his river originated. Using the river as the eastern boundary and working south to the sinking river, he would destroy or drive out all the wolves inside that area. It was an area of about one hundred square miles and constituted just a little more than half the valley on his side of the river. When that area was clear, sometime in late winter or early spring if things went as planned, he would take a break to do his planting. In the summer, he would clear the rest of the valley on his side and then cross the river and finish the job after the next fall's harvest.

All that winter, when he found the tracks of packs of wolves, he ruthlessly hunted them down. It was fairly easy at first because when they caught his scent they moved to attack him and this tactic allowed him to choose the ground where he would confront them. But as their numbers dwindled, the wolves grew wise. They couldn't know why this particular human, whose kind they were used to killing with ease, was now their most dangerous enemy, but they began assiduously to avoid him.

Aram realized that in order to continue to be successful he would have to find a way to mask his own scent. By early winter, when the first snow came down out of the mountains and frosted the ground, he'd already slain twenty-four of his enemy. But as midwinter approached he was generally given very wide berth and had killed only six more. One day after a storm left several inches of snow on the ground, he came upon an older wolf feeding on the carcass of a deer left by others and he slew it easily. It was a large animal and its odor was very strong. It gave him an idea.

He skinned the beast and made a coat and leggings from the wolf's hide. What better way to mask his scent than with that of his enemies? After this he found that he could make his way almost in among the packs of wolves before they realized the danger. By the time the first permanent snow fell he'd cleared the valley from the north all the way south to the main avenue and its junction with the north-south road by the pyramids.

One morning, in a shallow hollow between two long ridges south of the pyramids containing a small stream that meandered toward the river, he rounded a rocky corner and blundered into a company of eleven wolves, all of them large adults. Immediately battle was joined, and he was nearly overwhelmed.

The wolves attacked him en masse and at first it was only the outcropping of rock behind him that saved his life. Though he immediately killed two with his spears and wreaked havoc among the others with his sword, the situation rapidly became grave. There was no possibility of retreat. The rock wall behind him was too tall and too steep to climb and lacked indentations for use as cover. With so many concentrating their attack on him, they were bound to get lucky and do some damage.

As he dispatched one wolf with a thrust to the throat, his sword caught in the sinew of its neck and he was pulled down. Another leapt upon him instantly and before he could sink his dagger upward into its belly it had savaged him. His dagger stroke killed it but it had used its long sharp teeth well in its dying moments. Pain exploded up the left side of his chest and through his arm. Pulling his dagger and sword free, he rolled to his feet in time to defend against two more that came at him together.

He spun to his left and swung his sword into the neck of the nearest wolf, almost severing its head while the other was carried past him by the impetus of its charge. There were now just five able to do battle, four of them circling at a distance, looking for advantage. He turned just in time to parry an attack from the fifth, but failed to wound it seriously.

A terrible weariness began seeping into him and though his whole left side was soaked in warm blood, he felt suddenly very cold and his left arm hurt terribly. He was bleeding severely and he knew his wounds were serious. The wolves knew it too. They ignored their six dead companions and approached low to the ground. Aram backed up against the abutment of rock and waited for them to come. There was no avenue of escape. He was in deep trouble.

His left arm was quickly becoming useless and there was a dim, distant, uncomfortable buzzing deep inside his head. He realized that he didn't have much time. If he didn't end it quickly, he was finished and they would kill him. Drawing a desperate, shuddering breath, he yelled loudly and attacked.

Lunging suddenly to the right, he killed the first of the five wolves with a stroke, using its body for shelter. The others attacked in a frenzy. But now they had to come at him along a kind of alley between the rock wall and the pile of bodies. And they came. He was able to kill just two more before the remaining pair of wolves gave up and retreated. But they did not leave the area.

As if they knew that the serious nature of his wounds would eventually debilitate him, they went out about thirty yards and lay down in the snow watching him. They seemed to know that he was in imminent danger of collapse and had decided to let nature aid them. Aram knew that he had to stay conscious and somehow get back to the safety of the city, nearly five miles away. Warily watching the two wolves, he examined his wounds. He'd been slashed across the forearm and there was a deep gouge in the muscle of his chest just above his heart. Both wounds were streaming frightening quantities of his blood. He slipped his pack around and found a poultice.

He tied part of the poultice on his arm with leather thongs and shoved the rest deep into the ragged gouge in his chest. Then he slung his arm close to his body with a leather strap in order to put pressure on both wounds. He could not afford to lose much more blood. To fight the creeping dizziness, he washed his face with clean snow and shoved a handful into his mouth.

Keeping a wary eye on his remaining enemies, he got to his feet, grasped his sword firmly in his right hand and started up the draw. The sun had already slipped past noon. He had to get to the city before it set; he would never survive the night out in the open. In his condition, the cold would kill him even if the wolves did not. The two wolves got to their feet when he began to move and paralleled him along the low ridge top to the north. Walking helped to clear his head but sapped his energy and he felt a weakness overcoming him that he could not fight for long. He had to get back to the city.

He decided to ease up the ridge to his left and get on higher ground where he could make out the ramparts of the city and keep himself moving in the right direction. As he did this, the wolves stayed with him, slinking along the ridge to the north. It was as if they knew that the day's battle had devolved into a contest of attrition that they would eventually win.

Step by step throughout that long afternoon, he kept himself going, step by weary, painful step, toward the city while watching his enemies watch him. Slowly but surely as the sun slid down the sky toward the mountain he began to grow drowsy from the weariness induced by the pain and the loss of blood and the vicious, creeping cold of the winter evening. As if they knew it, the wolves gradually closed the distance to him. Once again, deep inside his fevered mind, there arose the desperate longing for a bow.

Finally, while he was still a mile or more from the great porch, the sun slid behind the crest of the mountain. Injury and the bitter cold overwhelmed his strength, and he could go no further. He stopped, leaning on his sword, and as best he could in his debilitated state, considered things. The wolves crept ever closer, patiently wearing out their prey. He knew without any doubt that he did not have the strength to get himself back to the city while having to defend against their constant vigilance. There was only one thing to do. If he was to have any chance for survival, the battle had to be rejoined—and ended—here.

Letting his sword slip down his thigh, he dropped to his knees and hung his head. He washed some snow over his face, stared at the ground, and waited. It felt good to abandon the exertion of dragging his damaged body through the snow but he knew he must stay alert while at the same time letting his enemies see that he was utterly spent. Hopefully, they would take the bait before his strength failed him completely. His right hand dangled near the hilt of his sword.

After circling him slowly and cautiously several times, the wolves became convinced that he was finished and took the bait. Whining in eagerness, they circled closer and then charged. With a roar born more of will than of strength, knowing that it was very likely the last thing he would do in life, Aram grasped his sword and came to his feet. Summoning the last dregs of his life's force, he swung the sword in a mighty circle. The blade severed the top of the nearest wolf's skull and sank into the neck of the other, killing both, but the combined weight of their bodies drove Aram to the ground and one fell on top of him.

He lay there for a while, listening to the silence of deep winter, struggling to breathe beneath the weight of the dead wolf, and knew that he was dying. He tried to shift the body of the wolf and found it impossible. His strength had gone and taken his will with it. Strangely, though, he found that it wasn't so bad. After all, he reasoned, he would die as a free man—a man that had known the joy of living at his own will and by his own wits, if only for a short time.

He closed his eyes and a pleasant warmth seemed to seep out of the earth and push back the pain and the cold. He released himself into its soothing embrace.

Aram.

As if from a great distance, someone called his name.

Aram, get up.

Louder now, and more insistent, the voice had crossed the distance and entered into his mind and it was a voice that he vaguely recognized. Sometime, somewhere, he'd heard it before.

With immense effort, he forced his eyes open and looked up. Bending over him in the gathering gloom of the evening was a cloaked and hooded figure. It was the same ethereal figure he'd seen on the ridge top the day Decius died.

Do you intend to give up and die here, today?

Given the events of the day and the current state of his health, Aram found the question somewhat offensive. "There's not much I can do about that; I'm very tired and badly hurt," he answered. "I've lost a lot of blood."

Indeed, I've lost more.

Aram considered that curious statement for a moment but could not fathom it. Hoarsely, weakly, he laughed. "I didn't know specters could bleed."

Specters can't, men can.

"Are you a man, then?"

Aram, you are the last of our hope. If you lay there and die the race of men will undoubtedly fail. Light will go out of the world, Manon will win it all; eventually, even the stars may go dark. The Maker will have to start over. Much depends on you. Will you abandon your destiny?

Even in his state of pain-induced delirium, Aram realized that he was hallucinating, but he decided to humor the delusions of his fevered mind.

"Why would anything in the world or the heavens depend upon what I do?" he asked, and the strain of speaking pushed him nearer to a darkness that was darker than the surrounding night. "I am but a slave, and the son of a slave. I have gone as far as I am able—don't put anything else on me."

You are the son of my line and no slave. There was a quiet and insistent fury in the specter's voice. *Get up, Aram, get up and return to the city of your fathers. You will not die today.*

A cold wind breathed over the valley and Aram's eyes cleared and the fever-induced vision faded. He stared for a moment straight up into the darkening sky where the first bright stars were making their appearance. The cold had helped his wounds to clot and he felt a small bit of his strength return. Rousing himself to great effort, he pushed the body of the wolf off him and sat up, gulping in weak gasps of the frigid air.

To the east, the very tops of the highest mountains were still colored with the last rays of the setting sun and the moon was in the sky. To the northwest he could just make out the dark ramparts of the city's defensive wall a mile or so away. Using his sword as a crutch, he wearily pushed himself to his feet with his good arm and shuffled stiffly and painfully toward home.

It was well into the night by the time he reached the city, struggled up the stairway, and made his way through the dark streets to his room below the tower. There, as if in a dream, weak and sick, barely alive, he cleansed his wounds, made new poultices, and started a fire. Then he collapsed upon the bed.

He dreamed. In his dream he walked through a thick stand of pines. Sap ran down their trunks and he put his hands into it and it stuck to his fingers and palms. Then, his hands covered in thick resin, he walked near a stream and with his dagger stripped the gray bark from a tall, thin tree. Inside the bark were sinews like tendons in the muscles of a beast which he then pulled free of the bark in long sections and wove into string. For some reason this made him feel a great and overwhelming joy.

Once or twice, in the midst of his fever, he sensed that he was not alone, that he was being watched over, even, at times, that someone spoke to him, but his eyelids were too heavy to lift and he did not care.

He woke three days later, cold and soaked in the remains of his fever. The fire had long been out. He was very thirsty and a bit hungry. His wounded chest and his arm were sore but not inflamed. And there was something from his long sleep that he needed to remember.

VIII

It was the depths of winter. For several days, he rested and recovered his health. Outside, the world was buried in snow. When he felt well enough, he went up to the tower and studied the valley. To his relief, wolves were nowhere immediately in view. There were only a few deer, digging in the snow with their slim forelegs to get at the grass below.

As he grew stronger, he remembered his dream. At first, he dismissed it as merely the subconscious response of his fevered mind to his deep desire to have a bow, but as the bitter weeks of winter crawled by he considered it again. The ancient people who had lived here had fashioned many weapons and they must have found the raw materials for those weapons in the world that lay before their door. He must do the same.

In the meantime, he waited out the winter. There were several large storms that dumped snow into his valley, making the trees beautiful and softening the rough edges of the wilderness. He was thankful for the stores of food he'd put aside, especially the extra deer. And, as his health improved, he practiced his swordplay.

Finally, the place of the sun's rising began creeping back toward the north, day by day. The snow began to melt and bare earth appeared along the higher ground. The stiffness from his wounds was gone and he was anxious to take up arms again before it was time for the spring planting.

He was implacable now. The wolves had to go or die. In his first few forays out of the city he stayed near the main avenue and was cautious. But gradually his old boldness came back, though now it was tempered by wisdom. He never traveled without his sword, two spears and four daggers stuck in his belt. Whenever he left the city, he was armed to the teeth.

One day in early spring as he was just east of the river, following the tracks of a large pack, he entered a stand of tall pines. As he leaned against the bark of a tall conifer, his hand came into contact with a sticky substance. He wiped his hand on his pants but the substance was difficult to remove. It was resin from the sap of the tree. As he examined it, the dream he'd had during his fever came back to him.

He ate all the food from one of his small leather pouches and used it to collect as much of the resin as he could find. Then he continued his hunt but the wolf tracks turned east and went up into the hills so he left them and crossed back across the river. From that day forward, he began to look for trees that resembled the tall, thin, gray-barked trees of his dream.

He didn't really believe in dreams but it didn't matter, the resin was real. Whether he'd simply noticed it before and it had subsequently appeared in his fevered dream was of no import. He now had an idea for a bowstring.

As winter crept northward back into the high mountains and spring entered the valley, he went back to war. His left side, especially his arm, had not recovered its full strength but it didn't deter him. His right hand and arm were, if anything, stronger and he was considerably wiser. Consequently, he slaughtered wolves by the dozens, even hunting them outside what he considered to be his area of control, eastward into the timbered hills, north into the long draws below the mountains, and south of the sinking river. And always he watched for tall, thin trees with gray bark.

One day he was far to the north in the foothills of the mountains, and up a long, steep sided hollow, tucked up against an outcropping of black rock, he found what he was looking for. It was a stand of tall slender trees with gray, closely woven bark.

There were no limbs on the trees for several feet from the ground and the trunks were perfectly straight. Eagerly, he took his knife and cut long furrows into the trunk of one tree and stripped away a long piece of bark. Forgetting all else he sat and carefully worked his knife lengthwise down through the strip of bark. And there they were—long thin cords threading like the white tendons of an animal through the bark of the tree.

Taking care not to girdle the trees, he gathered strips of bark from several of them and spent the rest of the morning separating the threads from the bark. By early afternoon, he had at least a hundred of the threads or more. They were very strong and flexible and looked as if they could be woven into strands. Maybe, just maybe, he had the material for his bowstring.

He left off hunting for that day and hurried back down the valley to the city. As he went, the sky clouded over and it began to rain. Over the next several days, the storm stayed over the mountains and the valley. This suited him. He was happy to stay inside the city and work on his bowstring.

He carefully braided the strands together and using the leather bow-string as a template determined its length and looped the string at both ends, weaving the strands back into themselves. Then he stretched the finished product between two heavy stones and coated it with the resin from the pine trees. He split some feathers he had gathered during his travels and cut grooves in the end of his arrows, attaching the feathers in the grooves with the resin.

Everyday for several days, he worked the resin along the length of the bowstring until it seemed ready. He had no experience upon which to judge its readiness, just his instinct and trial and error. Finally, he strung the bow. Going down to the broad porch, he nocked an arrow and loosed it into the sky and then shouted for joy as the arrow sailed into the heavens in a perfect parabola and sank into the damp earth more than a hundred yards from the wall. His greatest wish was realized—he had a bow, a weapon of distance.

Over the next few weeks he made several strings and many arrows, finally perfecting both processes. And he made a taller and stronger bow that would project longer arrows over greater distances. With the creation of the bow and arrow and the making of shafts for spears, a process he'd long ago perfected, he had, in effect, become an accomplished weapons maker. And as his weapons became better and deadlier, so did he.

All through planting time, at the end of each day's work, he practiced with the bow, aiming at targets placed at different distances, shooting on the run, even learning to use it from his weakened left side as well as his right, releasing the arrows with either hand. And he practiced shooting to either side as he ran. He wove willows into targets so that he could retrieve and re-use his arrows. Still he broke many, but he gradually became so proficient that within the distance of a hundred yards not much would escape his rapid and accurate shooting.

He went back to war as soon as the spring sowing was done. And now, wolves were brought down at ever-greater distances although, with his wolf skin clothing, he could usually get as close as he pleased. By the end of that summer, his second in the valley, he'd slain more than a hundred wolves. Their numbers had grown thin throughout the breadth and length of the valley, between the mountains and the twin rivers, and even across the river into the wooded hills beyond, an area of almost four hundred square miles.

Wolves that were not killed began to leave the dangerous valley for safer ground. After harvest, as winter was coming on, he sometimes went for several days without the sighting of a single wolf or even a track. He went farther afield, crossing the river more often and going so far from the city in every direction that he was often obliged to spend three or four nights away from his home. When he camped in the wilderness, he scattered steel arrow tips in a circular pattern around his camp so that anything that approached during the night would be injured and discovered before it could attack.

It was during this time, as he was becoming familiar with the whole of the valley and the uplands that surrounded it, that he discovered something he'd always suspected. The river that ran through his valley was the same one that had sucked him into the mountain on that rainy day more than a year ago. It made a sharp turn to the west at the extreme southeast corner of the valley where a low line of hills separated it from the river that he'd followed when he fled his bondage. That other river continued on to the east into the timbered mountains that bordered his valley on the east and southeast.

And he discovered another interesting thing. Here and there throughout the valley, there were ruins of sizeable settlements, all made of stone and laid out geometrically, with central squares, main avenues, and secondary streets. It was as if there once had been satellite towns, no doubt farming communities that traded with or serviced the city.

And there were remnants of ancient roads running throughout the valley that connected these scattered communities. The main road that intersected the broad avenue coming out from the city at the pyramids traversed the whole of the valley, north to south. In the north, it rose up into the foothills where another main artery, just as wide and as well constructed, branched off at right angles and went straight west, up though and over the gentler hills to the north of the great black mountain. The main road continued northward from this intersection and went out of sight toward the distant mountains.

To the south, the valley road angled to the southeast in a broad, sweeping curve, following the course of the river. There, at the extreme southeast corner of the valley where the sinking river turned back west, the road crossed the river at a wide, shallow place in the stream. Broad, flat paving stones had been set into the streambed to facilitate crossing.

Beyond the crossing, the ridge that separated the two rivers was more moderate in height and steepness here than at any other point. To the east it grew increasingly rough and rocky as it merged with the pine hills, finally being incorporated into them completely where a lone spire of rock jutted into the sky. Westward, the ridge rose slightly and grew ever narrower and steeper until it converged with the steep flank of the mountain above the place where the river sank and went into the earth.

Between the two rivers, a massive cut had been engineered through the ridge by the ancients so that the road arched gently over it in a straight line. The crossing at the southern river was similar in size and construction to the first. To the south of this river the road curved up and out of sight into jumbled hills that were largely covered in broadleaf trees. Curiously, after crossing the river, the road deteriorated in size and quality; there were places where the forest had reclaimed it.

The hills beyond the southern river resembled the green hills that Aram and Decius had bypassed two years earlier. As they trended eastward, south of the river that went generally straight into the east, there was very little change in their physical makeup other than a slight increase in altitude and roughness and a corresponding change from broadleaf forest to pine woods. Back to the west, however, the ground south of the river changed rapidly, becoming rougher and rockier, higher and wilder; until finally it became the sharp ridge forming the southern wall of the canyon through which Aram had passed when running for life and freedom almost two years before. Somewhere down there, two or three miles downstream, Aram and Decius had made their fateful crossing into the land that had cost Decius his life and brought Aram his freedom.

It occurred to Aram, as he stood on the ridge between the two rivers and gazed down into the dark canyon that he had never tried to recover Decius' body. Probably, it had been utterly consumed but even if not, Decius had been slain by the river's edge and the intervening periodic floods would have washed anything that remained of him to the west. Aram could do nothing for his friend now except that to which he was already committed—the destruction of the wolf packs.

By the time that second winter's snows forced him inside the city; Aram had a clear idea of the layout of his valley and the countryside immediately surrounding it. Snow came early and fell often throughout the winter and Aram spent his time adding to his weaponry and improving the room below the tower and its furnishings.

Four more years passed. At the end of that time, he was in unchallenged possession of the valley. He never saw wolves now unless he went into the hills to the north or the east or crossed the twin rivers to the south. He seldom did this. As long as they stayed clear of his valley he no longer went looking for them.

He developed the ground to the southeast of the defensive wall until it became a respectable farm with fields and orchards that produced in plenty. Wheat was now grown on an acre of angled ground above a small stream to the south. Bread was no longer a luxury; after collecting grain enough for his needs and for seeding the next year, he often left the rest for the deer.

And he had now become familiar with almost the entirety of the city. The great frescoed hall was in the center of the city on its lowest level, surrounded by smaller administrative buildings and many beautiful mansions. Behind it was the granary and just above it, on the next upper level, was the armory. The next few levels, rising up the mountain, consisted of lesser homes and buildings, including the infirmary, though none of the structures could be described as plain. His apartment, and the tower that rose above it, was located near the topmost level, with a view down over the city and the valley beyond.

Once, during his fourth winter, which had brought abundant snow and very cold temperatures and had locked him inside the city for a full three months, he'd taken torches and made the journey down through the long dark maze of corridors, stairways, and blocks of square rooms to the subterranean river. Perhaps, he conjectured, it all was intended to be defensive in nature. But there was no definitive clue that he could discover to explain the amount of work that had gone into accessing the river deep in the heart of the mountain.

He never went down there again, instead spending his free time in improving the city and exploring the regions near his valley. Always, now, as he roamed, he looked for signs of other people. He hated to admit loneliness, but many times as he walked the grand porch and gazed out over the valley, the thought came unbidden that the life he now lived could be greatly improved in one way—by the addition of a spouse and partner—a wife. A woman.

He had not seen another living person since the day Decius died and no evidence of others since he found the bodies of the two men the wolves had killed near the sinking river. As for them, he never found any clues as to who they were or where they'd come from.

One evening in late summer of his sixth year in the valley, just after sundown, he was looking for a suitable campsite along the top of a bluff above a small stream on the east side of the river in the southeastern corner of the valley. It had been a while since he'd checked that part of the valley for wolves and he was looking for any sign that they had been killing deer along the fringes of his domain.

The sun had slid behind the mountain and he was about to bed down in a stand of stubby pines clustered on the bluff above a sharp bend in the stream when the sounds of conflict erupted from out of the bottom of the draw. They were sounds that he instantly recognized—the snarls and eager yips of a pack of wolves on the attack.

Quietly he prepared for battle and then peered over the edge to see what it was that they'd cornered. He froze in amazement. Four men were backed up against a rock wall on the far side of the stream in a defensive line, swords drawn. Before them, circling and growling in preparation for attack was a full pack of wolves, eight in all.

Five of the wolves, the largest of the pack, had forced the men back against the cliff, while three smaller ones fed on a deer's carcass near the riverbank. The men held short, broad swords and lighted torches. It appeared that they'd defended themselves successfully so far but it was nearly dark down in the bottom along the river, and when the light failed completely they were doomed.

Carefully Aram positioned himself so that he had a clear shot with his bow down the small, narrow canyon. He decided to kill the three smaller wolves first. Nocking an arrow, he shot the first one in the body. Its head shot upward in shocked surprise and without making a sound it ran flat out head first into a rock, where it fell on its side, twitched for a moment and then was still. The other two looked for a moment at their companion's bizarre behavior, and then went back to gnawing on the deer. Aram let another arrow fly. He shot the second wolf in the neck. It stood up, stumbled sideways and fell silently. So far, then, so good. The men were still holding the five large wolves at bay, but the stalemate wouldn't continue much longer.

He aimed an arrow at the last small wolf. The light from the western sky had almost completely failed. For whatever reason, Aram's last arrow went slightly astray, striking the last of the smaller wolves in the haunches. It howled in furious pain and stumbled about on its two good legs, snapping at the offending wooden rod that was lodged in its hindquarters.

This attracted the attention of the five larger wolves. Unable to see Aram on the ridge above, they assumed that this injury to their young had somehow come from their cornered prey and instantly they turned and charged the men. Aram leapt off the bluff and ran toward the melee. He killed one wolf on the run and nocked another arrow as he ran. Then the remaining wolves realized the nature and source of the new attack.

They were evidently from a different area and had not encountered Aram before, for they turned to attack him. He dropped his fifth wolf by sending an arrow down its howling throat as it charged him. Then he dropped his bow and drew his sword. There were now just three. Leaping to the right, he slashed at the one on that side as it turned toward him. His blade cut a long gash in the wolf's side behind its front legs. Screaming in pain and fury, it went down as its guts tumbled out.

Aram's impetus carried him a short way past his attackers. He spun to face them just as the remaining two wolves whirled to continue their assault. He caught the second as it hurtled right at him and ran his sword deep into its throat. Bracing himself, he pushed the weight of the stricken wolf into the charging body of its companion. Pulling his sword free he buried the steel blade in the neck of the last wolf and with a twisting yank nearly severed its head.

After checking to see that he was uninjured, Aram went around and made sure every beast was dead. There was a bit of fight still left in the one he'd slashed in the side, but he dispatched it with a stroke across the neck behind its head. Then he turned to examine the men.

They had not moved from their defensive posture beneath the rock and were gazing at him open-mouthed. Aram lowered his sword slightly and approached them. He did not consider it until later, but he must have appeared quite a sight, stalking in out of the twilight after slaying eight wolves with apparent ease, dressed in his rough clothes made of wolves' skins, his hair hanging long, and his jaw bristling with a full beard.

He studied the men in the light of the torches.

"Are any of you hurt?"

A young man with blonde hair tinged with copper and a clean-shaven face stepped slightly forward. The young man was a bit above medium height and was dressed, Aram noticed with a start, in a long-sleeved shirt and trousers, both of heavy cloth of good quality, and a leather vest. He'd seen clothing like this before, on the bodies of the two men he'd buried on the ridge above the siphon four years earlier.

"All of us are hurt a bit, but none seriously, I think." The young man looked around at his companions for verification of this statement. They all nodded, staring at Aram. The young man turned back to him. "We owe you a great debt, sir, probably to the extent of our very lives."

Aram ignored the gracious statement as he studied the man. The copper-haired young man possessed a pleasant face, with an open and friendly expression, blue eyes, a firm nose, and a mouth that appeared as if it couldn't wait to break into a smile. He met Aram's fierce gaze with wariness and respect but without fear.

Aram had many questions he wanted to ask these men. Where were they from? How had they gotten here? Were they free men? Instead—

"What are you doing in my valley?" He heard himself ask gruffly, and was instantly surprised that his strongest feeling was a sense of trespass at their presence inside the boundaries of his land.

"Your valley?" The young man looked shocked.

"Yes, my valley. What are you doing here?"

"Well," the young man stole a glance at his companions and then looked back at Aram with caution dampening the naturally open expression of his features. "We're hunting deer. We usually don't come this far from home, but wolves are overrunning the whole of the country near our lands and deer are getting scarce. We didn't mean to trespass." He looked at Aram curiously. "I didn't know anyone lived in this valley."

Aram studied the men for a moment. They all looked healthy, fairly well fed, and were armed with short swords. On the ground near their fire were small bows and quivers of arrows, somewhat shorter than his bow but deadly looking none the less.

"Why didn't you kill the wolves with arrows?"

The young man shrugged apologetically. "We were eating supper. They caught us by surprise."

Aram frowned. The idea of being taken unawares had become foreign to him. "They took you by surprise? How could you let that happen?"

Without waiting for an answer, he walked over and retrieved his bow and examined the deer carcass, torn by the wolves. Then he turned to the men, and as he did, he sheathed his sword.

"Who are you?"

The young man with copper hair spoke. "I'm Findaen, son of Lancer, the Prince of Derosa. This is Jonwood, Mallet, and Wamlak."

Aram nodded at each man in turn, the short, tough looking Jonwood, the enormous, barrel-chested Mallet, and the dark-haired, lean Wamlak.

"How is the hunting?" He asked, taking care to lessen the level of hostility in his voice.

The men visibly relaxed. Findaen left the others and came over near Aram. "Not good. We've seen many more wolf tracks than those of deer. We were hoping to carry twenty or thirty pounds of meat each back to Derosa. If we found good herds, I hoped to make a few more trips before fall." He glanced at Aram. "We really didn't know that this was your valley."

Aram nodded grimly. "But it is. And I don't like others being here." He was surprised to hear himself say it, but knew that it was true. "Where's this place called Derosa? Is that your village?"

"Yes." Findaen nodded and pointed southeast. "Only, it's more like a large town. It's forty or fifty miles, maybe a bit more, beyond the hills."

"You're a long way from home." Aram observed. "And you have problems with wolves in your country?"

Findaen's pleasant face fell. "We're being overrun, as are all the deer herds everywhere, especially in the last year or so."

"Why don't you eradicate them?"

"What—wolves? You mean, kill the wolves?"

Aram looked at him and said nothing.

Findaen shrugged and glanced away. "You don't just kill wolves. Well, as we've just seen, you certainly do. We do, too, when we can, but they're as big as a man, some bigger, and we're farmers mostly, or were. We're not really trained to kill something as big and ferocious as a wolf, and not really equipped."

Aram glanced at the young man's scabbard. "May I see your sword?"

"Sure." Findaen drew his short sword and handed it over, hilt first.

It was made of poor quality steel, barely more than worked iron, and showed damage along the blade's edge where it had struck something hard, bone, probably. Aram handed the poor weapon back to Findaen and looked in the young man's eyes.

"Are you a free people or servants of Manon?"

Findaen's features contracted in anger and he spat on the ground. "We're still free so far, but we've lost much land. That's why farmers find it necessary to go hunting for deer. Manon's gray men have pushed us almost completely from the plains. Derosa is in a high valley, fairly secure against attack but the planting season is short and we have to supplement our harvests with hunting."

Aram turned from him and walked a short distance away, thinking. He liked these men, despite their trespass into his valley. And for some time now he had missed the company of other humans, but still he was reluctant to readily entangle his life. And for reasons that he couldn't quite understand he didn't want anyone to know of the existence of his city.

"I'll make a deal with you," he told Findaen.

"A deal, sir?"

"Yes. Where do your people normally hunt?"

Findaen swept his arm in a half-circle, indicating most of the country to the south and southeast. "Usually, in the green hills. In years past, they were full of deer. Now, each party we send out is often more concerned with avoiding wolves and staying alive than finding game. That's why we crossed the river and came up through the pine hills. When we saw this valley, we hoped to find deer rather than wolves. And, well, you know the rest."

Aram walked to the fire and motioned for the men to gather. "Here's what I'll do. I'll kill your wolves out of the green hills to my south and the pine ridges to my east. But you must stay out of my valley. Your people must stay to the south of the two rivers in the green hills and, in the eastern hills; you must not hunt farther north than the lone spire of rock that stands between the rivers. In return, I will kill all the wolves from that whole country. Is that acceptable?"

Findaen stared at him. "You'll kill all the wolves?"

Aram nodded. "All of them."

The four Derosans glanced uncertainly at each other. Findaen asked in an incredulous voice. "Would—would you like us to help?"

"No." Aram shook his head decisively. He stood a minute in silence, thinking. Looking at Findaen, he asked. "Can you track a man?"

Findaen indicated the slim, dark-haired man to his left. "Wamlak can track almost anything."

Aram nodded. "Good. I'll camp to your south tonight and start in the morning. I'll leave good tracks for you to follow. When I find deer, I'll kill them and leave them in trees for you to find. Maybe that will help you." He looked hard at the four incredulous men. "I'll keep my bargain. In return, you must stay clear of my valley."

Findaen nodded slowly. "I assure you, sir, we will never enter your valley again except by your leave."

Aram spun and went into the night, leaving the four astounded Derosans staring after him.

IX

For the remainder of the summer and into the fall, until it became absolutely imperative for him to return home and harvest his crops, Aram wandered to the south through the wooded hills and hollows, the western borders of which he'd admired so greatly when he first escaped into the wilderness. He found and destroyed nine separate wolf packs, forty-six wolves in all. Most he slew in surprise attacks, in direct conflict. The wounded, he followed and dispatched with mercy. Touched by evil though they were, he was loath to let anything suffer.

As he worked to the west into the swath of higher, wilder country along the river's canyon, he eventually came to the cave of the wolves that had chased him into the maelstrom. There were thirteen of them now and he slew them all. When he came opposite the mountain, where he'd slept on his third or fourth night of freedom, wolf tracks became scarce, and he turned back to the east to hunt out the pine covered hills on the east of his valley.

He killed deer for the Derosans when he could but only when there were at least three to a herd and he didn't slay females that might be carrying young for the coming year. Occasionally, he checked back along his trail and found that the Derosans were as good as their word. They found every deer he left them, and several times he spotted them, but they never saw him and he was reluctant for reasons he didn't understand to make contact.

One evening, just after sundown, he slipped close to them as they were seated around their campfire. As he was deciding whether or not to approach, he picked up their conversation and realized that they were discussing him.

"Who do you suppose he is, then," wondered Mallet, the big man. "And where in the world did he come from? Has he always lived in that valley?"

Wamlak poked at the fire with a stick, sending sparks flying into the twilight. "He acts like one of the ancients."

"The ancients are all gone, thousands of years ago," protested Jonwood.

"I just said that he acts like one. He has no fear and he kills wolves with apparent ease. And look at his weapons—I've never seen any like them."

Findaen stirred uneasily. "I don't know who he is or why he's in that valley, but there is something of the ancients about him. You know that it is said that there is a high city of the old kings somewhere in that valley—over on the other side, I think, near the mountain. My father said that his grandfather had actually seen it, years ago, and that it was still haunted by spirits."

"Maybe he's a spirit," whispered Mallet, and his eyes grew round as he stared into the fire.

Wamlak gazed at him with mild disgust. "He's as real as you or I, Mallet. I see his footprints every now and then. Spirits don't leave footprints."

"Who is he then, Wamlak—tell us." Mallet said defensively.

Wamlak stared into the fire thoughtfully, then lay back and gazed up at the stars. "Maybe he is one of the ancients, who survived somehow. It's said that they didn't die—they could be killed but they didn't die."

At this, the men fell silent and Aram turned away and slipped into the night.

By the time the first real frost came, he'd driven off or killed most of the wolf packs in the pine hills from few miles south of the southern river north to the spire of rock that stood at the point where the two rivers diverged, the southern river cutting eastward straight on into the hills and the valley river turning sharply back to the north. He left a final deer there for the Derosans to find and built an "X" of deadfall to warn them to keep their bargain. When he turned toward home, he stopped leaving easy tracks, walking only on hard ground and using streams and rocks to cover his trail.

The leaves were turning and the apples were ripe when he came back to the main street before his city. He'd been gone so long, living in the wild, that he cautiously explored the city for any sign that anyone had been there but he found no evidence of people or wolves. The city did have one new occupant, however. A young bear had moved into the old wolf's den under the south steps.

It was small and black and was terrified of Aram. He decided that if it didn't bother him, it was welcome to stay and he made a habit of leaving a few apples near the grotto for it to find. Aram worked hard to get all his crops in before the first big freeze or snowfall, and only just made it. Everything had produced well, even the wheat, but he'd been gone long past its prime and had lost most of it. Bread would be a luxury again rather than a staple.

Throughout that winter, he continued to work on improving his lodgings in the city, perfecting his weapons, and organizing the armory and infirmary. On days when the weather was moderate, he scouted the immediate area for wolves but saw none.

His sixth winter in the valley passed quietly. Aram was now twenty-nine years old.

At the first break of spring, he made several wide surveys of his valley and found two deer carcasses at two different locations near the river beyond the pyramids. He studied the tracks near both kills and discovered that it was a sizeable pack of large wolves. This concerned him. He'd thought that he had eradicated all the large wolf packs in the valley. But these tracks, when he followed them, led back across the river to the east.

When spring fully came, he finished his planting and packed a pack with apples and dried meat and his little bit of bread and went across the river into the hills east of the city. He was tiring of the killing. As much as he despised wolves for what they did to people and to the deer, he had come to regret the killing of them even as he saw it as a necessary thing. He wondered whether, if the evil that touched their existence could be lifted, there could be some kind of harmony brought back to nature and the creatures that dwelled in his valley.

Crossing the river, he found a draw that wound back up into the forested hills that had a substantial stream issuing from it. As he ascended, he found no evidence of the wolves and began to hope that they had done the wise thing and departed his lands.

But then he discovered the tracks of a large pack of ten or twelve animals crossing the draw from south to north. As he climbed further into the mountains, he came across occasional carcasses of deer. This didn't alarm him, for he didn't hunt these mountains nor did the Derosans. But then one afternoon, on the slope of an amphitheater below a pass between two high peaks, he discovered the carcasses of two entirely different animals that the wolves had slain and eaten.

These were enormous skeletons with large, elongated skulls and strange rounded hooves. The legs had been long and the animals had stood higher than a tall man's head. Aram didn't know what they were but there was a mystical familiarity to their structure and it appeared that, in life, these had been magnificent creatures. He was overwhelmed by a curious grief that these animals had died. The old anger rose in him again, and when he discovered that the general route of the wolf pack led up into the pass and over the mountains to the east, even though it was not his country, he decided to follow them and eliminate them for what they had done.

As he climbed the steep slopes, he remained vigilant for any movement of dark shapes against the pale gray rock of the mountain pass above him but saw nothing. He camped that night in a windblown copse of trees a few hundred feet below the summit, scattering two concentric circles of arrow points around his camp. The high, thin air was cool, but he did not start a fire. In the morning, as soon as it was light enough to see, he ate a cold breakfast, gathered his arrow points and moved on.

The high pass was rocky and devoid of vegetation, well above the timberline, and lay between two very tall gray peaks. The wind, as it blew through the pass, was bitter even though it was late spring. As he passed between the high ramparts of stone, he found banks of snow in places where the warm sun never shone.

He stopped just below the summit of the pass and looked back. Never before had he been able to see the whole of his valley lain out before him in panorama. It was about noon and the brilliant sun angled down from its position in the southern half of the sky, delineating the black, rose, and gold rock of his mountain far to the west. He could not make out details of his city but he could see its brilliant rectangle at the mountain's base and the main thoroughfare that ran almost directly towards him.

Turning to look east, out beyond the forested slopes that fell away below him, he saw a vast, high, rolling country, broken here and there by gentle ridges with serpentine lines of trees growing along their spines, and the whole of the country was carpeted by a lustrous green. It stretched away from him toward the east farther than his eye could see, and was bounded far away on the north by high, gray-topped mountains like the ones that bordered his valley and in the distant south by gentle, timbered hills. It was a broad and wide land, all of it beautifully green. No doubt, if they hadn't all been slain by wolves, this was a country for deer, or any other animal that grazed on grass. He thought about the skeletons far down the draw behind him and wondered if those great beasts had come from this wide, grassy land.

The tracks of the wolf pack led down through a steep, wooded cut, and Aram once again gave chase. There was water here, fed by the high snows, tumbling down in a headlong rush. Here on the eastern side of the mountains, the woods were deep and lush and cool, with many more fir and spruce than pines. Throughout the morning, as he rapidly lost altitude, the weather warmed toward the making of a fine spring day.

Noon found him still far up the mountainside and with the necessity of caution that prevented a blunder into the wolf pack; it soon became obvious that the day would wane away before he reached the valley floor.

At nightfall, he found the brow of a ridge that extended out from the side of the mountain and ended in a steep precipice. It was crowned by a stand of tall sweeping firs. After making certain that it could only be accessed from the mountainside, he scattered his arrow tips and camped, once again without making a fire.

After eating, he lay for awhile listening to the sounds of the forest around and below him and gazed up through the sweeping bows of the giant firs at the stars. They had never shone as bright and clear out on the plains of his youth as they did in this high thin atmosphere. Out over the broad land to the east, hanging in the perfect blackness of the heavens just above the horizon, there was an elongated circle pattern of red stars with a long slash of bright white stars extending from it halfway across the sky. His father had told him once, long ago, that it was the Glittering Sword of God.

As he lay watching it ascend into the sky from the east, he fell asleep.

He woke before dawn and ate another cold breakfast. As soon as it was barely light enough, he gathered his points and descended the ridge into the hollow below and crept down the mountain. It was his experience that wolves tended to fuss among themselves until late into the night and seldom awoke before full sunrise. Often because of this habit of theirs, he'd been able to fall upon them unexpectedly in the early morning.

He had no such luck this morning. Sunrise found him still among the firs of the mountainside following a tumbling, cascading stream. An hour after sunup he found where the wolves had passed the night. He was not far behind them now but still it was disappointing. He'd hoped to catch them and slay them somewhere along the route to the pass as a warning for all wolves to avoid his side of the mountain.

The ground began to level out and the tumbling stream flowed more gently, descending in short falls from pool to pool. Pines grew here, rather sparsely and the steep mountainside gentled out and crumpled into foothills covered with grasses and wildflowers.

The stream made a sharp turn to the left as it encountered a grassy ridge that bisected the mountainside and the tracks of the wolf pack went up and over the ridge. Aram followed. As he topped the ridge he heard the sounds of an intense struggle immediately to his front. The wolves had found prey.

Just below him and in front was a stand of trees where the stream flowed out around the end of the ridge into a small meadow. The trees masked his view of whatever was happening. He ran down the ridge top to the right until he was clear of the trees and looked into the meadow.

In the center of the small, circular meadow twelve wolves had attacked a very large animal. It looked exactly like the one ridden by the ancient warrior in the fresco on the wall of the great hall.

The animal was enormous and black with a beautiful coat of shining hair and a long tail and mane. Plunging and rearing, it was resisting the attack of the wolves mightily, had already slain two, and injured another so badly it could not walk but lay kicking ineffectively at the ground. But the remaining nine wolves were assaulting the great animal in a circular attack, and they had seriously bloodied the magnificent beast.

Even in the few seconds that he watched, Aram could tell that the great animal was weakening. Strips of flesh hung from its haunches, showing the stark white of tendons and bone and its legs were red with its own blood. The grass around was slick with it. The beast's attackers were leaping upon it in turns and slashing at it with their teeth. Aram could not bear to see such a magnificent creature die at the will of wolves.

He nocked an arrow and ran into the fray. The big beast was whirling and plunging and kicking with its hind legs and Aram did not want to strike it, so he angled to one side where he could shoot at the wolves without endangering the animal. Quickly loosing three arrows in succession, he killed one wolf outright and eliminated two others from the fight. Then four of them turned on him.

They were much larger than those he'd been used to, massive beasts, and they assaulted him eagerly, without fear. Dropping his bow and drawing his sword he plunged among them even as they attacked. His sword flew as he darted left and then right, parrying attacks from one side and then the other as he drove the steel deep wherever he could. These wolves did not die easily, but Aram's blood was hot with a lust to kill and a desire to save their magnificent prey.

He slashed forelimbs from bodies and stabbed at necks and drove his sword deep between ribs and into haunches. Finally, with a great swipe of the blade he cracked the skull of the last of the four that had attacked him and turned to find what had become of the great beast. The last two wolves had driven it to its haunches and were shredding its flesh. White tendons shone out through the crimson flood on its legs.

With a roar of anger he leapt on the remaining two wolves and slew them before they could turn and face him so intent were they on their kill. Aram quickly made sure every wolf was dead and then approached the great animal. It had managed to get back on its feet but stood with its head low, muscles quivering, and its breathing was labored and shallow.

Retrieving his pack, Aram set about stanching the flow of blood from its many wounds, working like a madman, making poultices and binding them with leather strips to shore up the torn flesh hanging from its legs and haunches.

He soon ran out of leather strips to hold the poultices in place, so he cut up his pack. In places the animal's flesh was ripped deep, exposing bone and tendons, but at least most of the tears in its flesh went with the grain of the muscle and not against it.

Some two hours later, he'd managed to bind the beast's wounds and still it stood with its head low, its nose almost brushing the ground, breathing in great shuddering sighs. Its eyes were half closed and the huge dark orbs were dulled with pain. Aram instinctively knew that if it went down it was finished.

To try to revive it he removed his shirt, dipped it in the stream and washed the animal down all over, removing the blood and grime of the battle. He cupped water into his hands and tried to get it to drink but it was not interested. Carefully, he went around the animal and checked all of his bandaging work, making certain the skin was re-attached properly and that no raw flesh was exposed. He checked its knees, making sure they were locked so that, hopefully, it would not go down accidentally.

Then, crouching down, he examined the great beast.

Despite the terrible wounds it had suffered in the fight for its life, it was beautiful, the most beautiful animal he had ever seen. The graceful lines of its body exceeded in the beauty of their form even that of deer. Its coat was as deeply black as a starless night. At its shoulder, it was at least a foot taller than he stood. The long mane and tail were thick and, if anything, blacker than its coat. It was exactly the same kind of animal depicted in the fresco in the great hall. In fact, it appeared to Aram as if it could very well *be* the same animal depicted in the fresco, as if this very beast had stood for its portrait with the ancient warrior on its back. Studying it, it seemed obvious to him that it had been created for the express purpose of carrying a man.

It seemed an obscene thing to him to allow the carcasses of the beast's attackers lie so near it in the hour of its agony—suffering that they had caused—so Aram hauled the bodies of the wolves one by one down to the bottom of the meadow and stacked them away from the stream. If the vultures did not do their work, then in a few days time, he would burn them. At least the area around the great animal was clear.

About mid-afternoon, when he approached it again to check that the bleeding had been contained, he noticed that the great animal was shivering. The loss of blood had reduced its body temperature. Aram gathered wood from the stand of trees on the small ridge and started a fire, near enough upwind that it would get the advantage of the heat but far enough away that it wouldn't frighten the animal. He couldn't be sure of the state of its consciousness. Since the end of the fight for its life, it hadn't moved from the spot where it stood and its head remained down, with its eyes nearly closed.

He tried before nightfall to get it to eat some of the new grass from the meadow but it showed no interest. That night he encircled the animal with a ring of small fires that he tended between fits of sleep. Every so often throughout the night, he checked the animal, always with the same result. It was no better, but if it was worse, Aram could not discern that either.

At sunrise, he ate breakfast and held an apple under the nose of the great beast. It did not eat, but for the first time exhibited signs of life by moving its nose at the scent of the fruit. Its large eyes, however, remained dulled with pain and again that day it did not raise its head. Toward evening, when Aram again tried to give it water, it succeeded in sucking in a small amount from the palm of his hand.

Over the next several days Aram did nothing but patrol the area for dangers and tend to the animal's wounds, changing poultices, cleaning the wounds to halt infection, and giving it water as often as it would drink. Finally, after more than a week, the beast lifted its head slightly and took a bit of grass. Aram was elated at the progress and became increasingly hopeful that the beast would not die.

After several days passed the animal eventually moved haltingly, painfully, down to the stream where it drank its fill. There it stood nearly motionless again for the better part of a day. On the days that followed its move to water, however, there were perceptible signs of improvement. Occasionally the animal would lower its head to the ground and bite a mouthful of grass and a day came soon after when it accepted an apple from Aram's hand. Slowly, but surely, the light of life came back into its large black eyes.

Aram continued to change the poultices, scrounging on the slopes about the small meadow for medicinal herbs. One spot just above the animal's knee on its right hind leg worried him. An inflamed swelling had appeared and instead of diminishing, grew ever larger and more inflamed. Finally, he decided that it must be lanced.

He sterilized his knife in the fire and prepared to do the deed. But he was unsure what the huge beast that had submitted to his ministrations in a docile manner thus far would think of his actions when he approached it with the sharp steel.

He approached the great beast head on and looked in its eyes, holding out his hand and showing it the knife.

"Listen, my big friend, I've got to do something that you may not like and I'd prefer it if you didn't kick me into the next life when I do it. I'm not trying to hurt you, understand?"

The great animal raised its head and looked at him with its luminous black eyes.

"*I understand,*" it said.

X

Aram stumbled backward and stared at the big animal in astonishment.

"Did you just speak to me?" he asked incredulously.

"*I did.*" The great beast answered. Aram heard its voice clearly, a rich deep baritone, colored by age and wisdom. But when the animal spoke, its mouth did not move. Its voice seemed to originate inside Aram's own mind. He studied it for a long time.

"How are you speaking to me?" he asked, finally.

"*Mind to mind,*" it answered. "*It is an ancient art. My kind spoke to your kind, mind to mind, long ago before the dark ages came.*"

"What are you?—I'm sorry, forgive me, who are you?" Aram asked.

"*My name is Florm; I am the third of my kind and—in the absence of my father and grandfather—the lord of all horses. I am grateful to you for saving my life. You are a great warrior and I owe you a great debt.*"

Aram shook his head slowly, in wonderment. "No, my lord Florm, you owe me nothing. I am honored to know you. I'm very glad to meet you. I've seen depictions of your kind before in the great hall of my city."

"*Your city?*"

"I didn't build it, but I found it deserted and I live there now. In the absence of its rightful owners, I guess its mine." Aram pointed to the west. "It's in the next valley."

Florm's head jerked upward and his neck arched. "*The city in the mountain—the city of stone?*"

"Yes. It's carved into the mountain. I think it's quite ancient."

Florm snorted. "*It's more than ancient; it's one of the oldest cities in the world. It was the city of the great kings, long ago, and no one has lived there in more than ten thousand years. When last men resided there—and they did so in splendor—I was barely more than a colt.*"

It was Aram's turn again to be amazed. "How old are you?"

"*I have walked the earth for more than eleven thousand years, since before the coming of the evil of Manon. Do you have any more of those apples?*"

Aram laughed. "I have several, my lord, and I can go home and get more if you wish. But I am loath to leave you here without an adequate defense until I'm certain that you are well."

Florm looked downstream at the pile of wolf carcasses. Aram had dragged them and piled them far enough away so that the odor of rotting flesh wouldn't overwhelm them.

"Yes," he said. "Let's talk about that. Did you slay them all?"

"No, my lord, you killed three yourself."

Florm studied him a long moment. "Who, may I ask, are you?"

Aram shook his head. "No one of consequence. My name is Aram. I was born a slave out on the plains but when they brought me to the edge of the wilderness to help open up new fields, I escaped. I could not bear to be a slave. After escaping and wandering awhile, losing a friend to wolves, and getting lost inside the mountain, I found the city of stone. As no one was living there, and it appeared to have been deserted for some time, I took up residence. That was seven years ago."

Florm glanced down across the meadow again at the piled carcasses. "No one of consequence, you say?"

"No," Aram replied. "Now I really must lance your sore."

He went around behind the horse and probed the swelling gently until he found a place between the tendons. Then he carefully pushed the blade into the skin and pressed out the foul infection with his fingers. When he was satisfied that it was clean, he applied a poultice to the wound and then washed his knife and hands in the stream.

"That should heal now." He told Florm.

Florm nodded his gratitude. "And how did you learn to fight so well, and to kill wolves with such impunity?"

"I had to survive." Aram answered simply.

Florm didn't respond but moved stiffly to the stream and lowered his nose into the cold, clear water. Then he grazed for a bit on the lush grass of the meadow. Aram took it as his cue to make his rounds on the ridges above and through the forests surrounding the meadow to check for signs of predators. When he returned, Florm was standing with his head down as if he were sleeping. Aram started a fire and rolled out his bed. The sun was behind the tall mountains to the west and a pleasant evening had settled over the meadow.

After a while, Florm stirred and walked over to the fire. He stood quietly while Aram ate, then he spoke.

"I was coming to find you, you know."

Aram looked up, startled. "To find me? Why?"

"Because you are the wolf-slayer and rumor of your deeds has gone about the land. The people of the free towns to the south speak of you with great admiration and wonder." Florm looked up into the deepening twilight of the sky. "The wolves used to be a natural part of the cycles of life on this world, but Manon touched them with his evil and they have become a blight on all life. They have increased dramatically in number over the last few centuries and have begun killing our colts. When two or more horses are together we can handle a sizeable pack of wolves, but when they catch one of us alone, well, you have seen the result.

"When I heard of your deeds, I sent my nephews, Haveng and Melchor, to find you and watch you and verify that you could do the things that were claimed. When Haveng and Melchor did not return, I came to find the answer to what had happened to them." Florm looked sharply at Aram. "Have you seen them?"

Aram stared into the fire and thought of the lonely, desolate skeletons beyond the mountain. He nodded sadly. "I believe I have seen them both, my lord." He looked up at the great horse. "They were killed by wolves on my side of the mountains. I was tracking their killers when I came upon you in the midst of your battle."

He looked down the darkening meadow toward the piled carcasses.

"Their killers are there."

Florm lifted his head, gazing out into the darkness, and was silent for a long time. The night deepened, stars filled the sky, and the Glittering Sword of God rose above the eastern horizon. Finally, Aram broke the silence.

"What is it that you sought me for, my lord?"

Florm stirred. "I already owe you a great debt, Aram Wolfslayer. I hesitate to ask anything further." He fell silent again.

Aram got up and went around the fire to stand by the horse and looked up into the deep sapphire of the eastern sky. The Glittering Sword of God hung at an angle just above the horizon.

"My lord," he said. "You have been alive longer than I can imagine. Your stature on this world is more than I could attain in a thousand lifetimes. If you wish me to kill wolves, it is a simple thing, I can do it easily. I will happily slay or drive out the wolves from all the lands that you designate. In return, if you wish, you could tell me, now and again, things that I do not know but wish to know. Perhaps we could make a bargain of that sort?"

Florm looked at him curiously. "What is it that you wish to know?"

Aram shrugged. "Everything. Who lived in the great city and why did they leave? What was life like before the tyranny of Manon? I don't even know the history of my own people."

"So, you are more than a talented killer. You wish to be a scholar."

Aram laughed. "That is probably overstating the case. I would say that at the least, I would like not to be ignorant."

"An accomplishment, indeed; one that few attain. My friend, I will tell you all that I know." Florm promised. "But still, I cannot ask you to risk your life further in the service of my people."

Aram laughed again. "Forgive the nature of this statement, my lord—but there is very little risk to my life. I was almost slain by wolves once, but I was not. I killed them, even in my extremity, when it appeared that my life would surely end. I believe that I have become a man that is difficult to kill. You need not ask, my lord. I will hunt and destroy every wolf on these plains of my own will. That is my promise. But I would like to have your friendship, nonetheless."

"You have my friendship, Aram, and you will have it always. I should tell you that none of my kind has spoken to yours in thousands of years, since our peoples broke fellowship, so you and I have already established a precedent."

Aram frowned at him. "Why was fellowship broken?"

"Long ago, many of your people joined Manon when he rebelled against the gods and altered the affairs of earth. My people joined those that rebelled against *him*. But the men who were our allies were all slain or enslaved, and the others began a long descent into madness, slavery, and barbarism, so we horses broke fellowship and went away from the rule of Manon into the wild. Since that time, no horse has communed with a man or carried a man on his back. Now you and I have altered the first constriction. When I am well enough, the second will be altered as well."

Aram was silent for a time. Then he went and lay down on his bedroll and looked over at the horse on the far side of the fire.

"Lord Florm?"

"Yes, Aram?"

"Sleep well, my lord."

Florm cocked one hind leg and lowered his head.

"And you, my friend."

While stars still shone overhead and the eastern sky barely colored with the promise of the coming day, Aram awoke to a distant thrumming in the ground. He leapt up and crouched, seizing his sword and looking about the meadow. He could hear nothing and could see nothing in the pale light of very early morning. He leaned his head back close to the earth. From a great distant, the ground throbbed, but whatever created the sound was almost certainly approaching. He stood and looked around for Florm. The horse lord was down near the stream, grazing quietly and unconcernedly. Quickly, Aram strode in that direction.

"I think we should go up into the trees on the ridge, my lord."

Florm looked up. "Why is that, Aram?"

"Something is coming—we need to find a more defensible position."

Aram could hear Florm's laughter ring inside his head.

"Actually, my friend, two somethings are coming. They are my son, Thaniel, and my nephew, Jared. You have impressive ears, Aram. They are at least five miles away and won't be here for another ten minutes or so." Florm lowered his head and returned to his breakfast.

So, Aram was to meet two more horses. He quickly ate and cleaned up the campsite. Ten minutes later the rumbling of hooves filled the close air of the meadow and two magnificent horses appeared from the east and galloped to Florm, bowing their heads low. Florm acknowledged them and they communed together a few minutes. Their conversation was closed to Aram. The two newcomers looked at him occasionally during the course of their communion and when it was ended Florm opened his mind and spoke to Aram.

"Aram, if you please, come and meet some of my family. This fellow," Florm indicated with a look the large, dark horse on his right, "is my son, Thaniel."

Thaniel nodded slightly to Aram. Aram bowed. Thaniel was a tall and solid beast, muscular and imposing. He was a bit taller than Florm and, if anything, blacker, though with a small, diamond-shaped blaze of white in the middle his forehead.

"And this is my sister's son, Jared." Florm indicated the second horse. Aram and the horse acknowledged each other. Jared was also muscular but somewhat rangier than the others and his coat was a deep rich brown.

"I am honored to meet you both." Aram said and then he stepped away to gather up his stray arrow points and to give the horses privacy.

Thaniel followed him. "My father has told me of your great service to us in saving his life. I thank you. I am in your debt. Florm is a great lord—the lord of all horses. We are all in your debt."

"With due respect," Aram replied. "There is no debt. I am honored to have been of service to such a great person but I would have saved anyone from the wolves in the same circumstance."

The great black horse was silent for a moment and it seemed to Aram that he was quietly distressed about something. After another moment's hesitation, Thaniel said, "My father has informed me that he intends to honor you by bearing you where you will. This is a great honor, indeed. But I must ask that you allow me to stand in the place of the Lord of Horses. My father has not borne a man on his back since the ancient kings were in allegiance with us. If you will forgive my bluntness, it would be unseemly. And, he needs time to recover. If you will allow it, I will bear you wherever you wish to go."

Aram instantly understood the reason for the horse's discomfort but it was for nothing. He had no intention of riding the great horse anywhere.

"Sir, I am honored. But the things that I have to do, now that you are here to guard your father's wellbeing, I must do alone. I need no bearing. Thank you for your offer but I prefer the use of my own two feet."

Aram turned away, a bit rudely perhaps; but he found himself nonplussed and irritated at Thaniel's seeming humiliation that a mere man had rescued his father. But Aram was unfamiliar with the ways of free people, let alone horses, and he didn't wish for any more entanglements in his life anyway. Let horses and all others be as they would. He had wolves to kill.

He gathered the rest of his arrow points and checked his supplies. He still had twenty arrows and his spear so there was no immediate need to re-supply his weaponry. He glanced toward the horses. They were standing together near the stream. As the sun peered over the eastern horizon, Aram secured his campsite and slipped away over the wooded hill to the north.

All that day he hunted out from the meadow in concentric circles, searching for wolves. Finally, late in the day, on one of the long wooded ridges between two streams to the northeast of the meadow, he found the tracks of a large pack of at least ten animals. The trail led northwest into the timbered hills and while it had been made that day was too cold to follow at such a late hour. But now he had quarry for the morrow.

He got back to camp just at twilight, intending to eat and go straight to bed so he could arise early and hunt due north in the morning, hoping to catch the pack coming down out of the hills at sunrise. The three horses were there, grazing near the stream. Florm still moved painfully and with a fair amount of stiffness, so in the fading daylight, Aram approached and sought permission to examine his wounds.

The great horse was healing fine, however, even on the hind leg where he'd had the swelling, but it would be some time before he was fully mobile and recovered enough to travel any distance.

"Do I need to scatter my arrow points, tonight, my lord?" Aram asked. He was anxious that nothing should delay his departure in the morning.

Florm chuckled. "Nothing will get past the ears of these youngsters. I doubt much would get past yours, either, my friend. Did you find your wolves today?"

Aram nodded. "A large pack with several mature animals a couple of miles north. I'm going after them tomorrow."

Florm stared thoughtfully out into the deepening twilight. "Long ago, they answered to Kelven and his laws, as did all living things, but Manon touched them with his evil. It is very sad. Our two peoples used to talk, once upon a time; we shared the earth in peace and settled any disputes we had with civility. Horses were never their natural prey. Now, they slaughter our colts, and our mares and sometimes even stallions are killed defending their young."

The great horse sighed. "It is Manon's doing. I have often wished that the evil of Manon could be undone."

Aram shrugged. "Maybe someday it will be. But one thing at a time, my lord. For now, we must protect your people." He frowned and looked at Florm. "My lord, I know of Manon, but who is Kelven?"

"Long ago, it was Kelven that ruled all living things besides men, as well as the air and the water and trees and all plants. In the great war, he fought with us against Manon, but Manon triumphed. Kelven has not been seen upon the earth since that time. This is one of those things that, when I am stronger, I will tell you in full, for it touches upon the history of your people, especially of those that dwelled in the city of stone." Florm looked at him and spoke with solemn intensity. "Thaniel is right, you know. The debt is on our side, you only increase what we owe with your deeds."

"Nonsense, my lord," Aram shook his head impatiently. "I know that your people are greater than mine, and I am certainly one of the least of all my people. Thaniel need not point this out in order for me to know that it is true. But despite the differences in our stations, is there any chance for friendship between you and me?"

"It already exists."

"Then that is why I will kill your wolves. For friendship's sake. There is no debt. Goodnight, my lord."

Aram laid out his bedroll at the base of the rock outcropping where he had an unobstructed view of the meadow. He believed Florm about the keenness of the horses' ears, but he had long ago learned that there was great value in not being careless.

XI

The next day, he accomplished something that he'd never done but had anticipated since the creation of his bow. As he had hoped, he found the wolf pack coming down out of the hills onto the plain about an hour after sunrise, running nearly single file along a streambed. Aram was concealed in a stand of thick firs on a gentle ridge to the south. As they came opposite him, he dropped one at about the middle of the pack with an arrow.

Instantly, the others were upon the fallen wolf, tearing at its flesh in a frenzy of bloodlust. As always, Aram was repulsed by the barbaric, unnatural behavior. Quickly, he felled three more. By this time, the wolves were confused at the quick, inexplicable deaths occurring among their ranks and began tearing around their fallen comrades in confused fury, howling and yapping.

In the midst of their confusion, Aram easily killed them all, eleven in total. When they had all fallen, he went down and dispatched those that were still living with his sword and recovered a few undamaged arrows from the bodies of the dead. He'd dropped them all with his bow, not once engaging in single combat. A sense of mastery over their kind grew within him. After making sure that they were all dead, he dragged the heavy bodies away from the running water so that the vultures could do their work without the stream being polluted.

As he was washing his arrows in the stream and watching the meadows and hillsides about him for danger, he spotted Thaniel and Jared observing him from the ridge top. He met the horses' gaze for a moment and then they turned away and went toward the south out of his sight.

That day he ranged further north into the corrugated grasslands, turning east when he found the tracks of another pack of wolves, only five or six this time, all adults. He trailed them eastward until the sun began to slide toward the hills then turned back to camp.

It was fully dark when he returned to camp, and the horses were out in the meadow, so he unrolled his bed near the rocks and went to sleep. At dawn, he was again on the move, heading northeast. At noon, he crossed the tracks of the wolf pack and turned east to follow them at a sprint. Three hours later, he caught them lying in the shade of a stand of pine trees, sleeping off the effects of a kill of two deer, a doe and a fawn. There were six wolves in all.

Pulling his sword, he ran in among them, slaying two instantly before they could rise and wounding a third. The other three pounced but he was ready, sidestepping to the right, nearly severing the massive head of the lead wolf, whirling and catching another in midair, running his sword deep into its guts. The remaining wolf, smaller than the others, turned and fled. Aram started to give chase, but the wolf was too swift for him and he didn't want to risk spending more arrows. He killed the wounded wolf and then turned southwest toward the meadow. It was already late and he needed to find a stand of ironwood to replenish his arrows.

Searching along all the streams as he went, he found a young, tall stand of the necessary saplings toward evening, within a mile of camp. As he was gathering enough to replace the arrows he'd lost the day before, once again he saw Thaniel and Jared trotting parallel to his line of march toward camp.

Later, as he was sitting in camp fletching the new batch of arrows, the horses approached and watched him for a while in silence.

"That is an ancient and amazing skill," Florm remarked finally. "One that I have not seen practiced in some time. Where did you learn it?"

Aram glanced up. "There are old drawings on the walls of my armory. I experimented until I discovered how to make it work. And I tried many different kinds of wood for bows and arrows until I found the right ones."

"Remarkable." Florm stepped forward. "We would like to speak with you, Aram."

Aram laid his work aside, stood up, and looked at him expectantly.

"My son spoke in haste the other day," Florm said. "He is used to the way things have been for thousands of years now. No horse has borne a man upon his back in all that time. It is often difficult to recognize the winds of change. But they are blowing.

"Jared and Thaniel have observed you at your work, Aram, and they recognize now that you are a great warrior and that you seek no reward for meting justice. But they also see that you are limited in the amount of ground that you can cover in a day. The foaling grounds of our people are very far away and are overrun with wolves. It is vital to us that those grounds be protected. We have an offer."

Aram stood in silence, waiting. He recognized the superior rank of the horses to his own station upon the earth especially that of the ancient and honorable Florm, but he intended to do no more groveling in the course of his life so he waited for them to tender their offer unsolicited. Thaniel stepped forward beside his father.

"My father is now able to make his way to the summer camps of our people." He said. "Jared will go with him to guard him on the way. I offer my back to carry you where you will to destroy our enemies. I will bear you gladly and will fight with you. Afterward, I will carry you wherever you wish to go. Will you accept?"

Aram looked down for a moment in surprised silence and considered it. The range that could be covered by a strong, fast horse would certainly solve his problems of distance. And he intended to free this land of its scourge of wolves—mostly just because it was the right thing to do but also because he now wished to cement a friendship with Florm and his people. But he had told Thaniel the truth when he said he preferred the use of his own feet. He looked up.

"I have never ridden. I'm afraid I would be a cumbersome burden."

"I will help you," Thaniel replied. "We will practice in the meadow for as long as is necessary, if you agree."

Aram studied the ancient face of Florm for a moment and then bowed to Thaniel in decision. "Thank you, I accept. Together we can speed the work of ridding your land of wolves."

For three days, Aram rode the great horse around the meadow, learning to leap upon the great back and ride while holding on to the mane. After he was comfortable, he practiced shooting from the horse, first as it was standing, then trotting, and finally, with it running at great speed. He practiced shooting to his right and then to the left with the bow while holding his spears in readiness across his lap.

A day after they all agreed that Aram was ready, they parted, Florm and Jared going off to the southeast and Aram and Thaniel to the northeast, toward the foaling grounds.

As if they'd been in league all their lives, the two of them became efficiently deadly. As the summer waxed and then began to wane, they slew dozens of wolves, destroying pack after pack, hunting ever further eastward across the vast country of the horses. Aram found it exhilarating, riding into the wind and the heat of battle astride the great thundering black beast. Thaniel communicated very little, but Aram was used to silence and they seemed to have an unspoken understanding of what each expected of the other.

In battle, they were seamless, moving together as one killing machine. Thaniel was a powerful animal and extremely quick. He would charge directly at a wolf pack while Aram let arrows fly. At the last minute, Thaniel would plunge left or right and Aram would lean out and deal death with his sword. Then they would run down those that tried to flee. None escaped.

Usually, except for dispatching the wounded, Aram did all his killing from horseback, much of it with the bow. At times, though, they would discover that a pack was filing down through a narrow, rough ravine where there was no room for the horse to maneuver and then he would instruct Thaniel to remain behind while he went down and fought at the level of the wolves. He had developed a preference for joining battle with the bow but sometimes, in thick growth or along very narrow draws, it was all sword work.

In one such ambush, Aram spied a pack loping down a narrow steep-sided defile. It was a large group of sixteen, something rarely seen. The defile was too close to risk mounted combat so Aram had Thaniel remain at the top of the ridge hidden in the trees while he went alone into the bottom where two spires of rock rose about twenty feet into the air a few feet apart. There was a space between them that would allow Aram to fight at close quarters while only defending two narrow openings, one to either side.

He waited, hidden in a cleft of one of the spires, until some of the wolves had gone past then attacked. He plunged the sword into the side of a great wolf running past and the battle was joined. They came at him from both sides but he spun one way and then the other, his sword quick and sure. The wolf pack circled him and plunged in at perceived opportunities but Aram was too fast and efficient. When it was over, dead and dying wolves surrounded him and yet he was nearly unscathed. Thaniel, watching this display from the top of the bluff, thought to himself not for the first time that this man must be very like those warriors of old of which his father often spoke.

Eastward, across the northern half of the high plains, they hunted and battled, crisscrossing the region between the mountains on the north and the winding river that flowed gently from west to east at the middle of the highlands. While many streams drained the grasslands of the horses, generally flowing eastward, this river, though not very grand in any sense of the word, was the largest of them all.

One day, on the gentle slope that rose above this stream to the north, while chasing a pack of fleeing wolves, they entered suddenly into an area of rough, bumpy, and rocky ground spotted with small patches of stunted brush and twisted, dead trees. Thaniel swerved suddenly, nearly unseating Aram and charged down toward the river, quickly exiting the unusual landscape.

When Aram had righted himself and Thaniel had plunged through the shallow river to the far side, he tugged on the horse's mane, bringing the animal to a halt. As Thaniel stood uneasily, snorting and wheezing from the sudden exertion, Aram turned and studied the odd ground across the river for a few moments. Then he looked down at the back of Thaniel's head.

"What troubles you, my friend?"

Thaniel swung his great head around and looked north, at the broken, lumpy ground, its trees all dead or seriously stressed and its scattered bunches of grass yellowed and withered though everywhere else across the highlands the lush green of summer possessed the land. The broad area of distressed earth stretched for three or four miles along the top of the rise.

"That is where the old world ended," the horse said simply.

Aram felt his heart constrict and his eyes widen as he gazed across at the wounded landscape. "I don't understand."

Thaniel blew great flecks of foam from his nostrils. "That is the battlefield where the ancient king Joktan fell, and his army with him. It is where Manon, the enemy of the world, cut him down, ending the age of kings. It is a place of evil." The great black horse was silent for a moment and then he spoke softly, almost reverently. "My grandfather and his father were alive then."

Aram stared across the quiet river at the troubled ground for several minutes, trying to imagine the sights and sounds of the great struggle that had occurred there. Then he looked toward the east and nudged Thaniel with his boot. "Let's go around it, my friend, and see if we can recover the trail of those wolves."

The partnership between Aram and the great black horse had two results. Wolves became increasingly scarce across the high grasslands, and the wolves that they did encounter traveled in ever-larger groups. This last fact troubled Aram and he mentioned it to Thaniel.

"Is it normal for wolves in this country to group up like this? I've never noticed it before anywhere else."

Thaniel laughed, a deep rumbling sound. "It is because of us, my friend. Rumor of an angel of death on a horse has gone throughout all the wolf people. I've caught word of it here and there when we've passed near to them."

Aram was stunned. "Do you mean that you can understand their speech?"

"Yes." At the moment Thaniel was walking southeast along a broad, grassy ridge. "Once, before Manon turned them, the wolves were one of the noble peoples, granted the gift of speech by Kelven. We often spoke, resolving issues of boundaries and of the keeping of the peace. Our peoples no longer talk openly but we can still hear them when they are in duress. Lately, because of you, they are in deep duress. So, they are gathering in ever-larger numbers for the purposes of defense. I watched you in the ravine, Aram. I don't think they could touch you with an army of a hundred."

"Tell me, Thaniel, who are the noble peoples?"

"There are six families of noble people that walk the earth. Men, of course, and horses. Then wolves, and the predators of the air—eagles, falcons, and hawks—and then lions and the family of great cats, and bears—though bears and the family of great cats use the gift rarely, I am told. There are some that dwell in the sea as well, but I have no knowledge of them."

"And these all possess the gift of speech?"

"Yes."

"Including those that live in my valley?"

"Of course."

"That brings up a point." Aram said.

Thaniel turned his head to listen but continued progressing down the ridge toward the southeast.

Aram looked out over the vast wide country. "Wolves are becoming scarce on the high plains and in two or three weeks I will need to be in my valley, far to the west beyond the pine mountains. Summer will soon end and I will need to harvest my crops. It's been some time since we've seen substantial numbers of wolves. How close are we, do you think, to clearing the entire country?"

"My father made it clear to me that you are in control of the schedule, Aram." Thaniel answered. "We have already cleared the foaling grounds and eradicated them in many other places. If you need to go west now, I will take you."

"How great a journey is it to the west of this land?"

"We are now three hundred miles east of the place where you saved my father's life. I can return you there in three or four days."

Aram considered that for a moment. "I have observed, Thaniel, that you are not easily tired."

"That is so."

"How far is it to the eastern borders of your land?"

"Less than a hundred miles," Thaniel answered.

Aram gazed eastward in astonishment at distant, snow-topped peaks, certainly farther away from their current location than a mere hundred miles. "Are you telling me that those mountains are within a hundred miles of our present position? They appear much farther away."

Again Thaniel laughed. "No, my friend, you are right, those mountains are at least two hundred miles distant, maybe farther. Between our lands and those mountains there is a large body of water, an inland sea, that borders our lands from the north where it is fed by many streams, to the south where a mighty river drains it out through the mountains toward the distant ocean."

"I would like to see this water." Aram said.

"It is but two days away."

"Then let's do this. Let us find this sea on the eastern border of your lands and then methodically and at good pace, search out all the land until we get back to the west. We will slay any wolves we find. Can we do that in three or four weeks?"

"We can. And that will bring you to your home in time?" Thaniel asked.

"Yes."

Thaniel turned off the ridge toward the east and broke into a ground-consuming canter. As they sped eastward, Aram saw something above the earth, far beyond the mountains to the northeast, something massive and elusive that seemed to fool his eye. When he looked away from it, it was there, at the side of his vision, but when he turned his head to gaze directly at it, it faded into the hazy blue depths of the sky.

"Is there something beyond the mountains to the northeast?" he asked.

"Yes." Answered Thaniel, but he would say no more.

After two days of traveling, they came quite suddenly to the sandy, reedy, and wind-blown shores of a large sea or lake, beyond which, at a great distance, there rose the heights of mountains. The water stretched away to the horizon, a vast blue-gray cauldron. Aram had never seen a body of water this substantial and he dismounted and walked for a time along the beach. The wind was up and the waves of a moderate surf rolled up onto the sand.

The air was pungent and rich with moisture but there was no smell of salt and when Aram tipped his fingers in the water and tasted, it was fresh. The sun glinted off the waves and for as far out as he could see, whitecaps dotted the steely surface. It was a pleasant aspect and called to something ancient and primordial deep in Aram's soul. The thought crossed his mind that a man could build a home back in among the trees and look out at this view for the rest of his life and not tire of it.

The shore was cut by small coves and sandy bays and every so often streams of varying size ran out of the highlands and added their volume to the lake. Long-legged water birds rose up before him in flocks, complaining loudly at the intrusion into their affairs. After a time, regretfully, Aram turned away and he and Thaniel went back to work.

They hunted northward along the edge of the sea for more than a day then angled back to the northwest toward the distant foothills, crossing many streams and rivers flowing from west to east toward the sea. Reaching the edge of the northern mountains, they swung back to the south, always searching for wolves.

Together, Aram and Thaniel scoured out the eastern lands, slaying scattered bands of wolves, and then they worked westward through the lands they'd already hunted. Except for the occasional lone wolf and small bands of two or three, the land was empty, though they often crossed the tracks of large groups of the animals headed north.

Finally, they turned resolutely in that direction. The land to the north of the grasslands was composed of long, furrowed, wooded hills that wound gradually upward into the domain of high, granite-peaked mountains. These mountains were wild and rugged, with sharply delineated peaks that were ever capped with snow though they looked toward the south.

In the middle of the second week, Aram and Thaniel broke over the height of a wooded ridge running east and west and down into a broad valley watered by a wide gentle river fed by streams that tumbled out of the hills. There were few trees in the grassy expanse of the valley, leaving it mostly open, and there were marshes scattered between the loops of the river.

Beyond the river, at the edge of the timber, where the foothills merged with the open slopes of the valley, was a long dark line of wolves, a hundred at least or more, sitting on their haunches looking south, as if they'd been waiting for the man and the horse.

Aram and Thaniel stopped at the top of the ridge and stood still and stared northward across the valley at the wolves. Nothing stirred anywhere. One lone eagle hovered motionless in the blue high above. The man and horse stared across at the wolves that in turn gazed back at them without movement or sound. Finally, Aram slid his bow over his head and spoke quietly.

"I think this may be the army you spoke of, Thaniel," he said. "Evidently they mean to end it here."

"Perhaps," the horse answered, "but I sense only anxiety."

"Can you hear what they are saying or thinking, if anything?"

Thaniel was quiet a long moment and there was wonder in his voice when he answered. "Yes. They want to speak with you."

Aram looked at him sharply. "With me?"

"They want to negotiate."

"Negotiate? To what end?"

"You'll have to ask them." Thaniel answered.

Aram slowly dismounted and walked out onto the grassy slope until he was more or less on level with the dark line of wolves across the way. He studied them for a moment and then spoke audibly.

"I am here." He said.

A lone black wolf of immense proportions separated himself from the line and advanced a short way, limping slightly on one paw as he came. He stopped and sat on the gentle slope about halfway between the trees and the river and a harsh, raspy voice broke in upon Aram's mind.

"I am Durlrang, chief of the wolves of the north. Why do you slay us without mercy, O my enemy? Is it your intention to destroy us all?"

"I kill your kind because you also kill, without mercy, those whom you should not touch." Aram answered slowly, still speaking aloud. "Before I came you seemed intent upon destroying all other life. By your barbaric actions you have unbalanced the natural world. You even devour your own kind. I have witnessed you tearing the flesh of your own kin while they yet live. This is unnatural and a great evil. Why should you not die? You disregard, in all your actions, the will of Kelven."

"Kelven is dead." Durlrang answered shortly.

"Is that why you abandoned the natural laws? Was it only his presence upon the earth that guided you and not the structure that he gave to nature?"

"The one that killed Kelven, he gave us new laws."

Aram let the words fall unchallenged. "What do you want from me?"

Durlrang shifted on his haunches. "Your conditions for peace."

Aram was surprised and astounded by Durlrang's declaration. Was this the way the war would end? After all the years of killing, after all the desperate battles and all the death, could it really end in a simple verbal agreement that it should? He let several minutes slip by in silence while he considered, then, in a gesture, he laid down his bow upon the long grass.

"Alright." He said. "My conditions are these. You must return to keeping the laws of Kelven. You must slay and eat only those creatures that were given to you for food at the beginning. You must never again touch the life of horse or man. And you must look to yourselves and raise your families with care and caution so that you do not overrun your own hunting grounds. You must never consume or kill your own kind. You must never again pass the borders of the high plains or the King's valley."

Durlrang stirred uneasily. "Some of these demands we can meet. But others go against the will of our master."

Aram considered that for a moment. Then drawing his sword with sudden decision, he held it straight out to his side.

"This I also demand," he said. "That you and all your kind acknowledge me as your master."

A furious commotion erupted among the ranks of wolves at this stunning statement. Many gave voice to angry yelps and howls and fights broke out here and there among them. Durlrang snarled harshly to regain calm. When his people had quieted, he gazed at Aram for a long moment.

"We cannot," he answered, and there was regret in his voice. "We already have a master."

"*Manon.*" Thaniel interjected.

Aram advanced a step toward the line of wolves across the valley.

"If you truly have a master," he thundered. "Let him now come and declare himself before us."

The wolves jumped and whined at this statement and some of them ran in fear for the shelter of the trees. The rest peered skyward in terror as if expecting bolts of angry power to blast out of the firmament and strike the man down. But minutes passed and the peace of the afternoon remained unbroken.

Finally, Durlrang, who'd crouched in horror at Aram's statement, lifted his head cautiously, looked carefully around, and spoke.

"He is not here."

Aram turned the bright blade of his sword over and back several times so that the waning sun flashed off its steel.

"I *am* here." He said.

Durlrang sat stiffly staring at the tall man beyond the river for a long time. Then he turned his head and there was communion among the wolves that was closed to Aram's mind. Several became quite agitated and broke from the line to run back and forth along it, snapping and snarling.

Finally, Durlrang stood up, faced Aram and dropped his head, and looking back between his forelimbs, pushed his forehead to the earth. "We will obey all that you have said and though we are but one of the many companies of wolves on the earth, for our part, we acknowledge you as our master."

Aram lowered his sword and let the silence stretch out for a minute or two, and then he raised his voice to all the assembled wolves. "Obey me and answer to the laws of Kelven, and keep these things and I will not only leave you in peace, but I will defend you as well. Obey me not, and break any of these sayings of mine and I will return and bring your end upon you. It may be that if you live as the Maker of old intended the evil that has touched you may be lifted."

There was a moment then of utter quiet, when the forest and meadow seemed to draw a collective breath and the wind and stream fell silent. In that instant, Aram could feel their combined will bend to his. The wolves bowed their heads over in unison, touching their foreheads to the ground. Those that had fled into the trees slipped back into the ranks and they all answered him as one.

"We will obey."

Aram slid his sword back into its sheath and picked up his bow.

"Durlrang."

"Yes, master." The great black wolf lifted his head.

"Come down to the river, I wish to talk with you."

Obediently, the big wolf trotted down to the shore, limping on his right forepaw as he came. Aram splashed through the shallow riffles at the bottom of a pool and met the wolf on a stretch of sand.

"Let me see your paw, Durlrang."

"Master?"

"Your paw. What has happened to you?" Aram knelt down and looked into the animal's eyes. They were black and deep as a starless night with ripples of ancient trouble in their depths.

After a moment's silent contemplation of his new master, Durlrang lifted his paw. "A month ago, I was running through a field of loose shale high in the mountains. I cut my foot and a piece of rock lodged inside."

Aram shifted around to the wolf's right side and bent the paw upwards. Carefully, he opened the mangled flesh on the damaged central pad and looked deep into the wound. Sure enough, there was sliver of sharp rock, shiny with blood, wedged across damaged flesh deep in the wolf's pad.

Aram looked up into Durlrang's eyes and drew his knife. "I'm going to remove the rock. This will hurt. Can you bear it?"

The great black wolf inclined his head slightly. The animal trembled as Aram dug deep into the raw flesh of its pad, but the rock came free after a few moments prodding with the steel. He squeezed gently on the pad to remove the pus, clotted blood, and infection, then crumbled some medicinal herbs and pressed them into the wound. Then he cut a makeshift pad from the flap of his pack and fastened it to the bottom of Durlrang's foot with leather strips that he wound up around the leg and tied above the knee.

"Be careful and move slowly—try to keep this on your foot. In a week or ten days you can chew through this and remove it. With care, your pad should heal by then."

In response, Durlrang did something odd and surprising. He made a small sound deep in his chest and licked the back of Aram's arm with his tongue. Aram set down the foot and touched the wolf briefly on the side of its shaggy head with the palm of his hand.

"Durlrang, do your people know how to fish?"

"I did once, long ago." Durlrang answered.

"Recall the skill then, and teach the others. In the winter, when many deer will migrate to lower country, the fish in these streams can sustain your people. Sometimes during the coldest parts of the winter, they will become trapped by ice in the shallows and are easy to catch. I've done it myself. In the meantime, I will alter the rule about trespassing on the highlands. You may hunt deer for the distance of one-half day's journey into the grasslands. But remember, you may never again slay a horse, a man, or one of your own."

"Upon my life," Durlrang answered. "It will be as you say."

Aram met the animal's gaze for a long moment and stood.

"Then farewell until we meet again." He said, and he turned away and crossed the river and strode up the slope into the trees where Thaniel waited. When he got there, he was surprised to find Florm and three other horses waiting with him. One was Jared and the others were a large dappled gray and another brown one like Jared but with a black mane and tail. Florm studied Aram with his great black eyes for a long time before he spoke quietly.

"So now you are the master of wolves?" There was a curious excitement trembling on the edges of the ancient horse's voice.

Aram shrugged. "Yes. It is a practical matter. They know that I will slay them all if they break their word."

Florm turned away. "I want to give you something," he said. "Thaniel will bear you. Let us go into the south."

XII

For three days they traveled toward the southwest across the heart of the high grasslands. To their front a great gray mass began to rise out of the plains. It dark top was sharp and pointed like a pyramid. As they drew nearer, Aram could see that the mountain did indeed have four distinct sides like a pyramid and that a thick forest of trees surrounded its base. Early on the fourth morning, they circled around the forest that surrounded the mountain, passing by it on the east until, turning back to the west, they came to about the middle of the dense woods on the mountain's southern side.

Florm stopped in a grove of trees on a small rise where a spring bubbled up from the ground and ran off toward the south. Aram dismounted and looked to the north. A tangle of thick, tall trees surrounded the base of the mountain, and spread out for at least a mile from it on all sides. Upon closer inspection, the mountain did indeed appear to be far too uniform and straight-sided to be natural formation. The woods surrounding it were so thick and dark that they looked impenetrable. The top of the mountain or pyramid rose dark and majestic above the forest. Aram looked curiously at Florm, but said nothing.

"You are a brave man, Aram, master of wolves. Are you brave enough to enter there?"

Aram looked into the gloom under the spreading trees. "What do you wish me to do there?"

"I wish to give you something." Florm answered. "It is there, inside the mountain of Joktan."

"What is this thing?"

"It is an object known as the Call of Kelven."

Aram gazed at the distant pyramid and the dark jungle that surrounded it and waited in silence.

"The Call is an ancient device of communication between horse and man. Long ago it was used by Ram to summon Boram, my grandfather. Later, it bound my father, Armon, in friendship to Joktan, perhaps the greatest king of old. I wish now to give it to you that it may bind us in the same ancient bonds of friendship. You may use it to summon me at any time."

Aram stared at him, stunned. "My lord," he protested. "I am but a servant. I will gladly retrieve this thing for you, but I am not worthy to summon you ever, anytime."

Florm's great dark eyes glowed in their luminous depths.

"My young friend, you are anything but a servant. By the strength of your own will, you have shed the chains of Manon and gained your freedom. You learned to survive in the wild, and you have become a warrior who's like I have never seen. You saved me and you have protected my people. You have exerted your own will, above that of the grim lord himself, over the company of wolves. You are anything but a mere servant. I'm beginning to think you may embody the answer to Kelven's Riddle. That is why I wish you to possess the Call."

Aram did not know what the lord of horses meant by Kelven's Riddle, and decided not to inquire. He looked at Florm. "Can we not communicate with our minds when it is necessary?"

"Only over short distances," Florm answered. "Mindspeak does not suffice beyond several yards between peoples of different kinds, and for only a few miles among those who are the same, as with horses. With the Call, you may summon me across a thousand miles. It is mine to give—I want you to have it."

Aram still doubted his worthiness to possess such a device or to use it in summoning as great a person as Florm, but he acquiesced with a slight nod. "What must I do?"

"You must make your way through the forest to the great stair at the base of the mountain. It will not be easy. These woods are ancient and troubled. You must proceed with care. Then you must find the door, enter the square mountain, and make your way into its depths by many passages, none of which any horse has ever seen. Somewhere in the depth of the mountain, at the lowest level, you will find another door, beyond which is the Call.

"The Call is kept by two Guardians, strange and dangerous creatures, who took it back there after Joktan fell ten thousand years ago. The Guardian on the left is named Ligurian, and the one on the right is Tiberion. You must say the right words or they will slay you. Say the right words and they will give you the Call."

"What are the words?"

"You must say this; 'I come in the name of Florm, lord of horses, son of Armon, son of Boram, for the Call that Kelven gave to men at the beginning of time.' Then you must speak their names, Ligurian first, Tiberion second."

Aram ran this over in his mind, making certain that he had it. Then he looked at Florm. "I will return," he said. He glanced up at the sky. The sun was rising toward midmorning as he turned away and entered the trees.

Beneath the trees there was sunlight-swallowing gloom. Within steps he was plunged into near total darkness. Not a single ray of light found its way through the dense, convoluted canopy to illuminate the thickly rooted floor. He had not gone far into the jungle before it was necessary to stop and wait for his eyes to adjust to the sudden gloom. Even then, objects mired in the shadowy murk beneath the trees revealed themselves but reluctantly. The only thing that was clearly seen was that his journey to the pyramid, no more than a mile or two distant, would be arduous and difficult.

There appeared to be nothing living in the dim world beneath the trees. No small animals moved in the undergrowth or scurried up and down the knotted trunks and no birds flitted overhead. It was a silent place, overwhelmed and choked into perfect stillness by ancient, gnarled wood.

Aram found it necessary to detour constantly as he went forward, hacking through thick undergrowth with his sword, and avoiding enormous tree roots that heaved up from the ground like huge coils of rope. In places, the massive tree trunks grew so close together that he could not pass between them. Often, he strayed further to either side looking for passage than he progressed forward.

Even after his eyes adjusted to the gloom, he could not see very far in any direction before darkness swallowed things up, removing them beyond the limits of his sight. Slowly, carefully, he negotiated the dim forest, gauging his direction by sighting along several trees at a time and choosing a particularly odd trunk that he knew to be in line with the direction he needed to go. Even if he had to reach the chosen tree by a circuitous path, once he succeeded, he would line up more trees, before him and behind, and continue.

He knew that without being able to see the sun or any landmarks above the close canopy of the trees, it was inevitable that he would go somewhat astray. A more serious problem was that, after a while, the twisted massive trunks of trees began to appear very similar to each other. Nonetheless, he trusted his instincts and his eyes, always studying the way before him and the path he'd come. Occasionally, there would be the whispered ghost of a ray of light from the sun. Always it appeared to come from behind him, to the south. Each time it seemed a confirmation that his sense of direction had not failed him, but he could not be certain.

As he struggled forward through the gloom, time itself seemed to dissolve in the murk. It was difficult to know how long he'd been wandering the forest floor. More worrisome, he began to suspect that his wanderings were in fact aimless, maybe even circuitous, and that he was becoming hopelessly lost. Even the tumbled walls of ancient rock that he occasionally encountered, apparently the work of men, though it was hard to tell from their crumbled state, began to appear very like one another.

Then, abruptly, after two or three—or perhaps four—hours he emerged from the trackless gloom of the jungle into an area of less dense growth where there were crumbled stone buildings and wide ruined avenues. Trees still grew thick and unchecked amidst the broken walls and towers and thrust up through the pavement but even so the going was much easier. He found one particularly broad avenue that went straight toward the pyramid and followed it. It was broad enough that there were gaps here and there in the thick canopy of the trees overhead. His heart lightened—he could see the sky.

There had once been a great city here, but unlike his city, which was carved from living rock, this one had been constructed from the foundation of the ground upward and was composed of hewn stone. At regular intervals cross streets intersected with the broad avenue. It appeared as if the city was laid out perfectly along straight lines of tangent, and if it could be seen without the crush of vegetation, would cause the observer to marvel. But now it was overgrown with ancient trees and thick underbrush. Even the main avenue was punctuated here and there by massive trees that severed the roadway, forcing Aram to detour to the right or the left as he made his way forward.

There were many large structures, in that they sometimes filled whole city blocks, but none of them was overly tall, none more than two or three stories. With only the broad grasslands of the high plains surrounding it, there had been no reason to check the city's lateral growth and build upward. It was a sprawling metropolis.

Eventually, as the day waned toward afternoon, he came out into un-hindered sunlight and the sudden end of the avenue's use as an access route to the pyramid. It ended abruptly at the edge of a deep, straight-sided chasm, a thousand yards across and at least half that deep. It was clear from the ruined remains of broken stone that jutted a few yards into empty space that at one time a bridge had spanned the gorge, but had long since crumbled into the depths.

Leaning over the edge and looking down, Aram could see, far below in the dimness of the abyss, the metallic glint of water. The sides of the chasm appeared to be almost perfectly perpendicular and there were obvi-ous signs of quarrying. This chasm, then, was manmade. The stone for the construction of the city had come from here.

Curiously, this quarry—if indeed that's what it was—had been delved in such a way as to render it exactly symmetrical in both directions. It was as if the builders of the city had quarried their stone from a perfectly straight seam of subterranean rock, resulting in a massive ditch that sev-ered the city in two. Perhaps, Aram thought, the quarry had once served a defensive purpose as well. But, if that were true, why not surround the city's entirety instead of just its central portion?

He glanced across the gorge, at the broken walls and towers rising above the jungle beyond. They seemed little or no different from those on the near side, in size or construction, but maybe that interior part of the city had been built at the first, the chasm surrounding it on all sides, and this outer portion had come later as the city grew.

Leaning as far out as he dared from the remains of the bridge, Aram looked along the canyon in both directions. He could not see the end of it either way but that was mostly due to the lateness of the day and the per-sistent gloom created by the overreaching trees. There was something he could see that lifted his hopes, however. A few hundred yards to the right on his side of the chasm there were steps, cut into the stone, leading down into the depths. Looking across at the other side, he saw that there were corresponding steps descending the opposite wall.

There was no other bridge that spanned the chasm in either direc-tion for as far as he could see, and it was pointless to try and fight his way through the jungle in hopes of finding one. It appeared that if he was to cross, he would have to use the steps, and there was no telling how deep the water at the bottom of the quarry would be. Well, he thought, he could swim; he'd done it before when necessary. In any event, the only visible solution was to use the steps and hope they'd retained their integrity down through the centuries.

Directly across from him the wide avenue went straight on toward the heart of the pyramid-shaped mountain, although it was as badly over-grown as on the near side. The jungle pressed in upon it from both sides. His journey toward the pyramid and the mysterious Call would get no easier.

He made his way toward the steps along the side of the gorge, scram-bling across broken masonry and through deep undergrowth until he came to the top of the stairway. The steps were narrow and steep and faded quickly into the gloom below. In the west, the sun was halfway down the sky, obliquely off to the southern side of the gorge and so had little impact on the depths.

The steps, however, though weathered, were still in very good shape, having been expertly cut from the natural rock, but were overgrown with a thick layer of spongy, damp moss. As he descended, he went with vigilant care, so as not to slip and plunge to certain injury and likely death over the side. It grew increasingly darker as he went down and he kept his right hand upon the wall as a guide and tested each step before descending.

The ribbon of water below him was dark as obsidian and still. No breath of wind troubled its surface. It appeared to him to be very deep, though there was no way to verify this. Along its edges where it touched the sides of the gorge, there was texture to the water, as if plants grew there. And there was something else. A pale strip of stone rose above the dark surface, cutting across it from one side of the gorge toward the other, and though it didn't touch either shore, appeared to be a bridge.

Down he went, into the gloom. Sunlight angled into the gorge from the southwest and touched the upper hundred feet or so of the wall oppo-site but what light the stones reflected weakened almost to nothing before it reached the depths. The moss on the steps thickened as he went down and they grew ever slicker.

Finally he stood at the edge of the water. The steps continued on down into the murk a short way and a few steps beyond where they entered the water and three or four yards out from the side of the chasm the span of a bridge rose from the water and arched toward the other side.

The ends of the bridge were under water for about ten feet from the walls on both sides of the quarry but the center rose clear of the water for the rest of its length. It was a gently arched bridge without railings, cut from the natural rock. The water beneath it was dark and its surface was splotched with patches of mossy growth. There was no telling as to its depth. Peering before him beyond the point where the steps entered the water, he could just make out the beginnings of the bridge in the murk.

Gingerly, he stepped down into the water. It was startlingly cold. As he descended the last few steps to the point where the bridge turned and spanned the chasm, the water rose above his waist to his chest and he felt his vital organs tighten and contract upward as if they were trying to avoid the bitter chill. He turned to face the bridge and found that he was a bit of-fline, as if he'd gone below the point where the beginning of it arched away from the steps. Evidently, the stairway continued on downward into the deep water. At one time, then, this bridge had spanned the gorge through open air. The bottom of the gorge was somewhere still far below—the water had filled it up over the centuries.

Easing back upward for one step and then two, he came into align-ment with the arched span of the bridge that rose above the water. He put one foot gingerly forward and felt its broad span beneath his boot. Testing its integrity by putting weight on his forward foot, he found it to be solid. He moved his other foot forward. Then he was on the bridge.

Moving carefully in the gloom, using his hands as outriggers in the icy liquid, he eased out over the unseen portion of the bridge and in a few steps came clear of the water. He continued to hold his hands out slightly for balance as he ascended toward the arched center of the bridge. The bridge was steep, steeper than it had appeared, and slick. His eyes were focused on watching the slippery, moss-covered stone as he progressed, but at the periphery of his vision he caught a glimpse of something moving in the depths.

He stopped and set his feet, and then leaned over as far as he dared and peered down into the murky water. Far below, down in the deep, flash-es of silver darted here and there. Fish. They were moving rapidly from his right to his left beneath the bridge. He straightened up and continued on, up the arched span, step by careful step, until he reached the apex and be-gan to descend toward the other side. Below him the silver flashes increased in number and speed, always moving from right to left.

It was even more difficult to descend the arch than it had been to climb up it. Always he was in danger of slipping on the slick moss and plunging into the icy lagoon. Fear of the water—of the dark, mysterious depth of it, began to rise in him. Unreasonable, and attached to nothing obvious other than the strange behavior of the silvered fish, it nonetheless filled him. His chest ached with tension and his breath came in short, labored gasps.

The surface of the water beneath the bridge suddenly boiled as schools of fish scrambled madly from right to left, fleeing—something. Aram fought a stifling fear as he tried to negotiate the downward portion of the arch. Then, once again, he entered the water as he neared the far stairway. Careless now of the danger of slipping, he surged through the cold water toward the steps, heeding a desperate urge to get clear of the icy murk. His chest constricted further as the water rose to his midsection and he struggled for each breath as he hurried toward the stair.

Finally, he stepped clear and began climbing, just as there was another movement down in the water. This time the object was not a school of fish, but something massive, broad and dark, blacker even than the surrounding murk, rising slowly and deliberately out of the depths. In a sudden spasm of fear, he turned and sprinted up the stairs, heedless of the slippery moss and weathered condition of the steps, taking them two at a time, stopping only when he was well above the surface of the water.

Then, breathing heavily from fear and exertion, he pivoted carefully on the mossy steps, digging the fingers of his right hand into a crevice in the stone for support, and looked down. The large dark something was falling back into the blackness of the deep, becoming one again with the underwater night. Aram turned away and moved on as quickly as he dared. Whatever the unknown thing was, if it came out of the water after him, he didn't want to face it on the slippery surfaces of the stairway.

He cleared the steps into full sunlight and turned to look down into the bottom of the gorge. The dark surface of the water was still once again, with not a ripple anywhere. He sat down on the top step and took several deep breaths while he waited for the pounding of his heart to cease. What, he wondered, dwelled in that deep, dark, icy pool? Whatever it was, it had sensed his presence on the bridge and had decided to investigate—or perhaps do something worse.

Before continuing on up the avenue, he examined the position of the sun, having a clear view of it for the first time all day. It had slid almost halfway down the sky to the west. He knew he must hurry or he would have to spend the night in this place. And he was positively terrified about crossing the dark water at the bottom of the chasm after nightfall with its unknown entity lurking in the depths. It would require all his courage to do so once again while the light of day lasted, let alone in twilight. It would be impossible at night.

He rose and turned toward the pyramid. Though the avenue was broken by the intrusion of trees as it had been beyond the gorge, the ruined buildings stood closer together on this side, impeding their wild growth somewhat, and he made reasonably good progress. Even after thousands of years, there were still a few stretches of level pavement among the heaved-up and broken stones. In another hour he came to the flanks of the mountain.

Only it wasn't a mountain. It was as it had appeared from a distance; a pyramid constructed of huge, beveled blocks of stone. Aram stared up its angled side in astonishment, marveling at the fact that men had once been capable of erecting such a structure. A wide stairway ascended the face of it from the center of a broad courtyard at the end of the avenue. Though the stone was worn and weathered and broken in places, it was relatively sound and not difficult to climb. Glancing once more at the sun, which was by now dangerously far down in the western sky, he headed up the stairway.

He soon rose above the riot of trees that stretched away from the pyramid in all directions like a green sea. What, he wondered, had caused this unnatural forest—temperate and deciduous in nature, yes, but tropical in the abundant lushness of its growth—to flourish about the base of this manmade mountain? It did not feel evil in itself, even when he had struggled through the depths of it, but it *felt* like it had been caused by malevolence. It was as if the ancient forest had grown thus in an attempt to cover the evidence of an act of evil.

As he climbed upward for hundreds of feet, then for a thousand or more, the stairway narrowed. The forest fell away, became indistinct, and he could see the broad and open plains beyond it. About a third of the way up, he came upon a wide, level place that indented the pyramid and split the staircase in two. This platform was bounded at the wall of the pyramid by a sealed doorway.

He could find no means of opening it, though he searched diligently for several minutes, so he went up the stairway to the right of the indention until the staircase became whole again and continued on. Three or four thousand feet later, winded and weary, he came to the top of the pyramid. There was an observation platform about a hundred feet square that topped the pyramid, and from it he could view the whole country of the highland realm of the horses, east to west, and north to south.

He pivoted slowly and examined it all. To the west rose the mountains beyond which was his valley. In the north, the grassy plains gradually gave way to rumpled hills and then to the high mountains, beyond which were the vast, even taller, snow-capped ramparts he had often viewed from his own tower in the city, and that seemed to go on to the edge of the world.

To the east was the great inland sea bounded on its far distant shores by impassable walls of more rugged mountains. Beyond those mountains to the northeast and rising above the earth there was *something* that his eye could not resolve. To the south the gentle green country rolled away until it was finally lost in the wooded hills that swung around from the west, beyond which, somewhere slightly southeast of where he stood, was the town of Derosa. Upon the highlands, a bit closer to him than those distant hills, there was the shimmer of another large body of water. Curiously, there were no roads or streets visible anywhere upon the plains beyond the limits of the city.

Encompassing the base of the pyramid, the forest spread away on all sides for more than a mile, with broken walls and towers jutting above its tangled tops. The gorge that he'd crossed in fear two hours earlier encompassed the pyramid as well, forming a dark line of demarcation in the forest equidistant between the base of the pyramid and the rest of the ancient city. It formed a square, its right angles corresponding to those of the pyramid. The broad avenue led directly away from him toward the south and there, by the wooded hill out on the plains beyond the reach of the forest, he saw the dark shapes of the horses.

He could find no way into the pyramid from the observation deck on its top and no staircase descended its opposite side. The sun was barely an hour or two above the horizon. He'd seen nothing that promised ingress into the pyramid but the sealed doorway below, so he descended to that point and examined it. There were no keyholes or handles or any sign that such devises had ever been present.

On either side of the door, however, in the floor about thirty feet apart, there were raised blocks of stone. When he stepped on the stone to the right, it depressed into the floor, grumbling, grinding, and complaining as it performed a task it had not done for millennia, but came up again when he stepped off. The other stone behaved in exactly the same way. Understanding came. He went down the stairway until he found a large piece of broken stone almost as heavy as himself and lugged it back up the steps to the flat place beside the door.

Placing the stone on one of the raised blocks, making sure it depressed fully, he went across and stood on the other. There was a distant, dim rumbling and with a groan, the doors swung inward. When he stepped off his block however, they quickly closed, so he had to climb back down and retrieve another block of broken rock. The sun was sliding far down the sky by now. In less than another hour it would touch the tops of the mountains in the west.

After carefully placing the stones to open the doors and keep them open, he went through the opening into the dark of the pyramid's interior. But there was a surprise here. Daylight came down through long shafts in the stone above the corridor and though it was by no means brilliant, it was light enough that he could see to make his way forward.

A few feet in front of him the narrow corridor ended at the top of a long stairway that went straight down into the heart of the pyramid. As he descended, it grew increasingly darker. Outside, the sun fell away to the west. On and on, downward he went, until he felt sure that he'd dropped below the level of the surrounding forest and the ground in which it was rooted. Finally, deep inside the pyramid, he came to a large chamber lit by a flame that ascended from a round pit in the middle of the broad, rectangular tiled floor.

He froze, listening, feeling vulnerable in the gloom, and looked cautiously about him. There was no sound or movement. Had the Guardians that Florm spoke of lit this fire? Or was someone or something else tending it? The room felt empty to his probing senses but that only deepened the mystery of the unattended fire. After several minutes, hearing nothing and feeling the pressure of the fading day upon him, he eased out into the chamber.

On the opposite side of the chamber, a raised dais held a golden sarcophagus, no doubt the final resting-place of a great man or woman. Joktan, perhaps, or someone more ancient even than him. The dais was twelve or fourteen feet high and its walls were too smooth to climb. It was difficult to discern in the darkness but it appeared to be composed of a slick, hard, dark-colored substance, like polished onyx. A foot or so above his head, a single word of seven letters was inscribed in the smooth black side of the structure, further sparking his curiosity. He would have liked to examine the sarcophagus. But Aram had no time for exploration or curiosity.

Florm had said that the Call was to be found at the lowest level of the structure. There were narrow passages providing egress from the rectangular room in the centers of the end walls on either side of the dais and after considering he went into the one on the right. It ended about fifty paces beyond in a small, round chamber lit by a single shaft from the outside. As there was little sunlight left on the outside world, and the shaft that illuminated it was oriented toward the east, the chamber was nearly dark. Aram circled its walls but found no further egress, doors or passages.

He backtracked through the central chamber with its sarcophagus and explored the passage that went beyond it in the opposite direction. It ended in a chamber that was a copy of the other, with no exit here either, so he went back to the main chamber and examined all of its walls. In the cramped, dark space behind the sarcophagus he found an open doorway beyond which another steep, narrow stairwell descended.

The stairwell was almost utterly in the dark and yet grew darker as he went down until, at the last, he was reduced to groping his way downward through cloying gloom. Then, finally, he came into a small foyer beyond which a larger room loomed. The foyer was totally dark but the room beyond was infused with dim light, the source of which he could not determine. Aram was about to enter the room when the sense of another presence riveted him in place.

He was not alone.

Drawing his sword quickly and quietly, he slid into a corner on the right hand side of the foyer and examined what was visible of the room beyond. He could see no one. Keeping his back to the foyer wall, he slipped sideways until he was against the angle of the other corner and could see into the rest of the larger room. Nothing. Unless there was someone flattened against the wall on either side of the doorway, the room was empty.

But there *was* someone. He could feel them.

Cautiously, his sword at the ready, he eased into the doorway.

Instantly, brilliant light erupted to either side and shining blades crossed in front of him barring the way. He leapt back and prepared to defend himself, but the light faded and the crossed swords were withdrawn. No attack ensued. Again he stepped forward and the spectacle was repeated. Unmolested, he took one step back, sheathed his sword and then approached the crossed blades that glittered like ice.

"Who comes into this place?" The voice was barely more than a sinister whisper but it contained in itself a curious echo, as if two spoke at once.

Standing utterly still, Aram answered. "I am Aram, friend of Florm, son of Armon, son of Boram. I am come for the Call of Kelven that was given to men at the beginning of time. I seek permission to do this from the guardians, Ligurian and Tiberion."

These were not the exact words that Florm had taught him but they were honest and felt right.

There was silence for half a minute.

Then, slowly, the glittering swords were withdrawn and the shimmering outlines of two entities stepped into view. Their bodies seemed to be composed of the night sky, dark and glittering with stars, and if they had facial features, Aram could not make them out. The entities were tall with curiously elongated bumps rising high above each shoulder. Power, latent and palpable, seemed to emanate from them.

They spoke as one, their voices mingling as the sound of rushing waters whispering over rock to fall into space. "Who are you that you would be master of the Call and of its Guardians?"

It was a challenge and suggested dire consequences should he produce a wrong answer. Aram knew instinctively that he could not stand against these creatures if battle was joined. Whatever they were, they were far above him. He wanted desperately to retreat but forced himself to stand his ground.

"I would not be master of the Call or its Guardians, or anyone else for that matter. Florm, the Lord of horses sends me here, to gain the Call and use it in need. If Florm, son of Armon, son of Boram has not the authority to grant such a thing, I will return to him and tell him that Ligurian and Tiberion will not lend it to me. Is this your instruction?"

The two beings shimmered silently for a moment then the stars in their bodies winked out and they disappeared but their presence remained. The voices of the whispering waters came again.

"Aram, son of Clif, you may take the Call to use as long as you live, and we will guard you. When your life ceases or is taken from you, we will return the Call of Kelven to the mountain of Joktan. You will not see us nor can you command us, but we will go with you and defend you in duress. Understand, we cannot protect you from all enemies, nor can we defend you from overwhelming circumstances, but we can make your presence as the presence of three or four men in battle. Go now, take the Call, and we will go with you."

The voices ceased and it seemed to Aram that he was suddenly alone in the dim light. How, he wondered, could these creatures know his father's name? Stepping through the doorway, he looked around. The chamber was square and featureless except for a peg hung on the far wall. Dangling from the peg was a shining cylinder suspended by a silver chain.

Aram crossed the room and slipped the cylinder off the peg. It was about the size of a small reed, maybe three or four inches long. He slid the chain over his head and hung the Call around his neck, tucking it inside his shirt. Then he left the room and began to negotiate his way back up through the dark interior of the pyramid.

It was now fully dark along the passages leading up. The sun must have set below the mountains, for no light came down the shafts through the stone, but in Aram's immediate vicinity, there was inexplicable light that seemed to emanate from either side of his body. He could not ascertain its exact source but it was bright enough that he could see the way before him.

The fire was still burning in the pit in the large room with the sarcophagus. He would have liked to ask his new companions about its purpose and meaning but he knew instinctively that querying such beings on any subject would be improper, perhaps dangerous. When he exited the pyramid onto the level platform before the door, it was dusk. The sun had indeed set behind the western mountains and there were deep shadows along the wide avenue leading away from the pyramid but it was not yet full night. He thought about the slippery steps leading down into the quarried gorge and about the thing that lived in its depths and he hurried.

The light near his body emanated from the spaces to either side of him and he understood that it came from the Guardians. It grew in intensity as the coming night overtook the earth and in its influence he hurried along the avenue, clambering over roots and around pits in the ruined pavement. He came to the gorge and found the stair. It was now utterly dark and without the light from the Guardians, passage would have been impossible.

He hesitated at the top and looked down into the darkened abyss. The Guardians had stated that they would protect him and aid him in battle. Did that mean they would guard him now?

Gazing into the indistinct blackness at the bottom of the quarry, he wondered how he would spot whatever it was that lurked in the depths of the water if it came for him. How could one see night arise out of blackness? Steeling himself to do what he must, he went down. At the bottom of the stair, he drew his sword and slipped into the water at the end of the submerged bridge. Gently he began easing across, slogging carefully through the water. Even with the illumination provided by the Guardians, he was in constant danger of slipping off the unseen stone beneath his feet and into the murk.

He saw the center of the bridge in the dimness and aimed for it. Slowly but surely, he came clear of the water. As he stepped onto the dry portion of the bridge on the near side there was a gentle gurgling in the water to his left. He stopped and cocked his head, listening. In the darkness out beyond the reach of the Guardians' light, the water boiled and waves slapped against the unseen shores of the quarry's walls.

His heart lurched suddenly in his chest. Something was coming. He turned to face it, peering anxiously into the gloom.

Something huge was ascending out of the deep toward the surface fifty yards away and it was approaching. It was coming straight at him. In the blackness of the gorge's bottom, caught in the center of a narrow, slippery bridge, there was no way he could outrun it. He must fight. He slid his sword into his right hand and held a dagger in his left.

With his sword at the ready, he braced himself, trying to see what would arise from the black water. He felt himself entombed in the heavy darkness at the bottom of the gorge and terror dug with vicious claws into his chest. The water heaved and boiled over. A great black mass arose from it.

The monstrous dark mass heaved itself up out of the water, high into the darkness above the level of the bridge, and grew terrifyingly larger as it surged toward him. In horrified desperation, Aram held his sword up in what he knew instinctively was a futile attempt to receive the colossal beast's attack.

Then, abruptly, light erupted from either side of him and he caught just a glimpse of shining blades splitting the darkness. In the sudden illumination, he saw to his front a great mouth that had opened to consume him but now emitted a shriek of pain and anguish as the pale, gleaming mass of hideous flesh behind it tried to abort its assault in the face of unexpected injury.

Aram almost stumbled backward off the bridge at the sight of this monstrosity. The thing turned itself ponderously over and dove into the depths to escape the wrath of the Guardians and the bridge shuddered as an enormous body crashed against its underside. Aram spun and made for the far shore, pushing heedlessly through the murk toward the stair.

When he'd gained the stair and had climbed a few steps, he stopped to catch his breath and he whispered into the darkness.

"Ligurian and Tiberion. I don't know if you can hear me, but thank you for my life." There was no answer and after regaining his breath he climbed the stair and came out of the pit.

He went back west along the top of the quarry until he gained the avenue and followed it out of the city. It was terribly overgrown for the last hundred yards or so and beyond the point where it ended, he once again had to fight his way through jungle. It was deep in the night and stars slashed brilliantly across the clear heavens when Aram came at last out of the overgrown city and the tangled jungle onto the open ground of the high plains.

XIII

The black forms of Florm and Thaniel approached out of the starlit darkness.

"I see you have been successful, lord Aram. And that you are not alone."

Aram looked sharply at Florm. "My lord, I deserve no such title. Why did you use it?"

"Not lightly, I assure you." Florm answered. "But anyone who commands the mastery of wolves away from Manon and now commands the Call of Kelven and enjoys the company of its Guardians is truly a lord in the world."

Aram shook his head. "I am not comfortable with such things, lord Florm. Less than seven years ago, I was among the lowest of Manon's servants. I am only where I am due to the exercise of my own limited strength, the blessings of the Maker Himself, and the good fortune of your mighty friendship. I am no lord."

"Nonsense." Florm seemed genuinely annoyed. "It is precisely such things that make men great. You have made your own way in the world and carved a destiny for yourself that cannot be diminished. Your actions have already come to the attention of one of the gods and will almost certainly bring the eye of Manon upon you. Do not resist your fate, Aram, embrace it."

"I did not flee into the wilderness to become the enemy of Manon, but to escape him. I am not seeking a destiny. I only do what I think to be right."

"Indeed." Florm looked at him closely. "You have meddled in the affairs of Manon already, with the wolves. He will not care about your intentions. He will want to know his new enemy. I'm afraid you have found a destiny, whether you sought it or not, and cannot escape it now."

Aram was tired after his ordeal and this discussion made him angry. "Fine. Let Manon come. Let him kill me or me him. Just let me sleep first. I have gone a long way today and was nearly eaten by a monster in the deep."

Florm chuckled. "Yes, I suppose I should have mentioned him, but he usually sleeps during the day and I knew that you would not be alone coming back. His kind is no match for the might of the Guardians."

"What is he—what is that thing?"

"No one knows. Something from the world that existed before our time, probably. He was loosed when the builders of the city quarried too deeply and pierced a subterranean stream. Anyway, he did not eat you."

Aram grunted and walked away into the stand of trees on the hill where he rolled immediately into his bed. He was asleep in moments.

Dawn broke over the high plains before Aram awoke. It was a cool morning, suggesting the coming of the end of summer. His muscles ached from the previous day's exertions and he sat up and rubbed his stiff joints. The five horses were grazing several yards away and saw him as he sat up. Florm and Thaniel came over and Florm spoke cheerfully.

"Good morning, lord Aram. Thaniel told me of your wish to go home before the end of summer. I will gladly bear you. On the way, we can commence with your promised education."

Aram stood and looked around him. It was a beautiful morning on the highlands with a bright sun in a clear sky and, though cool, promised later warmth. He nodded.

"If there is nothing further I can do here, my lord, and you do not mind the trip, I am ready to go see how my crops have fared." He grinned at Florm. "I am, after all, but a simple farmer."

Florm snorted. "I have learned that there is nothing simple about you, my friend. But let us go. Thaniel will return to our people for the remainder of the summer and I will join them on the foaling grounds in the fall."

They bade Thaniel farewell. The great black horse nodded low to Aram.

"It has been an honor, my lord."

"No, my lord Thaniel," Aram said pointedly. "The honor has been mine."

Thaniel met his gaze for a long moment and then turned and cantered away into the southeast followed by the other horses. Florm and Aram turned west. The sun followed them across the high plains as they put miles of rolling grasslands, coiling streams, and gentle forested ridges behind them. By sunset, they'd covered nearly a hundred miles and the pine mountains were less than a half-day's journey before them when they stopped for the night.

Before noon on the morrow, they were climbing the long draw above the meadow where Aram had saved Florm's life in the spring. When they stopped for a drink from the clear water of the stream Aram put into words the request he'd made so much earlier in the year.

"My lord Florm, you said that you were a colt when men last inhabited my city. Can you tell me the history of those days? In fact, would you tell me of the history of the world as we travel?"

Florm looked at him and chuckled. "I promised you an education but—of the world? That is a bit ambitious for one day's journey, don't you think?"

Aram shrugged. "I wouldn't know, my lord. Other than the names of my father and mother and of my sister that the servants of Manon took, I know nothing of my own history, let alone that of my people. Certainly, I know nothing of the history of the wider world in which you have lived for so long."

"Where would you like me to begin?"

Aram stood up from drinking and gazed out across the rounded meadow. "What do you know about the beginning, my lord?"

"The beginning? Of the world—or of your people?"

"Of everything." Aram glanced up an eagle circling high in the air above the brow of a distant hill. "I'd like to know about the very beginning—of life—if you don't mind, and about everything that's happened since."

"I can only relate to you those things that I myself have heard from my elders about events before the great war, Aram—I was not alive then, so I cannot bear eyewitness." Florm lowered his nose for one more drink. "But I will tell you what my father told me of such things when I was a colt."

The great horse lifted his head, nose dripping, and backed away from the stream. After Aram had climbed upon his back he turned toward the west and headed up the draw toward the heights. Within moments they were among the trees where the air was full of the pungent scent of evergreens.

Florm was silent for awhile as they trended up through the thick fir and spruce trees of the draw. The late morning was cool. Birds sang high in the branches and squirrels quarreled over the last of the summer's fare. As the trail broke out of the trees and they had a view back to the east of the great highland plains, the horse lord spoke.

"Long ago, there was nothing, only the Maker, and He was alone and lonely, and there was no light. He wandered the utter blackness until he came to the shores of a dark sea. The sea was filled with the waters of chaos. There was no order. But the Maker set Himself to organize and He ordered everything out of the raw materials of that vast sea. He made the stars and He made the worlds, and He made for Himself children, the gods of old.

"With the help of His children, He filled the earth with vibrant life and He put all things under the dominion of the ancient people that He made from the soil of the world. There were two of them at the beginning, Isher, the first man, and Chavah, the mother of all living. Out of the womb of Chavah came a great race. They built cities and roads and subdued the earth and it gave to them of its fullness. For thousands of years, the world was a paradise.

"But the ancients could not help but look at the stars that filled the heavens at night. And when they had fully developed the resources of the world, they lusted for the regions of the stars. Why, they wondered, should the Maker and the gods alone live out among the glorious vastness of the universe? They had become great, so why should they be confined to one world when there were undoubtedly many? Rather than petitioning the Maker on these questions with reason and humility, they took refuge in foolish and ignorant pride and fell into envy. And in their increasing envy, they came to despise the earth that sustained them."

Aram shifted uneasily. "How could anyone despise the earth, my lord? It is such a beautiful place. Were it not for the tyranny of Manon and the evil that he has unleashed in the world, it would be a paradise."

"True." The horse lord agreed. "But when life is too easy—something that you will have no concept of, my friend—people tend to become disillusioned with the wealth of all those things that come to them without the exertion of any great effort on their part. Perhaps it is guilt; I don't know, but my father use to say that when people no longer have to strive to better their daily existence, the end result, generally, is indolence, decadence, and moral decay. All of which may lead to the loss of self-control. That is, evidently, what happened to the ancients."

Aram was quiet as he considered this but he couldn't quite get his mind around it. Florm was right; his life had been so difficult that he could not relate to the problems of the ancients. Self-governance was a necessary attribute for survival in his world; it was hard to imagine a world where the concept itself was at issue.

"Shall I continue?" Florm asked.

"Please, my lord."

"Isher and Chavah spoke to their children and advised them to consider their dark thoughts. Was not the earth a garden of delights? Nothing was denied them and life was full and easy. And if they desired the stars, why not present their Maker with a respectful petition, one which in His wisdom and at His discretion, He would very likely grant to them? But the children of Isher would not listen to their father and mother. For there was someone else that had come among them.

"Aberanezagoth was one of the greatest of the gods of old, powerful among the children of the Maker, and he, also, was not content with his lot. He wished to sit on the throne of the Maker and rule the stars. The children of the earth allied with him for he promised them that they could enter the kingdoms of the heavens and sit in seats of power. And so there was a rebellion. Naturally, as all the power in the universe emanates from the Maker, the rebellion failed.

"Aberanezagoth was banished by the Maker to the unstructured darkness beyond the stars where he wanders in despair to this day and the people of the earth were destroyed. The world was turned upside down and was drowned in confusion. Isher and Chavah were allowed to ascend into the heavens to dwell among the gods. For a while, the earth was desolate and uninhabited.

"But the Maker did not like to see the work of His hands languish. So he told the gods, His children, 'make of it what you will, let the earth come alive.' The gods rebuilt the earth and renewed the face of the ground. And when the Maker saw what they had done with the earth, He made the humans, your ancestors to dwell here. He made plants and animals, fish and birds of all kinds and He made my people, too. Then he gave the care of this grand new world into the hands of His children, the gods.

"But the gods did not give full dominion to any of the peoples of the earth. Many, such as yours and mine were equal in stature and had to make alliances. And the gods determined to give the governance of the world to three of their own kind. Kelven had dominion of all things that grew from the earth and of all life but that of men. To him also was given control of the forces of the air, storms and wind and rain.

"Ferros was given control of the deep engines of the earth in order to maintain structure and balance. Into his hands was given control of the heat of the depths and the currents of metal and stone that flow through the heart of the world.

"To Manon was given the governance and guidance of humans."

Aram was stunned by this statement and blurted out his astonishment. "My lord, Manon is the rightful ruler of my people?"

"No, no," Florm answered quickly. "Don't misunderstand, my friend. Your people were made like mine, and the wolves, and many others, with a free will to decide whether they will act for good or for ill. When Manon was given the oversight of men, the emphasis was on guidance rather more than governance—it was intended that he should be more advisor than ruler."

"Then he has broken the laws of the Maker." Aram protested. "Why was he not punished?"

Florm was silent for a moment as he negotiated a steep, narrow place in the trail. "Perhaps you will have a hand in his punishment, Aram, for the story is not yet over." The horse chuckled quietly and looked around at his rider. "Nor, for that matter, is my narrative. Shall I continue?"

Aram grinned. "Yes, my lord, if you please."

"Well—all was well for thousands of years. The first king of the earth was Ram. He it was that allied with my grandfather, Boram. Under the guidance of Manon and Kelven, the world was restored to its former glory. The great king Ram built your city, Aram, twenty thousand years ago. It was carved from the living rock of the mountain. He gave it the name, Regamun Mediar, which means 'the Power at the Center of the World'.

"A succession of the kings of old dwelt there; Ram, Arphaxad, Meshech, Tiras, and Tobal. Each reigned for more than a thousand years and passed into the glory of the ages. Manon knew each of the kings and counseled them; they grew in wisdom and knowledge and with each generation they needed him less. After the death of Tobal, rule passed to his twin sons, Magog and Peleg.

"For a time, they ruled together in relative harmony with only minor disagreements between them. But Manon perceived that an opportunity had come for him to regain influence. He began to whisper in the ears of Magog and Peleg, especially to Magog who was more willing to listen. Minor disagreements soon became sharp arguments over policy.

"The peoples of the world began to align themselves with one or the other until, finally, there were, in effect, two nations—divided, but sharing the same cities and countryside, intermingled. Differences between Magog and Peleg translated into strife between neighbors and families. Ultimately, the social and political schisms became too great and there was civil war.

"The world of men devolved into chaos. Armies wreaked slaughter, cities were burned, and society was destroyed. Finally, Javan, the clever son of Verita, the younger sister of Magog and Peleg, had enough. He suggested that in order to end the war, Magog and Peleg should meet in single combat before the walls of a neutral city, of which there were few indeed. But the city of their sister, a city near the edge of the world called Sulan was one such place. The hatred between Magog and Peleg had grown to such a degree that they willingly accepted Javan's proposition.

"They met before the walls of Sulan in fierce combat and Magog slew Peleg in a pitched battle. Upon the death of one of his uncles at the hand of the other, Javan immediately invoked the ancient law that said that he who slays a ruler in violence must forfeit his own life and Magog was hanged from the walls of Sulan for the murder of his brother.

"Javan went to Regumun Mediar, put himself upon the throne, and set about to heal the breach caused by the war and the treachery of his uncles. But the damage was too great for one man and there was resentment toward Javan for his part in what had happened. Finally, he went into exile and gave up the throne in favor of the young son of Peleg, Joktan.

"Joktan was handsome and proud and strong in mind and body, but he was also wise and just. He re-established a government of law and ruthlessly put down any vestiges of rebellion while fostering equality and justice among all people. By the time he'd reigned for a hundred years, peace had come to all the land and the golden ages of prosperity returned.

"As I said, Joktan was strong and proud, and though he paid obeisance to Manon, he seldom sought his counsel for he suspected Manon's part in bringing the horror of the civil war upon them. Joktan reigned one thousand nine hundred and seventy-three years and he did not die but was slain. For as the reign of Joktan lengthened, he called upon Manon less and less and finally not at all.

"Manon was displeased and did not like being ignored by his subjects. Also, though know one knows what dark thoughts he harbors deep in his heart, he evidently felt that he deserved more respect from his fellows among the gods as well. It is believed that he made a journey into the nether regions of chaos and sought out Aberanezagoth and his counsel.

"When Manon returned in secret, he no longer walked among men but built a stronghold in the north which he named Morkendril, 'The New Beginning'. He built a tower of strength that reached into the sky and beneath it he delved deep into the domain of Ferros. After that, the disappearances began. Men and women that lived in remote regions of the earth or wandered alone into the wilderness vanished and did not return.

"Then, after a time, it was only the young women that turned up missing, especially in the regions near to Morkendril. Suspicions were raised that Manon was engaged in dark arts that he had learned of Aberanezagoth. Finally, Joktan sent agents to speak with Manon and learn of his works, but none returned.

"About this time other evils appeared upon the face of the earth. Wolves, which had always been a fierce people but had remained loyal to the laws of Kelven as denizens of the wild regions, abandoned that law and began to slay men along the borders of their country. When appeal was made to Kelven, and he went to learn the truth, the wolves refused to hear him.

"Then Joktan himself went with an army to confront Manon at Morkendril and learn of his deeds and intentions. When Joktan was upon the plain before the great tower, Manon suddenly unleashed a great army of fierce beings never before seen, the spawn of his vile experiments with the race of men. These were the lashers and they fell upon Joktan and his army with terrible fierceness. Joktan barely escaped with his life. And so the battle for control of the world was joined.

"Manon loosed his armies that he had created in secret upon the peoples of the earth. Death and darkness fell across the whole of the land. Joktan and the free peoples fought against the armies of Manon but everywhere they were pushed back. Finally, an appeal was made to Kelven and Ferros.

"Kelven joined with the race of men against Manon and looked to the gods for help, but they were embroiled in troubles of their own for Manon had made confederates among their numbers. You see, he wished to control not only the world but the heavens as well. It was, in fact, a reprise of the rebellion of Aberanezagoth. The Maker had long since gone away to His far home and left all to his children. The gods were embroiled in confusion among their own ranks and so the battle for the world was left to Joktan, Manon, Kelven, and Ferros.

"Kelven readily allied himself with Joktan but Ferros decided to behave defensively rather than risk outright war with Manon."

"Excuse me, my lord," Aram broke into the narrative.

"What is it?" Florm inquired. They were just then passing between the tall spires of the mountains and Aram's green valley was spread out before them to the west.

"You said that men and women were taken by Manon for his dark purposes."

"Yes."

Aram shifted uncomfortably. "Does this mean that the lashers were made by Manon of the race of humans?"

"Well, they were certainly not a creation of the Maker. No one knows by what horrible means Manon made the lashers, but they are absolutely the result of his tampering with nature. Why?"

"My sister was taken by Manon's overseers more than eleven years ago."

Florm was silent for a long moment. "Ah, my young friend, that is a sad and terrible thing indeed. I am truly sorry, my friend, but there is no doubt but that Manon is still engaged in his dark practices."

They passed through the high gates of the mountain and began to descend toward the valley floor through the tall pines. Aram felt his throat tighten. "Can anything be done for my sister? Can she be found?"

"Eleven years?" Florm asked.

"Twelve this winter."

"It is almost certain that she no longer lives. I am truly sorry, my friend." The horse answered quietly and then he was silent for several minutes before he spoke again. "Shall I continue, Aram?"

Aram swallowed at the lump in his throat and nodded. "Please."

"As I said, Kelven went to war with Manon, but Ferros would not, and there was no help from the gods, who had troubles of their own."

"Why wouldn't Ferros help?"

"Because he was too busy trying to discern what was done by Manon in the deep places of the earth. Manon's ambitions are greater than just a need to be acknowledged by the race of men. It is still not known what the fullness of his intentions may be. But he has meddled in the affairs of both Ferros and Kelven. Wolves went readily into his service. Others, as well, joined him; among them were vultures and serpents.

"Despite the help of Kelven, the war went badly for Joktan and the race of men. Then things grew worse. Men began to defect from Joktan and willingly join Manon. Finally the great city of the kings—your city—was breached and abandoned. Joktan and the remnants of his race came into the high plains where they were closer to Kelven's power than to Manon's. For three hundred years there was a sort of stalemate with only scattered skirmishes. It was during this time that Joktan built Rigar Pyrannis, the great city where you recovered the Call.

"Ultimately, however, under the cover of a great storm—for he had also devised means to tamper with Kelven's dominion—Manon came with a vast army out of the mountains to the northwest and was upon the plains before he was discovered. He came himself to this battle. Rigar Pyrannis was besieged and finally Joktan went forth in desperation with his armies and was defeated and was slain by Manon himself and the peoples of the earth were scattered and killed and taken into bondage.

"But as Joktan fell, cut nearly in two by the sword of Manon himself, he suddenly stood upright, tall and fierce. With the blood of life pouring from his body, he cursed Manon and named him the enemy of the world. He said, 'today you have slain me but as surely as I die, know this—my blood will arise from the earth where you have sent it and bring your end upon you.' It is said that Joktan refused to go to his long home after his death and wanders the world to this day, looking for the man of his bloodline that will avenge him upon Manon.

"My father and grandfather were both killed in this great battle upon the plains to the north of Rigar Pyrannis. My father bore Joktan into battle and was killed beneath him. It was at this time that fellowship between my people and yours was broken.

"Then Manon turned his attentions to Kelven and attacked him upon his mountain. Though he suffered great loss, and was weakened for a long time, Manon was ultimately successful and control of most of the world passed into his hands. And there it remains to this day. Unless someone can destroy him or the Maker Himself intervenes, the whole of the world will fall fully into, and remain under, the darkness of Manon forever."

"But there are still free peoples, like those of Derosa." Aram protested.

"Not for long, my friend." Florm answered. "Manon has recovered most of the strength he lost in the final battle with Kelven and he will not rest until all the peoples of the earth are in his chains. He presses upon them even now."

Aram was silent as the afternoon waned and they came down out of the hills to the river. As they rode up the broad avenue toward the city Aram asked.

"What can I do, lord Florm?"

Florm was silent a moment before answering. "I think that is the indeed question, lord Aram. What *can* you do?"

XIV

When they came opposite Aram's vegetable garden and the orchards, Aram dismounted and examined his crops. The apples were making a fine crop, as were the plums, with few worms, and his vegetables had done well. There had been plenty of rain that summer. Even his wheat, which was nearing readiness for harvest, had made enough that there would be flour for bread that winter.

While Aram checked his crops, Florm grazed on the grass near the stream that issued from beneath the walls. Except for the calls of birds and the subtle movements of scattered groups of deer, the valley was calm and quiet. Aram was grateful that there had been no disturbance in his absence. Even the bear in the cave of rubble under the south stairs made an appearance. He was fat and sleek.

Florm and Aram moved on and ascended the stairs onto the great porch.

As they entered the city, Florm looked around in wonder. "It's been a long time since I was here last, just after the city was sacked. You've done much, Aram."

Aram shrugged. "It's my city."

"Indeed."

Aram could find no evidence that anyone had been inside the city in his absence. The door to the armory was closed and everything inside was as he'd left it. As Aram came out of the armory into the courtyard, Florm turned suddenly away and went toward the lower parts of the city.

"You're not leaving, my lord, surely?" Aram asked.

"No," Florm answered. "I'm going to view my old guest quarters. If you have any lamps, you'll need to bring them."

"I have a few resin torches I use in winter."

"Good, bring them."

Aram followed him wonderingly. Florm descended to the lowest level and went around behind the great hall along the wide avenue. At the end of the avenue, where it split and wound up to either side into the heights of the city, Florm went straight ahead, down the broad, central passageway into the dark. Aram had never paid much attention to this part of the city because it was so dark. He'd always assumed it contained storage rooms for crops.

"If you would light the torches, we could see." Florm stated pointedly.

Aram put flint to steel and flames blazed forth in the reeds of his torch. He lit another from the first and held them aloft, one in each hand.

The large subterranean room was, in fact, a stable with rows of what once had been well appointed stalls to either side. Florm went to a large stall at the rear.

"This was mine, once—"he stopped in amazement. "Well, look at that."

Aram stepped around him to see what had engaged the horse's attention. Florm was gazing at a pile of black metal trimmed in gold that gleamed in the light from the torches.

"My father's royal armor. I did not know it was still here." He turned to Aram. "My father was not here when the city was breached and new armor was created for him for the battles that were fought on the high plains. This was evidently abandoned along with the city and never used, for no horse ever fought with Manon."

The horse returned his wondering gaze back to the pile of armor. "This is a magnificent development, Aram, for if you and I ever go to war together, I will be armored." He was quiet a moment, and then continued in a thoughtful tone. "I have to admit, however, that it is more likely to suit Thaniel's frame than mine, for his build is more like my father's than my own."

Florm walked slowly around the large compartment. "This brings back pleasant memories, Aram. I was a guest here many times with my father and mother when Joktan sat the throne. I was very young then—ages have passed and much has happened."

Aram sat on a bench along the wall and watched his friend wander the gloomy stable. Finally, Florm turned to face him. The ancient horse spoke in calm, measured tones, but there was youthful ferocity in the old voice. "This city," he said, "must rise again. The Maker meant for men to govern this earth, not to be slaves in it. The Maker's intentions must be reasserted. And for that to occur, Manon must be pushed from the world."

Aram answered him just as quietly, but with as much conviction. "Both of these things seem to me to be beyond the reach of the most outrageous ambition, my lord. Why do you speak to me of them?"

"So that you will know," Florm answered, and his voice seemed to expand beyond the reaches of Aram's mind and fill the room. "That should you find the desire and the will to attempt either, or both, I will aid you in every way that is possible."

Aram studied him for a moment. "It appears that you expect that I will involve myself in these grand schemes in some way. Why?"

"Oh, I don't expect you to involve yourself, my friend, I expect you to lead the effort."

"Again, my lord, why?"

"Because," Florm's great dark eyes glowed in the light of the torches. "I have come to suspect that you embody the answer to Kelven's Riddle."

Aram leaned forward. "You mentioned this 'riddle' to me before, and I let it go unquestioned. What do you mean by it?"

The great horse came close and spoke earnestly. "Long ago, after the battle in which my father died but before the meeting with Manon in which he was disembodied, Kelven spoke to us, the horses, and said to remember this:

'He comes from the west and arises in the east,

Tall and strong, fierce as a storm upon the plain.

He ascends the height to put his hand among the stars

And wield the sword of heaven.

Master of wolves, friend of horses,

He is a prince of men and a walking flame.

"There was once another line to the riddle; somehow we've forgotten it and it is lost. But think of it, my friend. Your coming from the west into the east, breaking free of the chains of Manon to become a mighty warrior, and then gaining the mastery of wolves and the friendship of horses, all this speaks to the heart of the riddle. Kelven must have foreseen your coming."

Aram shook his head slowly. "I have no sword of heaven, I have never been to the stars, and I assure you that I am not a prince among men. And I doubt that I resemble fire when I walk."

"Perhaps some of it was meant to be allegorical," Florm answered. "I don't know. I do know that your coming has changed things. We are no longer without hope." The big horse stopped pacing and stared out into the darkness of the stable. "I was very young when Manon defeated Joktan and my father was killed. When the battle on the mountain between Kelven and Manon occurred, it seemed as if the world had exploded—mountains cracked and fire plunged down the sky. It was a horrific cataclysm of sound and fury, as if it signified the end of all things. And then afterward it was quiet for a long time, for centuries.

"For a while it seemed to me that horses were the only people left in the world. Then, gradually, others appeared, small animals, hawks, and finally, even a few of your people here and there." The horse hesitated and glanced at Aram. "Including some that I had known before."

He turned away again and gazed into the gloom. "We did not know whether Manon had survived the battle—for a long time it seemed he had not. We came to be certain, sadly, that Kelven had not survived it. We thought that a new age had arisen, a wild age, one that would be unstructured by the guidance of higher powers.

"Then Manon began to make his presence felt. We discovered that he had indeed survived the confrontation with Kelven but that he had been reduced. He was, however, slowly regaining his power and working to rebuild his armies. He still intended to rule this world at his own whim and now there would be no one to oppose him.

"For centuries, we were left alone, far from the frontiers of Manon's influence. But the evil grew, men were enslaved, many were altered, and lashers appeared again. Still, it did not touch us, until the wolves were changed, and then Manon's evil began to ravage our people. The world has grown increasingly darker and more savage these last few centuries. Manon must be nearing his full strength again. I tell you, my friend, lately I have known the terrible despair of overwhelming hopelessness.

"And then, when it seemed that all hope would be driven from the world, you came. Out of nowhere, you came, like one of the kings of old reborn, and you began to alter the will of Manon. You fight with the skill and the strength of the ancient warriors. And with your coming, Kelven's riddle is being answered, line by line. That is why I say that we are no longer without hope."

Aram frowned with chagrin at these astonishing assertions. "Don't expect me, my lord, to be anything more than I am. I despise Manon, I always have, and I would willingly resist him anywhere. But I have no armies, I lead no one, and I am certainly no prince."

The great black horse quivered with irritation. "You ask me not to expect more of you, my friend—I would warn you not try to be less than you are. You cannot escape the consequences of what you've already done. You wrested the mastery of wolves from Manon after having slain many of their number. Do you think he will not learn of this?

"The free peoples to the south talk of the return of one of the kings of old, living in the high city of the kings. Do you expect that these things will not come to the ears of Manon? Do you think that his eye will not fall upon you? Believe me, he already knows that he has an enemy and he will want to know who that enemy is.

"As to your lack of armies, Aram—the oppressed will always be drawn to the strong that are willing to lead the fight. Men need someone to follow. This has always been true and you are the strongest man I have ever known. Men will follow you." The horse gazed at him curiously for a moment in the dimness. "By the way, as to the part in Kelven's riddle about a 'walking flame', well, Thaniel says that you are as fast as lightning in battle, and, even now, the Guardians to either side of you lend you a certain glow. Perhaps that part of the riddle is allegorical after all."

Aram had forgotten about the presence of the Guardians and he glanced self-consciously to either side. He could make out no figures in the gloom but there was a faint sliver of pale light on both his right and his left.

He stood and walked over to Florm. "My lord, I don't care about Kelven's riddle, but I will tell you this—if it were even remotely possible to bring about the downfall of Manon, I would forfeit my own life to accomplish it."

Florm shifted uncomfortably. "Don't talk lightly of forfeiting a life that you have only just begun to live. I cannot see the future, my friend. I don't know what will befall any of us. But I believe that your life—your being alive—may be the thing that the whole world has been waiting for."

"How am I supposed to consider such a statement?" Aram asked and again he shook his head in consternation. "I am nothing extraordinary. I am just a man who does what he finds it is necessary to do and what he thinks is right—no more."

"Yes." Florm agreed. "And I can tell by looking in your eyes that you don't know what a rare thing such a man is."

Aram turned away. "I'm hungry, my lord, and I'll bet you are, too. There might be some ripe apples on the smaller trees."

They went topside and made their way down out of the city. The sun had gone behind the mountain and evening had settled over the valley. While Florm grazed in the grass near one of the springs, Aram checked his trees for ripe fruit, finding five apples that were just beginning to color. He picked them, and turned to see the bear, sitting carefully near the safety of its grotto, watching him closely.

He chose one of the apples for himself, two for the horse, and rolled the others along the ground in the direction of the bear. Then he walked down to join Florm.

The horse sniffed the apples offered to him and refused them, his low laughter rumbling in Aram's mind.

"If I ate those, I assure you I would regret it. They are still too green. Give them to the bear. His insides are not as sensitive as mine."

Aram complied and then sat on a rock while Florm continued to graze, and watched the eastern hills color with the orange light of the waning sun. He realized suddenly, with a start, that he had been homesick. It seemed to him, sitting there in an evening saturated with the pungent scents of late summer, that he had lived in this valley for the whole of his life and that there had been nothing before. His old life had receded into the realm of vague memory.

Florm wandered up and they watched silently as the sunlight left the earth and the blue of the sky deepened toward black. Eventually, the stars came out and pierced brilliant holes in the dark fabric of the night.

Aram turned to Florm. "Surely you'll stay the night here, my lord?"

"Yes. I'll go home tomorrow. I thought I would sleep in the orchard."

Aram nodded. "It's a pleasant night—I think I'll join you."

"I wanted to tell you about the Call, Aram, how it works." Florm said. "You simply blow into it like a reed and it renders a note that I can hear for a thousand miles or more. One note means that you need to see me. One note and I will come alone. Two notes means that your need is urgent and I will bring help, Thaniel certainly, and probably Jared, or maybe Huram. Three notes will tell me that the situation is dire and I will come quickly with all the help that I can bring. Do you understand?"

"Yes, my lord. One note if I need to see you. Two, if I'm in trouble. Three, if it's desperate. But tell me, does it work the other way? What if you're in jeopardy and you need me?"

"No, it doesn't." Florm chuckled. "But don't worry, my friend, I won't let myself get into another situation like the one that introduced us. I am, after all, quite old enough to know better."

Aram got to his feet and stretched. "I just remembered that I have apples stored in the granary from last fall's harvest. Would you like me to fetch some?"

"Not tonight." Florm said. "Perhaps in the morning." He arched his neck, drew in a great breath of the fragrant air and expelled it loudly from his nostrils. Then he turned and went into the trees of the orchard, where he cocked a hind leg and lowered his head.

Aram retrieved his bedroll from the great porch and stretched out by the side of the wide avenue where he could look up through the branches of the trees and see the stars. He thought about all that Florm had told him and wondered if somewhere out among the distant suns and their worlds, the gods were still troubled by the works of Manon.

He thought about Kelven and his end, and wondered why the Maker had allowed the destruction of one of his children by another. Had the Maker tired of the strife among His creation? Had He perhaps gone away and started anew on other worlds leaving the earth to end however it would?

He considered himself, then. He'd asked Florm earlier what he could do; now he asked himself what he would do. Was it his destiny to oppose Manon on behalf of the world? Was he, in fact, the subject of an ancient prophecy? Aram frowned at that thought and dismissed it. He didn't believe in such things. When the Maker created life, He gave it a free will to do what it would for good or evil. Aram could not believe that anybody was fated to behave in a certain manner by the words of ancient riddles.

Gazing out across the immense vaults of the universe, feeling the cool, rich breeze of freedom caress his face, he decided that if an opportunity arose for him to resist Manon in any meaningful way, he would seize it. For the sake of the free peoples of the world, including Florm and his people, and for all those that yet languished in the bondage of Manon, he would fight. Not for the sake of old, obscure riddles, but because it was right.

His chest tightened in an odd manner at the resolve of this decision and involuntarily, he thought about Findaen and his companions and how Lord Florm had stated that Manon "pressed upon them even now." He resolved to go south as soon as his crops were in and see about the state of the people of Derosa. Then, finally, he slept.

Florm nudged him awake in the early morning.

"It's a full day's journey to get across the mountains, Aram. I need to put many miles behind me today."

Aram sat up and rubbed his eyes. "Okay," he said. "Let me grab some apples and I'll go with you."

Florm stared at him. "Go with me? Why?"

"To guard you, of course." Aram looked at him in surprise. "At least until you get over the mountains."

Florm's laughter rang in response. "My good young friend. You did indeed save me from disaster once, and I shall always be grateful. I understand your sense of protectiveness but I assure you I will be fine. I have gotten through several thousand years, after all."

"I'm sorry, my lord." Aram looked down at the ground in embarrassment. "I know you can take care of yourself—I didn't mean to offend."

"I'm not offended, my friend, nor am I surprised. You have become a great warrior with immense confidence in your own strength. A great warrior's only true weakness is a failure to understand that others have strength as well. You have been alone for so long—don't forget that you may sometimes have to depend upon others to do their part." Florm glanced toward the eastern hills. "Besides, there's no need to worry; Thaniel and Huram are coming to meet me, probably near the summit of the pass."

"When will I see you again, my lord?"

"Not until spring unless you call me. In a couple of months, we will gather and go to our winter quarters in the south, near the lake. But I will visit you when the snow leaves the passes next year." Florm looked at him closely. "I believe that you will miss me."

Aram smiled slightly as he returned his gaze. "You are my only friend."

"Ah, now that is certainly not true. Thaniel grows increasingly fond of you and holds you in the highest regard." The horse answered. "And I would not underestimate the feelings of Durlrang the wolf—he is more important than you know. Then there are the men of the southern towns, whose friendship only requires a bit of effort on your part. And there is that bear over there."

"Well, then, you are my first friend."

"May it always be so." Florm lowered his head a moment. "I really must be going. If you need me, call. I will come, even in winter."

Aram blinked at the sudden stinging in his eyes and stiffly raised his hand. "Farewell, my lord. Go carefully and winter well."

"And you, my friend." Florm turned and cantered away down the avenue. Aram watched him until he passed the distant pyramids and went down the slope out of sight toward the river. Then he moved off the avenue among his crops and went to work.

The successive days grew shorter and cooler, leaves changed color and the fruit ripened and there were mornings when frost rimed the grass in the low places around the valley. Aram harvested his crops as they matured and stored them in the granary. The last vestiges of summer left the earth gently and the promise of a long peaceful autumn followed.

One morning, Aram watched as the bear tried without success to turn a large rock in order to get at the grubs underneath. On a whim, he went over and, when the bear backed cautiously away, took a long wooden pole and wedged it beneath the stone. Using a smaller rock as a fulcrum, he rolled the rock over, exposing the prizes beneath.

After Aram had retreated, the bear returned and eagerly dug the grubs from the exposed earth and shoved them in its mouth. Smiling and satisfied with himself, Aram went back to his work.

A while later, as he was lying on his back in the grass resting, he noticed the bear approaching his position in a series of hesitant, cautious movements. He watched the animal out of the corner of his eye and took care not to give any alarm. Florm had suggested that the bear was a "friend". Aram decided to test this proposition by allowing the animal to get as close as it wanted.

Finally, when the bear was a mere two or three yards away, it stopped and lay down, resting its head on its enormous paws, and stared at him. Aram turned slowly and returned the gaze, smiling.

"What do you want, my friend?" He asked in a quiet voice. "More apples? You may have as many as you want—there are plenty for both of us this year."

The bear lifted its head and looked into Aram's face. "I want to...ask a thing." It said and the voice inside Aram's mind was low and slightly muffled, as if it came from a distance.

Aram froze, startled. He'd grown used to the fact that he could commune with horses and even wolves; he no longer considered it unusual. But Thaniel had stated that bears rarely used the gift of speech.

Regaining his composure, he pondered the bear's words. "You want to ask a question?"

The bear was quiet a moment, then, "Yes." It said.

Aram nodded slowly. "Okay. Ask what you will. I will answer if I can."

"You..." the bear sat up and seemed to struggle with its response.

"Me? You wish to ask something about me?" Aram asked.

The bear blinked its small, narrow eyes. "Are you...god?"

Before he could stop himself, Aram let out a shout of laughter, startling the animal. It jumped to its feet and turned its body skittishly, as if in preparation for flight. Aram quickly held his hands out, palms open, in a soothing gesture.

"Take it easy, friend. You just surprised me, that's all. It's okay."

Slowly, the bear calmed down and, after a few moments, returned to its sitting position on the grass. Aram turned to face it fully.

"You asked if I was a god?"

"Yes. You are god?"

"No." Aram shook his head and smiled. "I am a man."

The bear considered this and seemed unconvinced. "You are a man. But man is god. This is true?"

"No." Aram repeated firmly. "It is not true. I am not a god. I am a man. Just a man." He tapped his index finger on his chest. "I am Aram, a man."

The bear gazed intently at him. "Aram...man."

"Yes. Aram, a man." He pointed at the bear. "Do you have a name? What are you called?"

Aram could hear the distant rumbling of the bear's thoughts as it sorted the question. Then it focused carefully on him again and the answer came in the low muffled voice.

"I am Borlus."

"Borlus." Aram nodded with satisfaction. "That's a pleasant name—and it suits you. Well, Borlus, you and I might as well be friends since we essentially share the same city. What do you say—friends? Do you understand this word?"

It took Borlus some time to digest this, and then he looked intently at Aram. "You and I, Aram and Borlus,...are friends." It was a statement, not a question.

Aram nodded gravely, affirming the matter. "You and I are friends."

"Good." Borlus looked out over the valley for several minutes as if deep in thought. Finally, he turned back to Aram. "In the spring, Borlus will find a mate."

He went silent and it took Aram a few moments to realize that he expected a response to his statement. He nodded slowly.

"You, Borlus, are going to find a mate in the spring. That's good. I'm happy for you."

The bear's tiny eyes were serious. "Mate will live with Borlus in the cave?"

It was a question. Aram realized that in his clumsy way, Borlus was asking for permission. He smiled, even though he was unsure of whether his facial expressions had any significance for the animal.

"Of course," he answered. "Your mate must live with you in the cave. Indeed, have a family. That cave is yours, Borlus, for as long as you want it."

Borlus continued to gaze at him with an odd intensity until finally the silence became awkward. It was time for Aram to return to work anyway, so he got slowly to his feet and addressed the bear.

"Is there anything else, Borlus?"

Borlus stirred. "You are a good friend. Borlus is happy."

Aram nodded, smiling and repeated the earlier words of Florm. "May it always be so."

After that first awkward and clumsy conversation, Aram and Borlus became companions, the bear following Aram on his sojourns around the valley and staying near when he worked his small farm. They seldom spoke because it was such a difficult task for the bear, but Aram often reached out silently and ruffled the thick fur behind Borlus' ears, something the bear seemed to enjoy immensely.

One afternoon, as they went southward along the face of the mountain, with Aram looking for material for spear shafts and Borlus digging under random stones for grubs, they were startled by the furious, high-pitched keening of a hawk and the sounds of conflict coming from a stand of trees to their front. Aram nocked an arrow in his bow and ran forward.

High up in a dead snag, a pair of hawks was plunging and diving at something just below the level of their nest. Coming closer, Aram realized that a large snake had managed to climb the dead tree and was endangering the nearly grown but still flightless offspring of the pair.

He slid to one knee and took quick aim. His arrow caught the serpent in the thick part of its body about a foot behind its head and it came coiling to the ground where he dispatched it with one sweep of his sword. Curiously, even after the head was severed, the body of the serpent continued to move, writhing and twitching. The hawks fluttered overhead, uncertain of the meaning of the sudden turn of events.

Turning from watching the odd behavior of the serpent's body, Aram looked up at the hawks and decided to try communication. The conversation with Borlus had suggested the possibility that he could talk with any of the noble peoples of the world.

"I am Aram, a friend of Florm, the lord of horses," he said slowly. "Is everything alright with your family?"

The hawks circled and came to rest on the branches of the snag a few feet over Aram's head. A thin clipped voice broke in upon his mind.

"You are he that dwells in the city of kings."

Aram nodded. "I am."

"I am Willet and this is my spouse, Cree. You have saved our children, lord Aram. We thank you.'

Aram glanced up at the nest where two roughly feathered youngsters were peering over the sides. "Isn't it a bit late in the year to be raising young? Winter is less than two months away."

"This is our second brood." Willet answered. "Do not fear—they will fly before the snow comes."

Aram laughed. "It's not my affair, anyway. By the way, this is Borlus, my friend."

In the moment of silence that followed, the bear and the hawks considered each other but neither spoke. Finally, Willet turned to Aram.

"I thank you, lord Aram, for protecting my family. Is there any service I can render you in repayment?"

"There is no repayment required or desired." Aram answered. "We must all work together in this valley to make it a place of peace and plenty. Be certain that I will defend you and your family at any time that such actions are necessary. You only need call."

"Why would you, a man, take such an interest in us?" Cree asked, and her voice was sharper than Willet's.

Aram looked at her. "Why would I not?"

She studied him but had no answer. Aram let the silence stretch out and then turned back to Willet. A thought had touched his mind again that had come unbidden several times in the last week.

"There is something you could do for me, if you would. Not as repayment but as the act of a friend."

"Speak it, my lord." Willet answered quickly.

"Do you ever fly over the green hills across the rivers to the south?"

"Sometimes." Willet said. "But it is not our usual hunting ground. Why?"

Aram looked south toward the rumpled, forested high ground beyond his valley. The grassy hillsides had yellowed and there were patches of red and gold among the distant stands of trees.

"I want to know if there are men there. Men in leather and cloth, who hunt deer. If there are, I wish to know where they are so I may meet with them."

It was Cree who answered. "My sister lives on the ridge above the sinking river. She and her mate hunt those hills. I can ask her."

"I would be most grateful." Aram said. "If it is not too much trouble."

"I will be back before evening." Cree answered. She leapt off the limb, climbed rapidly skyward and flew into the south.

Willet watched her for a moment.

"She will not be gone long and she will find you wherever you are in the valley when she returns, lord Aram," he said, and then he went back up the dead tree to his young.

Aram studied the dead snake for a moment. It was about six feet long and black, with a pattern of yellowish lines crisscrossing its back. He remembered that Florm had said that serpents were aligned with Manon and he wondered if he should be cautious of the species. After moving the carcass out into the open where scavengers could readily find it, he and Borlus turned toward the city.

Just before sunset, Cree returned and found Aram resting on a rock at the edge of his orchard.

"I have news," she said.

Aram watched her as she lit on a low branch of an apple tree.

"There are men in the hills to the south, four of them, hunting deer. They have been there for the past six days, and there are three more coming."

Aram nodded. "Probably to help them with their take. They must have found success."

"The four have had success." Cree agreed. "But my sister, Frinna, says that the three who come look troubled and come with great speed. Also, there are clouds of dust to the southwest, they darken the sky. Something stirs out on the plains. Frinna thinks it is this that troubles the men who come with speed."

Aram stiffened. "Cree, where are the four men who hunt?"

"A little west of due south. The three who come will find them tomorrow."

Aram was already moving toward the city. "Thank you, Cree. I must go. Borlus, come here."

The bear rumbled over to Aram as the hawk circled up and away to the south. Aram grasped Borlus' head in his hands.

"Listen my friend. I am going away. You must stay here. Lie low and trust no one that comes. But, if anyone does come, you must watch and tell me what is done here in my absence. Whatever you do, though, stay out of danger. Do you understand?"

Borlus growled in deep, troubled tones, but he answered. "Borlus understands. I will stay and watch the city."

"And stay out of danger."

The bear gazed at Aram with his small eyes. "Yes. Aram will come back?"

Aram grabbed a handful of the matted fur behind Borlus' ears and shook the bear's head gently but firmly.

"I will be back," he said. "You be careful."

XV

Early in the morning, as dawn was coloring the sky, Aram slipped out of the city, heading southeast toward the crossings. He was heavily armed, carrying as much weaponry as he could manage while still being able to move quickly and make good time. By noon, he was across the twin rivers and moving quickly up a draw on the south side west of the dilapidated roadway. He hoped to intercept Findaen or whoever it was that headed the hunting party before they returned to Derosa.

It was a clear day and when he topped the ridge and looked to the southwest above the trees, he saw immediately what Cree had been talking about. The far horizon, south of the rumpled hills, was fouled with the dusty evidence of great movement. Something indeed was moving out on the plains. Something substantial.

Aram examined the ground along the top of the ridge and in a few minutes found evidence of the three men going west from Derosa, but as far as he could tell no one had returned along the track. The men of Derosa, then, were still to his west.

He eased off the ridge top and moved west throughout the afternoon through the trees on the south side of the crest, watching and listening. Just as the sun was angling toward the western hills, an hour from sunset, he saw seven figures coming toward him.

When they were near enough that he recognized that their leader was in fact Findaen, he stepped out where they would notice him. They were moving rapidly and resolutely and didn't see him until they were very near. The second man in line, the dark one called Wamlak, spotted him and swerved toward him, warning the others to a halt.

They drew swords and formed a semicircle as Aram approached, and then Findaen recognized him and lowered his weapon.

"What are you doing here, sir?" he asked.

Aram ignored the question in favor of one of his own. "Where are you going so quickly? What troubles you, men of Derosa?"

Findaen came near him and pointed back toward the dusty blotch on the sky in the southwest. "Do you see that? That is an army of Manon, going toward Derosa. Our scouts tell us it is a body of five or six thousand men and assorted beasts, plus lashers. It may mean our end."

Aram looked at him sharply. "Your end? Why would you say such a thing? Will you not fight?"

Findaen spat on the ground and returned his gaze bitterly. "Of course we will fight. But seven or eight hundred men, against six thousand? How will we stand for very long against such a host?"

Aram ignored him as he studied the dark smudge in the southwestern sky. It occurred to him that it was the second time in his life that a column of dust hanging in distant air had boded evil things. "When will they approach your city, do you think?"

Findaen followed his gaze. "Well, they seem to be in no hurry. The scouts say that, at their current level of progress, they will approach our defenses within nine or ten days, maybe less. We go now to prepare as best we can."

Aram studied the men. They were obviously shaken, their faces pale and their eyes haunted by the certainty of the peril. Even the stalwart Jonwood's features were the color of ash. They appeared to Aram's eyes as exactly what they were—good men trudging bravely forward through a morass of fear to go and look in the face of death.

He felt the cold thrill of unavoidable destiny arise in him. An opportunity to oppose the will of Manon had come, more quickly than he could have expected. Manon was sending his minions into Aram's part of the world to bring ruin upon those that Aram wanted for his friends and over whom he had begun to feel a curious sense of proprietorship. With sudden decision, he spun toward Findaen and his voice rang with command, startling the Derosans.

"Go now, all of you, and prepare for battle. But know this—you will not fight alone. I know someone who will help. I will find him and we will return before the army of Manon reaches the gates of your city."

He pulled the extra sword from his belt and handed it to Findaen, along with two spears and two of the fine daggers from the storehouses of Regamun Mediar. "Take these. Tell your Prince that help will come."

Without waiting for a response from the men of Derosa, Aram turned and plunged down a ravine toward the north. As soon as he passed from their sight, he drew the Call of Kelven to his lips, and after considering the situation a moment, blew two notes into the small silver reed. He needed

Florm, and he needed Thaniel as well, but he hesitated to raise a general alarm until he could consult with the horses and tell them what he had in mind. As he blew into the Call, he heard nothing, but there was a tingle along both his shoulders as if the Guardians were alerted.

After sunset, throughout the night, he traveled eastward along the rivers until he could make the crossings, and then he turned to the north, aided by the last half of the harvest moon. He reached the city before daylight and, before heading inward toward the armory, blew two more notes on the Call.

He checked his armor and helmet and found his heaviest boots. He chose another sword to replace the one he'd given Findaen, then he filled two large quivers with arrows and equipped himself with three spears of the heaviest weight. Afterward, he went down to the stables, gathered the horse-armor and carried it topside.

For the next several hours, as the day wore away, he worked to replace all the leather fittings and catches on the armor, testing them for soundness and strength. Then, as the sun dropped toward the mountain behind the city, he ate a quick meal and went out to the great porch and looked along the avenue toward the river. It was empty.

He went to the south end of the porch so that he could see the grove of trees where the hawks had their nest.

"Willet. Cree." He called, as loudly as he could.

Within minutes, the hawks came circling down out of the sky. Aram looked in their shining eyes and pointed toward the river.

"Please, if you will aid me, go and see if there are two horses coming toward the city from the eastern hills."

Without answering, the hawks wheeled away toward the east but came back almost immediately.

"There are three horses, Lord Aram, just now coming onto the avenue." Cree's sharp voice rang in his mind and a glance along the avenue confirmed the information.

In a few minutes, Florm, Thaniel, and Jared came clattering up to the walls below the porch.

"We are here, Aram." Florm's rich voice reverberated up the masonry. "What is your need?"

Aram went rapidly down the stairs, out the end of the alleyway between the porch and the defensive wall and greeted the horses. "It is my friends, the Derosans," he said. "Manon sends an army against them and I wish to aid them in their need. Will you help me?"

The horses wheezed with the exertion of their speedy trip across the mountains from the highlands and flecks of foam were spattered back along their necks and shoulders. Florm drew in a deep, shuddering breath.

"An army? How large is the force that Manon sends?"

"The scouts figure it to be between five and six thousand men. I haven't seen it myself." Aram answered. "They are led by lashers and Findaen said that there were also some 'beasts'."

"Did he? And how many warriors can your friends field?"

Aram shook his head. "I don't think many of them are 'warriors'. Just farmers with poor quality weapons, no more than seven or eight hundred, but they are tough and determined and will fight to defend their homes and families. I intend to put at least one experienced fighter on their side of the field. Will you help me, my lord?"

"Of course we will aid you," Florm said, and he seemed strangely pleased. "What is your intention?"

Aram sat down on the large stone at the edge of the orchard. He was tired from the lack of sleep, but at the same time, energized by the decision to engage in the coming action. He considered Florm's question a few moments, then decided to ask one of his own.

"My lord Florm," he asked, "when was the last time that any of Manon's servants went into battle against an armored, mounted man? When was the last time such a thing was seen?"

Florm gazed at him for several moments and his large, dark eyes seemed to smolder in their ancient depths. "Very good, very good. I told you this day would come, my friend, and I am happy to see it. The last time anyone faced a mounted warrior on a field of battle was more than ten thousand years ago. It was a fearsome thing then, and now that it is unheard of, and unseen, I suspect that the impact of a knight on horseback would bring an unhealthy measure of fear to the ranks of any enemy."

Aram looked at him steadily. "I intend to bring more than fear to the enemy, my lord. I intend to bring death."

Florm studied him for a long moment. "And so you shall. Let us prepare my father's armor and I will bear you."

"Not you, my lord." Aram shook his head firmly. "Thaniel, if he will. He and I know each other well, we have fought together, and you told me yourself that your father's armor would more readily fit your son's frame than your own."

There was a long, uncomfortable silence while Aram and Florm gazed at each other, finally broken by Thaniel. He stepped forward and looked into his father's eyes. "Lord Aram speaks the truth, father. It is my time that has come."

Florm hesitated a moment longer and then sighed. "Yes, youth must prevail. And it is true that the two of you have experience in battle. Go, my son, bear lord Aram with honor."

"A moment, my lord." Jared moved forward and spoke impatiently. "I would go as well. You have said that the day would come when we must all resist the evil of Manon. I would do my part. Do not deny me."

Aram stood, pre-empting any answer from Florm. "You may go with us, Jared, and help with preparation and the devising of strategy, and the day will come when you will fight as well. But for now there is armor for only one horse, and I would not have anyone die or be injured unnecessarily. I have an idea, and if it works, Thaniel and I, and most of the men of Derosa will escape death. Many of the servants of Manon, however, will not."

He approached the horses and knelt down and drew a line in the dirt. "If Manon's army moves forward in a line, and I suspect that it will, his men will be vulnerable to an attack from the side." He drew an arrow in the dirt that impacted the line from the left. "A well-armed man attacking unexpectedly from the side would, in effect, face only one enemy at a time, at least at first. And if he caused enough death and confusion, the superior numbers of the enemy would be negated somewhat."

Florm nodded his great head in enthusiasm. "You are a natural warrior, my friend, I always knew it. That particular tactic is called a flank attack. Joktan used it many times against the armies of Manon—though usually with much more than one mounted man—and it does precisely what you think it does, if executed well."

Aram looked up at him. "Thaniel and I will do more than execute it well, my lord. We will shock and surprise them."

The great horse had been quivering with tension, but now he calmed himself and bent his head toward the ground. "I am pleased, my friend, that at last there is someone to lead the fight against Manon. Thaniel will bear you. Jared and I will follow in reserve, if needed. We are at your service, lord Aram. What are your orders?"

Aram stood. "My armor is ready, as is Thaniel's, though his needs some checking to make certain that I have interpreted its disposition properly. I want to go south in the morning, at first light."

He looked up at the sun, just then preparing to slip behind the mountain. "I'll get apples from the granary. We should all eat well and then rest. I'll make a pack of extra weaponry and provisions." He looked at Jared. "If it is not too great an imposition, perhaps my friend Jared will carry these extra supplies?"

Jared, still disappointed by his disbarment from the coming fight, nonetheless nodded his head in agreement.

"Good. Thank you." Aram turned and looked intently at Florm. "And I would never think of going into battle without the benefit of your wisdom, my lord. Perhaps when we have looked upon the enemy and seen his intentions we may discuss how best to affect those intentions to his dismay."

"The world is about to witness something it has not seen in a long time." Florm answered thoughtfully. "A mounted knight in full armor. It will have an effect, perhaps enough for this battle. But there will be more battles. You understand that we are going to war and there is no turning back? If we survive this and have any measure of success in rescuing your friends, Manon will not let it stand, he will return and he will seek you."

Aram smiled grimly and turned to go up the stairs into the city. "From what you told me yourself, my lord, the world of men has been at war with Manon for ten thousand years. We will fight this battle and then we will see. I will bring apples for supper and then I will join you, my lords, at first light."

He sprinted up the south stairway and went first to the granary, then to the armory. After preparing the pack that Jared would carry, he took apples down to the horses and went back and laid out the armor for him and Thaniel for the morrow. Then he tried to sleep but it was deep into the night before he was successful. He felt like a man who had embarked upon a broad, dark, and unknown ocean in a small craft, unsure of his destination, or of his return, certain only of the righteousness of the journey.

At dawn, he lugged the mounds of armor down the steps a bit at a time and, with Florm's guidance began to assemble it on Thaniel's powerful frame. There were adjustments that had to be made and some of the fittings needed retying but, when he was done, shining black metal trimmed with beaded gold overlaid and protected every portion of Thaniel's body, including his head, ears, eyes, and hooves.

Across the horse's chest and just above his knees, wicked-looking spikes protruded from the armor. Long, sharp, and curved, they looked like they would do severe and obscene damage to any infantryman unlucky enough to be impacted by the passage of the great horse. Aram felt strange as he examined them. Florm was watching him and spoke quietly.

"You said you wished to bring death to the field of battle, my friend. You will be two against very many—you will need all the advantage this armor grants to your mount. It makes of Thaniel a weapon."

Aram nodded solemnly. "I understand, my lord, it's just that I've never killed my own kind before."

"If this is truly an army of Manon," Florm answered. "They will not really be your own kind."

Aram looked at him sharply. "The Derosans said it was an army of men."

There was sadness in the voice of the horse. "They once were—or those they came from were—but they have been altered by Manon, reduced to animals that follow orders and do not think for themselves. They are called 'gray men' but in truth they are not men at all. They are, however, dangerous. They will fight like a pack of maddened wolves."

"Do they know fear?"

"Oh, yes." Florm answered. "Manon cannot breed that out of them. They will not be your match in any aspect if you are able to inflict enough damage right away. Kill enough of them and the rest will run like rabbits. But there will be lashers also and they will not run, nor die easily."

Aram nodded and began to don his own armor, black like Thaniel's but without the gold trimming. "Actually, my lord, I've thought about that. I intend to attack the lashers first, if possible. If I can kill one or two of them, it might demoralize the army and give the Derosans a chance."

Florm was silent for a moment, studying the disposition of Thaniel's armor. Then he turned to Aram and spoke with frank directness. "Lashers are not like wolves, my friend. They are strong, fierce, and intelligent and they fight for Manon as sons fight for their father. A lasher can be killed, but only with great difficulty."

Aram looked at him steadily. "But they can be killed."

"You and Thaniel are a deadly team, I've seen it myself, but these are greater enemies than either of you have ever faced. I would not want to lose my son, or you, at the very beginning of the war."

Aram finished strapping on his armor and began deploying his weaponry in the places provided by Thaniel's. "We will not do anything foolish, my lord, and you will be there to advise us. I don't intend that Thaniel and I will prevail on our own, just that we will even the odds a bit. You told me that others must do their part and the men of Derosa will do theirs. They will fight."

The sun was topping the wooded ridges to the east when they set off to the south. Borlus sat forlorn at the entrance to his grotto and watched them go. Aram rode Thaniel and the two of them spent the morning's journey becoming familiar with the art of moving in tandem while being so heavily armed.

By midmorning they had negotiated the shallow crossings in the rivers and started up through the long draws that led into the hills to the south. After several hours, Thaniel and Aram had become comfortable with being so heavily armored and were both functioning more easily in the confines of the thin metal.

It was the middle of the afternoon when they topped the wooded ridge south of the twin rivers and saw the cloud of dust to the southwest. It was closer, farther east, but still some days away from coming up due south of their position. Since Aram had never seen the gates of Derosa or the plains to its front where the battle would occur, he decided to check that out first.

They progressed southeast down the spine of a long, broad-topped ridge until, toward evening, they rounded a spire of jumbled rock and saw, two or three miles away, the rolling southern plains. There was plenty of grass where they were standing and a spring that issued from a grove of tall beech trees, so they decided to pass the night in that spot.

After removing his and Thaniel's armor, and discussing with the horse some necessary changes in its disposition for the morrow, Aram scaled one of the taller trees and gazed out upon the plains. Off to his right, to the south and southwest, the plains went away from the verge of the green hills into the haze of the evening toward a distant flat horizon.

To the east and southeast, on Aram's left, the wooded hills arched away from him in a gentle curve into the south. In the middle of the curve, a few miles distant, a large stream issued forth upon the plain to be joined at intervals by the many smaller tributaries emanating from the hills around Aram. The river coiled lazily southwestward through a broad but shallow valley in the gently undulating plains until it disappeared into the line of the horizon.

At the point in the southeast where the river flowed from the hills, his eye could make out hints of human construction, as if the river flowed from beneath a wall. Beyond the hills, smoke rose from disconnected fires. He decided that the smoke must come from the homes of Derosa.

Turning back to his right, to the southwest, he tried to make out the movement of the army, but the hour was too late and the sun too far gone. There was only an indistinct orange haze along the horizon in that direction. As he descended the tree, the wind came up from the south and brought with it the subtle smell of the sea.

In the morning, they continued on down the diminishing ridge until they stood at the edge of the hills upon the plains before Derosa. There were scattered buildings and fenced areas, evidently farmsteads, but they were deserted and the plain was empty of people. Aram walked to the top of a low, grassy ridge above a small stream and gazed eastward.

The sun was just topping the hills slightly to his right, but even with its light in his eyes he could make out the wooden wall of the town's defenses. The wall completely traversed the narrow valley where the river left the hills and entered the plains. It arched over the stream and there was a gate in it to the left of the running water. A well-used road led away from the gate and wound away toward the southwest, generally following the course of the river.

There were no signs of any people. Evidently, they intended to fight from behind the wall. Aram examined the plain on the near side of the river by the road. It was gently rolling to flat, cut here and there by the rivulets that issued from the hills behind him. He could see nothing but advantage for an army of superior numbers in that eminently maneuverable space.

He looked westward. In the morning sunlight, the dust raised by the approaching army appeared almost white. He estimated the distance and decided that if the army moved at the pace of a normal man's walk, it would arrive on this spot in four or five days. He had time, therefore, to go west and examine the army and its strength, and discuss possible plans with the horses.

Aram decided to leave the Derosans alone and not inform them of his arrival and his plans but to let them deploy as they would. If there was to be any advantage in the surprise of a mounted man appearing suddenly upon the battlefield, he thought that it might work both ways, for his friends and against his foes. Besides, he was used to operating by himself, at his own volition. Perhaps that aspect of his life would someday change, but not now.

He rejoined the horses and found that Florm agreed with his assessment.

"If there is a weakness we can exploit in the enemy's deployment," the horse lord said, "we'd best do it on our own and surprise everybody. They won't know at first that it is just one man—it might be the thing that turns the battle in our favor and gives courage to your friends."

Aram remounted Thaniel and the four of them went back up the long ridge to the top of the main spine between the rivers and the plains and turned west. The horses were strong, powerful and fast and ate up the ground quickly; by the end of that day, they had come upon the trail that Aram and Decius had walked years ago and were nearly due north of the cloud of dust out on the plain. They camped at the bottom of a wooded draw.

The next morning, they eased southward through the trees along the top of a ridge, with Aram going ahead to watch for scouts that Manon's army might have sent among the hills as outliers. But there were none. They made it all the way down to the end of the green hills and stopped in a copse of woods at the base of a slope. The plain spread before them. Looking to the south, Aram felt his blood freeze and his insides constrict. The cold hand of fear reached into his chest and squeezed his heart with fingers of ice.

Out on the plains a mile or so distant, their pikes held high with the metal points glittering in the sun, were three very long columns of soldiers, trudging eastward. It was an enormous clot of humanity, more men than Aram had witnessed during the whole of his life. At the head and rear of each column, the tall, black figures of lashers moved the masses forward. Behind were dozens of wagons, pulled by oxen, no doubt full of provisions.

For one chilling moment he wondered whether he might just as well turn around and retreat into his valley. How could one man, three horses, and seven or eight hundred farmers defeat such a grim host?

But then he calmed himself and glanced over at the horses to see if they were affected as he was and if they had witnessed his spasm of fear. There was no indication that they'd noticed, or had had similar thoughts. Florm gazed intently southward for several minutes and then turned to Aram.

"It seems as if your friends let fear get the better of their eyes." He said. "There are no more than three thousand men, maybe a few more, about half of what we expected. Still formidable, but less so. There are, however, six lashers. One would be a challenge; six will be daunting, especially if they fight as a group on the battlefield. But—there are only six. Manon must either think this will be an easy thing, or he can't spare more. If the latter were true, it would be suggestive."

Aram watched the long, glittering black lines moving eastward across the prairie. "How long before they reach the walls of Derosa? Three or four days?"

Florm nodded. "Just about."

Aram pivoted and moved back into the trees. "Then there is enough time to return and examine the ground where we will face them."

The horses turned to join him when Jared suddenly stopped, peering at the wagons following the tramping army. "What is that?" He asked and the others followed his gaze.

At the very rear of the army was a large wagon, pulled by eight oxen. Mounted on the wagon was a tall dark cone, its pointed top capped by shining metal, like a spear point. It was surrounded by tramping guards in black armor, two or three rows deep.

"I don't know what that is," answered Florm. "Perhaps it's a commander's tent. A new breed of lasher, maybe, or something else. I cannot guess. I know very little of Manon's chain of command. Aram?"

Watching the unknown object, surrounded by its dark and formidable guards, Aram felt a strange coldness in his belly. Even at that distance, the black cone emitted an aura of evil. He had the sudden feeling that whatever lurked inside it was a thing he would not want to face.

"We should go," he said, and they started back up the wooded draw toward the distant ridge top. Thaniel had learned to move easily in his armor even when Aram was aboard, so, in order to make better time, Aram rode the tall black horse though for the moment he let Jared carry his own armor as a pack. By nightfall, they were back on the long ridge to the west of Derosa that sloped down to the site of the coming battle. They camped in the copse of trees by the spring again and Aram and Thaniel once again discussed the disposition of the horse's armor, making final adjustments for the task ahead.

The next day was spent examining the ground where the hills verged the plain for possible routes of egress and ingress, depending upon how Manon's army was ultimately deployed. Every so often, Aram would climb to the top of the nearest ridge and check on the progress of their enemy. Toward sundown, the advance contingents of the army were in view, dark specks on the distant plain, less than two days away.

They agreed that the next day was to be spent in rest, though Aram went down the ridge alone in the early afternoon and checked on the army's progress. The men of Manon were barely two miles away. Aram hid on the crest of the ridge and watched them approach.

About an hour before sundown, the army stopped and spread out across the plain in two or three ranks, and they sent scouts into the hills barely a mile from Aram's position. This was worrisome. He'd hoped to hit the army by surprise, upon its left flank, but if he had to deal with scouts, the element of surprise might be compromised.

By nightfall, the army had camped and fires were burning across the plain. Scattered fires also burned along the ridge tops to the west, in the hills north of the army. On the morrow, Derosa would be assaulted, and Aram would be at war with his own kind for the first time in his life. He slipped back up the ridge toward camp in the darkness with something that felt very much like real fear thrumming deep in his chest.

There was no moon as yet, only stars in the sky, and the physical features of the ridge top were reduced to gray shadows and black shapes. The only serious source of light was the Glittering Sword of God, slashing obliquely up the sky a few hours above the western horizon. As he rounded a rocky spire surrounded by gray-barked trees, he was suddenly confronted by a tall, dark figure, standing alone in the dimness upon the open ridge beyond the trees.

The steel of his blade sang sharply in the stillness of the night as he pulled it from its scabbard and brought it to the ready to challenge the stranger. The man was hooded and cloaked and did not respond to Aram's threat. He stood perfectly still as Aram eased to his left, searching the ground with his boots for a better purchase.

When he was on solid, level ground and slightly above the stranger's position, he forced himself to breathe deeply twice and then spoke quietly.

"Identify yourself," he demanded.

The man stared at him from the deep blackness of his hood while Aram waited with his sword pointed at the figure's chest. At last the stranger stirred.

"So, Aram," he said, "you will fight tomorrow, is that so?"

Aram jumped. It was a voice he'd heard before. This same specter had leaned over him that evening in the snow when the wolves had savaged him and he had prepared himself for death. He lowered his weapon slightly and peered into the shadow under the hood.

"*You.* You seem to show up every time I'm in peril."

The hood bent forward slightly in assent. "May it always be so."

"Who are you?"

The cloaked figure ignored the question, and repeated his own instead.

"Will you fight tomorrow?" He asked quietly.

Aram swung his sword over his shoulder and slipped it into its scabbard.

"Yes." He answered. "I will fight tomorrow."

"And you are afraid." It was a statement. "You, who have attacked entire packs of wolves without fear and slain so many of their number, are afraid."

Aram shrugged. "I am. These are men, and there are thousands of them. There are lashers as well. Yes, I am—afraid of tomorrow."

"Fear is a wise man's friend, it makes him cautious. As long as it does not overwhelm him and render him impotent. Are you afraid that tomorrow you may die?"

Aram laughed quietly. "No, I do not fear death. I never have." He turned and gazed behind him at the gray expanse of the darkened plain, lying indistinct and featureless under the stars. The fires of the enemy camp were further west, out of sight. "I am afraid of failure. I do not want to die and have the homes of my friends plundered, and perhaps cause the death of a horse and have it all mean nothing."

"You will not fail. And you will not cause the death of a horse under any circumstances."

Aram looked at him. "But I will be mounted."

"Yes, but Thaniel goes into battle of his own will. Horses do not go into battle any other way. They are an amazing people, strong, wise, and courageous." Aram felt the unseen eyes upon him. "What is your plan of attack?"

"I intend to strike them unexpectedly upon their flank, after they are in line but before they can assault Derosa."

The figure nodded. "These are the servants of Manon and they will fight as they always have. They will be mostly pikemen; each of them will be also armed with a secondary weapon, probably a short sword. They will line up across the field in one or two ranks with reserves in the center. But there will also be archers. After the pikemen are on line and the field to the front secure, the archers will be ordered forward. As they are passing through the lines, then is the time to strike."

"There are lashers, also; I've seen them." Aram informed him. "Six in all. I intend to go after each of them as soon as I can, if at all possible. Lord Florm warned me that they might be unconquerable if they fight together."

The cloaked figure shook his head. "They won't. They will be spread along the line. Manon expects that this will be an easy thing. Of course, he doesn't know about you." He hesitated a moment. "About the lashers. Young Florm is right in that they will not kill easily. But they *can* be killed. And, like any other creature, they do know fear. A lasher will fight ferociously, but, if he sees the imminence of his own death, he will run from it if he can. If you can kill even one or two, the others will not be so certain of victory and your task will be easier. Their armor is of hardened leather and is very strong but it has its vulnerabilities, especially about the head and neck."

The cloaked figure leaned forward and studied Aram quietly for a moment and then stepped back, standing erect.

"I see that you are not alone. There are Guardians with you. Though you may not command them, they will aid you. Believe me; they are worth more than a company of the best swordsmen. You will not fail tomorrow, Aram, I am sure of it."

Standing there on the darkened ridge top in the still of night, listening to the specter's quiet voice, Aram felt his confidence begin to return and his earlier fear recede. As he gazed with renewed confidence at his advisor, the cloaked and hooded figure began to fade into the blackness of the trees behind him. He realized suddenly that the specter was leaving. He stepped quickly forward and held out his hands.

"Wait, please, sir. Tell me who you are."

The figure shimmered darkly on the edge of visibility for just a moment. "I am all that remains of what was once a man. Be very careful tomorrow, my son, even as you are brave. I would not have you die now, at the beginning."

Then he was gone. Aram stood staring into the black and gray tapestry of the night and thought about what Florm had told him of the ancient king, Joktan, who would not leave the earth until he was avenged upon Manon. Then, though he did not know if he was heard, he spoke quietly into the shadows along the top of the darkened ridge.

"I know who you are, my lord." he said, but the darkness returned no answer.

XVI

After he returned to camp, Aram tried to sleep, but found that the tense anticipation of the events to come on the morrow prevented it. The Glittering Sword had fallen into the west and was sliding beyond the edge of the world when he finally gave up on sleep and concentrated on forcing his body to be still so it could rest.

As soon as it was light enough to see, Aram ate a cold breakfast and eased down the crest of the ridge to the west to watch the movement of the enemy's scouts. An hour past sunrise he saw them come, three or four of them, fifty yards apart, moving furtively but in a straight line from west to east, cresting the ridges and then disappearing for a time as each negotiated the narrow draws between. The nearest one would pass well to the south of him.

For a moment, he considered killing all of them with his bow, but thought better of it. Such an act might alert the main body to the fact that there was a threat on its northern flank. He did not want to sacrifice the element of surprise; it would be his best friend in the first minutes of the coming struggle.

After the scouts had traversed the ridge where he and the horses had camped and gone out of sight to the east, he returned to the horses. The main body would come into position down on the plains by mid-morning or early afternoon. It was time to prepare for battle.

Florm was grazing calmly on the western slope of the ridge but Thaniel and Jared were standing out on the top, looking stolidly toward the south. Aram went over to Thaniel.

"How are you this morning, my friend?"

Thaniel swung his great head around and focused on Aram. His large eyes were shining and black. "I am...tense. But I am ready. And you?"

Aram placed a hand on the horse's shoulder and looked south. "Tense is a good word for it." He drew a deep breath. "The enemy will be in position in a few hours and the scouts have gone by. We should prepare and go."

"Then let us go."

As Aram was armoring Thaniel, Florm came up and watched. After a few moments, he spoke.

"I heard you talking in the night, Aram. Were you praying?"

"No, my lord, though probably I should have. I met an old friend; a ghost who seems to show up every time I'm in duress."

"A ghost?"

"Well, a specter, anyway." Aram thought about it a moment and then shrugged. "Sometimes I see him, but mostly I don't."

Florm studied him. "Indeed. And did he give you advice?"

"Oh, yes." Aram smiled slightly. "He is familiar with Manon's methods and he seemed to think that we would not fail today. And he knows you, my lord—he called you 'young Florm'."

"I see." There was an odd tone in the ancient horse's voice that made Aram turn and look at him.

"What is it that you see, my lord?"

"How things really are." Florm answered quietly. He turned to Thaniel. "I know that you and lord Aram have fought together often and well, my son, but today's effort will need to be perfect and seamless if you are to prevail, or even survive. After the battle starts, Jared and I will move forward and watch from the ridge. I will be in contact with you should the need arise. Do not die before my eyes."

Thaniel shifted his bulk under the armor. "I will not die, father. Lord Aram and I will not fail."

When Thaniel was fully armored, Aram checked every fitting and every strap and made certain the saddle was cinched to Thaniel's satisfaction and comfort. Then he slipped his spears through the rings at the front of the saddle and tied two quivers of arrows to the rings on the back.

He dressed into his armor and pulled his horned helmet over his head, leaving the visor up for the moment. After checking his sword and bow, he slid the sword into the scabbard on his back and slipped the bow over his head. Then he mounted the great black horse and they went to the bottom of the draw and headed south.

Before the middle of the morning, they stopped in a dense copse of trees a quarter mile from the open plain. Removing his helmet, Aram left the horses hidden and crept cautiously forward on foot. From the open plain to his front came the sounds of shouted orders and the ringing of metal and the tramping of many feet. The army was already within an arrow shot of the walls of Derosa and was forming up for the assault.

It was difficult to crawl wearing his armor but he managed it. At the top of a small embankment where the stream at the bottom of the draw made a loop through a stand of willows before flowing out into the level ground, he gazed upon his enemy.

The columns of lean, hunched men were spilling their contents to each side, forming a double line across the plain, bristling with spears. Their discipline was impressive. The line was forming just short of the crest of a small rise to Aram's left, on the eastern side of the stream. Aram watched, fascinated, as the long columns broke into segments and then spread like water poured on stone, filling the gaps in the line.

The near end of the line, anchored by a large lasher armed with a spiked ball suspended on a thick chain, began about a hundred yards out from the trees clustered at the base of the bluff that defined the end of the ridge to Aram's left. From there the line extended across the plain southward for nearly a half-mile. Six lashers stood behind the lines, one about every two hundred yards.

Back to the west, to Aram's right, a mile or so behind the line, the wagons of provisions pulled into blocks of six or eight and stopped. Just in front of them was the wagon bearing the tall dark cone, topped with shining metal, guarded by its cadre of heavily armored men.

After the pikemen were on line, prodded by snarling lashers, a second, smaller group of men began forming a line to their rear. These men were armed with bows and bore quivers of long arrows. They were the archers that Joktan had mentioned as being key to the timing of Aram's attack and they were forming quickly. Even as he watched, there was a roar from the lasher at the center of their line and they moved forward.

Aram realized suddenly that there would be no preamble to the battle. Manon's army meant to assault Derosa at once. If he did not get into the battle now, the opportunity suggested by Joktan would be lost.

He slid rapidly back from the crest of the rise and ran as fast as his armor would allow back to the horses. The three of them stood rigidly, their large black eyes unblinking, and watched him come.

"We must go immediately," he gasped, and he pulled himself up onto Thaniel's back. He felt the great horse quiver beneath him. "We must attack now or we will miss our chance."

"Then go." Said Florm.

Thaniel blew a great blast from his nostrils and bolted from the copse, down across the stream to the grassy bank on the far side and out through the trees toward the plain. Aram slammed his visor down and drew his sword, holding it downward alongside the surging flanks of the armored horse.

As Thaniel crashed through the stand of trees, the spikes on his armor tore at their trunks and ripped off branches, but Aram could hear nothing but the wind whistling through the ear holes of his helmet and, far away, the pounding of the horse's great hooves.

Then they broke into the open and came out onto the field under the noonday sun.

The archers were within two steps of the main line and moving forward. The lasher with the spiked ball had moved southward along the line and there were about fifty men between him and the northern end when Thaniel thundered from the trees and charged the enemy.

The minute that it took for Thaniel to close the distance to the enemy's line seemed to Aram to lengthen and stretch beyond the bounds of reality. Time slowed almost to a stop. Through the slit in his visor, he saw the grim, gray faces of Manon's soldiers turn toward him and their mouths open to release shouts that he could not hear. Turning in response to the tumult, the lasher roared in fury and came loping northward just behind the line of archers. The archers stumbled through the line to the front as the pikemen began to wheel toward this new and unexpected threat, their lances twisting and lowering.

At the end, just before the great horse crashed into the line, Aram saw the eyes of the soldiers widen, and in the flat, black depths, there was fear and awe.

Then, with a horrific explosion of sound, Thaniel smashed into the flank of the army. Men screamed as the deadly spikes in Thaniel's armor severed limbs and wrought terrible injuries. And Aram went to work with his sword.

The Guardians of the Call of Kelven awoke to action. Light erupted to either side and any lance that threatened Aram was struck down and its bearer reduced to death. When a small number of archers managed to group up beyond the line and aim their missiles his way, the arrows were deflected by unseen blades.

In the meantime, Aram dealt death with his sword as his mount plunged forward. As they penetrated deeper into the line, the cohesion of the pikemen was lost and the line snarled into a confused tangle of wounded, dead and frightened men. As the bodies began to pile up and men tried to flee only to trip themselves and their fellows, Thaniel's forward progress was in danger of being halted.

And the lasher approached.

As he slashed and parried and thrust with his sword, Aram saw him come and realized that to face this enemy, they must get clear of the clot of soldiers.

"Thaniel, go right!" he shouted above the din, even though he knew the horse heard him with his mind. "Move right. We must face the lasher on open ground."

Thaniel wheeled and stumbled free of the mass of confused, frightened and dying men. The lasher was a scant thirty feet away and was swinging his spiked steel ball in a vicious circle above his head.

"Charge him." Aram told Thaniel and this time it was a silent command. "Jump to the right at the last second and wheel in a circle just out of range of his weapon. Make him miss and then get me close."

With a powerful lunge of his back legs, Thaniel rushed at the lasher. The lasher stopped and planted his wide feet, his mouth open in a roar, showing his long, pointed teeth. Both of his clawed hands were on the chain of his weapon and his muscles rippled beneath his armor as the spiked ball cut deadly circles through the air. His eyes were slits of malevolent black.

At the last moment, Thaniel lunged to the right and Aram leaned away from the trajectory of the lasher's weapon, but one of the steel-tipped spikes caught him a glancing blow on his upper arm. Though his armor prevented the spike from piercing his flesh, pain exploded through his shoulder. With the explosion of pain, though, there also came a surge of fury.

"Wheel, Thaniel, wheel," he shouted.

Digging into the soft soil of the plain with his massive hooves, Thaniel turned sharply, spun around and charged forward, just to the left of the lasher.

The lasher had made two errors. First, he'd aimed his spiked ball at the rider instead of the mount, so that the trajectory of his weapon had caused it to circle in a high arc and bury itself in the soil behind him, losing all its momentum. Then, instead of dropping it and drawing his sword, he attempted to lift the ball and swing it again.

Before he could do this, Thaniel was upon him, driving his great shoulders against the lasher's body. Losing his grip on the chain of his weapon, the lasher roared and tried to dig the claws of his right hand through the armor and into the muscles of the horse's chest. With the other, he attempted to pull Aram from his mount. But Aram was ready.

Though the lasher was very tall, Aram, sitting on the back of the taller Thaniel, and standing high in the stirrups, had the advantage. Grasping his sword with both hands, Aram drove the steel blade straight down into the lasher's open mouth, feeling it stop abruptly as it encountered bone somewhere deep in the cavity behind the creature's teeth.

Howling with pain and rage, the lasher clamped his teeth down on the steel and grabbed at the offending blade with one hand while he pulled at Aram with the other. Aram strained to keep the pressure on. He could feel the immense strength of the lasher as he struggled against them. Even through the steel of Aram's armor the enormous claws threatened injury.

"Forward," he screamed at Thaniel, "forward."

The horse leaned his full weight into the struggle. Then, suddenly, there was a dull 'pop' and Aram felt something snap deep inside the lasher's head as the blade slipped inward a little further. A torrent of putrid, black liquid erupted from the depths of the lasher's maw. The beast's great hands slackened their grip, the slatted eyes opened wide and the flat blackness of their depths went even flatter. The lasher crumpled.

With tremendous effort, Aram pulled his sword out from between the teeth of the beast as it fell and then Thaniel lunged away. They'd made their first kill. Looking around, Aram took stock of the situation on the battlefield.

Near him, the ordered line of pikemen had devolved into clumped groups of frightened and uncertain men who'd just seen their commander destroyed by this terrifying figure on a black and deadly beast. Even more terrifyingly mysterious, when any found the courage to attack, their spears were inexplicably shattered and mysterious explosions of light killed the attackers.

Beyond the line, the archers were also in confusion. The arrows that they loosed toward the black rider were reduced to ash. It seemed as if the man on the horse was protected by lightning. And now there was no one to command them. Fear began to make its awful presence known.

To the rear of the army, Aram saw two lashers running away from him toward the mysterious cone, a half-mile or so away. He didn't want to abandon the fight at the front just yet and give up the advantage by crossing open ground. Turning and looking over the top of Thaniel's head along the line, he spotted his next two opponents. Several hundred yards away, one lasher was trying to turn his men to face the threat posed by Aram and Thaniel, but closer, loping directly toward them behind the line of pikemen, was another.

"Do you see him?" Aram asked Thaniel.

"Yes." The horse answered.

"Go."

Thaniel heaved forward and thundered toward this new enemy. The lasher was armed with a large, flat-bladed sword and he held it out to the side as he sprinted resolutely toward them. About a hundred yards of open ground separated them. Aram slid his sword into its scabbard, pulled his bow over his head, and nocked an arrow.

Standing in the stirrups, he let the arrow fly. It was a clean shot, but the lasher dodged, swung his sword round with surprising speed and flicked the missile away. Aram shot again, but again the result was the same. The lasher avoided a third arrow and the gap was rapidly closing.

"*Aram.*" Thaniel's voice was anxious.

"I know." Aram answered. "I'll get him. Keep straight on."

He had to find a way to get an arrow through the lasher's defenses, if not, they would have to either sheer off or get into close combat. Aram didn't want to consider either option. Veering away would lessen their momentum and perhaps ease the fear they had instilled already in the body of Manon's army.

And he didn't like the thought of dealing with this lasher and his huge sword at close quarters. The problem was that his quivers were tied to the saddle behind him and bringing the arrows up into play was slow and awkward. There was only one thing to try.

Retrieving two arrows from the quiver to his right, Aram held one vertically in his bow hand while he nocked the other, took aim and released. Not waiting to see the result of this shot, he quickly released the second, sending it right after the first. The first arrow was knocked aside like the others but the second sank into the breastplate of the lasher's leather armor.

Roaring in fury at the sudden, sharp pain, the lasher didn't even break stride but grasped the offending arrow with his left hand, broke it off, and tossed it away. But Aram already had two more arrows screaming toward him across the diminishing distance.

The first of this second assault broke against the flat blade of the lasher's upraised broad sword, but the second struck him in the face, lodging deep into the lasher's right eye. The lasher stumbled and went to his knees, dropping his sword and clawing at the shaft of the arrow in torment.

"Slide to the left of him." Aram shouted at Thaniel and he slid his bow over his head and freed a spear from the rings in the saddle.

The lasher raised one clawed hand to ward off the horse and rider, but Aram, grasping the spear with both hands and standing hard into his stroke as Thaniel crashed into the kneeling beast, drove the sharp point of the spear deep into the lasher's other eye. The steel tip slid through the cavity, scraped against bone, and then found its way into the softer tissue beyond. Without another sound, the lasher crumpled onto the grass.

As Thaniel thundered past, Aram let go of the shaft of the spear, righted himself in the saddle, and looked toward his next opponent. The lasher in command of the center of the army had succeeded in turning his troops to face the threat. Several hundred gray soldiers now marched in a line toward them, driven forward by their snarling commander. Aram once again slid his bow over his head and into action.

Behind them, the left side of Manon's army was beginning to dissolve in fear and confusion. Its two commanders had been slain in quick and decisive fashion, many of their fellow soldiers were dead or injured and the dark-clad enemy on the black horse seemed untouchable. And now, a new foe threatened them.

For at that moment a sudden, loud noise erupted out across the plain from the direction of Derosa. Turning to take a brief look, Aram saw a dark line of men sweep out from the wooded hills around the gates of the city and charge toward the left side of Manon's army. Encouraged by the amazing events they'd just witnessed, Findaen and his farmers had decided to leave their defenses and join the fray.

Aram looked back to his front over Thaniel's head. There was now a solid line of pikemen, four or five hundred at least, advancing toward them. Just behind their center, the lasher in command strode back and forth, roaring orders and whipping them forward. He was armed only with a multi-thronged whip and a short sword. Thaniel didn't wait for instructions from Aram but immediately began to close the distance to the line of upraised pikes.

The lean, hunched warriors of Manon were lightly armored with leather breastplates, shoulder pads, and broad strips that hung from their belts to protect the fronts of their legs. Such armor was no match for the missiles from Aram's long bow and he went to work creating a gap in the line. Every arrow brought a soldier down, either dead or rendered useless. The center of the lasher's line of pikemen began to grow thin.

Finally, as the great black horse and its deadly rider galloped down upon them, thinning their ranks, they broke, streaming to either side like water around a rock. The lasher was left alone. And Thaniel's blood was up. He crashed straight into the massive horned creature, driving him back. The lasher spun to his left, going down to his hands and knees for a moment, but got up again immediately.

As Thaniel whirled around, Aram pushed his bow over his head and drew his sword. The lasher was dazed but turned to face them. As Thaniel thundered by, Aram swung his sword with all his might at the beast's head. The blade clanged off the lasher's horns, doing little damage, but the beast was staggered. Thaniel turned again.

This time, the lasher raised his arms to protect his head and Aram's sword slashed through muscle. One of the clawed hands dropped and brackish fluid erupted from the arm. Aram's own arms ached from the collisions with the bones of his enemy but he was filled with the fury of battle and he urged Thaniel to go around again.

But the lasher had had enough and was running away. Thaniel was on him in a few strides and Aram brought his sword down on the neck of the beast at the base of his skull. The steel found a gap in the bone, the sword bit deep, and the lasher went down in a heap, kicking at the ground with his clawed feet. Thaniel spun and charged again but the lasher had stopped moving. There were now three of them gone.

They swung back to the left, toward the right-side remnants of the army. But by now the army was falling apart. In small, disorganized clumps, Manon's troopers were ditching their weapons and streaming toward the rear. Sudden, inexplicable destruction had come down upon them from the hills that even lashers were powerless to stop. It had become apparent to them that to stay was to die. They feared the retribution of their commanders less than the fury of this new and terrible enemy. Besides, it appeared that, very soon, there would be no commanders left on the field to exact retribution. And so, they ran.

Two lashers had already gone to the rear, toward the strange wagon, three were dead, and only one remained at the front. Aram and Thaniel now set themselves to destroy this last one, the commander of the army's right. He was larger than the others, with enormous, shining horns, and he was striding furiously toward them. As he came, he swung his great sword in deadly sweeps about him, killing his own men as they tried to leave the field.

When about a hundred yards separated them, he tossed the sword aside and picked up a long pike discarded by one of his men upon the plain. Sprinting to the top of a low mound, he spread his thick legs wide, brought up the pike, and prepared to receive their charge.

As the space between them narrowed, Aram felt a twinge of warning. This particular beast was huge and if he succeeded in positioning the pike just right, the force of the great horse against the tip might allow the steel to penetrate Thaniel's armor, injuring the horse, maybe killing him.

"Thaniel, break off. Circle him at a distance." he ordered, and Thaniel responded to the earnestness in his voice. "But keep him turning, off balance."

The horse complied, charging around the lasher in a tight circle, close, but just out of range of the deadly pike. Aram swung about in the saddle so that his leg hung over the back behind the quiver that was attached there. Drawing arrows and releasing them as fast as he could, he assailed the lasher with a storm of missiles.

Surprised by the sudden change in his opponent's tactics, the lasher was caught off guard. Twisting around slowly on top of the mound so that he could keep his face to his enemy, the lasher was assaulted by a hail of arrows, and he was sustaining damage.

Though few of the arrows penetrated his hardened leather armor deep enough to cause serious injury, they were nonetheless penetrating some, and were causing pain and loss of blood, and forced the lasher to keep his head down or turned away from the assault to protect his eyes.

Finally, he could take no more and he charged down off the mound, both hands on the pike, aiming for Thaniel's broad side. Instinctively, the horse turned toward his attacker, but Aram knew that a collision with the lasher's pike would be a disaster.

"No, Thaniel," he screamed. "Turn away!"

The horse veered to the right at the last moment but the lasher lunged forward and drove his pike into the horse's flank. Because of the angle, the tip did not penetrate the armor but slid upward and through the gap between Aram's leg and the saddle. Aram seized on the opportunity.

"Go right—now!" He instructed the horse, and with his gloved hand, he fastened onto the wooden shaft of the pike just behind its metal tip. The force of the horse's sharp turn ripped the pike from the lasher's grasp, leaving him standing defenseless on the open plain. Thaniel turned to charge.

The lasher saw that his fate was sealed but was apparently determined to take his enemy down with him. Extending his clawed hands wide, with a roar, he rushed the horse and rider.

They came together in a horrific, shuddering collision. Aram lost his grip on his sword and was nearly thrown over Thaniel's head by the sudden loss of forward momentum. Like a rabid wolf, the lasher tried to sink his long, sharp teeth into the horse's shoulder, ripping and tearing at the metal armor even as blackish blood spouted from his mouth. Thaniel strained to push his opponent backward, trying to force the spikes in his chest plate through the lasher's armor and into flesh. For a long moment there seemed to be no sound in the world but the groaning of the two great beasts.

Momentarily stunned, and nearly unseated, Aram drew several deep breaths and then finally righted himself and pulled a dagger from his belt. Leaning forward along Thaniel's shoulder, he drew his arm back and plunged the dagger deep into the flat black well of the lasher's eye. The lasher howled in agony and let go of the horse, slipping to the side, grabbing at the offending dagger with one hand and the rider with the other.

The loss of tension caused Thaniel to surge forward suddenly, stumbling, and Aram was thrown from his back. As he crashed to the ground, face first, his helmet rang against the steel of his dropped sword. Instinctively, he grasped its hilt and rolled over to find the lasher almost on top of him.

He brought the tip of the sword up but the lasher grabbed the blade and tried to yank it from Aram's grasp. Fortunately, the lasher's claws were slick with blood and he struggled to grip the steel. For a moment there was a silent tug of war that Aram realized he could not help but lose against the superior strength of the lasher.

Then, suddenly, like the descending mass of a black thundercloud, he saw Thaniel appear behind his enemy and he released the hilt of the sword and rolled away just as the great horse rode the lasher down from behind. The creature gave out a peculiar grunt as the sword pierced his body and he crumbled slowly forward, impaled upon the blade by the raw force of Thaniel's size and power.

As the lasher collapsed, Aram got to his feet, gasping for breath, and glanced around the battlefield. They were nearly alone upon the plain. Manon's army was running to the rear, toward the wagons, pursued by the ragged, shouting line of the men of Derosa. The two remaining lashers were farther to the rear, atop the wagon with the metal-tipped cone, working furiously.

With Thaniel's help, Aram heaved the lasher over and pulled his sword from the body. Then he remounted the horse and they turned to overtake the remnants of the army. Quickly, they surpassed the men of Derosa and caught the fleeing soldiers but Aram decided to ignore them and go on toward the rear and take out the remaining lashers, if possible.

They surged far ahead of the retreating soldiers as Thaniel drove westward across the plain. Topping a small rise above a stream they saw, a hundred yards distant, the two lashers standing on the ground by the wagon. They were bathed in a pale green glow. The unearthly light emanated from the figure of a man standing on the bed of the wagon in front of the cone, which now had a dark opening in its angled sides.

The figure standing on the wagon bed was tall and thin, clothed in full- length silver robes, entirely wreathed in the strange luminescence. Even in the glare of the midday sun, the figure glowed, emitting waves of the evil greenish light. His forehead was high, and his large head was bare and bald.

He looked straight at Thaniel and Aram, watching as they approached with a slight smile on his face, seeming to welcome their appearance. Commander or king, whoever he was, he was unarmed.

Thaniel turned toward the strange figure and Aram reached for his remaining spear. If this were the commander of Manon's army, he would not live to command much longer. But at that moment, Florm's voice boomed down out of the hills and crashed into Aram's mind.

"Thaniel! Aram! Turn away—turn away! It is a fellring of Manon. It will destroy you. Turn away—quickly! *Run.*"

The panic in Florm's voice was unmistakable and irresistible. Thaniel spun away from the wagon so quickly that Aram was again nearly unseated. He grabbed desperately at the horn of the saddle and leaned low against the horse's neck, trying to regain his balance.

As they tore away from the eerie figure standing atop the wagon, they again topped the small rise in the ground, beyond which was the stream they'd passed over moments before. Thaniel thundered across the lip of the rise and down toward the stream with Aram hunched over his shoulders just as a small, but mysterious and frightening sound, like the single tolling of a heavy bell in a distant, deep, and dark place occurred behind them.

Time stopped.

The sun dimmed.

A soul-wrenching wave of pain passed through Aram's bone and sinew.

In one terrible instant, it seemed as if he was torn from his body and thrown out into the vast darkness beyond the world. The sun had gone out. Before him, he saw the circle of the world as it hung among the sweeping fields of stars against the black curtain of the universe. Nothing moved anywhere. Across the surface of the earth, everything was still. The mightiest rivers halted in their courses and raindrops hung suspended in space.

Life had ceased.

Time had stopped.

All was still as death.

And then, fitfully, painfully, time started again.

Like a guttering candle, the sun flickered back into existence.

As if detached from the event and watching it happen as slowly and as hesitantly as the snowflake drifts to earth, Aram saw Thaniel stumble and go to his knees. Inside his own head, thunder rolled against the bone of his skull and pain and nausea whipsawed through his body unchecked.

Thaniel slid to a stop by the stream and Aram rolled slowly earthward from the back of the horse. The impact with the ground seemed to occur at a great distance from him and added nothing to the intense pain. Darkness rose up out of the earth in a venomous cloud and enveloped him. He desperately needed to vomit and tried to remove his helmet but found that he could not raise his arms. As his head rolled to the side, his visor popped up and he saw, inside an ever-constricting cone of darkness, Thaniel's great head drop forward.

As Aram watched, the horse's large, lustrous eyes dulled over and rivulets of red formed in the great nostrils, pooled, and dripped onto the grass. Aram tried to speak but he could not find his voice; it was lost somewhere in the fog of his mind, and then the sun winked out again and he went into darkness.

XVII

"Thaniel, Thaniel, my son, my son." From far away, Aram heard Florm's desperate cries and through the fog of pain and nausea inside his head, he heard the thrumming of thunder sweeping along the ground, growing ever louder.

He opened his eyes but could see nothing. The world was shrouded in darkness with only one tiny, hazy point of light directly in front of his eyes. Slowly, he became aware of the fact that he was lying on his back. Even more slowly, memory returned.

He remembered then, vaguely, that he and Thaniel had been injured by a terrible detonation. He recalled the immense struggles of the battle and, at the last, the tall ominous figure of a man, wreathed in evil green light, smiling a venomous smile.

The tiny point of light before his eyes grew in intensity until he could no longer bear it and he turned his face away. Something large and black was to his left. Out of it came the sounds of torment.

Thaniel.

"Thaniel, can you hear me?" His voice sounded dry and cracked.

"I hear you, Aram." Thaniel's reply was faint and there was agony in its delivery.

"Are you hurt badly?" Aram asked.

"Yes."

The thunder grew louder and, as Aram's vision cleared, he rolled his head the other way and saw the approach of Florm and Jared. Florm was obviously in panic as he slid to a stop and dropped his head near that of his son.

"Thaniel, my son, speak to me. How badly are you injured?"

Thaniel could not raise his head but he blinked his eyes.

"I am hurt, father. I do not know to what extent."

Aram rolled onto his belly and pushed himself, trembling, onto his hands and knees. As he did so, his visor clanged shut. He did not have the strength to remove his helmet so he left it on and examined his friend through the slit in the visor. Thaniel was still bleeding from his nostrils, the blood dripping into an increasing pool in the grass. But his eyes were open and though dulled by pain, had regained some of their depth.

Florm rubbed his head gently against that of his son.

"What can I do for you, my son?"

Thaniel heaved a great, shuddering sigh. Clots of blood were ejected from his mouth and nostrils. He breathed in several quick, shallow breaths.

"What was that—the thing that attacked us?" he asked.

"It was Manon."

Aram looked sharply at Florm, the quick movement of his head causing his ears to ring. "That was Manon?"

"It was a fellring—a projection of himself. He no doubt intended for it to kill you, Aram. But we have no time for this discussion, now." He pushed gently against his son, shoulder to shoulder. "Can you walk, my son? We need to leave this place."

"I need water, father. I am so thirsty."

Using Jared for support, Aram got shakily to his feet. "There's a stream just over there—I'll bring some water in my helmet," he said.

"No." Thaniel stopped him, and his voice was a bit stronger. "I can walk, Aram. Lord Florm is right. We need to leave this place. There may still be some danger to us here and neither of us has much fight left in us."

Aram glanced around the plain. They had dropped down out of sight of the wagon where the deadly apparition had appeared but, in his field of vision, there were no soldiers or lashers. The army had gone, probably still fleeing into the west. Since the fighting had occurred farther east, there were no bodies about, either.

"I see nothing to threaten us, Thaniel. There is no reason to rush. We should be certain that you are well enough to move. I'll bring water." And he turned toward the stream.

But Thaniel lifted his head and blew out a breath, flecked with blood. "Thank you, lord Aram, but I wish to leave this place. I can walk, though I cannot bear you, and you do not look so well yourself. Jared will bear you."

Aram leaned unsteadily against Jared's brown shoulder and nodded his head weakly. "You are right, my friend—if you are able, we should go."

Florm came around and, with his head, helped Aram get astride Jared. "Can you sit, Aram?"

Aram nodded. "I can sit, my lord."

"Then I shall help steady Thaniel as we go."

Florm faced his son and lowered his head until they touched. Pushing against his father, using his strength, Thaniel was able to get off his knees and put his feet firmly beneath his body. For a moment, he stood trembling and breathing erratically. Then he glanced toward the small stream.

"I need water," he said.

With Thaniel leaning much of his weight against Florm and Aram on Jared's strong back they went haltingly down to the tiny rivulet. Thaniel put his nose in the water and drank deeply. Aram thought that the water looked very inviting but he was afraid that if he left Jared's back he would never get back up so he deferred getting a drink until later.

As Thaniel drank, Aram glanced to the east, toward Derosa. From the vantage of Jared's back, he could see over the rise onto the plain beyond. Standing on that plain, a quarter-mile or so distant, were the men of Derosa, watching the horses and the rider that had saved them. They seemed hesitant to come any nearer and Aram was glad of this. In his current condition he did not want to see anyone but the horses.

Just beyond the ragged line of the Derosans was the main field of battle. Scattered across it, from north to south, were dozens, perhaps hundreds of bodies. Here and there, Aram could see the larger mass of one of the lashers he and Thaniel had killed.

Swiveling his head and shoulders, he looked to the west and was stunned by what he saw there. Where the wagon with the cone had stood there was a blackened crater in the plain, surrounded by a spreading ring of fire, slowly licking at the dry grass. Of the wagons, the men, and the lashers that had been near the fellring, nothing remained but bits and pieces of charred wood, flesh, and bone.

Beyond the ring of the worst devastation there were, here and there, signs of movement in the grass. Horribly wounded soldiers of Manon cried in agony and thrashed about as their pitiable lives ended in anguish. The main body of the army, including the wagons that were still serviceable, was just barely visible in the distance, fleeing across the plain to the west. The battle was over.

When Thaniel had drunk his fill, they eased to the top of the rise and turned north toward the hills. Aram pushed his visor up and as they went, he turned his head and looked at the Derosans, who had grouped up and come a bit closer.

Aram still did not want to talk to anyone and he was sure he could not be recognized in the dark depths of the helmet through the narrow opening provided by the open visor. He looked up and down the line of men for Findaen. Finally he saw him, standing with another man, who was tall, clad in robes, and gray-haired, just a bit in front of the main line. And there was someone else.

Beside the tall man with the gray hair there was a woman.

Aram could not help himself; he stared at her.

Even across that sizeable distance, he could see clearly that she was beautiful. Long dark hair framed an alabaster face. The distance was too great for him to see the color of her eyes, but they were large. She was of medium height and slender, and she carried a small sword and shield.

Finally, Aram turned his face away and the four of them went steadily across the plain and into the trees that he and Thaniel had exploded from an hour before. He turned for one last look at the woman before the trees obscured their view of the plain.

All that afternoon, they went slowly on to the north, up the draw with the stream. Thaniel stopped often to drink and sometimes just to lower his head and breathe deeply for a time. Aram got off his mount once or twice to drink but the effort and the cold liquid, though necessary, often made him nauseous.

It finally occurred to him, in the midst of his illness that he ought to remove his helmet. He was surprised to find that the interior sides of it were smeared with his blood. The detonation of the fellring had caused him to bleed from his ears and, when he put a finger inside his right ear, it came away damp and red. But he breathed better with the helmet gone and the cool autumn breeze felt good on his face.

Toward evening, they found that they'd progressed no further up the draw than the site of their camp the previous night, so they stopped. Thaniel was able to go no further anyway. Aram was deeply concerned for the welfare of the big horse but he was in no condition to do anything but collapse onto the grass, so he left the care of Thaniel to Florm and Jared.

Jared checked with Aram to see if he needed anything but Aram just wanted to lie as still as possible, so the big brown horse went over to help Florm keep the wobbling Thaniel upright throughout the night. It was the belief of both of them that if Thaniel went down again, he would never rise. As he tried to sleep, unsuccessfully, Aram heard the labored breathing of his friend rise and fall throughout the night in great, painful waves.

The night grew cold with threat of frost or maybe even a freeze and it took a toll on Aram's body. As ill as he was he could do nothing to prevent its assault on him. He was too weak to build a fire and this skill was beyond either of his well companions. Curiously, though, the chill air cleared his brain somewhat and he was able to think more clearly even as his body suffered.

He realized that he and Thaniel had come very close to death. He did not feel now that he was going to die but Thaniel's future was obviously still very much in doubt. The horse's mind was untethered because of the pain and Aram was occasionally subjected to an intrusion into Thaniel's thoughts. They were wild and confused and overlaid with fear. Aram was pained that he had brought the great brave horse to this terrible pass.

But Florm and Jared succeeded in keeping Thaniel on his feet though the night and, when dawn broke, the injured horse went to the spring on his own volition stumbling on trembling legs to drink deeply from the cold, clear water. After sitting in the warming rays of the rising sun until he felt able to move, Aram followed suit. It appeared that they were both on the mend.

This day, however, proved to be worse than the previous. By midday, Thaniel's wounds, which were not visible to the eye, had taken him fully. They tried to make progress up the long ridge toward the top but Thaniel could move no more than a few yards at a time before coming dangerously close to collapse.

Aram, who sat on Jared the whole time, found that he was improving as the day wore on, even as Thaniel seemed to fail. Finally he thought clearly enough to realize that Thaniel did not need to carry the added burden of his armor, so during one of the frequent stops, he untied the straps and loosed all the catches and removed the armor from the horse.

He also took off his own armor and tied all of it into two great bundles which he then fastened on Jared, using the saddle as a pack frame. Then he went over and checked Thaniel all over but could find no exterior injury to the horse. Still, Thaniel worsened as the day drew on. And he shivered almost uncontrollably.

That night when they stopped, still far from the top of the main ridge above the river, Aram gathered wood and started a fire. Once again, Florm and Jared stood on either side of Thaniel, straining to keep him erect throughout the night. Aram slept fitfully, rousing every so often to refurbish the fire so that both he and Thaniel could benefit from the heat.

The next morning, the big black horse was still upright but no better. That day they traveled again in spurts and were still among the tangled green hills when the sun went down. Toward evening, however, Thaniel seemed to improve enough to once again find his way down to the stream and drink. But then he stood trembling and the other horses again held him up through the night.

Thaniel was better, though only just, on the third day since the battle. He drank more often but still refused to eat and he did not speak. But they made enough time that day that, by evening, they were at last on the top of the ridge and could see across the twin rivers into Aram's valley.

They camped in a copse of trees just below the ridge top where there was a spring. The night was the coldest so far and Aram, who felt better than he had since the battle, stayed awake most of the night, feeding the fire so that Thaniel would stay warm.

It took three more days, with Thaniel limping painfully along, for them to descend the ridge, cross the rivers and go the five miles up the valley to Aram's city. When they had got Thaniel ensconced in the orchard near a stream, with Jared for support, Florm asked Aram to accompany him up into the foothills south of the city.

"I want to find something," he told Aram. "A remedy that I learned of long ago from one of your forbears."

With Aram walking next to him, the lord of horses went up along the broad slopes of the foothills where brush mingled with rock at the base of the mountain.

"Look for a small bush with gray-blue leaves and a twisted, woody stalk that smells of smoke." Florm instructed Aram. "It has always grown here among the taller brush."

In less than an hour, Aram located a patch of the pungent plant and, following Florm's instructions, gathered several of the leafy stalks.

"Build a small, hot fire." Florm told Aram. "And when it is blazing, feed the brush onto it a bit at a time."

Aram complied and in a few minutes, thick gray-blue smoke rose up in a cloud. Florm had Thaniel stand with his nose into the smoke, breathing deeply of the pungent mist.

"What is this stuff?" Aram inquired.

"It's called bloodbane. It clears fluids, especially blood, from the lungs. I believe that my son has been injured internally and may be drowning, as it were, in his own blood. This smoke will help him to cough it up. You should breathe the smoke as well, Aram. You have also suffered damage." The great horse was thoughtful a moment. "It's fortunate for both of you that you were able to get over the rise and below the level of the ground before Manon was able to detonate his fellring. It would have certainly slain you otherwise."

Aram watched Thaniel for a minute. The horse was breathing deep breaths of the smoke and exhaling it in great clouds. His eyes were closed and his head was low but he no longer trembled. Aram turned back to Florm, who was also closely watching his son.

"Perhaps you'll tell me now, my lord. What was that thing?"

Florm glanced at him then continued to watch his son as he spoke. "It was a piece—a very small piece—of Manon himself. It is one of the dark arts he is believed to have learned from Aberanezegoth. Manon learned long ago, in the great wars, that he could send a piece of himself—project it—to great distances across the world, as long as it was properly protected. In this way he could seem to be involved in many battles at once.

"But then he learned that if he destroyed that piece of himself, if he separated the bit of spirit from the bit of flesh, the resulting explosion wrought great damage, killing everything within a certain perimeter. This is what he intended for you, my friend.

"He was not sure where you were, or who you were, only that you were alive in this part of the world because of that which occurred with the wolves. He may not yet know that you dwell in this valley, but he will discover it. By attacking Derosa—where, in fact, he may think you live—he hoped to draw you into close combat and eliminate you before your influence gets out of hand. All in all, it was a close thing."

Aram stared into the fire and inhaled the smoke thoughtfully. It had a sharp, bitter tang to it that burned his lungs but seemed to improve his breathing. "Did I understand you, my lord? Did you say that it was but a small piece of Manon's power that we witnessed?"

"Yes, a very small piece. Even now, he cannot afford to sacrifice much of his being. It shows just how dangerous he thinks it is that a man is once again allied with horses that he did it at all. He hoped to kill you both."

Aram scowled at him. "If that was just a very small piece of his power, how will we ever confront Manon himself? Who on earth can stand against such strength? How can we ever expect to win this war against power like his?"

The horse made no answer.

Aram stared into the fire a moment. "Lord Florm, tell me. What is to prevent Manon from coming into this part of the world in power and destroying all of us with impunity?"

"Theoretically, nothing." Florm answered quietly. "In actuality, many things."

"Things? What things?" Aram asked in exasperation. "Certainly not me. He nearly killed me with what you describe as a tiny bit of his power."

"That is so, my friend. But he did not kill you. And you are not the only threat on his horizon. There are many. Although, you are by far the most dangerous—but he may not know this yet. As to his coming personally to this part of the world, well, this is only a part of the world and he wishes to subdue it all. There are still many cities and peoples not under his sway and though some of them will fall by deceit and negotiation, many will have to be subdued by the sword. And he can only stretch his armies so thin. He will not come here until he understands the scope of the threat that you represent to his plans. Even then, he may prefer to try and draw you to him."

Florm went around the fire and stood next to Thaniel, listening to his son breathe. Thaniel stood quite still with his eyes closed but after a few moments, Florm seemed satisfied. He looked across the flame at Aram.

"You must understand that Manon cannot do what he did six days ago very often. He may be a god, but producing and destroying a fellring is still a dangerous proposition for him. And it is the only way he can produce such power. Not but that he is powerful enough, anyway. He is. But he has vulnerabilities all the same."

Florm gazed out into the gathering darkness of the valley. "Manon is very cunning. His plan is to rule the world and, eventually, the stars. Any threat to his plans will be dealt with accordingly."

He looked at Aram solemnly. "You are something new—something unexpected. I don't believe he ever intended to destroy Derosa. They are much more valuable working their farms for his benefit. When you appeared on his horizons, it troubled him, but he decided to solve two problems at once—by drawing you into battle and killing you—then he would subdue Derosa once and for all. They would be placed back on their farms out on the plains with his servants to oversee them. You know what that is like."

Aram nodded, but the frown stayed upon his face. "I still don't see how we are to defeat such power as we saw six days ago. At least, not with swords and lances."

Florm sighed. "Nor I, my friend. But does that mean that we do not wage this war?" He looked up at the dark walls of the city. "You are in a very secluded place here and my people inhabit the high and remote plains. It is no doubt tempting to think that we could remain out of this struggle for the remainder of our lives. But we cannot even if we wished it. Manon has seen you and he has seen Thaniel. Most importantly, he has seen you *together*."

Aram looked at him sharply. "My lord, I am not tempted by such thoughts. I, for one, am in this fight to one end or the other. I just believe that we must find a more powerful means of combating our enemy. But what do you mean when you say that Manon has seen us?"

"Before the fellring detonated, it looked at you with its eyes." Florm answered. "They were the eyes of Manon. He heard me warn you of the danger and saw you turn away from him at the last moment. He knows now that he has a powerful enemy in this part of the world and that his enemy probably survived the meeting."

Aram folded his arms and stared out into the night. "Good enough; let him send his armies. If necessary, I will kill all of his servants one at a time—men and lashers. But then, what? How do I defeat Manon himself?"

Florm sighed again. "I don't know. It was precisely this problem that defeated Joktan. Finally, in his frustration, he challenged Manon to single combat. He was destroyed. You, my friend, must be wiser than that."

Aram shook his head. "I don't see how, my lord."

They were both silent then and the night deepened. Finally, weary and tired, Aram threw the last of the bloodbane on the fire, rolled up in his blanket and slept for the first time in days. Florm and Jared settled in on either side of Thaniel. Borlus, hearing the angry voices subside, came out of the darkness and curled up beside Aram.

For three days more, Aram gathered bloodbane and fed the fire. He brought apples to the horses and finally, on the third day, Thaniel showed interest, taking a couple of bites.

By the time another week had passed, and the nights had grown bitter, Thaniel was walking with his head up and his lungs were clear. Florm watched his son grow stronger with joy but at the same time, glanced always up at the pass with trepidation. Any day now, snow would fall in great enough amounts to close the way over the mountain. Florm, while not wanting to rush Thaniel's recuperation, nonetheless was anxious to get across the mountains and south to his winter quarters. If not, they would be forced to spend the winter in Aram's valley, leaving their people to wonder at their absence.

After Thaniel began moving about the area before the city, his health improved rapidly. Aram was overjoyed to see his friend cantering along the avenue, testing his lungs. It was now clear that, not only would Thaniel live, but also that he would recover completely.

Finally, one morning when the sky was gray and the wind blew cold, Florm decided that they should get across the mountain pass and onto the high plains. Thaniel was moving well by this time, his head was up and his eyes clear. Aram and Borlus stood on the avenue and wished them goodbye. Aram bowed to Florm.

"Thank you, my lord, for coming to my aid in defending my friends."

Florm looked at him sharply. "Are they then your friends?"

"They will be." Aram answered somewhat sheepishly; and secretly he thought of the woman. "In the spring I will go and get to know them better."

"That is good." The horse answered. "It is not good for you to be alone so much. And they will need your leadership in the difficult days to come. For difficult days *will* come."

"Being alone doesn't bother me, my lord." But as he spoke, Aram could see with the eyes of his mind the slender woman standing proud and beautiful upon the plain and knew that it wasn't as true as it once had been. He turned to Thaniel and put a hand on the horse's broad chest. "My brother, I am overjoyed to see you well again."

Thaniel looked at him a moment with his large dark eyes. "My lord Aram, I am well, thank you. And I am also proud. Going into battle with you has made me a warrior. Know this, my lord—I will bear you into as many battles as you wish. When you go to war, I will go with you ever."

Aram stared at him, stunned. He had almost expected rancor for his part in getting the horse injured. Instead the great black horse made a declaration of fealty. He did not know how to answer. Then Florm interjected.

"Lord Aram, our two peoples are once again allied. You and lord Thaniel have won a great victory, like those of old. But there is a greater war coming. I do not think that even Manon knows this. There will be a need for this alliance. You must rally your people and I will prepare mine. Dark and desperate years will come upon us all as we seek to frustrate the will of Manon."

"I do not intend to simply frustrate his will, my lord," Aram answered sharply. "If possible, I mean to discover a way to destroy him."

Florm stared out across the valley as if seeing these things unfolding before his eyes. Then he turned to Aram and his ancient voice shook with intensity. "You have come into the world, my friend, just as Kelven foresaw. I do not know how you will succeed where Joktan did not, but somehow you will. I believe this. Somehow, you must. And my people—all my people—will aid you. As they did in ancient times, my people will bear yours into the very teeth of battle and into the jaws of war."

Jared trembled with excitement at this speech. "Yes, my lord, we will all do our part. There are many of us who wish to be as Thaniel."

Aram turned to him, sobered. "You have already done much, Jared, and I thank you as well. Lord Florm is right; there are dark times before us. There will be more than enough war for us all before it is finished."

As he spoke, a single snowflake drifted to earth. All of them looked skyward.

"It is time to go," Florm said. "If we do not get across the mountain before this sky opens up, we will be your guests for the winter."

"That would suit me," Aram answered.

Florm laughed. "But not me—there is someone I do not wish to be apart from for that length of time."

Aram said nothing but it was the first time he'd heard Florm mention a special person. And he did not wish to intrude into the horse's private matters. He bowed.

"Go well, my lords. May the Maker bless your path."

The horses lowered their heads. "Winter well, lord Aram. We will see you in the spring."

Aram watched them canter out the great avenue, past the distant pyramids and over the slope toward the river. Then he sat on the bottom step and studied the sky. With the absence of the horses, Borlus came up and laid his head in Aram's lap. Aram absentmindedly rubbed the hair behind the bear's ears. After a while he looked down.

"Are you well, Borlus? You seem tired."

"Only sleepy, master." Borlus did not raise his head. "It is time for Borlus to go into the cave for the long sleep. I wanted to see if you—if there was a need of doing anything before I go."

Aram frowned at him. "Is this normal—this long sleep?"

"Oh yes. My people have done it every winter, as long as there has been time. I will awake in the spring."

"Then—is there anything I can do for you, my friend, before you sleep?"

Borlus rolled his shaggy head groggily. "No, master. Thank you. Borlus will go now."

Aram watched the bear wander off to the cave beneath the steps and then he was truly alone. The sky lowered and grew heavy although it still produced only scattered flakes of snow. There were no birds in the sky or small animals moving in the thickets. The world was still and he was alone in it. And, for the first time in his life, he felt it.

XVIII

It did not snow that day or the next, but the sky grew increasingly heavy. Aram took stock of all his provisions, checked his stores of food, and made certain of his winter's supply of firewood. By the end of the second day, the sky had lowered to the point where the tops of the mountains to the east were hidden as well as those north of the valley, and the great mountain behind the city was lost in the heavy gray overcast.

Then, three days after the horses left him; the sky opened up and covered the world with snow. It stormed for five days. At the end of it, when the clouds had divested themselves of their burden and shredded and had gone, and the sun rose over the world, the snow was more than three feet deep out on the great porch. Aram was effectively shut inside the city.

As the winter deepened, and it snowed again and again, Aram pondered the events of the year. When he considered it, he was astounded. Barely seven months ago, he had been utterly alone and friendless in the world. Then, over the course of a summer and a fall, he'd met and befriended the horses, Florm, Thaniel, Jared and others, reached a truce with Durlrang and the wolves, and met Willet, Cree, and Borlus. Then he'd fought with allies and defeated an army of the lord of the world, slaying four lashers in the course of it.

His life of quiet, lonesome self-sufficiency that had persisted for more than half a decade in the valley was irrevocably altered. And Florm was right—Manon had seen him and would no doubt move against him, and Derosa, again. In the spring, he must go to Derosa and get to know its people and somehow find a way to turn farmers into warriors.

There would be no trouble with arming them. Aram had enough munitions in his armory to equip thousands. The problem would be with organizing them and convincing them that they must do more than fight a defensive, delaying war here on the edge of Manon's realm. Would they follow him, as Florm believed? Aram didn't know.

But these thoughts galvanized him and he passed the bleak days of the worst winter he'd ever seen in making hundreds of spears, lances, and arrows and bows, using up his entire stock of military wood. As the winter persisted, he also did something he'd intended since finding a particularly fine piece of yew. He made the longest, strongest bow yet for himself.

Shooting down the length of the great hall into his ranks of firewood, he was able to sink arrows so deep into the stacks of oak and hickory that he had to sacrifice the shafts in order to retrieve the steel tips. It was a powerful bow. He was certain that it would pierce the tough leather armor of the lashers.

He counted his swords and daggers, and found that the swords had been manufactured to serve men of various sizes. He possessed more than fourteen thousand swords and almost two hundred daggers. After his stocks of wood were used up, he still had uncounted tens of thousands of spear points and arrow tips.

And still winter gripped the valley. With nothing further to do, he decided to fully explore the city; a task he'd never completed. He knew the grand lower parts well enough but in the city's upper reaches there were many passageways he'd never gone far into, mostly because they went into darkness and he'd always suspected they were for storage.

In fact, this turned out to be true of the majority of the passages. But there was one passageway, going straight into the mountain right behind his apartment below the tower that was obviously not for storage. This shaft went somewhere, purposefully.

Narrow vertical shafts that were cut at angles upward through the stone dimly lighted it, reminding him of the technique that had been used inside the pyramid on the high plains. The tunnel went straight on through the very heart of the mountain and finally came to an end on the other side at the lip of a precipice. Lying on his stomach and peering over the edge, Aram saw, far below, a room lit by the angled rays of the afternoon sun. He'd come completely through the mountain and found an egress to the other side.

Peering over the side of the precipice, he could see no footholds or handholds or anything else in the smooth rock that would allow it to be climbed, but beside him on the floor of the tunnel was a pile of rotted wood and material that may, once upon a time, have been a rope ladder. And there were steel rings set into the rock on either side that had once been stays. But if he were going to be able to use this passage as a quick way to access the western side of the mountain, he would have to construct his own ladder out of deerskin or something similar for that purpose.

That is how he spent the rest of the winter. Using smaller limbs of hickory wood that he'd gathered for firewood, and lashing them together with strips of deer hide, he finally made a ladder strong enough and long enough to get him down over the edge of the precipice and into the cave below.

The room let out onto the spine of one of the jumbled foothills above the broad rocky slope that he'd often gazed upon back in the days of his captivity. Far away to the west he could see the broad smooth and white snow-covered expanse of the field that, once upon a time, he'd helped to create. He could not imagine what would arise that would engender a need for him to access this side of the mountain but if it did arise, he could now do so.

·The novelty of this new discovery wore completely away as the cold, dreary days stretched out, and still winter lay over the valley. So, he made furniture for his room below the tower. He constructed a table and chairs, lashing the legs together with thongs. And he made a chair just to sit in, with deer hide cushions. It turned out to be somewhat more comfortable than his bed so, rather than improving the bed, he often slept in the chair.

Then, at last, the long-overcast skies cleared and the sun shone into the valley with increasing energy. The snow began to melt. And once the weather moderated, spring came quickly. The warming sun cut deeply into the banks of snow every day. Out in the valley, Aram could see the broad silver mass of the flooded river moving ponderously toward the south and hear its muted thunder.

Within two weeks, the snow was gone from everywhere except the deeply shaded northern sides of the corrugations in the valley floor and Aram moved out into the world again. He rejoiced in the warmth of the sun as it came back northward. The ground would be too damp for some time for him to plant his crops, so he wandered, counting deer and checking on the damage done by the flooded river.

One afternoon, as he returned from a trek into the southern part of the valley and visiting with Willet and Cree in their grove on the flank of the mountain, he found Borlus sitting sleepily in front of his cave. Aram went gladly to him.

"Borlus, my friend, did you winter well?" He looked closely at the bear, noting that his fur hung from him in loose wrinkles. He frowned. "Are you well, Borlus?"

Borlus groggily licked Aram's hand. "I am well, master. But I am hungry. I will need to go hunting for grubs. It was a long winter."

"It was that, indeed," Aram agreed. "But there's no need for you to hunt while you're still weak. Will not apples satisfy your hunger, my friend?"

Borlus raised his small eyes. "I would not ask my master to provide me with food."

"Nonsense. I'll return quickly."

Aram brought Borlus a bushel of apples and sat with him, enjoying the spring evening, while the bear munched happily on the treat. It was the warmest day so far of the new year. He got up and went down onto his worked land and pushed his fingers deep into the soil. In another few days, if the good weather persisted, he would begin planting his crops. Then, he would go to Derosa. The thought gave him an inner thrill.

The good weather did persist, although it stayed cool to the point that it still frosted at night. Up on the mountains, the heavy snow stayed. It would be some time before the pass would be open to the high plains. He didn't know when the horses would return north from their winter lands, but he would probably have time to finish his planting, go to Derosa, and return before Florm and Thaniel made their promised visit.

He was excited at the prospect of seeing the horses again, but his thoughts turned most often to the woman. He wondered about her; who she was and what she was like. Mostly he wondered what she would think of him. And then a sobering thought occurred to him.

What if she already belonged to another man? For that matter, she might even be the wife of Findaen. He knew nothing of the man's domestic matters and she had stood very near him upon the plain on the day of the battle. He didn't believe that she belonged to the tall gray-haired man. For reasons he couldn't justify, Aram believed him to be her father.

Not being able to resolve all these issues troubled him greatly, but they drove him to finish planting his crops as expeditiously as possible. And finally, they were all in the ground. He checked everything well and then put together a pack of enough food to get him seventy miles to the southeast. He would not be mounted this time and the trip would consequently take substantially longer.

He found Borlus on the north side of the avenue digging for grubs and informed him that he would be gone for at least a couple of weeks.

"Borlus, too, master Aram."

"You're leaving also? Where are you going?" Aram asked him.

The bear turned his broad snout north and looked at the jumble of rugged foothills beyond the upper reaches of the valley.

"To find a mate." He answered.

Aram followed his gaze. "Yes, of course. You told me. Do you know where she is?"

Borlus rumbled deep in his throat; a sound that was suspiciously akin to laughter. "No. That is why I must find her." He looked curiously up at Aram. "What about you, master? When will you find a mate?"

Aram felt his chest tighten. "Actually, Borlus, that is why I am leaving. I think maybe it's time I found a woman as well."

The bear's small eyes grew very sincere. "I wish you well, master."

"And you, my friend," Aram patted the beast's shaggy head. "I hope you find the mate you want."

That night, Aram bathed in the spring and using a sharp knife and the magnifying glass in the tower, trimmed his hair and beard. Then he laid out his best clothes. He decided that he ought to take gifts for his hosts, so he chose two swords and two daggers, including one sword that had a green jewel embedded in its handle. It was a beautiful weapon and Aram had often admired it, but it had never felt right in his hand.

The next morning, Borlus was absent, having gone northward at first light. Aram shouldered his pack and went out and stood on the great porch and looked up at his city for a few moments, and then he went down the stairs and turned southward along the mountain's base. When he came to Willet and Cree's grove, he found Cree on the nest.

"I'm going southeast to a town by the plains," he called up to her. "If the horses come before I return, is there any way you can get word to me?"

"If the horses come, lord Aram, you will know." She answered shortly.

"Thank you, Cree." He told her, ignoring the sharp tone she always seemed to use when speaking with him, and then he turned southeast and went toward the river.

It took him four days to cross the twin rivers, climb the southern ridge and make his way along the familiar long ridge top southward through the green hills to the plain. But at last he stood at the base of the bluff among the trees and gazed eastward at the gates of Derosa. It was about noon.

He scanned the plain for signs of people and saw that, here and there, there were men working the earth, but none of the dwellings exhibited signs of being inhabited. Looking back to the east, he saw two men carrying tools coming along the road toward him. Cautiously, he stepped out where they could see him. Startled, they stopped dead. Aram held out his hands, with his empty palms turned upward.

"My name is Aram," he said. "I am a friend of Findaen. I would like to speak with him. I was—"

He stopped himself in time. How would it look, he wondered, if he claimed to be their savior of a year ago? He changed tactics and spoke carefully.

"I am a friend of the man on the horse that came to the battle last fall. Ask Findaen; he will know that I speak the truth."

They dropped their bundles and stared at him. Finally they approached and the older man spoke.

"Are you he that sent the Black Rider?" he asked, and his awe was obvious, if uncertain. "If you are, Findaen speaks often of you."

Aram decided that it was a tack that would work for the moment, so he answered simply. "I am he."

The man studied him closely for a moment and decided that he spoke the truth.

"Come," he said, "I will take you into the city."

They crossed to the road and went east toward the gap in the hills where the river exited. Aram's suspicions of the previous year proved correct. The gate, beginning at a rock bluff in the hill to the left, or north, crossed the road and arched completely over the broad stream to its southern shore and was anchored by stone pillars on each bank.

At the gate they were challenged by a sentry and the older of Aram's escorts shouted up excitedly.

"This is the man that sent the Black Rider!"

A face stuck itself out of a high window. It was the big man, Mallet.

"Yes, I know this man. Hello, friend from the valley. Welcome and come in. Open the gate," he called down to someone inside.

The gate swung back and Aram went through. Mallet swung in beside him and gestured for him to go on up the road. The road curved up a high bank and angled away from the river. It was lined on both sides by small wooden defensive positions.

After it topped the hill, however, it went through a thick stand of pines and broke out into a large circular valley. The river had angled away and flowed along the southern edge of the valley. The valley floor was broken into dark squares of freshly plowed farmland.

On the north side, against a backdrop of wooded hills was the town, a large square mass of wooden structures, many of which had two or three stories. In the center, at the end of the road that became an avenue lined by businesses as it entered the town, stood the largest building. This, Mallet made him to understand, was the home of Findaen and his father, Lancer, the Prince of Derosa.

As Aram passed up the avenue, which was paved with rough cobbled stones and much narrower than the avenue before his own city, and was lined on either side with places of business, people stopped and stared at him. He became increasingly conscious of the fact that he must look like a savage compared to most of the town's citizens.

The men all wore coats and trousers of cloth, and the women wore dresses. As they passed one low, dark building, from which raucous laughter and loud voices emanated, Findaen suddenly appeared from its depths to welcome him. Grinning broadly, he faced Aram and bowed low.

"Welcome, welcome, my lord." He said effusively and as he did so he emitted a peculiar aroma. "You are most welcome here." Bending to peer into the interior of the building he'd just left, he shouted. "Jonwood, Wamlak, come out here."

Aram studied him and then looked up at Mallet, who was also grinning at Findaen. "Why is he so happy?"

Mallet chuckled. "He's been drinking, my lord. All day, by the look of things."

"Drinking? Drinking what? Something other than water?" Aram stared at Findaen, puzzled, while Findaen grinned back at him.

Mallet roared with laughter. "Oh, yes. Something much other than water."

Jonwood, Wamlak, and several others joined them, and Findaen looked at him more seriously. "Forgive me, my lord. We finished planting just an hour ago and for people like me, who detest farming, it was an excellent reason to get drunk. Now that you're here, of course, we have an even better reason."

He stood quietly for a moment, looking at Aram. "My lord, I don't know your name—you've never told me. Would you honor us by giving your name?"

Aram smiled slightly. "It's no great honor—my name is Aram."

Findaen bowed again, with a flourish. "Welcome to our humble town, lord Aram. It's nothing so grand as yours from what I hear, but it suits us."

Aram looked around. "It's a fine town, full of people." He looked back at Findaen. "I'm glad to see you, my friend."

Findaen took his arm and pointed him up the avenue. "My father will want to meet you, lord Aram."

Aram looked at him. "I am no lord, Findaen."

Findaen didn't meet his gaze but spoke more quietly, and this time there was no jesting in his voice. "Such a statement will not be believed in this place, my lord."

Mallet, on the other side of Findaen spoke up. "He sent the Black Rider, you know."

Findaen spoke coolly. "Sent him or *was* him, I wonder."

Aram looked at him sharply. He'd already decided that his visit would be more comfortable if he was not believed to be the town's savior. He decided to refer to Thaniel as their benefactor in all his discussions, though not by name. "No, Findaen, I sent him. Well, not even sent, actually, he is simply a friend."

"Then you have very powerful friends, my lord, I must say." Findaen looked at him sidelong. "I'm glad that you are *our* friend."

Aram nodded and glanced around at the growing crowd of people. The tall building at the end of the street loomed above them. He stopped.

"Is something wrong, my lord?" Findaen looked at him curiously.

Aram hesitated and glanced at Findaen. The man's cheerful face was clean-shaven, his blond hair was combed and his clothes were of good cloth. Beside him, Aram felt barbaric.

"Findaen, is there something I can do about my appearance? I don't wish to meet your father looking this—rough."

Findaen grinned. "I don't think you look so bad, my lord, but sure, we can take care of that for you. Right this way." And he led him back the way they'd come toward a small narrow two-storied building set between many others of similar design.

Aram hesitated again and pulled Findaen to a stop. He'd never been involved in commerce of any kind but he understood instinctively that some sort of currency must change hands in order to keep these businesses operating.

"I don't have any money," he said. "Is it possible to trade something of worth for clothing and, well, are there people here who—?"

Findaen cut him off with a laugh. "My lord, I know precisely what it is that you desire and if you had money, it would be of no use here. Come, we'll get you trimmed and combed and my tailor will get you clothes. My father would evict anyone that charged you a cent."

A large crowd had gathered in the street by this time and on the fringes, Aram could hear Mallet proudly informing everyone that this was the man who sent the "Black Rider" and "killed the wolves" and that he was, in fact, a particular friend of Mallet's. Findaen led Aram into the narrow shop where a tall thin man was attending to another citizen seated in a chair before a mirror.

"Jaffa, this man needs the works—I will pay." He turned to Aram." Do you want the beard trimmed, my lord, or shaved completely?"

Aram rubbed his hand over his face. "Just trimmed, I think. I wouldn't feel like myself without at least some hair on my face."

"There you go, Jaffa. Treat him well; many of us owe our lives to him." His voice hardened a little as he glanced around at the assembled company, most of who were grinning at Findaen's jovial treatment of the tall, rough-looking stranger. "It is no joke, my friends. This man is a great warrior. Let no one forget it."

Findaen turned back to Aram and looked him over with a critical eye. "I will leave you with Jaffa while I go and talk to my tailor, my lord. We'll work on getting something put together. I'll be back before you are ready." And he spun on his heels and left the shop.

Jaffa had not finished with the other man and he approached Aram and bowed low. "Would you like to bathe, my lord, while I finish with Hender? There is water and a basin in the back, and soap for your hair." He blinked at Aram and swallowed, as if suddenly realizing that he might have offended this dangerous man in suggesting that he needed cleansing. "It's just that it makes the trimming easier."

Aram smiled. "Thank you—I will."

The warm water felt marvelous on his skin. For seven years he'd bathed only intermittently, almost always in cold running streams. He dressed and after Jaffa finished with him, he felt more human than he had in the course of his life. Findaen returned and led him further back down the avenue to a larger shop where a portly man named Suven was waiting with a variety of garments.

Aram was finally dressed in black trousers with a deep green shirt and a vest of dark leather. Though the mirror told him that it was a much more civilized look, he felt self-conscious. And he could not stand in the soled boots Suvan found for him—he was too used to his boots made of deerskin, so he decided to forgo that one luxury.

Findaen eyed him approvingly and suggested that they have something to eat. Aram was hungry so he agreed. He added his old clothes to his sizeable pack and started to follow Findaen. Mallet stopped him.

"My lord, I would be honored to carry your pack for you." He offered.

Findaen agreed. "Good idea, Mallet. In fact, why don't you take it up to my father's house and put it in a room. And tell my father to expect a mighty guest for supper."

He led Aram back up the street to the low, dark building from which he'd appeared earlier. Inside there was a long bar along one wall and scattered tables with chairs. Findaen lead the way to a table with four chairs in the back. He held up five fingers to a stout woman carrying a tray while Wamlak brought another chair.

Findaen turned to Aram. "Do you drink, my lord?"

"Water." Aram answered dryly.

"Oh, this is better than water, my lord."

"What, exactly, is it that is better than water?"

Findaen grinned. "There are various names for it—rotgut, panther piss, sludge—but for the sake of the moment—and because we can't prove otherwise—we'll call it whiskey."

"Whiskey."

Findaen nodded and narrowed his eyes. "And you've never had any, my lord?"

Aram shook his head.

"Well, then, we'll go easy for today. And we'd better get some food into you as well."

The stout woman brought five glasses filled with an amber liquid. She stared admiringly at Aram the whole time until Findaen shooed her away, advising her not to return to the table without a plate for the tall stranger. As she left to get Aram's lunch, citizens of the town began to file in, filling up the available seating. Mallet had evidently been generous in his reporting. By this time everyone knew that the man who'd sent the "Black Rider" was in town.

Aram tentatively held the glass containing the amber liquid up to his nose. It smelled strong and bitter like the pools of black mud he sometimes found oozing from certain veins in rocky hillsides. He tasted it and found that it burned his tongue like it was on fire. And it burned going down. It was all he could do to keep from gasping.

"Well done, well done." Findaen nodded at him approvingly. He leaned across the table and looked narrowly at Aram. "How do you feel, my lord?"

Aram frowned at him. "Why, is it supposed to have an effect?"

"Oh, it will have an effect, even on such a man as yourself, never fear."

Aram's frown deepened. "What 'effect'?"

Findaen grinned. "It makes you happy—like me. Unless you're like Mallet there. Then, if you have too much of it, you'll get all morose and want to fight everything in sight—even the women."

"I've never laid hands on a woman." Mallet protested.

"Really." Wamlak cut in dryly. "Then where did all those little Mallets come from over at your house?"

The big man bristled and Aram half-expected violence to break out but then Mallet grinned sheepishly. "You know what I meant," he said.

Aram looked around the table at them, the dry-humored Wamlak, the tall, blustery Mallet, the solemn Jonwood, and the ever-smiling Findaen, and decided that he liked these men. And, after a few more sips, he decided that he liked the whiskey as well.

The afternoon passed in this agreeable manner until Aram was feeling quite mellow from the drink. Findaen finally decided it was time for them to go up to the house but when Aram stood, he found that his feet had become a bit unreliable. Findaen took his arm.

"It's okay, my lord," he said, and he grasped Aram's elbow, "whiskey takes a bit of getting used to. We should probably have taken it a bit easier.

I'll get you settled into a room in my father's house and then we'll go down to supper. You can meet my father and my sisters."

Aram looked at him. "Sisters?"

"Yes," Findaen replied. "I have two of them—Ka'en and Jena. Great pair of girls—you'll like them. I don't suppose you have any sisters?"

Aram scowled as he stepped out into the bright sunlight of the evening. "I had a sister once. The servants of Manon took her away long ago."

Findaen stared at him a moment. "I'm sorry." He said quietly.

The room that Findaen put him in was at the back of a long exterior veranda on eastern side of the building's topmost level, reached by navigating three flights of stairs. They entered it from the outside, although in the opposite wall there was another door that opened from it into an interior hallway. After Findaen got Aram and his pack settled, he went through this door and into the interior of the house, promising to return within an hour.

The room was large, entirely composed of wood, and it was furnished with two chairs and a wide bed, which had cloth blankets. And there was a basin filled with water that had a washcloth near it. After he unpacked and laid his old clothes out in a corner, Aram chose the finest sword from those he'd brought, the one with the jewel in the handle, and put it on the bed. This he would give to Findaen's father.

Then he went out and stood on the porch and looked over the valley. His room was on the east of the house and most of the town was to the south, so he had a fine view of the surrounding countryside. The valley which contained Derosa was lush and green with spring grass beyond the river and dark brown squares of newly-plowed farmland across its center on the near side of the stream. The valley was almost perfectly circular. The hills that surrounded it were not tall but they were rugged, with spires of rock, and they were thickly wooded.

The town was laid out in neat rectangles of buildings separated by flat straight streets. It was a town made of wood and appeared to have stood for some time. There were no buildings out among the farmland. The valley was not overlarge and open arable land was precious, so the Derosans had built their town on the rocky northern fringe of the valley and left the good ground clear. By walking to the south end of the porch to the top of the stairs that they had come up earlier, Aram could see obliquely down the main thoroughfare of the town.

Findaen returned as promised dressed almost entirely in blue, except for his shirt, which was startlingly white. He flung the door wide and gestured toward the hall beyond.

"Let's go down, my lord, they're waiting."

Aram felt his stomach tighten. He was not used to so many people, or the familiarity with which they addressed one another, having never spent time in anything resembling civilized society. He wanted to ask Findaen about the woman he'd seen on the plain and whether she would be at supper, but ignorance of her identity and situation prevented it.

They wound down through many hallways to the second level and then down a broad staircase to the first. At the bottom of the staircase, Findaen turned to his right, toward the west side of the house. After crossing through a small gallery, they went through two broad doors, which were standing wide, and entered the dining room.

Aram stopped. The room was filled with light and noise. And people. He had expected three or four people but, at first glance, it appeared as if the whole town was present. Mallet appeared from the crowd and grasped his hand.

"Hello again, lord Aram."

"Yes, yes, Mallet, but he's here to meet my father," Findaen said impatiently, pushing Aram forward through the crowd.

As they passed people crowded near, women lowered their heads to him and man after man shook his hand. There were round tables covered with cloth everywhere, encircled by chairs. Finally they came to an open area in front of a long rectangular table lined with chairs on either side and there she was.

The woman from the plain.

XIX

She was standing behind the table beside the same tall, gray-haired man she'd stood beside on the day of the battle. Aram froze and felt his knees buckle at the sight of her. She was astoundingly, achingly, unbelievably beautiful. Her hair, which had appeared dark in the noonday sun that day upon the plain; here in the artificial light of the lamps, seemed alive with color, chestnut, auburn, and gold.

She was slender and dressed in a wine-red gown, trimmed with black fur that showed the contours of her body. But it was her face that was stunning, with skin that glowed like snow blushed with the rays of the setting winter sun. Her eyes were large, dark, and set deep under long eyelashes. Her nose was perfect and her mouth was red like the petal of a rose.

Surely, she must be the queen. Probably, the tall, older man beside her was, in fact, her husband.

Dimly, Aram became aware that Findaen was speaking. "—my father, Lancer, Prince of Derosa."

Aram yanked his eyes away from the woman and found the grace to acknowledge the tall, gray-haired man. The Prince was dressed in velvet finery and bore himself in a stately, dignified manner. His face, though lined with the care of years, was still handsome. Aram bowed low.

"I am honored, my lord."

"No," the tall man said quietly. "The honor is ours. My son tells me that you are the one that aided our cause and won the day last fall by sending the Black Rider."

Aram hesitated. "I did not—send him, my lord. I asked him to aid us and he complied."

"Well, we are grateful beyond bounds. It was, I am not ashamed to say, our salvation that rode upon the field that day." He frowned as if remembering something. "Tell me, was he or the horse badly injured by the evil device of the enemy?"

"Both were injured." Aram answered. "But both have recovered."

"Thank the Maker for that." The room had grown silent as everyone listened to the exchange, and Lancer stared at the floor and seemed to struggle with what he wanted to say next. Finally he looked up at Aram. "Forgive me, lord Aram, but might we know the identity of our champion?"

Again Aram hesitated. "I'm sorry, my lord, but I'm certain he would rather remain anonymous," he answered truthfully.

"As is his right." Lancer acknowledged and nodded slightly. "Suffice it to say that you have powerful friends, lord Aram—for which we are ever grateful. Come, meet my daughters."

Ah, thought Aram, and his heart soared, *his daughter.*

Taking the woman by the hand, Lancer brought her from behind the table. As she came close, Aram became painfully aware that his heart was pounding so loudly that he could barely hear. He suddenly developed a measure of difficulty breathing and it seemed to him that his muscles, and even his bones, trembled.

"My daughter Ka'en, lord Aram." Lancer said and she held out her hand.

Findaen leaned close to his ear. "Take it and kiss it," he whispered.

As Aram hesitated, uncertain, Findaen whispered again.

"For heaven's sake, man, take her hand and put your lips on it."

Numbly, Aram complied. The skin of her hand smelled wonderful, like grass and flowers in a mountain meadow after a spring rain. He thought in that moment that he could be content to get lost in her scent and the nearness of her presence, but Findaen was tugging him erect. He looked up into her eyes. She smiled, softly, wrecking him further.

"It is a pleasure to meet you, lord Aram," she said, and her voice matched in its tone and quality the vision of her loveliness.

"The honor is mine." He croaked out and his voice sounded distant and harsh to his ears.

"This is my other daughter, Jena," Lancer said then, forcing Aram's attention away from Ka'en, and the spell was broken to the extent that he could acknowledge the Prince's other daughter.

This woman was younger, barely more than a girl, and reminded Aram of his own sister. She was pretty, with golden hair like summer wheat. Aram took her hand and kissed it.

"My pleasure," he said.

"You're getting good at this." Findaen whispered, chuckling.

"Now, then," Lancer said, raising his voice. "Let us sit and eat, my friends. Come, lord Aram, sit across from me at my table."

Lancer, Ka'en, and Jena sat against the wall, a daughter on each side of their father, with other finely dressed people on either side of them. Aram and Findaen sat opposite with their backs to the room. Ka'en was to Lancer's left, on Aram's right. Jonwood sat next to Aram. He was accompanied by, and entirely occupied with, a plump and pretty young woman with red hair who sat beyond.

The food came, served on platters. Metal utensils were placed beside each plate, the use of which seemed obvious, but Aram watched surreptitiously until he was certain of the protocol. Except for meat that was clearly venison, he didn't recognize anything on the tables. Nonetheless, he helped himself to a portion of everything offered.

One item in particular he found to be wonderfully delicious. A whitish vegetable with a dense texture had been cut into small pieces and browned in a pale yellow sauce. He had never tasted anything like it. He looked up at Ka'en, intending to inquire of her as to what it was, but Lancer anticipated him.

"Is everything to your liking, lord Aram?" He asked.

"It's very good, my lord," he answered, and he indicated the portion of white vegetable. "This, in particular, is wonderful. What do you call it?"

Ka'en leaned across the table toward him, smiling. "Have you never had potatoes, lord Aram?" She asked in her soft voice.

"I do not think so—I would have remembered something this good." He answered.

"Those are potatoes, fried in butter." She laughed quietly, a marvelous sound to him. "We call them, obviously, butter fried potatoes."

He smiled back at her, wanting to hold her attention. "But what are they, my lady?"

"They are a root crop, grown in the ground, one of our staples." Findaen interjected, rounding on him with a surprised expression. "You've never seen them?"

Aram was disappointed in the interruption but curious, nonetheless, to discover the nature of this tasty treat. "Could I grow them in my valley?"

"Sure." Findaen replied. "When you go home, I'll send some seed portions with you. It's getting a bit late in the spring to plant them now, but you could store them in a cool place until next year."

This offer reminded Aram of the swords he'd left in the room. He looked across at Lancer. "My lord, I brought you a gift. It's in my room. Perhaps I could retrieve it later this evening?"

Lancer inclined his head. "There is no need for a gift, lord Aram, but I am honored to accept it. The young people will dance later. Then will be a good time."

Findaen laughed aloud at the insinuation in his father's remark. "I know he doesn't look it, father, but lord Aram is as young a man as I am. He may wish to dance also."

Ka'en caught Aram's eye. "Yes, lord Aram, you must dance."

Aram knew nothing of dancing and the prospect of attempting it in such a large company, no doubt with the result of disappointing the lady, made his insides grow cold. There was nothing to do but admit the truth. "I'm sorry, my lady, but I—know nothing of dancing."

A slight smile touched her perfect mouth. "I will teach you, my lord."

It was at this moment, gazing transfixed across the table at her that Aram noticed the young man sitting next to her. He was husky and broad-shouldered with blonde hair and as he studied Aram, there was undisguised dislike in his eyes. He tended to lean, rather possessively, toward the princess.

Aram wondered about their relationship and was surprised to discover that, while knowing nothing at all about the light-haired young man, he disliked him intensely as well. He decided to ask Findaen later, point-blank, about his sister's domestic situation in life.

In the meantime, the meal wound to its conclusion, a delicious drink called wine was served, and the younger men began to push the tables, except for Lancer's, to the walls. It was time for the dance. Aram was treated to another novelty in his young life—music.

Four musicians with curious stringed instruments took their places along one wall and within moments, the hall was filled with music. Young men led young women out onto the floor and began twirling in time to the meter of the melody. Jonwood took his plump companion out onto the floor while Findaen went in search of a suitable partner.

Aram was petrified at the idea of attempting to dance, even with the beautiful Ka'en, so, to hide his discomfiture, he turned away and looked out at the couples and smiled slightly, as if happy to just be a spectator. In truth, he wished he were miles away, alone with her. But the ruse backfired. When he turned his head slightly to look at Ka'en, she was gone.

Startled, he glanced around for her and then he saw her. The broad-shouldered young man had usurped her and the two of them were dancing in the middle of the floor, surrounded by laughing couples. Watching them, he felt a curious constriction in his stomach. And anger. He hated the way the young man was holding Ka'en and tried to look away but couldn't.

Finally, he swallowed and gained control of himself and studied the other couples. Wamlak was dancing with Jena and on the other side of the room Mallet was dancing with a surprisingly small blond woman. She no doubt looked smaller than she was, wrapped in his giant arms. He turned back to the table and found that he and Lancer were left alone. The elderly Prince was gazing absentmindedly out toward the dance floor, tapping his fingers on the table in time to the music.

Aram felt a desperate need to escape. He stood and bowed to Lancer.

"My lord, would this be a good time to present you with my offering?"

"If you wish, lord Aram." Lancer said pleasantly.

Aram bowed again and left the table, working his way around the wall to the double doors. Once out of the hall, he glanced up the staircase toward the building's interior, and then decided to go outside and up the exterior stairways to his room. It was a pleasant spring evening, the sun had set and there were a few of the brighter stars already in the sky.

Aram stood gazing out over the valley, glad to be away from the tumult in the hall. He thought of Ka'en and the possessive young man. What were the circumstances of their relationship, he wondered? He hated to think of her in the young man's arms, whirling to the music, even though he had no rights where it concerned her, or any expectation of them. Fighting a curious gnawing in his stomach, he turned away from the night and went into his room.

He wrapped the jeweled sword in deerskin and returned to the hall and slipped around the walls to Lancer's table. Findaen was again seated with his father when Aram laid the weapon down before the Prince of Derosa.

"My gift, my lord. It was made long ago by—my fathers." Aram slid the blade from the deerskin and set it on the table before Lancer.

Findaen sucked in his breath and Lancer's eyes widened. Gently the Prince lifted the shining steel.

"But this is of the finest quality. Ancient quality. My lord Aram, are you certain you wish to part with this? It must have been in your family for some time."

Aram nodded gravely and decided to believe, in that moment, that he was indeed Joktan's heir. "Thousands of years, my lord. Please, accept it."

Findaen, standing behind his father, looked up at Aram with a different light in his wide blue eyes. Holding Aram's gaze, he walked slowly around the table until he stood next to him.

"Lord Aram, my friend, who are you, really?"

Aram shook his head. "I told you before, no one of great consequence."

Lancer looked up at him with gravity deepening his pale blue eyes. "Lord Aram, we are not fools. My son has told me of how easily you slew the wolves that threatened him and his men. We know that you live in the city of the ancient kings. You command the Black Rider—nay, don't protest, I know that you do.

"And now you give me a gift that is fit for the ancient kings. Indeed, it appears to have belonged to one of them. Do not think me impertinent when I ask this thing." He stood to his feet, holding the sword next to him as if he feared that it would vanish if he let it go. "Who are you, my lord?"

Aram gazed back at the two of them, uncertain as to what he should answer. It was true that he'd been born the lowest of slaves. It was also true, as Florm was wont to point out, that he was more than he himself could have ever guessed. Perhaps it was the wine or the proximity of the beautiful Ka'en, but he decided to return an answer that surprised even him to hear, and one that, once enunciated, he immediately regretted.

"I have been told," he said, and he stood very still and looked straight into Lancer's eyes as he spoke, "that I may be the answer to Kelven's Riddle."

Lancer frowned at him and blinked his eyes. "Kelven's Riddle? I have not heard of this thing. The Lord Kelven has not walked the earth in thousands of years."

"That is true." Aram answered carefully. "He was disembodied in the great battle when he failed to destroy Manon. But he left behind instructions for our times, though most of them are yet hidden from my eyes." He leaned forward and placed his hands flat upon the table and spoke quietly.

"My lord, you have resisted Manon for the whole of your life—you and your people—alone. But you are not alone. I am with you now and we have friends in the wilderness—friends that, when the time comes, will matter."

He glanced around to make sure he was not overheard. "The day is coming, my lord, when we must resist Manon to the death. We must either defeat him or surrender to chains. I will not surrender to chains."

Findaen, standing by his father stared back at him wide-eyed. "I knew it. You are the Black Rider."

Suddenly, Aram felt in control of the situation. "If I were the Black Rider, as you call him, would it be wise to disseminate that information, Findaen? Would it not be wiser to rally your people, and others, to action without the belief in a champion? When Manon returns, and he will, everyone must fight. Do you dispute this?"

Findaen shook his head slowly. "No, my lord. But you must understand, we have resisted Manon alone for so long—we have been pushed from our ancestral homes out on the plains. To know that there is someone now, on our side, strong enough to face him on his own terms is the greatest cause for courage imaginable."

Aram laughed harshly. "On his own terms? He nearly destroyed me."

"Yes." Findaen nodded solemnly. "But he didn't." Then his blue eyes widened and he looked sharply at Aram. "So, you acknowledge it. It *was* you—you are the Black Rider."

The music ended. People were drifting back to the tables. Aram gave his hosts a hard glance and spoke low. "Let's speak no more of this for now." He looked at Lancer and bowed. "I'm glad you are pleased with the gift, my lord. And I have one for you as well, Findaen, though perhaps less magnificent."

Wine was brought to the tables and soon everyone was seated again. Ka'en sat next to her father and the morose young man pushed his chair close to hers, though Aram was pleased to see that she leaned away and did not seem to share in a mutual depth of feeling. She looked across at Aram.

"Did you enjoy the dance, lord Aram?"

He smiled wryly. "I enjoyed watching, my lady. Luckily, I escaped having to join in—that would have been disastrous, I promise you."

She returned his smile. "And I promise you that you will not escape so lightly again."

This statement caused the young man next to her to deepen his scowl. But Aram ignored him, happy that her attention once again was centered on him. He smiled at her as long as he dared, then glanced down at his glass of wine. Feeling Findaen's eyes on him, he looked that way and found him grinning knowingly. Aram felt his face go hot.

The conversation turned to lighter subjects with the women back at the tables and Aram was content to listen and join in only rarely. He drank a substantial amount of wine and felt it going to his head. Then Jonwood came around with several small cylinders of a brown leafy substance.

"Have you ever had a smoke, lord Aram?" he asked.

Aram shook his head. He'd never encountered the word in any other context than that of a campfire.

"Well, you'll have to try one of these. Came out of my patch south of the hills. My Fiera rolled them herself. Ask anyone here, she makes the best smokes."

Findaen took two from Jonwood and handed one to Aram. "A truer word was never spoken," he said. "Fiera makes the best."

Aram looked at the small, five or six-inch cylinder. Then he watched Findaen slide his under his nose, closing his eyes in pleasure. Aram followed suit. It smelled pungent and woody. It was not unpleasant. Findaen lit both of their cylinders and Aram sucked in the pungent smoke, almost choking. Instantly, Findaen slapped him on the back.

"Don't inhale it, my friend, just roll it around in your mouth to get the flavor and then blow it out. Otherwise, it will make you sick as a dog."

Aram glanced up at Ka'en, embarrassed, but she only smiled at him. Again, as he looked at her, Aram was struck by the perfect beauty of her features and the utter smoothness of her alabaster skin. No wonder the young man next to her seemed so possessive. He reminded himself again to ask Findaen about their particular situation.

After a while, Lancer excused himself, nodding solemnly to Aram, and went upstairs, carrying his prized sword like a babe in arms. Shortly afterward, Findaen's sisters also said goodnight. Aram was talking with Mallet and didn't see them go. Aram looked up to see the morose young blond-haired man sitting alone. Good, he thought, at least the possessive young man, apparently, was not a permanent fixture in the household. The next time he looked up, the blond-haired young man was also gone.

Eventually, Findaen wandered off in the company of a slim, redheaded girl, Mallet left with his small, plump wife, registering an effusive good-bye, and Aram was alone. He was feeling a bit woozy from the wine and Fiera's smoke so he decided to go upstairs and find his room.

Foolishly, he decided to try and negotiate the interior passageways of the house. It was a large house with a confusing maze of passages. He knew that his room was on the eastern side of the house on the third floor near the back, so he went up and to the right and toward the back whenever he could. Eventually, however, with his head buzzing and his eyes blurring, he found himself at a juncture of two hallways, completely lost.

As he stood there looking one way and then another, a door opened behind him and he heard Ka'en's soft voice.

"May I help you, sir?"

He turned. She and Jena stood just outside an open door on the left side of the hall, dressed in robes and holding lighted candles. Ka'en leaned her head quizzically to one side and looked at him seriously, while Jena stifled a giggle with her hand. Aghast, he realized that he had wandered into the private compartments of Lancer's house.

He stared at her. "I'm sorry, my lady. I've had some wine tonight and I—that smoke was a new thing, too—I was looking for a way…" humiliated, he trailed off.

Jena burst out laughing. Ka'en shushed her and moved her back into the room, closing the door. Then she turned to Aram.

"May I help you, my lord?"

He looked at her miserably. "I cannot find the way to my room."

"I understand." She held out her hand. "Come. I'll take you."

He looked down at the hand she offered. It was small with beautifully tapered fingers and nails like clear shell. Like everything else about her, it seemed almost artificially delicate. Even in his inebriated state, it was like being offered the treasures of the world to be offered her hand.

Numbly he held out his own rough hand. She grasped his fingers—it was like being touched by lightning—and led him back along the hallway he'd just traveled. She smelled wonderful. Turning right at the next corner, she led him to a stairway and up. Then they went to the right again, left around another corner and finally stood before the door to his room.

"Here you are, my lord," she said and to his regret, released his hand. She turned her head to one side and looked up at him. "Will you be al-right, now?"

He nodded while trying desperately to gain control of his feelings. "Thank you, my lady. I—thank you."

The wine had hit him hard and the unfamiliar strength of the smoke had contrived to muddle him, but it was the nearness of her that was blinding. His senses were overwhelmed. He tried to think of something clever or at least reasonably intelligent to say in order to salvage the situation, but in the end just stared at her in mute and unabashed admiration.

She smiled gently. "Goodnight then, my lord."

She turned and moved away down the hall.

He watched her until she turned the corner out of sight and then went miserably into his room. Besides feeling ill from the excessive partaking of unaccustomed delights, he'd ruined a chance to get to know the beautiful Lady Ka'en better. And her younger sister had laughed at his ineptness.

He flung himself onto the bed and lay on his back, staring up into the darkness. He felt an utter fool. Ka'en—even just her existence—confused everything for him just when he was gaining some clarity of the meaning of his own life. Seven years ago he would never have guessed that he would become anything more than a vagabond in the earth, trying desperately for the rest of his life to stay one step ahead of Manon's servants.

Instead, he'd become something else. Men and horses and wolves called him lord and master. He had discovered within himself a prowess for waging battle. Manon, who already ruled most of the world and intended to govern the courses of all life, had seen him and no doubt by now considered him a personal, and special, enemy. That thought sobered him and he sat upright.

If Florm was right and the battle of the plains was Manon's attempt to draw him out and discover his base of support, then his proximity to Derosa placed that town and its inhabitants in special danger. Which meant—the realization of this appalled him—that his acquaintance with Ka'en would not mean just slavery for her and her people if Manon had his way, but death.

He went out onto the balcony and prowled back and forth along it like a panic-stricken cat, tormented by the idea of the beautiful Ka'en being killed or reduced to slavery. Gradually, though, his mind cleared and he was able to sort his thoughts intelligently. He realized that there was no hope for remedy now, anyway. Manon probably meant to destroy Derosa all along.

Aram had no knowledge of what kind of resistance Manon faced along his other frontiers but the people of Derosa had certainly struggled to retain their freedom for some time. Probably, Manon meant to kill the adults in any event and put the children to work producing for his empire. This was no doubt what had happened to Aram's own people sometime in the distant past but the certain knowledge of that event was lost in the deep wells of time.

None of this mattered. Manon knew now that he and Derosa were in league with one another and whatever else he was doing throughout the world, he would certainly bring his power and his evil plans to bear here on the southern plains as soon as possible. The fight would come and it would come to Derosa. He must use whatever time he had to prepare for it.

He walked to the end of the porch nearest the town and looked southward over the moonlit valley to the hills beyond. Somewhere, far to the south, was the sea. He'd always heard that there were great cities there. Were they aligned with Manon, under his boot, or were they yet free? These were things, he realized, that he must discover. Seven or eight hundred farmers, no matter how well armed, would never withstand the might of Manon when it was brought fully to bear. They needed allies.

Finally, as the moon wheeled west and the shadows grew long in the dark streets, he tired and went into his room. He lay for awhile, trying to sort out his thoughts but now that he was relaxed, found that he could think of nothing but Ka'en, of her gentle kindness and her astounding beauty. A feeling rose up strong inside him—though he'd never felt it before, he recognized it instantly. It was desire. Desire for this lovely, elegant, and graceful woman. It was spiritual, intellectual, and physical. He wanted to know her, to have her, and to be loved by her. For there in the darkness, he knew that he loved her.

XX

He awoke after a few hours to find the rising sun streaming into the room through the window. It was just past dawn. He went to the washbasin, stripped off his shirt and bathed. Then he went out onto the porch. Here and there in the valley, in the flat, orange light of early morning, men were making their way to work in the fields.

Aram had always hated his lot of tending the earth but now he wondered if he would feel differently about it if rather than wearing the chains of bondage; he had always been able to work his own piece of ground at his own volition. Thinking about it, he doubted it. He didn't mind attending to the few crops he grew in his valley but they were nothing compared to the labors of these farmers. These men worked large pieces of ground every day. Watching them bend into work that would undoubtedly last the day, Aram realized that he would rather go into battle a thousand times than face such an unending task.

Hearing boots ring on the deck of the porch, he turned. Findaen came toward him, bearing two steaming mugs.

"Good morning, my lord Aram." He extended one cup toward Aram. "Kolfa?"

Aram frowned at him.

"Your morning cup of kolfa, my lord." Findaen shook the mug slightly. "You know what they say—never start the day without it."

Aram took the mug and looked inside. Thick, black, pungent liquid sent steaming acrid aromas into his face. He smiled sheepishly at Findaen.

"I've never had kolfa." He confessed.

Findaen stared back at him, grinning. "By the land and all its bounty, you really are a barbarian, aren't you? A splendid barbarian—it's true—but a barbarian nonetheless. Go on—try it."

Aram brought the cup up and tipped it into his mouth. It tasted bitter and was very hot but to his surprise, he liked it instantly. Findaen's grin broadened.

"See? It's good stuff. Gets your blood pumping." He sipped from his own mug and then tapped it gingerly with his forefinger. "Used to be—we could drink this stuff like water but it's getting hard to come by now. We have to trade for it in secret. Comes from Kolfaria, an island in the ocean, I think. And the more power the grim lord has, the harder it is to do business. Back before he showed up, when we farmed all the plains, we—"

He stopped suddenly and leaned on the rail and gazed out over the valley with his head turned toward the west. When he spoke again, there was a tone of wistfulness in his voice.

"Lord Aram, I don't know of your history with Manon but until the time of my great-grandfather we had never heard of such a person. Our people lived out on the plains south of the green hills. Though there were a few towns, including Derosa, which has not always been our capital, my ancestors were mostly farmers. They traded with the seaports to the south—our leaf and wheat for their kolfa and exotic fruits.

"Then, the overseers of Manon showed up and with the protection of the lashers, began controlling all the trade routes. We had to pay taxes in goods and gold—then they began demanding young people as slaves." He glanced at Aram before continuing. "Our people had never encountered the concept of slavery—time out of mind—and they resisted. They fiercely believed that it was wrong for people not to be free. Then the killings began.

"At first it was small parties of traders that were ambushed and slain, but then whole families would disappear from outlying farms. The parents would be found dead and the children missing. So we fought back. We traded for weapons from Durck, a port city to the southeast, known for avoiding the official law, if you know what I mean.

"My ancestors organized patrols to fend off the overseers of Manon, but he sent an army with lashers, who were too fierce and strong to be resisted. Our fighters were slaughtered. Stell, our capitol, was lost. Finally, our people pulled back from their western lands behind the wide river that flows out from under Burning Mountain and destroyed all the bridges. We still couldn't kill lashers but we made any attempt at crossing extremely unpleasant for them.

"Then, somewhere on the other side of the world, there was a rebellion, and we did not see the servants of the grim lord for sixty years while he was occupied elsewhere. We half hoped that he'd been defeated.

The first warning that he'd returned was when the cities along the coast stopped trading openly with us and our people reported that there were lashers among them. Then, bands of the gray men came and began killing our people, taking their children, and burning our farms and villages. That was ten years ago.

"There were a few of our people that tried to farm lands in hidden dales and hollows of the plains but most of us pulled back into the hills to avoid the roving bands of gray soldiers, and occasionally, lashers. Last year was the first time Manon sent an organized force against us since the fall of Stell. After what you did," he glanced sidelong at Aram, "some have gone back out to their farms on the plains, but is it safe to do so? How long will it be before he returns with an even larger army?" He turned and looked full at Aram. "Or was he destroyed in that explosion?"

Aram shook his head slightly. "No, my friend, that was but a small bit of his power. He may have suffered a wound but it was slight." He scowled. "And you are correct—he will return. I don't know how soon it will be but certainly he won't wait very long. We are now a very black thought lodged solidly in his evil mind."

Findaen drained his cup and grinned fiercely. "Well—to hell with him and his evil mind. Enough of these dark thoughts on such a bright morning. Let's go down to breakfast—Ka'en will be there."

Aram looked at him sharply but he had turned away and was moving down the stairs. Aram followed him to the lower level.

Breakfast was served in a bright room on the eastern side of the house by the kitchen. A familiar aroma struck Aram's nose as he entered the hallway between the two rooms and he glanced around to discover with surprise that Ka'en was standing next to a metal, flat-topped stove, stirring potatoes. He'd assumed that because of her exalted station, she would be exempt from doing the menial work of the house.

She looked up and smiled at him. "Good morning, my lord. I hope you don't mind potatoes two meals in a row?"

"Not at all, my lady, I think they may be my favorite food." It sounded maudlin and he grimaced as he turned away toward the table but Findaen, sitting with his arms folded across his chest, grinned up at him.

Jena was seated next to him, frowning at her sister. She gave Aram a quick, lopsided smile and tossed her yellow curls. "What do you think of that, lord Aram?"

He frowned at her. "Of what, my lady?"

Jena pointed toward the kitchen. "Of my sister, cooking like a servant."

Aram smiled gently. "I cook all my own meals—over a fire. Have done so for many years. And they are barely worth eating. But, my lady, had I known that such behavior offends you, I would have trained Borlus to do it."

"Who's Borlus?" She asked, politely enough, but her mouth pouted at him.

"He's my bear. And I think he actually eats without cooking at all."

Her mouth dropped open. "You own a bear?"

"No, I don't own a bear, my lady. Who can own another creature? He's a friend. He lives in a cave near the walls of my city."

She stared at him. "Could I see him?"

"If you come and visit me, yes." He nodded. "Although, like myself, he is a bit shy."

She laughed. "You're not shy—you nearly came into our room last night."

"*Jena!*" Ka'en came quickly in from the kitchen, but Findaen shouted with laughter.

"Oho!" he roared. "Tell me about this, girls."

Aram felt his face go red.

"There's nothing to tell, Fin." Ka'en stood in the doorway with her hands on her hips and frowned at Jena. "Lord Aram got lost in the halls last night and I helped him find his way to his room."

Findaen leaned back in his chair and raised his eyebrows. "Did you now?"

Ka'en sighed and turned to Aram. "I'm sorry, my lord. The behavior of my brother and sister is abominable. Please excuse them."

Aram returned her smile, gazing up into her marvelous eyes. "It's alright, my lady, I had had too much of that wine. I was—"

"Drunk!" Interjected Findaen.

"Is that what you call it?" Aram asked him coolly.

"Yes." Findaen grinned at him. "Fun, huh?"

Aram thought about it a moment and then smiled wryly. "Actually, last night was pleasant all the way around." He glanced up at Ka'en. "The most pleasant time of my life."

She smiled at him, shot Findaen and Jena a frown and turned to bring the food to the table. The conversation at breakfast was pleasant enough but was dominated by Jena, who plied Aram with questions about his home and his bear, and Findaen, who teased everyone mercilessly.

Aram wanted to find time to visit exclusively with Ka'en but didn't know how to accomplish it. In the end, he bade the two women to have a fine day and accompanied Findaen to the council house where, Findaen informed him, Lancer was dealing with the day's municipal matters.

The council chamber was beside Lancer's house on the west side of the main street. When Aram and Findaen entered and sat in the back, Lancer was dealing with two men involved in a legal civil dispute. Lancer sat in an elevated chair with a tall back carved with an eagle's head. To his right, also in elevated chairs, were six citizens of the city with whom Lancer occasionally conferred.

Lancer acknowledged Aram with a polite nod of his head but kept his attention centered on the two men arguing before him. Looking up on the wall behind Lancer, Aram saw that his gift of the jeweled sword had been placed conspicuously on the wall behind the Prince's chair.

It soon became obvious that the city's business would consume most of Lancer's day so Findaen suggested that they go out into the town and the valley so that Aram could see how the Derosans lived. Aram spent the morning in meeting the various business men along the main thoroughfare and then they lunched at the tavern.

In the afternoon, Findaen took him out into the valley and showed him the various crops that they grew, including brown and gold leaf, from which the smokes were made, and potatoes. The farmers Aram met were all quite alike, sturdy, quiet men who seemed content to pour their strength into the soil. Once again, Aram realized that this was how the Maker intended his people to be—working happily and freely at whatever toil made them content.

Supper brought Aram another disappointment in that there were many guests and most of them wished to monopolize his time. He was not able to exchange more than a greeting with Ka'en. And the blond-haired, sturdy young man was there again, sitting as near to Ka'en as possible. Aram learned from Findaen that the young man's name was Kemul and that he had "designs" on his sister.

Wine was again poured in abundance, though tonight Aram was wiser in his consumption of the delicious liquid, and there were more of Fiera's fine rolled smokes. Aram was completely occupied by those sitting near him and when he looked up for the hundredth time late in the evening, Ka'en was gone.

Then Lancer rose and everyone turned to listen.

"I'm turning in now, my friends, and I wish you all a pleasant evening. For those of you on the military council—remember that we meet here at ten in the morning." He looked at Aram. "I would be pleased if you would join us, lord Aram."

Aram rose and bowed. "If you wish it, my lord."

Lancer nodded, turned away and left the room. Shortly afterward Aram followed suit. He didn't wish to offend but he'd had enough of bawdy and pointless conversation and Lancer's exit provided him with a protocol to do the same.

Again that night his thoughts were full of Ka'en, of whether a relationship might develop and what the nature of that relationship might be. It was deep in the night before he was able to sleep and Findaen roused him early the next morning.

They breakfasted in the great hall with Lancer and other men of the town, including Mallet, Jonwood, and Wamlak. All of those present were obviously of a more militant bent than their fellow citizens. Findaen's sisters were nowhere in sight. Nor was Kemul. This meeting dealt purely with the defense of the city. When the food was gone and the cups were filled with kolfa, Lancer brought the meeting to order and immediately turned the proceedings over to his son.

Findaen stood and looked around at the assembled men. "Fellow citizens, we are fortunate to be seated here still able to discuss how we may resist the grim lord of the north. This is almost completely due to the efforts of lord Aram—of lord Aram's friends, for which we are grateful beyond our ability to express it."

He bowed toward Aram and the men seated around the table looked in his direction with varying degrees of curiosity, respect and sincere admiration on their countenances. Aram acknowledged their attention self-consciously and looked down at his hands folded upon the table. Findaen continued.

"Our captain of the guard, Jonwood Cansel, has suggested that some of us do a reconnaissance as far as the Broad River to see whether we might return to work on some of the lands in that direction. Also to see whether or not the enemy has intentions of moving against us any time soon."

He looked around the table. "Wamlak Shurtan has expressed interest in going. Is there anyone else who can take time away from their family and work to accompany them? We'd like to send four or five."

There was a moment of silence as everyone looked at everyone else or studied the table thoughtfully. Then a large sturdy man of middle age stood up. Findaen acknowledged him.

"Dane Sekish?"

The man nodded. "My ancestral home is along Broad River. If I could work some of that bottom land, even for just one season—it would help us all. I'd like to go along."

Findaen nodded. "Good. Anyone else?"

A small, slim man with long blond hair got to his feet.

"Erak Barris?"

The man grinned. "I don't have any particular reason for going across the plains like Dane here. I'd just like to go. My dad is always saying I'd make a better soldier than a farmer."

"Good enough." Findaen said. "Anyone else? Okay, you four will go. Go and come back as expeditiously as possible. I'd like you to go west just south of the green hills as far as the river, then swing south to Dane's old farm and come back that way. Don't get into any fights if you run into Manon's men. And certainly don't challenge any lashers."

He glanced down at Aram. "Lord Aram, you know more of these things than we do. Do you think it likely that they will encounter any enemies?"

Aram considered a moment. He felt as if he should maybe offer to go along but he didn't think Manon's men would come back upon the plains except in force and that would likely not occur for some time. More than anything else, he wanted to stay around and get to know Ka'en. Also, the horses would find their way into his valley at any time and he would have to return home. He shook his head.

"Probably not. Manon will come back, certainly, but he will be more cautious next time and he will want to come in force. I can't say for certain, but I doubt that he will return before some time late this year or next."

Findaen nodded thoughtfully. "That makes sense. All right, you four get ready and leave as soon as possible. If we're going to be able to use any of the farms on the plains for a crop this year, we need to know as soon as possible. Now, on to other things."

The rest of the meeting dealt with details of the town's defenses and repairs to the wall over the river. By the time it was done, it was nearly noon. As the men drifted away, Findaen drew Aram out into the street and up the side stairs of Lancer's home to the second floor.

"I have a gift for you, my friend."

Aram glanced at him sidelong. "A gift?"

"Don't worry." Findaen chuckled. "You'll approve."

He led Aram into a small room that opened out onto the veranda. Inside, there was a small round table with two chairs. It was set for a meal. Findaen waved him into a chair.

"Have a seat, my lord. I've arranged for lunch and conversation."

Aram shrugged. "Well, I am hungry. What do you want to discuss?"

Findaen laughed. "Oh, not me. You'll have to talk to Ka'en."

Just then the interior door opened and she entered. She gave Aram a quick smile and looked expectantly at Findaen. "You wanted to see me?"

"Only for a moment. I have things to do." He grinned. "I wondered if perhaps you might join lord Aram for lunch—I hate to see him dine alone."

She stood very still for a moment. Aram got to his feet, but Findaen stepped back and gazed at them, his demeanor suddenly serious. "I apologize for any imposition but there really are things that require my attention. I will not be able to attend lord Aram for the next few hours. I thought Ka'en, that you—" He spread his hands wide. "Look—I really must go. I will see you later, my lord."

He bowed slightly, spun quickly on his heels and left the room.

Ka'en gazed after him for a moment and then turned and smiled uncertainly at Aram.

"I have no other engagements, my lord." She moved toward the table. "If you are free also, then we might as well not waste my brother's efforts."

Aram went around and pulled back her chair as he'd seen her father do for her. "Actually, my lady, I prefer this."

When she was seated, he went to his chair and sat and gazed down at the table frowning.

"Is something wrong, my lord?"

He looked up at her. "No, my lady, not wrong, exactly. It's just that—do you think that we could dispense with calling me 'lord'—at least between us?"

It was her turn to frown. "But you are recognized as the master of a land to the north, equal, at least, to the Prince of our own city. Everyone else will call you lord, and rightly so. How could I not?"

"But not between us." He insisted and he waved his hand over the table to indicate the two of them. "Not when it is just us."

She leaned her head slightly and smiled. "I see—when we are alone."

"Yes, my lady. In private I would prefer it if you simply called me by my name."

Just then a young man and woman in white brought the food to the table. Ka'en lowered her eyes and was silent until they left. Then she looked up at him. Her smile was full, giving him a glimpse of startlingly white teeth, and her eyes twinkled.

"I will call you Aram if you will call me Ka'en—in private. In public, we must continue to be formal."

He returned her smile. "Thank you—Ka'en." It was remarkable, he thought; even her name tasted delicious, like honey on his tongue when he spoke it.

She pushed at her food with her fork and glanced up at him. "I saw you before, you know."

"Before?" He gazed at her without comprehension.

"I saw you that day on the plain."

"But—how could you? The distance was—it was so far."

She smiled triumphantly. "See? It *was* you. You've just admitted as much."

He watched her closely for a moment, trying to gauge her mood, but she was not being mischievous. Instead, she simply seemed pleased with herself and returned his gaze with her honest, lovely eyes.

"How could you tell?" He asked.

"You looked right at me."

"Yes." He acknowledged, and continued on before he could stop himself. "I did. It was a strange, terrible day. And then, after everything that happened—to look up and see you standing there, it was amazing. You were so beautiful. I'd never seen anyone like you. It was—startling."

She blushed in the face of his blunt admiration. Then, putting her fork down on the table, she folded her hands in her lap and met his eyes with hers. "Who are you, Aram?"

He hesitated. "What do you mean?"

"Everyone says something different about you." She explained and she shrugged slightly as she said it. "Findaen thinks that maybe you were sent here by the gods. My father believes that you are a descendent of the old kings. Some people—Mallet, for one—think you *are* a god. No one knows for sure. Will you tell me?"

Sitting in the quiet of that room, gazing at her beautiful, placid face, it seemed to Aram that the world had constricted until it held just the two of them. He'd been alone for so long and he had never shared himself with anyone. Perhaps, now, it was time for all of that to change. He realized that if he would tell anyone about himself, it would be her. And so he told her.

Hiding nothing, he told her of his youth as a slave in the nondescript village on the plains, of the taking of his sister and the death of his parents. He described the terrible transport into the hills, watching her closely to see if she thought less of him because of what he'd been before. But she just gazed back in rapt silence.

When he told of the escape and of Decius' subsequent death, her eyes grew moist. She shuddered slightly when he told of the flood that had sucked him into the mountain. He described the long climb up through the dark and told of the discovery of the city. And then he told her of the finding of the two dead men and of going to war with the wolves.

"That would have been Calar and Harsl." She said quietly, almost in a whisper. "They disappeared six or seven years ago. Calar was my cousin."

He nodded in silent commiseration and then, after a moment, continued his narrative. As he was telling of his contest with the wolves on the cold, snowy night when he'd nearly died, he was staring down at the table as he spoke. Hearing a soft noise, he looked up at her. She was weeping.

"I'm sorry, my lady. I didn't mean to upset you—I assure you, it wasn't as bad as it sounds."

She wiped her eyes and shook her head. "It's just that it—it makes me sad to think of you going through something like that and being so alone."

He didn't know how to respond so he just smiled gently. "Well, I did get through it alright. Turns out I wasn't as easy to kill as the wolves would have liked. And it wasn't really their fault, anyway. All the evil things they have done can be laid at Manon's door." He waited while she dabbed at her eyes. "Would you like me to continue, my lady?"

She looked up at him in quick reproof. "Only if you call me Ka'en."

He felt his insides grow warm. His story, rather than making her see him as he'd thought it might—a lowborn slave from the plains who'd become nothing more than a savage, barbarian killer—seemed instead to be having a very different and profound effect upon her. And so he told her everything, about Florm, and Thaniel, Durlrang, and Borlus the bear. The only thing he left out was of the finding of the Call of Kelven and the two Guardians.

"And then Thaniel and I came to the battle," he finished, "and you know the rest."

"That thing that exploded; did it hurt you badly?"

He shook his head. "No, not me. But it was a close thing for several days whether Thaniel would live or die. Fortunately, he is well now."

"What was it—that thing?"

"Manon," he said, more savagely than he intended. "Or at least a piece of him. Florm tells me that it's one of Manon's favorite tricks. It didn't work like he intended this time and in the future, I'll know better. He won't catch me off guard a second time."

She looked down at her plate suddenly and then at his and her eyes flew wide. "I'm so sorry! You haven't eaten a thing. It's bound to be ice-cold by now."

He laughed. "It's no great thing—I've gone without meals before."

"I'll send for more." She rang a small silver bell and then looked at him wistfully. "You've seen so much of the world, Aram. I've been in this valley all my life. I'd like to see the things you've seen."

"You've never been away from this valley?"

She shook her head. "My father and mother came here when they were children, years before I was born. It had become too dangerous every-where else. Even during the years of the respite, when I was a girl, my father did not want his daughters to venture out onto the open plains.

"The day of the battle, when I first saw you—that is as far as I have ever gone from Derosa." She sighed. "My people have been at war with Manon for the whole of my life. My mother died when Jena was born; after that my father seemed to grow older and more tired very quickly. I helped raise Jena and Findaen has tried to relieve him of the burden of defending our people."

She looked up at him with a strange emotion deep in her eyes. "My brother is a good man, Aram, as I think you know, but he is young and not experienced in war. I am glad that you have come to lead us."

Aram frowned, surprised and unsettled by her statement. "But no one has asked me to lead the men of Derosa, Ka'en."

"It doesn't matter. If you lead, they will follow. I know my brother, Aram. You are a natural leader and he recognizes that and is not jealous. Since you have come, his burden is lighter and he has re-discovered his youth." She leaned across and touched his hand. "You must lead us. Everyone, including my father, knows that it is what must be."

The door opened and the young man and woman brought more food. Ka'en took her hand away and was silent until they'd left, then she smiled. "You must eat now, but perhaps afterward you might tell me more of the places you've been and seen."

Emboldened by her act of familiarity, he leaned forward eagerly. "I would start by telling you about my valley, Ka'en. It is long, wide, and green, watered by many clear streams and a river that flows out of the mountains far to the north. It is the most livable place I have ever seen. And the city of stone that was carved out of the black mountain on the west of it—well, you have to see it to believe it and appreciate it."

"I would love to see your city."

He let the words hang in the air for a moment while he looked at her. Her delicate eyebrows arched a bit as she returned his gaze.

"Would you?" He asked finally.

She seemed surprised. "Yes, of course, I meant it. Would you show it to me sometime?"

"As soon as it is safe, I will take you there."

"And when we go—can I ride a horse?"

He grinned. "I believe I can arrange it, yes."

"Then I will hold you to your promise." She partook of her meal and, with a glance at his plate, encouraged him to do the same. "Besides your city and your wonderful valley, where else would you take me? What other wonders have you seen?"

The course of the conversation was making him feel drunk, giddy, as if he'd been drinking too much wine. With an effort, he forced himself to focus simply on answering her questions and not on the implications inherent in them. He drew a deep breath and let it out slowly. "In the center of the high plains, where Florm and his people live, there is a city of the ancients, broad and wide and overgrown with trees. In the heart of the city there is a pyramid of stone, four or five thousand feet tall, built by the ancient king Joktan." He took a bite of his food while she stared at him. "It is a marvelous thing to see."

"I would love to see it." The words came out breathlessly.

He nodded. "If you like, I'll take you there—when it is safe."

She frowned. "I'm not a child, Aram, and I am not easily made afraid. Why do you qualify every promise with the words—*when it is safe*? I am not afraid of the unknown. I would go today."

"I believe you, Ka'en. But it is not the unknown that is a threat. It is what I know is out there that presents the real danger, and I would never put you at risk."

She allowed a slight smile to touch the corners of her mouth. "I would be with you. Wouldn't you protect me?"

Secretly, he thought it was a wonderful idea. "Of course."

"Then I would go today."

Despite its delightful insinuations, Aram decided to alter the course of the conversation away from dangerous ground where he might become lost and say something impetuous that could erode what was happening between them.

"Far to the east of Florm's land there is a great inland sea, a hundred miles across and more than twice that distance in length bordered by groves of magnificent trees and bounded on the far side by great mountains."

He gazed out the window at the brown squares of newly plowed farmland. "When the war is over and Manon is destroyed, I am going to ask Florm to let me build a summerhouse by its shores, back in among the trees. I'll sit on my porch every evening and watch the moon climb the sky. Perhaps you'd like to come and see that house when it's built?"

He turned and smiled at her but found that she'd grown suddenly tense. She put her fork carefully down on the table. "What do you mean by what you said, Aram—when Manon is destroyed?"

He was confused by her question. "When he is dead, of course."

"I don't understand—why must he die?" She sat very still. "And how can anyone so powerful be killed?"

"I don't know," he answered truthfully, still trying to decipher the meaning of her question. "But I intend to find a way."

"Then it's not over?"

"Over?"

"The war."

"Oh, no, Ka'en. No. It's just begun. Manon will not rest until we are his subjects or he is defeated."

She gazed at him for a long moment while comprehension dawned in her eyes, then she looked quickly down at her hands. "You must think me a fool. I guess I thought that when you defeated his army that he would sue for peace—that there would be some kind of truce. That he would leave us alone and we would not bother him. What you're talking about is—"

"—a fight to the death." He quietly finished her sentence. He understood her now. She had been protected from the world and was not aware of the true nature of their enemy. Now that he considered it, he realized that probably no one in Derosa fully understood the scope of the coming war.

For three generations, they'd been fighting a contracted war of attrition with an enemy they had never seen and whose evil intent they did not truly understand. They no doubt suspected that he simply wanted their lands and their treasure. Like Ka'en, they thought that there was a point where bargaining was possible and Manon might settle.

Aram had come to understand fully the hopelessly wishful nature of such sentiments. Manon's dark heart lusted for more than could be imagined. More than was contained in the whole of their world. And he would not stop until he had it all.

There was nothing to be gained from encouraging false hope. He leaned toward her and spoke gently. "Listen, Ka'en, you might as well know. Manon will never rest until the entire world is in bondage to him. All of it—and everyone. And if Florm is correct, he means to rule the stars as well. That must not happen. It would be the end of all things. No, he must be destroyed and it appears that I must have a hand in his destruction."

"Why you?"

"Because—it has to be done." He looked at her and shrugged slightly. "Besides, who else is there?"

She shook her head slowly. "I did not know. I've never—I didn't know that there was so much at stake. We know so little of Manon and his designs. You think—you're certain that he will never give us peace?"

"I know that he won't."

She looked down and moisture collected in her lashes and dropped onto the table. "I didn't understand, Aram. I thought when you came onto the field that day and scattered his army that we might be near the end of all this."

"I'm sorry." He said quietly. "But we are only at the beginning."

She looked up. "And there will be other battles and more people will die."

"Yes," he admitted, but there was a quiet ferocity in his voice. "I assure you, Ka'en, more of his than of ours will die."

She shook her head. "But some of ours will die as well. You can't always be as successful as last time. You surprised his army, but he will be ready for you now. We will lose people. My father perhaps, or Findaen or—you."

She slid her eyes away and looked past him out the window. The silence lengthened out and she did not speak. He realized that she was coming to grips with the truth of what he'd told her. Finally, after a few moments, he decided to move the conversation back to more comfortable subject matter.

"Ka'en," he spoke her name gently. "My summerhouse—near the sea? Would you still like to see it when it's done?"

Her eyes came back and settled on his face but her expression remained somber. "Yes."

"Listen to me, Ka'en. Someday I will show you everything I've told you of. If you want, I will show you the world. We'll go travel it together if you like." He felt a sudden, desperate need to regain the easy conversation that they'd shared earlier.

She smiled at him with her lips but her eyes remained serious. "Yes." She said. "I would like that. But how likely is it that it will come to pass?"

He found that he couldn't lie to her or patronize her. "Time will tell." He answered simply.

She stood suddenly and moved toward the exterior door. "It's a lovely day. Let's take our wine and sit outside on the veranda."

They didn't talk for a while, just sat quietly and enjoyed the early afternoon and when conversation resumed she asked him to tell her more of his valley and of his travels. They did not discuss Manon again. Ultimately, the wine did its work and she relaxed and Aram was sorry to see the day wear away. Finally, though, Findaen's boots rang on the steps and the most pleasant interlude of his life was at an end.

Reluctantly, he stood and offered his hand to Ka'en. He spoke low as Findaen strode toward them.

"Is there any chance that we could do this again?" He asked.

She stood and looked up into his face. "Share lunch? Yes, of course. Everyday, if you would like."

He tried not to let his sudden joy spill out over his features. "Tomorrow?"

"Yes." She met his gaze for a moment and then took her hand slowly from his and inclined her head slightly as Findaen approached. "Tomorrow then, my lord."

She turned and entered the house.

XXI

Aram knew he should go home. With every warm day that passed, the sun ate away at the banked snow up in the mountain pass that closed the way between his valley and the high plains. When that pass opened, Florm had promised to come. And in the back of his mind, a nagging voice reminded him that his city was unprotected in his absence.

But he could not pull himself away from the afternoons spent with Ka'en. Nothing was declared between them, but Aram felt his affection and need for her grow with every day that they spent together and believed that she reciprocated. As yet, however, he had not found the courage to broach the subject openly.

And there was the issue of Kemul. Derosa was a small place and word of how the princess and the tall, dark lord from the valley spent their afternoons was soon disseminated about town. No one said anything to Aram or Ka'en but Kemul, who continued to come to dinner at the palace and stubbornly take his seat to Ka'en's left, glowered his disapproval across the table at his rival even as Ka'en acknowledged him less and less.

Aram largely ignored Kemul but sitting in his seat of honor across from Lancer, he could feel the waves of disapproval that emanated from the broad-shouldered young man devolve over time into sullen hatred. The issue of Ka'en's regard would have to be addressed, Aram realized, first with her and then with Kemul. The stalemate couldn't, and shouldn't, continue.

On the afternoon of the sixth day as Aram and Ka'en sat in the shade of the east veranda on a particularly warm day, a pleasant lull developed in the course of their conversation and Aram decided to take the plunge. But, just as he turned toward her, a clear, sharp voice suddenly penetrated his mind.

Lord Aram. Lord Aram from the city of Kings.

Startled, he looked at Ka'en. Her eyes had gone very wide. Aram leapt to his feat and went to the rail overlooking the valley. The voice repeated its call and when he saw no one below him on the ground, he instinctively looked up. High in the air, riding the wind on broad, majestic wings was an enormous golden eagle.

"Here." Aram said, as loudly as he dared.

The eagle spun down out of the sky and hovered on the currents a few feet above the roof of Lancer's house. Ka'en stood beside Aram along the rail as the eagle spoke into his mind.

"Lord Aram, I am Alvern of the great spire of rock that stands between the two rivers. Frinna, sister of Cree, asks me to convey the message that there are many horses in your valley."

Aram stared at him. "Many horses? How many?"

"More than ten. More than a hundred." The eagle answered. "The use of numbers is not a strength of the lords of the air. We are very clever with distance and direction, but with numbers not so much. I myself have looked down upon the whole of the world from Kelven's Mountain to the Tower of Manon, and south to the great ocean. But I cannot use the numbers of men easily. There are more than ten, and more than a hundred."

"It will suffice. Thank you, lord Alvern." Aram inclined his head. "Please send word back that I am on my way and will be at the city in three days. I am very grateful for your time and effort. If there is any way I can repay your kindness, please speak it."

"There is no need, my lord. I have heard of your deeds and am honored to serve. You may count on me in any circumstance."

With that, the eagle angled his broad wings and with a few mighty strokes went away to the north over the roof of the house. Aram turned to Ka'en. She gazed back at him with wide eyes.

"Aram, you can speak to creatures? Well, I know you can—I have just witnessed it. I heard its voice as well. How is such a thing possible?"

He looked at her intently. "You heard the eagle's voice? Inside your mind?"

"Yes."

"It is an ancient ability—gone from the earth for a long time. But this is a new age, and such things have been recovered—*you heard his voice, too?*"

She laughed lightly. "Yes, I told you, I did."

Only enormous strength of will kept him from sweeping her into his arms and twirling her about. Instead, he smiled broadly and nodded.

"That is a marvelous thing. I'm glad, Ka'en. I'm glad not to be the only one." Then he frowned. "But it means that I have to go away. Florm and Thaniel have come and I need to see them."

He gazed at her lovely face for a long moment. He wanted very badly to kiss her but since as yet nothing was established between them he resisted the compulsion. Though he felt reasonably confident of her feelings, she had not uttered any declaration on which he could base taking such an action.

She looked back at him with her delicate eyebrows arching ever so slightly. Finally, when he did not speak, she smiled.

"But you will come back."

"Would you like me to come back?" Instantly, he felt foolish for asking it, like an inexperienced boy.

She started to laugh but stifled it quickly. "Of course—why would I not?"

It wasn't the answer he wanted but it would have to do.

"Then I will come back in a few weeks. I have to see what Findaen's men have discovered to the west, anyway," he finished lamely.

She touched his arm gently with her long, tapered fingers, and let her hand rest there a moment, making his flesh burn under his clothing.

"I will be here." She said.

Reluctantly, he turned away from her and went to his room to collect his pack and his weapons.

He did not wait for evening but found Findaen and Lancer and took his leave of them, explaining the situation. Findaen informed him that he expected Jonwood and his companions to come back from their reconnaissance of the western plains within a ten-day period.

"Good enough." Aram said. "I may be detained for a while longer than that but I will return as soon as I can."

The sun was still three or four hours in the sky when he left the river road west of the town and headed north into the hills. About midnight, he slept by the spring where, the previous fall, he and the horses had waited for the arrival of Manon's army. The second night, he camped near another spring just below the summit of the great east-west ridge.

Three days after leaving Derosa, he crossed the rivers and entered his valley. It felt good to him to be home but in a larger sense, home seemed empty. Ka'en was not here. Then, as he turned the corner of the intersection of the roads by the pyramids and started up the avenue toward the city, he began to see horses grazing in the fields off to either side. They appeared to number in the hundreds.

As he passed, they turned curious eyes upon him but did not speak. When he neared the orchard, Florm and Thaniel exited the trees and came pounding up to him. They gazed at each other for a moment and then Aram flung an arm around the neck of each great animal. A strange and potent feeling surged inside of him.

"My friends! My lord and my brother! It is so good to see you." He stepped back and looked at them. Both horses appeared sleek and looked well. Florm chuckled deep in his throat.

"You have been lonely then, lord Aram?"

Aram grinned. "It was a long winter and I missed you both."

"It has not been winter now for some time. Have you been alone all this while?"

"Well, no, not exactly." Aram answered sheepishly. "I've been to Derosa."

"Ah—so that is where the hawk sent the eagle? Good." Florm nodded. "Excellent. And how was your visit there?"

"They are very grateful for what we did for them."

"All fine and well," Florm agreed, "but I'm more interested in the future than the past. Did you make friends among your own kind?"

"Yes. One—well, two or three, actually, in particular."

"I am happy to hear it." The horse lord turned and looked toward the city. "Your bear seems to have been successful in finding companionship also. We've tried to give him space but he seems to have developed as strong a sense of proprietorship toward this city as you have. I think he finds our presence here somewhat irritating."

Aram stepped aside and looked around the horses. Borlus sat in front of his grotto gazing about him with his small eyes. Beside him was another bear, smaller, with reddish fur like rusted iron. When Borlus spotted Aram, he stood up eagerly on his hind paws like a small man.

"I should go speak with him." Aram said.

"Yes," Florm agreed. "And when you are finished, there is someone I would like you to meet as well."

Aram looked at him curiously. "Indeed. I will return momentarily."

Borlus fairly quivered with joy when Aram knelt and put his arms around the bear's neck.

"It is good for you to return, master."

"I'm happy to see you as well, Borlus." Aram answered. "Who is this?"

Borlus turned toward the small, cinnamon-colored female and coaxed her forward. "This is my mate, master. Her name is Hilla."

Aram bowed solemnly. "It is a pleasure to meet you, Hilla. Welcome to our valley—may it be your home for a long time."

Looking into the tiny eyes, he thought he saw surprise. When she finally spoke, her voice was soft and muffled.

"Thank you...lord Aram. Borlus is good."

He stifled the quick surge of laughter and spoke quietly. "Yes. I am aware of that. Borlus is my friend. I am glad that you are here, Hilla."

Again, he thought he saw surprise in her small, shrewd eyes. He turned to Borlus. "Has anything of note happened while I was away, my friend?"

"No, master. Except for the coming of the horses, all has been quiet."

"Good." Aram touched the bear on the shoulder for a moment, gently grabbing a quick fistful of fur. "I have to take care of something with the horses now. In a day or two, you and I will take a trip around the valley and check on the state of things."

There was pride in Borlus' voice as he answered. "Yes, master. Good."

When Aram returned to Florm and Thaniel, two horses—Jared and another, had joined them. This new horse was one Aram had never seen. It was almost pure white except for a hint of cream its mane and tail, and the lines of its body were gentler. He was certain it was a female.

"My spouse," Florm said. "Ashal."

Aram bowed low. "It is a great honor, my lady."

"My husband has told me much of you, lord Aram." The voice was low and smooth like quietly flowing water, without the innate and ancient tone of worldly wisdom that often pervaded Florm's or the solemn intensity of Thaniel's. But it was cultured and gentle, like that of someone highborn and yet humble. "We are fortunate that you have come into the world."

Aram felt himself in the presence of a queen and at a loss for the proper thing to say. He bowed again, clumsily. "Thank you, my lady, but I am but a simple man."

"My husband speaks of you quite differently—and in my experience, he is seldom wrong." It was a gentle and kind reproof. Aram acknowledged it with a slight smile and a glance at Florm and he bowed again.

"I am pleased to meet you, my lady." He said simply.

Florm stepped forward. "Will you come to the end of the avenue with me, lord Aram? There is something I wish you to witness."

"Certainly." Aram took his pack that he'd dropped earlier and moved it to the side of the avenue and then he accompanied Florm, Thaniel and Ashal back down the avenue toward the river until they reached the intersection by the four pyramids. Florm made a sound deep in his throat that seemed to carry around the valley then he turned and addressed Aram.

"Lord Aram, allow me to bear you to your city."

Aram looked at him. "Bear me—? "

"Yes."

Puzzled, Aram mounted the back of the great black horse and with Ashal on his left and Thaniel on his right, Florm walked slowly with high, proud, and deliberate steps toward the city. Out of the fields and orchards to either side, hundreds of horses came and lined up along each side of the avenue. As Florm, Aram, Thaniel, and Ashal passed, each animal separated its forelegs, moving one back and the other forward, and bowed its head low.

At the end of the procession, as they approached the walls of the city, Aram saw that the lines of horses stretching along the avenue were anchored by Jared on the left and the great dappled gray horse, Huram, on the right. When they reached the wall, Florm turned to face down the avenue and asked Aram to stand before him.

Obediently, Aram dismounted and walked out a few paces and turned to face Florm, uncertain as to what would happen next. Florm, Thaniel, and Ashal bowed to him. Then Florm spoke and though he spoke with his mind, his voice filled the valley.

"Aram," he said. "Lord of the city of kings, heir of Joktan, and enemy of Manon the enemy of the world, hail. We, the people of Boram, the ancient and honorable father of horses, declare today our allegiance to you and the renewing of our alliance with men.

"Command us and consult with us; we are your allies. Find riders from among your people that we may bear into the fires of war and onto the fields of battle. This alliance shall stand as long as you, and we, live, and until the enemy of the world is driven from earth or we are separated by death. So say we all."

Aram stood in stunned silence as all around him, from up and down the great avenue, the chorus of voices swelled inside his mind until it seemed that his skull would burst.

"So say we all."

Florm straightened up and looked at Aram who was still too astounded to speak. "My friend, the die is cast. You have become Manon's greatest enemy. He may not know this but we do. It is clear to us that we must either cast our lot with you or suffer his wrath and see our own destruction if we will not wear his chains. We choose to cast our lot with you.

"All who would be free, man and beast, must rally to you. Kelven, in his wisdom, foresaw your coming. Now you have come. Let us dissemble no more. Together, let us do what must be done.

"Now, what say you, my friend?"

Aram pivoted slowly and looked down the broad avenue, lined with several hundred horses, all watching him. And suddenly, something happened to him. The slave from the plains dissolved completely away. A man of strength and will stood in his place. He felt the mantle of destiny fall across his shoulders as surely as the sun shone upon his head.

Perhaps it was simply a natural result of all that had happened in the previous seven years. But certainly, the metamorphosis was contributed to by the realization that someone like Ka'en was alive in the world. If men were allowed to rule their own destinies and those like him and Florm governed the world perhaps he and Ka'en could come together and build a life of peace and contentment without the specters of war and death always nearby. He looked around at Florm.

"Can everyone hear me?"

"Yes." The horse answered.

Aram stepped to the center of the avenue. "I cannot see the future." He said. "I can barely see the road immediately before us. I don't know whether we will all live or die before the resolution of this matter. But this I do know. We will fight for our liberty.

"I will rally my own people and instill in them the resolve that I see in you. I will find men who can ride and who can use the sword, the lance, and the bow. When Manon sends his armies against us, we will destroy them. And when he has no more armies to send, we will go to him and draw him out.

"I do not know how Manon may be brought down. But the Maker did not intend that the world should languish in the chains of slavery. There is a means, there is a weapon, and there is a method by which Manon may be ejected from the world. This I promise—before the end, I will discover it.

"May the grace of the Maker be with us all."

When he ceased speaking there was silence for a long moment. Then, slowly at first but gaining in volume, there arose a sound that began at the deepest limits of his hearing and became a roar that filled the valley. It was the sound of the horses' approval.

Standing there, surrounding by the unearthly sound rendered from the minds of hundreds of unmoving horses, Aram realized that a line had been crossed. The world had entered a new age. And it was largely up to him to determine the direction that age would take.

The sound died away and Florm released the horses to go back to their grazing in the lush grass of Aram's valley. Then he turned to Aram.

"What news of the enemy since last fall, if any?"

Aram sat down on his favorite rock by the orchard. "Nothing moves upon the plain near to Derosa and there is no word from the hawks that anyone has entered this valley. Findaen, the son of the Prince of Derosa, has commissioned four of his men to go west below the hills and discover whether Manon's army has regrouped or if another has replaced it.

"They are expected to return within the next two weeks. Later, I will go and hear their report." He paused and gazed around the fields at the horses. "It appears that I must also find men from among their ranks that are willing and able to be borne by your warriors, my lord."

Florm spoke sharply. "There are no warriors here, lord Aram. Not among my people."

Aram looked at him in surprise as Florm continued. "There are only two people here that have ever been to war—you and Thaniel."

Aram stared. "But you, my lord—"

"I never went to war, my friend." The horse answered quietly. "I told you that I was but a colt when this city was breached and abandoned. It's true that I came of age before the battle on the plains that ended the war but there was great attrition among your people before the end. There were always more experienced horses than there were men to ride them into battle.

"I had two older brothers, besides uncles and cousins. More men died in those battles than horses. I was given rudimentary military training but never was there a man for me to bear into battle." He hesitated for a moment, gazing down across the valley as if uncertain in his mind about something, and then seemed to come to a decision. "Besides, there was another task for me that day, required by the great king himself, which took me far away from the battle." He looked back at Aram. "So you see my lord, you and Thaniel are the only warriors here."

Aram considered this astonishing news. "Well, we are starting from the very beginning then. Everyone will have to be trained."

"Indeed. There is a need for training, for horse and man alike." Florm answered. "Horses first, I think, and then men."

Aram nodded. "Yes, and we'll need armor for both. There are crafts-men in Derosa that may serve. We can use Thaniel's armor and mine as templates. When men and horses are paired up then armor can be fitted to each." He looked out at the many horses. "One thing is certain—we are going to need more men."

"Have you gone to any cities of the south and southwest?" Florm asked. "I have heard that there are those that as yet have not come under bondage to Manon."

"Findaen mentioned as much," agreed Aram. "But I have not gone."

"Perhaps such a journey should be undertaken sooner rather than later, my friend," Florm suggested gently. "We have many more horses than men at the moment."

"I know. But raising an army is a new thing for me. Those of the southern plains and the cities along the sea do not know me. I am not sure how they will be convinced to join us."

The great horse shifted his weight and gazed south. "You will find a way, my friend. I am confident of it."

Aram was silent a moment. "We might as well begin with what we have. There are many good men in Derosa. Besides," he continued thought-fully, "whatever the scouts say when they return; I need to go west and look with my own eyes to see if the enemy has devised anything new for us."

"I will bear you," Florm offered. "Or Thaniel can go."

Aram shook his head. "Depending upon what Findaen's men say, I believe we have time—a year or two perhaps. I don't think Manon will strike blindly again. He himself will send scouts. I would rather go alone and be able to move quietly and unseen. Then I will know how much time we have and how we can use it wisely."

Florm acquiesced to this with by saying nothing. The two of them watched the grazing horses in silence for a time. Aram thought about Ka'en and how he would like to get back to Derosa. But Florm was right—they needed to train these eager young horses and the level fields and rolling pastures before his city were as good a place as any to begin that process.

"How long can you stay?" He asked Florm.

"Two months, maybe three. I don't think we should leave our mares and colts alone much beyond the middle of summer."

"Then we'd better devise a system of training your people quickly and make the most of our time."

Over the next few days, Aram, Florm, and Thaniel discussed how best to train horses to behave on the battlefield based on Aram and Thaniel's limited experience. There were eight hundred and seventeen of Florm's people who were able and willing to fight. Calling upon Florm's remembrances of ancient fighting tactics, Aram decided to divide them into five regiments with the older horses in the first three that would lead any charge in battle and the others in two reserve regiments.

He taught them to charge straight across the open field at an imaginary line of enemy represented by shafts of willow stuck into the ground and then cut to the left or right at the very last moment. By moving sharply left or right in unison at the moment of contact they would strike the lances of the enemy at an oblique angle rather than straight on, limiting injury to themselves.

He taught them to wheel, to flank, and to move together. Even though he was acting on instinct rather than formal military training and the horses were all as equally inexperienced, by the end of spring they looked quite solidly martial maneuvering around Aram's green valley.

Most of the time, Aram rode on Thaniel during the training sessions but sometimes he would leave it to Thaniel to lead and then he would watch from the walls as they charged, wheeled, and retreated from the field. Then he would try to think like an enemy and imagine the actions he might take when facing the host of horses. When he conceived of something that might be done to debilitate the charging horses, he would make the necessary adjustments.

Ultimately though, until they faced a real enemy in battle, everything they practiced was based upon conjecture. Nonetheless, they learned to obey orders in a unified manner and to maneuver upon the ground while running flat out and they learned to keep a firm line as they rapidly covered the ground.

By mid-summer, Florm and Aram were both satisfied with the progress that was made. Florm was anxious to return to the high plains and check on his people and Aram was just as anxious to return to Derosa and hear the report of what Findaen's men had found to the west. Mostly, though, he just wanted to see Ka'en again, though he said nothing of this to Florm.

There was another ceremony when the horses lined up on a pleasantly warm summer morning to bid Aram goodbye and then the great host turned and went in an orderly manner toward the river and the hills beyond. The many hooves pounding upon the stones of the avenue sounded like thunder rolling across the valley. Florm, Thaniel, Ashal, and Jared stayed behind momentarily to take their private leave of Aram.

"I am pleased." Florm said, watching his host of young recruits flow down the avenue.

Aram nodded. "As am I, my lord. If I can find enough good and strong men as willing as your people, we'll have the beginnings of a cavalry that can face anything Manon sends against us."

"You will need infantry as well."

Aram nodded again. "We'll start with the men of Derosa. Those that can ride will ride. Others will be pikemen, swordsmen, and archers. If we can then stand up to—and make some progress against—the armies of Manon, others may join us."

"The men of the world have a simple choice, my friend—to join us or go into darkness. They must be made to understand." Florm looked at him. "I will come back before winter to hear what you have learned, Aram. Communication between us is important now."

"I will have Alvern the eagle watch for your return so that if I am at Derosa, I may come and meet you."

"Are eagles in your service as well, my lord?" Asked Thaniel.

Aram laughed. "No one is in my service, lord Thaniel—we are all in league with one another."

"That cannot be—there must be leadership, lord Aram." Ashal said quietly. "The race of men has always led the fight against Manon—and you must lead this one. We have promised you our allegiance, others will, too. Accept it. The whole world must join this fight. My husband believes that you are the man to lead it. Lead it."

Florm chuckled and his great black eyes shone. "There is wisdom speaking, my friend. I think nothing further need be said. Farewell, lord Aram, I will see you again before winter."

"Farewell, my friends," Aram answered, and he felt his heart swell as he watched them canter down the avenue and out of sight.

Aram spent another week checking his crops and making his long-delayed promised inspection of the valley near to the city with Borlus. He visited with Willet and Cree and spoke to Alvern once when he spotted him high in the air above the southeastern corner of the valley.

He harvested his wheat and a few squash and made certain everything else would be fine until fall, and then he prepared to return to Derosa. He wore only the breastplate portion of his suit of armor and he took his best sword, his long bow and one quiver of three dozen arrows.

By traveling fast throughout the long days and resting only a few hours in the depths of night, he came out of the hills and looked upon the river road on the evening of the third day. Before exiting the tall, green hardwood forests, he freshened up in the clear stream.

The guard at the gate knew him and sent a runner ahead of him into town to inform Findaen of his arrival. Findaen met him on the main street in front of the tavern. The copper-haired young man bowed low and grinned.

"Welcome, my lord, welcome. It is good to see you. They are just now sitting down to supper in my father's house. Please join us."

Aram grinned back. "Hello, my friend. Yes, I am hungry."

Mallet came tearing out of the tavern with his plump wife on his arm.

"Lord Aram—you are well met!"

"Hello, Mallet. Hello, Mrs. Mallet." Aram offered the big man his hand and the latter pumped it vigorously while his wife beamed.

Ka'en was at supper, seated next to her father. Kemul, as if he'd never moved, was seated stubbornly next to her. She was as breathtakingly beautiful as he remembered and suddenly the familiarity he'd shared with her in the spring and had hoped would continue deserted him. She smiled at him and he felt his face warm under the influence of a foolish smile as he bowed stiffly.

Lancer stood and offered his hand across the table.

"Welcome, lord Aram, again to my house." He said graciously.

As the conversation flowed, Aram found no opportunity of speaking directly with Ka'en and was silent for a while. Finally, feeling a need to involve himself verbally he looked over at Findaen.

"What news from the west? Did your men discover anything?"

Findaen glanced at his father who responded only with a slight lifting of his eyebrows. Findaen looked carefully around the table, and then studied his plate thoughtfully for a moment. Finally he looked up.

"I guess there's no one here that can't receive this." He said. He looked at Aram. "There is news, my lord. We haven't quite decided just what it signifies, but—perhaps it would be better for Jonwood to tell it, as he was there."

He glanced across at Jonwood, seated two places from Aram's left and made a motion with his hand. Jonwood finished chewing, lay down his knife and fork, and looked at Aram.

"We went west across the plains as you know, my lord, all the way to the Broad River. There we found a bridge that Manon's army had constructed. We had orders not to proceed any further than the river but we had encountered no one anywhere upon the plains, and there was no one in sight on the opposite bank, so we crossed over and went on along the edge of the hills toward Burning Mountain.

"A day later we encountered a patrol of six armed men like the kind you defeated last fall. We barely avoided them and hid in some trees until they had passed. A while later, we saw them going back west across the plains about a mile to the south, like they were making a regular patrol. We waited until it was clear and then we went carefully on until we could see the hills around the base of Burning Mountain."

He picked up his fork and pushed it into a piece of potato. "Have you ever been to Burning Mountain, lord Aram?"

Aram shook his head.

"It sits alone out on the plains at the end of a line of hills that jut out to the southwest at the very borders of our lands. It's a big mountain, and occasionally spits out molten rock and sets the forests on fire. That's why we call it Burning Mountain. It's surrounded by smaller hills made of the same material.

"There was a lot of activity upon the hills around its base, particularly on Flat Butte, a mesa that sits kind of by itself at the southern foot of the mountain. Lots of men. Some lashers, too.

"And there were wagon trains going into the forests to the north. We couldn't get close enough to see exactly what was going on but it looks like they're building something on Flat Butte."

Aram looked at him sharply. "Building something?"

Jonwood nodded. "They're bringing logs out of the woods by the hundreds. Whatever they're building—it looks like they mean to stay awhile."

Aram was troubled by this news. He'd thought that when he'd defeated Manon's army and avoided the trap of the fellring that Manon would have to fall back and regroup—that maybe they wouldn't be compelled to defend themselves again for as long as two or three years.

But if Manon was building fortifications within a hundred miles of Derosa it could only mean that he meant to stay in this part of the world and return in force soon to the plain before the walls of the town. And it would be a force that could be re-supplied and reinforced quickly. He looked at Jonwood.

"You say that you saw lashers?"

Jonwood nodded slowly. "I think so. We couldn't get close enough to tell for sure but there were some much larger figures moving among the men."

"You look troubled, lord Aram," Lancer said quietly. "What are your thoughts?"

Aram glanced up at the gray-haired, dignified man. "I just thought that we might have more time to prepare after last fall, my lord. I spent the last two months training horses and hoped by next year to have men from among your ranks to learn to ride and fight. Now it appears that we won't have the luxury of any time at all."

Wamlak leaned around Jonwood to look at Aram in amazement. "You've convinced the horses to join us—to carry us into battle?"

"I didn't convince them of anything. It was their decision. What horses do, they do of their own volition."

Wamlak glanced around the table. "Do you know what this means? It means that we will be the only mounted army on earth." He looked back at Aram. "I would like to volunteer to join your cavalry, my lord."

Aram nodded. "We need about eight hundred volunteers."

Findaen stared. "Eight hundred! We could put every man in Derosa on a horse!"

"Not me," Quickly interjected Mallet. "When I fight, I'll stand on my own two feet, thank you kindly."

Aram laughed. "There will be many who feel like Mallet." He said. "And we need an infantry anyway." He glanced over at Ka'en before continuing. Her lovely eyes and features were serious and stoic but she made no move to leave the room. "War is coming upon us and we must learn to fight with discipline and order. Your people, Lord Lancer, must decide what they will do—in a military sense—in the days ahead."

The Prince of Derosa smiled gently. "I have spoken with my son, lord Aram, and we have discussed it with the council. You are the only warrior among us and you have the alliance of the horse people. You must lead. The men and resources of Derosa are at your command."

Surprised, Aram stared at him and then looked around the table. Every man's eyes were fixed on him in agreement with the Prince's statement except those of Kemul. The broad-shouldered young man glared sullenly downward at his plate.

"Alright." Aram nodded slowly. "As you wish, my lord."

Findaen leaned toward him across the table. "So what do we do now? If Manon moves upon us this year, we are not ready."

Aram glanced again at Ka'en. She gazed steadily back and he could not read her expression. He turned to Findaen. "We'll have to buy time. I'll go west to Burning Mountain and see what Manon is doing there and—if I can—disrupt his plans. If I can make that location seem too dangerous, he might decide to relocate his activities further west. That would give us some time to train, at least a little more than we might have now."

Ka'en frowned. "What do you mean—disrupt his plans?"

Aram gazed into her eyes for a long moment, but found that he still could not read her expression, so he looked at the others. "I mean this—if I can kill a couple of lashers and as many overseers as possible, it might discourage the rest of his men. I have no doubt that most of the work is being done with slave labor; perhaps I might even set some of them free.

"Manon will know then that his feet are too close to the fire and that we might be stronger than he supposed. It will make him more cautious and it might buy us a year or two. That's what I mean."

Ka'en frowned down at the table but Jonwood spoke with enthusiasm. "I'll go with you, my lord. I would sure as hell like to see you kill a lasher and maybe learn to do it myself."

"You're not going without me," broke in Mallet, and several others nodded.

Aram frowned and spoke carefully. "There is no need for any of you to go. This is something I can do alone and—"

Lancer held up a hand and replied in calm, measured tones. "My lord, none of us doubt that you can do this alone. We have seen what you can do. But it is perhaps time to start bringing others up to your level. You cannot defeat Manon by yourself and the more experience these young men can gain under your leadership; the more they can pass it on to others. Does this not seem like sound military doctrine?"

Aram felt the sting of the rebuke but knew the words to be true. He smiled. "You are right, my lord." He thought a moment. "We do not need such a large party that we cannot move undetected, however. Perhaps six or eight men—no more."

He looked around the table and then at Findaen. "So, who's going?"

"Me, for one," Findaen grinned. "I 'm going for sure."

A chorus erupted from around the table. Every man except Kemul expressed a desire to be in the party. Aram held up his hands, silencing them. "Findaen will choose eight men. I want to leave as soon as possible." He glanced at Ka'en but her eyes were directed downward and she did not look up. "We'll leave tomorrow. We'll go to my city and equip every man properly, then go west along the river."

Mallet's eyes widened. "We're going to see your city, my lord?"

"The weapons are there." Aram said simply.

The men then turned their attention to Findaen, each expressing reasons why he should be in the party. Aram returned to his meal, quietly distraught. He desperately wanted to continue trying to develop his relationship with Ka'en but the news that Manon might be constructing fortifications within a hundred miles of the town could not be ignored. He glanced up at her but she was talking quietly and earnestly with her father.

He focused on finishing his meal, which had grown cold but was still better fare than he was used to. Then, suddenly, he heard her soft voice.

"Good night, lord Aram."

Startled, he looked up. She and her father were standing and obviously quitting the hall. She seemed upset, angry, and uncertain, as if she was unsure of where to direct her anger. He stood and bowed.

"Good night, my lady—my lord." She smiled very slightly and left the hall on her father's arm. Aram watched her go and, once again, found himself fervently despising Manon for the havoc he wreaked in the most basic aspects of people's lives. Instead of more quiet interludes on the veranda that might lead toward the fulfillment of his deepest desire, Aram was forced to once again bend his thoughts to war.

Findaen put him in his old room and promised to have the men assembled and ready to leave at daylight.

XXII

There were seven men gathered with Findaen in the morning. Jonwood, Mallet, Wamlak, Erak, Dane, Mallet's cousin, a very large man named Aberlon, and Dane's son, Alred. Through the mists of early morning, Aram led them northward up the long ridge west of town. Four days later, they were gazing about them in awe as they filed up the great avenue toward Aram's city.

He left them wandering the great porch in amazement while he led Findaen through the city to the armory. Findaen's head swiveled from side to side as he gaped at the great stone magnificence that surrounded him on all sides.

"You are lord of a magical place, my friend." He told Aram.

"This city has had greater lords than I." Aram answered.

Findaen looked at him with a new light in his eyes. "That remains to be seen, does it not?"

Aram shrugged. "One of the former masters of this city was an ancestor of mine and he was most certainly greater than I."

Findaen watched him a moment and then spoke soberly. "And was he defeated by Manon?"

"Yes," Aram acknowledged. "Manon slew him with his own hand."

Findaen stopped and looked at him with widened eyes. "What does such a history bode for you, my lord?"

Aram swung around and faced his friend, returning his gaze without expression. Then he smiled slightly. "My ancestor did not die easily, Findaen." The smile slowly disappeared as he looked up and around at the multi-hued stone mansions and towers. "And I don't intend to die at all."

"But you or Manon—one of you must die. Is this not true? How else can it end?" Findaen watched his friend through narrowed eyes. "How will you kill someone like him?"

Aram shook his head slightly but the wry smile returned and he continued on toward the armory. "I have not discovered that as yet."

As he followed his friend, Findaen gazed at the splendor of the amazing city around him. "I don't understand any of this—I've never heard the history of this place." He lowered his gaze to Aram's face. "Where did all the people go? Did Manon kill them all?"

Aram nodded. "Most of them, yes."

"When?"

"A long time ago—thousands of years before you and I were born." Aram glanced over at him. "We are part of a very old and very long story, Findaen."

Findaen stopped walking again and faced him. "You told us once that you were the answer to something called Kelven's Riddle. Kelven was a god—I know that much from the legends. Were you sent by the gods?"

"No." Aram answered simply. "And I don't know what to think of Kelven's Riddle. All I know is that the horses believe in it."

"Will you tell me what it is?"

Aram studied him for a moment. "Sometime, yes," he answered finally, and he turned to continue on but Findaen put out a hand and stopped him.

"Lord Aram, what strange power did you employ to stop the lances and arrows of the enemy that day on the plain? We all saw it as it surrounded you, flashes of brilliant light—it looked like lightning."

Aram studied the ground for a moment, considering, and decided that the Guardians were something he was not willing to discuss. He looked at his friend and put a hand on his shoulder. "Someday, my friend, I will tell you all about it. Suffice it to say that the power is something I don't control. Come, let's go on."

Obediently, Findaen followed him up through the streets to the armory. A while later they had chosen a selection of swords to be distributed among the men and one of Aram's long bows with arrows for Wamlak. As they were preparing to transport them down to the great porch, Aram paused and looked hesitantly at Findaen. Findaen caught the look and gazed back with raised eyebrows.

Aram took a deep breath and let it out. "May I ask you about Ka'en?"

Findaen sat down on the long table at the center of the armory. "What about her?"

Aram turned away and began to pace back and forth without looking at his friend. "You told me that Kemul has 'designs' on her. What did you mean?"

Findaen sighed. "Before we quit the plains entirely and abandoned our capitol of Stell, Kemul's family governed, under the lordship of my father, in Derosa. His father is dead but his mother lives there to this day.

"They are a wealthy family and have had among themselves for a long time an understanding—not necessarily shared by any of the rest of us—that Kemul and one of Lancer's daughters would marry and Kemul would have claim to the throne of my people."

Aram stopped pacing and looked at him. "Does your father share in this 'understanding'?"

Findaen shook his head but looked away and gazed out the door across the city and sighed again. "My father is old and tired and up until now Ka'en has not overtly objected to Kemul's attentions. I think my father is willing just to let it play out however it will."

"And does Ka'en object to Kemul's attentions now?" Aram stood very still and watched his friend closely.

Findaen looked back at him and grinned. "Come now, lord Aram, don't tell me you don't know where Ka'en's interests lie?"

Aram shook his head. "I don't. Not for sure."

"With you, my friend—*with you*."

"How do you know?"

Findaen snorted in exasperation. "I'm her brother and I pay attention."

"Has she said anything to you?"

"No," Findaen admitted. "Ka'en isn't like that. But I know that she prefers you to Kemul."

Aram resumed his pacing. "What do I do about him?" he asked.

"I don't know." Findaen answered quietly but then his voice assumed an undertone of ferocity. "But I'm not thrilled about the future he sees for himself—and that includes my people as well as my city. I don't want to see that weasel in charge of anything." His face lit up in a sudden bright smile and he looked at Aram. "But now that you're here—he won't be."

"So Ka'en isn't promised to him?"

"Not in anyone's mind but his own."

Aram frowned. "How much support does he have among the people?"

"As long as my father is alive—none." Findaen answered. "He and his mother intend that their plans should come to fruition after my father's death. And if Kemul is married to Ka'en by that time—well, then," Findaen shrugged. "Who knows?"

"I love her." Aram stated flatly as he stared out the door.

"I know, my lord," Findaen answered quietly. "And it will work out. You'll sort it out like you do with everything else."

Aram's face darkened as if a cloud had settled between him and the sun. "This affair is not the same as fighting lashers, Findaen, and it can't be settled with a sword stroke."

"There's an ancient saying," Findaen replied. "Perhaps you've never heard it. 'All is fair in love and war'."

"Does she love me then?"

"I believe so."

"But you don't know."

"But I believe so."

Aram sighed and moved toward the weapons they'd collected. "Alright, then, I'll sort it out later. For now—let's collect the men and go see what Manon is doing in the west."

They carried the cache of weaponry down to the others and matched the swords with soldiers. Mallet and his big cousin elected to carry lances and short swords. Wamlak's eyes shone when Aram handed him one of his best long bows. He ran his hand over the stock.

"This is wonderful. What kind of wood is this, my lord?"

"It's ironwood," Aram answered. "It grows along streams in the hills to the north. There may be some near Derosa. I'll show you how to make one when there's time."

Each man collected a pack and filled it from Aram's stores of fruits, dried meat, and meal. Then, as there were still several hours of daylight remaining, they left the city and moved southward along the flank of the mountain. At the river, they angled eastward to the upstream crossings below the ruins of the ancient farming community.

Sunset found them in a copse of trees below the top of the main east-west ridge by the spring where Aram had camped with the wounded Thaniel a year before. Aram sat quietly while the men talked around a fire and the stars came out and filled the sky.

In order to make better time, Aram decided to go westward across the plains rather than along the wild ridge. Two days later, they reached the plains just to the west of Derosa and turned west, traveling at the verge of the forested hills. The plains rolled away to the south in an immense green expanse, watered in plentiful fashion by the many streams and small rivers that emanated from the wooded hills to their north. Abandoned farmsteads of the Derosan's ancestors were tucked into every hollow.

For five days they moved purposefully west until they reached the Broad River, a wide, shallow stream of clear water a half-mile or more across. The bridge built by Manon's army was still intact. Depending on what happened in the days ahead, Aram thought that it might be a good idea to destroy it and fortify the near side of the river. When he mentioned this matter-of-factly to the others, they stared at him in wonder that they themselves had not considered such an option.

Findaen rubbed his chin ruefully. "Thank the Maker you're here, my lord. It was obvious to you in a heartbeat. We never even thought of it."

Jonwood pointed west across the river. "We encountered the patrol on the road about a mile further on."

"Alright." Aram nodded. "Then we'll stay near the hills after we cross and move forward with caution."

Once across the river, they eased northward toward the green hills through the tall reeds and grasses that grew in and among the shallows that bordered the wide stream. Near sunset, they came upon an amazing sight. At the base of limestone bluffs at the edge of the hills, the headwaters of Broad River rose out of the earth in a massive, rolling, blue-green spring; a huge pool of deep water that surged from the hidden depths of the world as if all the rain that fell on the green hills in a year and seeped down into the earth made its way to this spot before erupting from the ground in an astonishing display. The men stared in awed silence at this marvel for as long as they dared and then moved around the vast roiling pool and into the timbered hills beyond.

That night they camped in a thick grove of trees within sight of Burning Mountain, a tall, conical, black rock rising out of the plain to the southwest, much taller than the green hills and surrounded by smaller and very rough versions of its immense self. On its southernmost flank there was a flat-topped butte with steep sides jutting up out of the plain. Even from that distance they could see that it swarmed with activity.

There was no fire that night and Aram insisted on each man taking a watch throughout the night. In the morning they eased farther up into the hills and moved westward through the trees. At noon they came upon a sizeable stream tumbling quickly down out of the hills to the north.

It plunged rapidly southward at the bottom of a rocky, steep-sided canyon and they were obliged to go even further to the north in order to find a good crossing. The country became rougher and more thickly wooded as the green hills curved southwestward toward Burning Mountain.

A little further and they came out on the top of a ridge above a sizeable, lush valley filled with tall conifers mixed with hardwoods. From below them arose the sound of tumbling water and from the other side of the valley came the sound of work, steel against wood and the shouts of men. Occasionally, they heard also the deep-throated voice of a lasher.

Aram spread the men out along the ridge in a defensive position and told them to stay put and remain quiet while he and Findaen went ahead. The two men eased down through the tall, thick woods toward the sound of the stream. It was a good-sized stream and fell in a series of falls from pool to pool toward the south. Thick ferns covered its banks. They found a narrow place in the stream and waded across.

The sound of axes and the familiar cursing of overseers drew very near. Aram motioned to Findaen that they should get prone and crawl as they went forward. Easing west and south they came at last out on the crest of a rocky ridge among tall conifers and looked across at an open area that had been cleared of trees. Into this area, from the south, ran a road.

The trees had been cut from a gentle slope comprising several acres. Above the road, slaves, chained in pairs, worked under the watchful eyes of four overseers and one lasher, felling the tall trees, while others stripped them of limbs and loaded the logs onto wagons. There were about forty slaves in all.

Aram and Findaen watched for awhile, then went back to the others and moved cautiously southward along the ridge until they could look out over the plains. The expanse of Burning Mountain rose above them with the bulk of its mass just to the south of due west. The road from the clearing wound out of the trees on the ridge opposite and meandered through the broken foothills about the base of the mountain and then climbed toward the flat top of a black, steep-sided butte, almost due south of their position.

They were close enough now to see the flurry of activity and plainly see its purpose. A fort was being constructed on top of the butte. Tall walls of timber nearly surrounded the heights of the cliffs. Where the road wound up the less steep, but still rough, northern side of the butte, there were tall gates in the walls through which it entered the fortress.

On the plains just to the east of the butte and to the south, fields had been turned and the dense green of row crops cut vivid swaths across the prairie. Rows of small huts were being constructed before their eyes. Out on the plains in every direction from the butte but mostly to the east and south, small parties of armed men roved back and forth.

It was a large operation. Aram could plainly see that Manon had come to stay. The purpose of everything in view was of an obvious military nature. It was intended to be a stronghold from which his armies could launch operations to the east toward Derosa and to the south toward the sea. Aram could see plainly that Florm's worst fears were being realized—Manon's strength had grown and was waxing toward its apex.

He felt his heart grow cold within him. When he'd heard that Manon was constructing something on the western frontiers of Derosa, he'd hoped to discover an outpost, a temporary foothold, intended solely as a launching point for another assault upon Derosa. This was something completely different, a very large footprint; the first of many Manon obviously intended to impose on the southern plains.

From his tower in the far north, he was reaching out now to lay hold on the whole world. And he meant to control this part of it with the same iron fist that had governed the plains further north and west where Aram had spent his youth. Manon was mobilizing and if he were unchecked, Derosa and the seaside cities to the south would soon feel the full measure of his tyranny.

Findaen looked at him with rounded eyes. "What do we do now?"

Aram glanced up and down the line of men. He saw shock, even awe and a touch of raw fear, but no cowardice. These farmers had resolve. They would at least attempt whatever he asked of them. He looked back out over the plains and the flat-topped butte with its new and ominous construction.

"We can't hope to fight this host on open ground, not now. We can't even confront it," he said. He watched the tiny dark figures of the distant scattered patrols moving slowly across the plain and then he turned and looked back up the timbered valley toward the sound of the men felling trees. He smiled grimly at Findaen. "But maybe we can wreak enough havoc to divert their attention away from us for awhile. Buy some time."

Findaen gazed out over the massive works of their enemy and then looked at Aram through narrowed eyes. "Time to do what, my lord?"

"To raise and train an army." Aram answered.

"And where will we get this army?"

"From among your farmers, Findaen."

"Seven hundred farmers is not an army, my lord."

Aram smiled. "They are if they are mounted. One man on an armored horse is worth at least ten of Manon's foot soldiers. Next spring the horses will come and train with us."

"So the horses are really willing to bear us into battle?"

"Yes." Aram nodded. "But there is much to do—armor to make, and the men and horses must learn to work together—they can't go into battle untrained. And training requires time—time, it appears, that Manon does not plan to give us. So, we must force the issue—make him more cautious." He moved back deeper into the woods and turned up the valley. "Let's go see what we can do to disrupt his plans."

He led the small group of men back up the ridge until they were opposite the workers. Instructing all of them to leave their packs and move quietly and deliberately, he led them down through the valley and up to the crest of the small ridge where they could see the road and the open area.

The day was waning and the last of the four wagons were being loaded. As they watched, overseers chained the workers together and two of them drove the last wagons southward out of the clearing. The remaining overseers and the lasher then marched the slaves in the same direction.

When they were gone, Aram told the men to stay while he went across and examined the road and the work area. Cautiously he went down the road for a short distance. After it left the clearing toward the south, the road entered a thick wood. The trees were not as tall and big as those being harvested at the western and northern edges of the clearing and they grew closer together. Low brush abounded beneath the trees and bordered the road on both sides. Consequently, there was good cover to either side of the road for men who wished not to be seen.

The road wound across the wooded slope for about a mile before it exited the forest upon the spine of a rocky ridge. From there it went generally southward toward the distant flat-topped butte. The mass of Burning Mountain rose to the right. Halfway between Aram and the unfinished fortress, the wagons and the line of slaves were just entering the shadow cast by the mountain.

The sun was on the horizon when Aram returned to the men. He led them back across the wooded valley and beyond the eastern ridge. There, in a small bowl below the crest, there was a clear spring seeping from the ground. Aram examined the area in the dying light.

"We'll camp here. Tomorrow we'll watch and make our plans." He studied the men. "Findaen, Alred, and I will take first watch—about three hours—then Jonwood, Aberlon, and Erak next, followed by Wamlak, Mallet, and Dane. Wamlak, wake me before dawn."

Wamlak nodded and Aram studied the darkening sky. "As soon as it is dark enough that our smoke can't be seen, we'll start a fire and eat but we won't keep it through the night just in case someone decides to wander these hills."

The night passed without incident. The sky was just beginning to pale in the east when Wamlak touched his shoulder and Aram came awake.

"It will be dawn soon, my lord."

Aram nodded in the gloom. "Let's have a small fire and make up some of Findaen's kolfa—and maybe cook a hot meal of wheat cakes for everyone before it gets too light."

By the time the sun topped the hills to the east behind them the nine men were spread out along the crest of the small ridge northeast of the clearing, watching and waiting. An hour later they heard the sounds of wagons and the men, the overseers, and the lasher came into view.

There were six wagons. The day's work began. As soon as two of the wagons were filled with logs, about midmorning, two of the overseers climbed into the seats and drove them away while the other two overseers remained behind. The lasher stayed at the bottom of the clearing, striding back and forth along the road, watching the men, the overseers and the woods around him.

The overseers driving the wagons made three trips throughout the day. When they came back into the clearing after the third trip, they stayed until the end of the day when all the men and wagons left for the fortress just as they had on the previous day. Aram had seen all he needed to see. Since they could not risk attacking the fields on the plains below the fortress, this was the next best place to wreak havoc on Manon's operations. It was project's weakest and most vulnerable link.

That night, back in the natural bowl below the eastern ridge, he laid out for the men what he expected of them on the morrow. He looked around at the men carefully and liked what he saw reflected in the low light of the fire. These men might be farmers as Findaen said but they were tough enough to be turned into warriors.

Next to Findaen sat the short, stout, and capable Jonwood with a stubble of red beard on his serious face. Beyond him were the lean, dark, and clever Wamlak, and the slight, quick-moving Erak, with his tangled mass of blond hair. Mallet and Aberlon were near copies of one another—large, barrel-chested, and muscular with square jaws and pug noses.

Dane was older and round-shouldered and looked like what he was—a farmer, but his son Alred was tall and athletic and had the build and temperament of a soldier. These were good, dependable men and Aram felt a secret pride as he looked at them. They were the core of what might one day be a formidable force. It was a beginning. And tomorrow, they would be initiated. He stood up, gaining the men's attention.

"My friends, what we see out on that butte and the prairie beneath it is the coming of evil. It is the same evil that pushed your ancestors from their homes. And now it is come in force. If Manon succeeds in constructing a fort from which to assault our lands, it will mean death and chains and slavery for us and for those we care about. It must be stopped and we must start now."

He studied the faces reflected in the firelight. "Have any of you killed a man before?"

The men looked at each other and Wamlak shifted uncomfortably. "I think I brought a soldier down with my bow on the day of the battle, but I'm not sure."

Aram nodded. "Well, we are going to kill tomorrow. You must understand this and prepare yourselves. I will handle the lasher but you will have to help with the overseers. None must escape. Our lives and our futures depend upon this fact."

Jonwood glanced around at his companions then looked at Aram. "What about the workers—the slaves? What do we do with them?"

Aram considered that a moment. He really did not want to deal with the complications represented by a large group of slaves, and yet, he himself had been in slavery once and he believed fervently that all men should be free. But he also knew that some had been in chains for so long that they would fear the uncertainties of sudden freedom more than the sure oppression of their current masters.

He thought for a moment longer before answering. "We will set them free, of course—if they wish it. But I've known slaves before. Some of them will not know what to do with freedom and will wait for their masters to come for them.

"Whatever I say to them tomorrow, don't dispute it. If some or all of them wish to remain in their servitude, it may present an opportunity to deflect Manon's thinking in a way that will make him cautious and buy some more time."

Alred frowned into the fire upon hearing this and then glanced at his father. Aram saw the look. "Speak your mind Alred."

The young man looked up uncertainly. "I—I was just wondering why anyone would not want to be free."

Aram looked slowly around the circle of faces. "It's hard for men who have never known slavery to understand how the spirit in a man may become so broken that he no longer trusts the concept of liberty, but it happens. Trust me, I have seen it."

He let that sink in and then continued. "Here's what I want to do. Before the workers arrive at the clearing, I want all of you except Wamlak and myself to be hidden on either side of the road to the south. After the first two wagons are loaded and leave the clearing, Wamlak and I will kill the lasher. When the overseers run—and they will—the rest of you will ambush them on the road. Neither must escape. Any questions or suggestions?"

Wamlak looked up. "How will we kill the lasher, my lord?"

"With our bows."

"But he is armored, is he not?"

Aram nodded. "With standard leather armor. Our ironwood bows are more powerful than those you are used to, Wamlak. Just aim for the biggest part of him and pull back with your might. Our arrows will penetrate, I assure you. It will take both of us to bring him down, but we will bring him down."

Wamlak nodded and said nothing.

"Alright," Aram said. "Same schedule as last night, except for Wamlak. I want him to sleep through. Mallet, you and Aberlon will have the last watch. Wake the rest of us before dawn."

Before daylight, as the sky grew pink behind them, they were easing through the wooded valley toward the clearing on the slope opposite.

Sunup found them in the clearing. Aram distributed the men in the undergrowth on either side of the road to the south. Then he and Wamlak hid themselves in the trees on the north side of the work area and waited.

Within an hour they heard the wagons rumbling up the road along the top of the ridge. They came out of the woods into the clearing and stopped in a line along the bottom. The overseers immediately put the slaves to work, chained together in pairs like before, and the lasher took up his patrol along the roadway at the lower edge of the clearing.

It took most of the morning for the slaves to fell and strip enough trees to load the first pair of wagons then two overseers turned their oxen around and left for the distant butte. Aram waited until the wagons were too far away to hear what happened behind them, and then he touched Wamlak lightly on the arm. Wamlak swallowed and nodded. Aram let the lasher reach the far end of his patrol, turn, and start back. Then he caught Wamlak's eye, got to his feet and stepped out of the trees onto the road.

"Aim for the biggest part of his body." He told Wamlak evenly and he took aim. The lasher had not yet seen them. He was looking up the hill at the slaves. Aram's arrow caught him in the chest just below his chin. Wamlak's struck a second later in the upper part of the lasher's left arm.

The lasher grunted in pain and surprise and dropped to one knee, dragging at Aram's arrow with a clawed hand. The two remaining overseers looked around curiously. Then the lasher looked up and saw Aram and Wamlak standing on the road, drawing their bows back for a second volley. With a roar of anger, the great beast came to his feet, snapped off the shafts of the arrows and charged.

He pounded toward the two men in great long strides, eating up the distance, swinging his sword and his whip. But Aram could already see a black stain spreading quickly down over the beast's huge chest. His first missile had found something vital.

"Hold steady and let him come," Aram told Wamlak. "He's already hurt worse than he knows. Pull your bow back as far as you can and put your arrow right in the thickest part of him."

Aram pulled the long bow back until the wood groaned and held his fire. When he heard the twang of Wamlak's bow, he released his own missile. The lasher flicked his whip and partially deflected Wamlak's arrow but Aram's caught him high in the chest near the where the other had struck and sank deep. Brackish blood spewed from the wound.

The beast grunted and went to his hands and knees, sliding forward in the gravel of the roadway. He struggled to regain his feet but Aram's two arrows had done considerable damage and his great strength was failing. Deliberately, Aram nocked another arrow and put it near the others. The lasher was mortally wounded and though he scrabbled at the ground with his enormous claws, could not rise.

For a moment, now that the beast's head was on a level with his own, Aram considered dispatching it with his sword for the effect it would have on the men but thought better of it. He approached the lasher as it continued trying to rise and put a last arrow in its eye. The missile shuddered as it pierced the brain and struck the back of the lasher's skull. The beast collapsed.

Above the roadway, the overseers had watched the scene in stunned paralysis but now they abandoned their posts in the face of this astounding and terrifying event and fled down the road. Findaen and his men leapt from the undergrowth and felled the two overseers with quick and numerous—albeit clumsy—strokes of their swords.

Aram checked their work and then turned his attention to the slaves. For the most part, the workers, forty-two in all, had dropped their tools and hunkered back in among the trees, fearful and uncertain of the meaning of events. Aram slung his bow over his head and approached them. He stood for a moment and looked them over. The pitiful sight of the thin, frightened men brought back momentary yet painful memories of a life that until now had begun to seem very distant from him in space and time.

"We are free men," he addressed them in a loud voice. "We answer to our own will and not that of any other." He pointed to the west through the trees behind them toward the jumbled rocky wilderness of hills that formed the region to the north of Burning Mountain. "We dwell in the wilderness behind you. Your masters have invaded our land and we will not tolerate it. If they continue to destroy our forests, they will all die."

Out of the corner of his eye, Aram saw Findaen's eyebrows go up at this astonishing series of statements but the younger man remembered Aram's admonishment of the night before and remained silent.

"We were once like you," Aram continued, "slaves to the whims of the servants of Manon. Now we are free. We mean you no harm. Join us and know what it is like to have liberty."

He fell silent and waited for an answer from the slaves. Most stared at the ground before them, trembling in fear, and refused, or were simply unable, to meet his gaze. Finally, two men stood up, straining against the chains of their fellows who remained on the ground. They stood proudly and looked him in the eye. Aram studied the two. They were a similar pair and looked very much alike, lean and wiry with sandy colored hair, though one was slightly taller.

"We'll join you." The taller one said. "My name is Ruben and this is my brother Semet. We were taken prisoner when we were boys—our parents were slain. But we remember freedom. We will join you."

"Where are you from?" Aram asked. "Where was your home?"

Immediately, Ruben pointed toward the south. "We lived on a farm on the plains near the town of Gerontus which is on the sea. Ten years ago the gray men came with one of the horned beasts. Our village was utterly destroyed. All who resisted them were slain and the young girls taken away and all the boys like us put into chains."

"When were you brought here?" Aram asked.

"Last year," Ruben answered. "Before that we were made to work farms to the west near the great marsh."

Aram motioned for Mallet to join him and he went close to the young men and examined their chains. "Can you break through these by striking them with a sword against a rock?" He asked Mallet.

Mallet nodded slowly. "I think so—but it will probably ruin the sword."

"We have more." Aram answered simply. He looked at the two men chained with the brothers. "Stand up." He ordered and the slaves complied meekly.

While Mallet led the men away to find a flat rock and break the chains, Aram sent Jonwood and Wamlak down the road to watch for the return of the wagons and then he went back and examined the other slaves. They were a frightened-looking lot, thin and threadbare, and it was obvious that most of them had known nothing but slavery for most, if not all, of their lives.

He addressed them in a way he knew they would find familiar. "Stand up," he said loudly, "and form a line in the open."

Cautiously, the slaves lined up along the edge of the clearing in front of the standing trees, watching Aram with furtive and fearful eyes. This tall, dark-haired man had slain a lasher—a beast they feared with sound reason. If this man could kill one of their masters, what kind of man must he be? They stood trembling, most of them afraid to meet his gaze.

"I said I would not harm you and I meant it—now or ever. I offer you three choices. Join us in the wilds—go free on your own—or remain in your chains. Which will it be?"

One man, who seemed to be of about middle age—though it was hard to tell—finally looked up and met Aram's gaze for a moment. When he spoke, his voice was barely more than a whisper.

"The grim lord has taken our daughters and threatened all of us with pain more terrible than death if we do not do what he wishes. If we disobey him and go with you, we will never see our daughters again and our wives and children will suffer his terrible wrath. I cannot do this."

Aram gazed at him in pity and decided that he could not be so cruel as to tell the poor man that his daughters were lost forever, no matter what he did now. He spoke gently.

"Where are you from, my friend?"

The man appeared to be taken aback by Aram's kindly tone. "We— well, most of us here—are from the land of Bracken, near unto the tower of the grim lord." Anticipating Aram's next question, he continued. "We were brought here a year ago. It took many days, in many wagons, and many died."

Aram nodded in silent commiseration. He had memories of his own concerning such matters. He sighed.

"I understand. Perhaps the day will come when we can free all of your people, including your families. In the meantime, know that we will never harm any of you. Now, are there any others among you that will accept our offer of freedom today?"

None other answered. Aram let the silence stretch out as he watched them. They had been slaves for so long that they couldn't grasp the fundaments of rebellion, or even decision-making. Gazing upon their pitiable physical state and their mental paralysis, born of generations of servitude, his soul ached within him. Finally he turned and looked at the men from Derosa and indicated the slaves with a wave of his hand.

"This is what is in store for our people, for countless generations, if we don't win this war." He turned back to the workers and spoke gently. "Sit, then, and be quiet until our business is finished. Then we will leave you."

Mallet had succeeded in freeing Ruben and Semet and he brought the two slaves that had been shackled with the brothers back and set them with the others. Dane approached and asked Aram to go with him down to the remaining wagons. He indicated the two pairs of oxen hitched to the wagons.

"These are some pretty fine beasts," he said. "They haven't been fed as well as they should have but they're young and good oxen are hard to come by these days. Is there any way we could take them with us?"

Aram considered. They were a good four or five days from his valley and one or two further from Derosa—and a good portion of the distance was rugged and covered with woods. But the main problem was how easy the animals would be for their enemies to track.

"I don't know," he answered Dane honestly. "How valuable are they? What kind of risk are they worth?"

Dane looked at him. "As you saw, lord Aram, most of our farmers work their ground by hand without any beasts at all. These are valuable, and there are four of them. They will make a great difference."

Aram nodded. "Yes and there are four more coming, which we could take as well. Unhitch these, Dane, and take them into the trees over there"—he pointed to the north side of the clearing—"and secure them until later. Let's see how things go before we decide."

He gave instructions for the slaves to be given water—they couldn't spare any of their food—and then he went down the road to join Jonwood and Wamlak. The two men had positioned themselves on the ridge where the road curved away to the south and went out into the brush of the open ridge. They could see down the road for a good two miles. As Aram approached, Jonwood pointed to the south.

"They're coming back."

Just coming into view, rounding a curve in the road below the great black mountain, the wagons of the two overseers were returning. Wamlak glanced sideways at Aram.

"Do we need to kill these men as well?"

Aram met his gaze with cold eyes. "Did you get a good look at those slaves back there, Wamlak? Did you see the state to which men who were once like you and me have been reduced?"

Wamlak nodded silently.

"Alright, then." Aram indicated the approaching overseers. "These men have had a willing part in that evil. They deserve death. Even at that, however, there is a more important issue here. There is a sound reason why we're going to leave no one alive but the slaves.

"They'll tell the story we gave them about us living out in the wilds," he said and he swept his hand over the rugged, rocky country to the west, "and Manon and his commanders will think they have other enemies besides us. Enemies that, until now, they hadn't known of. So we can leave no one alive who might suspect otherwise. The way I see it, when the wagons don't return this evening, someone will come to check—hopefully another lasher, or perhaps a pair of them.

"The more of them we kill, the fewer we'll face later and the more cautious Manon will be. If they don't come tonight, we'll keep the slaves here and wait until morning. As long as they don't send a large party, we have the advantage on this ground and we need to make as big an impression as possible."

He looked into the eyes of the two men and waited until he saw that they understood and then he turned toward the clearing. "Let's join the others and get into position."

Within an hour, the returning overseers were dead, brought down by arrows from the bows of Aram and Wamlak. Dane spent the rest of the afternoon hitching the oxen together and herding them north into the trees along the ridge top. Aram sent Jonwood and Wamlak back down the road to watch for scouting parties of the enemy and he put the rest of the men, including Ruben and Semet, to work destroying the wagons.

The sun went behind the bulk of Burning Mountain and the day waned away. Finally, just before sunset, Jonwood came hurrying into the clearing to alert Aram.

"Two lashers, my lord. They're coming on the run."

"Only two?"

"That's all we can see. They're coming straight up the road."

"How far away?"

Jonwood considered a moment. "They should be here in about twenty minutes."

"Good." Aram said. He was pleased. Two was not too many to handle, but was enough, when added to the one they'd already killed, to make a lasting impression on Manon and his local commanders. He gathered the men and led them down the road. He glanced southward. The lashers had covered about half the open distance.

"Same as this morning," he told the men. "You get into cover on both sides of the road. Wamlak and I will step into view when they're close enough that we can do some damage. When we've wounded them, the rest of you can help, but don't get close enough to be wounded yourselves. Mallet, you and Aberlon use your pikes."

He looked around sternly. "Hear me. Don't any of you get too close to these beasts. Even badly wounded, a lasher can kill a man easily. Hopefully, Wamlak and I can finish them with arrows but if not, Mallet and Aberlon, be ready to help."

Aram and Wamlak went back up the road toward the clearing, warned the slaves to be silent, sent Ruben and Semet into the woods with the oxen and then hid behind trees to each side of the road. Aram looked across at Wamlak.

"We'll both aim for the nearest one first then the second—if they come together, the one nearest you first, then the one nearest to me. We want at least one arrow in each of them as quickly as possible." Wamlak nodded that he understood.

Luck was with them. The lashers sprinted into the woods in unsuspecting haste, angry that they had had to come at all, and one was several yards in front of the other.

"Now." Aram said firmly. He and Wamlak stepped into the road and drew down on the leading lasher. In the dusk, the lasher was unable to deflect either missile. Surprised and suddenly injured, he stumbled and crashed sideways into the woods. His companion roared in quick fury and charged the two men, brandishing his sword. Aram and Wamlak sent two more arrows at him. Struck hard, the lasher stumbled but came on. Again, they fired. Aram aimed for the head and his arrow found an eye and pierced the creature's brain. The lasher crumpled, kicking at the rough surface of the road with clawed feet as he died.

Hearing a great commotion from the wood, Aram ran toward where the other lasher had fallen. He found Mallet and Aberlon with their pikes in the fallen beast, straining with their might to keep the giant creature pinned to the earth. Drawing his sword, he hacked at the beast's arms, rendering them useless, then, avoiding its kicking, clawed feet; he drove his sword into its neck and heaved his weight on the hilt until the beast fell still.

There was no time for celebration. The sun, behind the bulk of the mountain, had evidently left the earth, for the sky grew rapidly dark. Aram ordered the men to move the oxen and the slaves north of the clearing into the trees. Then he went down the road for one more look to the south along the darkening road. Nothing moved in the shadowy dusk along the flank of Burning Mountain. He glanced at the sky. It was a clear evening and there would be a moon later.

He rejoined the men and addressed the slaves one last time. "I told you I would grant your freedom. You may go with us or on your own."

None answered.

"Alright. Line up and move along the road toward your homes. There will be a moon after a while and you should find your way easily enough. If ever you decide to escape you may join us in the wild. Now go."

Obediently the workers shuffled in their chains across the clearing and onto the road. Aram watched them trudge from sight. Then he turned to the others.

"There won't be much rest this night. Move the oxen ahead of the men, Dane, in single file along the top of the ridge. I'll lead and Wamlak and Jonwood can bring up the rear. Let's go."

In the deepening night, Aram led them northward through the woods along the top of the ridge. When they came out onto the rocky, brush-covered hills south of the bend in the river that Aram had followed during his escape seven years before, they turned east. An enormous moon came up over the edge of the world and rose into the sky before them.

XXIII

With no trail, the going was rough and moving the oxen was difficult but Aram had also become convinced of their value and considered the trouble and danger inherent in bringing them along to be worth it. By midnight, they had covered a distance of about three miles along the top of ridge. When they found a flat place, Dane tied the oxen in a stand of stout trees and they rested for a few hours until the sky lightened in the east.

They made better time in the daylight and by noon found the trail he and Decius had followed so long ago. When they came to a copse of trees above a long ridge rolling into the south where there was a spring, they again rested. Alred looked at Aram with a mixture of sadness and curiosity.

"Why didn't more of the slaves join us, my lord? I heard what that one man said, but still—why would they choose to remain in such a terrible state?"

Aram glanced at Ruben and Semet resting on the grass before answering. "It really wasn't a matter of choice, Alred. Most of those slaves no longer even understand the concept of choice. They have been in the service of Manon for so long that they are broken. They and their people have no doubt been slaves for generations, time out of mind. They have been reduced to the point where they can't grasp the idea of being free."

The young man looked at Aram anxiously. "Can that happen to us?"

"No." Aram shook his head emphatically. "It can, but it won't. We will resist Manon and we will win."

"Pardon me, my lord, but how do you know for sure that we will win?"

Aram answered him in even tones. "We will win."

Ruben, the freed slave, had been listening and now he interjected. "Why are we going east, sir? You told the others that you lived in the wilds north of the black mountain."

Aram laughed. "Yes, I did. And that's what they will tell their masters as well. It may not divert them for long—it depends on how well they can track us and whether they have anyone among their number who is adept at such things. Although with these oxen we are certainly leaving a trail that is easy to follow.

"My hope is that when they find the bodies and see our tracks going north out of the clearing that they will believe the story we told to the slaves. When they return in force to find us perhaps they will waste time searching the badlands before discovering the truth." He glanced up at the sun and got to his feet. "Let's move on."

When they came to the point where the trail angled off toward the south through the green hills, Aram decided to move the oxen along it in order to make for the better traveling conditions of the plains. If their enemies had managed to track their eastward movement, there was no further need for subterfuge. Speed was more important.

Once he was sure that Dane, Alred, and the oxen would get to Derosa all right, he intended to take Findaen and the rest of the men, go to his city and fetch weapons. The sooner they could accomplish that and start preparing the citizens of Derosa to defend themselves, the better he would feel about everything.

The green hills proved to be as lush a place as they had appeared to him and Decius all those years before. There were acres of tall hardwoods spilling over the rounded hills and filling up the gentle slopes above clear, cold streams. Herds of deer, rabbits and many other creatures bounded through the forests or scurried through the tall grasses of the meadowed bottomlands.

Findaen, walking by Aram, gazed up through the canopy of the trees with a peculiarly wistful look in his eyes. "I remember my father telling of hunting for herbs in these woods when he was a boy before my people were hounded from the plains. My grandfather had a house built entirely of chestnut in Stell, made from logs harvested in these forests." He sighed. "That's all gone, now."

Aram answered him quietly. "You will see the return of those days, my friend, I promise you."

Findaen glanced at him but said nothing.

Four days later, they came within sight of the walls of Derosa and Aram sent Dane and Alred on with the oxen. The rest of them turned north, traversed the green hills again, sleeping at night under the tall trees, crossed the twin rivers, and came back into Aram's valley. As they marched up the main avenue toward the city, Ruben and Semet looked at Aram in awe.

"Are you lord of all this, sir?" Ruben asked.

Before Aram could answer, Mallet laughed aloud. "Not just of this place, my lads—Lord Aram is lord of all the lands that you see."

Aram smiled slightly. "Easy, Mallet. There is far to go before anyone is truly lord of anything in this world."

The sun had gone behind the mountain. Borlus and Hilla watched with apprehension from the mouth of their grotto as the column of men came up to the walls of the city. Aram sent them a comforting, quieting thought and moved his companions on up the stairs, across the broad porch, and settled them in the great hall. He brought deer hides for blankets and stocks of food from his stores.

That night they had a feast, wiping the memory of the previous two weeks' short rations away. Afterward, they discussed their adventure, marveling at the things they'd accomplished. Eventually, attention turned to Ruben and Semet, who told them of their lives far to the south by the great ocean and of their years of bondage. Aram listened in silence as Ruben stated with vehemence how he had always known that someday he and his brother would be free.

Ruben looked around the darkened hall until his eye fell upon Aram. He stood and bowed. "We will be forever grateful, my lord."

Aram nodded. "I am only sorry that you spent so much of your youth in chains. I know what that is like."

The men turned and gazed at him in puzzled amazement. Findaen frowned. "But how could you know what that is like, lord Aram?" He asked.

"Look around you, Findaen." Aram answered. "What do you suppose happened to my people after this city fell? Where did they all go? Manon did what he always does—he slew the men and women and took the children away into slavery. It is his way."

Findaen stared. "You were—?"

"I was a slave as a child." Aram replied and he heard gasps from the circle of men.

"But how did you—?"

"I would not wear his chains." Aram answered simply. "I would not be a slave. I will never submit to that. Now," he said to his gaping companions, "let us sleep, for tomorrow brings stout work."

Using his store of deer hides Aram constructed packs for the men to carry weapons back to Derosa. He missed the horses during this operation. A few horses could have carried munitions for hundreds of men. He decided that he would talk to Florm of this when he saw him next. For the moment, he and the eight others would have to serve as pack animals.

Mallet and Aberlon each carried six of the twelve lances that Aram had made besides dozens of metal spear points that would be attached under Aram's supervision later in Derosa. The other men carried ten swords each, wrapped in deer hides. It wasn't much more than a start but it was a start. They left the city as the sun topped the pine-covered hills to the east.

Borlus watched them go. Aram hesitated and then went over to the bear. He knelt down and looked into the small earnest eyes. "I'm sorry that I haven't been around much, my friend, and I apologize for the all the disturbances. But there are many things which require my attention just now."

The bear studied him for a moment and then answered. His voice was firm and determined. "My people are not great, master. And there are not many of us left in the world. But if I can help you fight the bad one, tell me. Borlus will fight."

Aram stared at him, stunned. "Do you know what this is all about, my friend?"

"All people know, master. All know of the bad one. And all people know that you are the man of hope. I know this, too."

Aram reached out and ruffled the fur behind the bear's ear. "I wish that you didn't know it, Borlus. I wish your life was free of such things."

The bear gazed back at him with devotion shining in his small eyes and was silent. Aram stood.

"I have to go away again for awhile but I will be back before fall. Is there anything I can do for you before I leave, my friend?"

Borlus looked back toward the interior of the grotto. "I must find a bigger place, master, but that is not a thing for you to help."

"A bigger place?" Aram frowned. "Has something happened to this place?"

Borlus looked up at him with pride. "Hilla will have children in the winter."

Aram knelt back down and grinned. "Well, now that is something to celebrate, my friend. I am very happy for you. But why will this place not do?"

"It is too small for a family. We will go to the hills to the north."

Aram frowned. "There is no need for that, my friend. You may move into the city. There are many places there."

Borlus laughed. "Thank you, master, but my people like earth, not rock. We will not go far."

"Okay." Aram smiled at him. "I will look you up when I get back. Go with care, my friend."

"And you, master."

Four days later Aram and the others returned inside the walls of Derosa. Aram was anxious to see Ka'en again but he also felt twinges of uncertainty. The information Findaen had given to him about the designs of Kemul served to complicate the matter. He was not skilled in politics and he knew very little of the history and traditions of these people. Also, there was the simple fact that nothing had ever been declared between himself and Ka'en and they'd not seen each other in a long while.

It was late in the afternoon when they trudged up through the main street of the town, carrying their burdens of steel. Findaen suggested that they put the weaponry away in the armory and have a drink at the pub before getting cleaned up and joining his father for supper. Aram agreed and spent the rest of the afternoon listening to Mallet and Findaen regaling the locals with stories of their adventures in the west.

Aram was given his old room in Lancer's house. After washing and putting on his town clothes, he went down to supper. Ka'en smiled at him as he entered and nodded her head slightly. Kemul was seated to her left as usual, accompanied by another, equally burly young man. The broad-shouldered, blond-haired Kemul scowled at Aram as he sat down across from Lancer.

Lancer bent his aristocratic gray head. "Welcome to my house once again, lord Aram. Findaen has told me in general of what occurred to the west. Perhaps you and I could talk further of these matters tomorrow?"

"Indeed, my lord," Aram answered. "I will be at your disposal. Thank you again for your hospitality."

Out of the corner of his eye, Aram saw a sneer mar Kemul's handsome features at the tenor of this exchange.

"It is nothing, my friend." Lancer's features grew serious. "It grows daily more clear that our welfare is to be in your capable hands."

At this statement, the sneer vanished from Kemul's face. He shifted his weight angrily and scowled down at the table. Aram glanced at him and then at Ka'en, who smiled slightly and looked away. He turned his attention back to Lancer.

"I will be happy to discuss all these matters with you at your convenience, my lord."

Lancer nodded stiffly, aware of the bit of drama playing out to his left, and the meal went on with Mallet telling all those assembled in wonderful detail of how they had slain three enormous lashers and the four overseers and freed two slaves and eight oxen. Aram ate in silence. After supper, Ka'en stood and excused herself.

"Good night, father," she said, and then she looked pointedly at Aram and smiled. "Good night, lord Aram—perhaps I could also place a claim on your time tomorrow?"

Aram stood, his heart suddenly pounding. "It would be an honor, my lady."

She smiled again and left the room.

Kemul exited shortly afterward followed by his burly companion, speaking to no one. Aram glanced at Findaen who simply shrugged. Lancer excused himself then and shortly there was only Findaen, his friends and Aram left at the table. Findaen glanced around, checking to see who remained, and then addressed Aram.

"Dane tells me that we have about three weeks with which to train before most of the men have to attend to their crops, my lord. Will that be enough time to accomplish anything?"

"Certainly," Aram said. "We can gather ironwood and put some of your best craftsmen to work making pikes while those who are suited to using swords—at least seventy of them at a time—can begin practicing." He looked down the table at Wamlak. "We'll need to gather enough ironwood to start making bows as well—and arrows. We can teach men the basics and they can practice through the winter."

He looked around at those remaining at the table. All of the men who'd been with him in the west were there except for Ruben and Semet, who were lodged in a room above the tavern. Besides Findaen and his companions, there were also three elders of the town, Lestar Hayesh and his brother, Rayj, cousins of Lancer, and Wamlak's father, Donnick, a tall, dark, and solemn man.

"If we are not molested before winter—and I think now that we will not be—the horses will come in the spring and we can begin creating an armed force that can take the field against Manon. In the meantime, we need to make as many weapons as possible and begin the training of men in their basic uses. In the spring, I will have the horses bring enough swords to arm every man in Derosa."

Jonwood leaned forward. "How will we know which men suit which weapons?"

"Trial and error." Aram answered. "Let every man take a shot with the bow and see which ones have talent. Some men will be more comfortable with pikes and lances, whether they are mounted or not, and some—like Mallet—won't want to be mounted under any circumstances." He raised a cautionary finger. "Every man, however, will be issued a sword as his most basic weapon and be expected to gain a certain proficiency with it. Those gathered at this table will need to learn quickly so that you can teach others."

Donnick spoke thoughtfully. "Young Kemul is a very good swordsman. He is not here now but perhaps he could be persuaded to serve as a teacher."

Aram glanced at Findaen who simply frowned down at the table, and then he looked back at Donnick. He nodded slowly. "That is a good idea. Anyone who can help the men get up to speed quickly in basic skills should help."

It was getting late and Aram wanted to be alone. He stood. "Alright then, first thing tomorrow morning, the men should be assembled on the open area near the road south of the town and we'll begin. Good night."

In the morning, seven hundred men of the town gathered in the street. Findaen ordered them into groups and marched them south into the grassy field. Kemul did not show, so Aram set Wamlak to helping each man discover whether he had talent with a bow while he instructed everyone else in the basic use of a sword. Mallet and Aberlon he sent with four others to search the river bottom for ironwood suitable for making pikes and lances.

The morning wore away and just before noon a man came from Lancer requesting Aram's presence at lunch. He told Findaen to send everyone into town to find refreshment with instructions to return in two hours. Then he went into town himself, climbed to his room and cleaned up and went down to the hall. Lancer was alone. Not even Findaen was with him. With regret, Aram saw that Ka'en was also absent.

He bowed. "Good day, my lord."

"Hello, lord Aram. Please, be seated." The elderly Prince seemed distracted and kept silent until the meal was served. "Shut the door," he told the servants as they left the room.

Aram waited, eating in silence while the old man pushed his food around the plate with his fork. Finally, Lancer looked up.

"I am not a warrior, Aram. I never have been. None of my people are good at war."

Aram gazed back at him and slowly shook his head. "No one should have to be good at war, my lord. It's not what the Maker intended."

"That is not the point." Lancer said in sudden irritation and then seemed to immediately regret his behavior. "I apologize, lord Aram. I am getting old and I'm afraid that the times are moving beyond me, that's all."

Aram allowed the expression on his face show that he was not offended and waited in silence. The older man sighed and nodded.

"I am getting old, Aram. I feel it." He looked into Aram's eyes. "I want to know that my people will be alright when I am gone."

"You have a fine son, my lord. Findaen will do well."

Lancer shook his head. "It doesn't work like that. The governance of my people descends through the female line. It always has. I became Prince when I married the eldest daughter of Ralphon of Stell. Whoever marries Ka'en will become Prince of Wallensia—that is the proper name of this land—when I am gone."

Aram felt his heart jump but remained silent. Lancer held his gaze for a long moment.

"Lord Aram, you seem to know much of the history of the ancient world." The old Prince let the statement hang in the air between them. Aram wasn't sure whether it was meant to be a statement or a question. He nodded slowly.

"I was told most of what I know by a reliable source—someone who was there at the end of the last great war. He is the lord of horses; his name is Florm. From him I have a general idea of how the world came to be as it is."

Lancer shook his head sadly. "We know very little. The history of my people is limited and does not spring from deep in the depths of the well of time. Before the coming of the tyranny of Manon, we were simple farmers for as long as anyone can remember—time out of mind.

"We had heard the ancient stories of Manon, Kelven, and Ferros—and of the great king Jogdan. But we thought them to be little more than myth based upon scattered shreds of someone else's history. Nothing had ever touched us. Then Manon came and we knew that there was more to the ancient stories than tales told over drink at night by old men. Now, danger crouches at our very door.

"We always thought that we were fighting alone—fighting against a foe we had never seen, whose servants behaved mercilessly but one that, ultimately, when he'd gained enough, might let us be. When word came of the host that was marching against us last fall, I saw our end coming upon us and I despaired. I prepared my people to die upon the thresholds of their houses.

"And then you came upon the field like a warrior out of legend. You scattered and routed the forces of the enemy and frustrated his will. You saved my people. I believe that now it must fall to you to guide and protect them forever." The lines of the Prince's face set. "I must know, my lord Aram—who are you?"

Aram returned his gaze steadily. He was gladdened to see the depth of concern the old man felt for his people. Any people with such a governor could not be easily lost. He smiled. "His name is Joktan."

Lancer raised his eyebrows in confusion. "Pardon me, my lord?"

"The great king in the stories—and they are true, by the way—his name is Joktan. I am a son of his line."

"I am not surprised." Lancer said. "I think I could have guessed it. So he really did defeat Manon long ago and give the world an age of peace?"

It was Aram's turn to be astonished. "Is that what your legends say?"

"Yes." Lancer answered and he frowned at Aram's look of surprise. "Why? Is it not so?"

It occurred to Aram then that different parts of the world might have diverse understandings of the events of the days of Joktan, especially if they weren't directly involved in those events. Lancer's people—all the people of the southern plains, in fact—might have no direct knowledge of what had happened on the high plains around Rigar Pyrannis or in the meeting of Kelven and Manon. Their legends of those events would be vulgarized, just as Joktan's name had been. He shook his head.

"No, my lord. That is not what happened. Manon slew Joktan in single combat in the last great battle when the forces of men were destroyed.

It was Kelven that reduced Manon—at the cost of his own life—and gave the world an age—a wild age—of relative peace."

Lancer stared at him. "So Kelven really is dead?"

"Yes."

"And your ancestor did not defeat Manon?"

"He defeated his armies, certainly, several times, but not Manon himself. Manon cannot be defeated by force of arms. It must be done another way."

Lancers eyes grew wide and troubled. "And now we do not have Kelven to aid us. What will you do?"

"I will find that other way."

"Do you have any ideas—or access to any secret knowledge that might aid you in this?"

"No."

Lancer leaned across the table toward him. His hands trembled. "You do not know how to defeat Manon." It was statement but he wanted verification. Aram met his gaze and shook his head.

"I do not. Not yet."

Lancer stared down at his plate in silence and began picking at his food with his fork. "I am a good administrator, Aram, even an engineer of sorts. In my time I have kept my people alive and fed even as we lost access to our best lands. I have designed and built roads. I even improved this town—its structures and its infrastructure." He looked up. "I am a good administrator."

"I believe you, my lord."

"But I am not a man of war, Aram. War requires a different sort of man than I am. It requires a man of steel and fire who can kill and is skilled at killing, and who does not hesitate in his work even when the field around him is covered in blood." He shook his head slowly and deliberately. "I am not that man. You are that man."

"I do not like war any more than you do, my lord. No man should."

"No, but you are a man who knows how to wage it. And war is coming, is it not?"

"It is already upon us."

"Yes, it is. I have seen that it is so." There was deep sadness in Lancer's voice. "Soon the whole world will be aflame with its fire. And it is a war that we do not know how to win."

"There is a way, my lord, I believe it, and I will discover it."

The old Prince gazed at him without expression. "Is it even remotely possible for us to negotiate for peace?"

Aram sighed. "If it were possible, I would do it. But Manon does not need to negotiate, nor does he mean to. He means to enslave the whole world. And his strength grows daily toward that end. No, my lord, our only choices are to fight or to submit to his chains. I will not submit to chains."

Tears erupted from Lancer's eyes and his hand trembled as he laid down his fork. He hung his head and Aram watched in awkward discomfort as the gray-haired Prince gave himself over to grief. He did not know what to do, so he waited in silence. The Prince sobbed quietly but his chest heaved with the force of his emotion. Finally, Lancer wiped his eyes and raised his head.

"I'm sorry, lord Aram."

"No, my lord—I understand. How may I help?"

Lancer sighed deeply and wiped his sleeve across his face. "I always hoped, even when we were finally pushed from our ancestral homes out on the plains and had to fall back behind the walls of Derosa that, if we could not prevail, we might at least delay the inevitable. That we might push back defeat for a generation or two.

"When I saw the might that was arrayed against us last fall, I knew that such was not the case. I knew that we had come to the brink. And now we know that the armies of the enemy are gathering in force less than a hundred miles from our gates."

The old man seemed to diminish in size. Even his eyes, as he looked up at Aram, seemed to droop. His voice was thick with emotion. "I cannot bear the thought of my daughters and my son dead in the very cream of their youth, or bound in the evil chains of slavery. I cannot bear it."

Aram leaned across the table and grasped the old man's hand with a firm grip. He spoke evenly. "That will not happen, my lord, I promise you."

"You will take them away, beyond Manon's reach?"

"If necessary, yes. But I intend to destroy Manon before his reach extends across the breadth of the whole world."

Lancer blinked his eyes and spoke with an edge of bitterness in his voice. "But you admitted that you did not know how."

Aram released his hold on the old man's arm but held his gaze. "I told you once of Kelven's Riddle."

"Yes, I had never heard of it."

Aram nodded. "That's because Kelven left the knowledge of it only with the lords of the horses. It tells of a man who comes into the world and finds a mighty weapon. A weapon that I believe is the key to defeating Manon. I intend to discover what he meant. I intend to find the weapon."

"Are you the man the riddle speaks of then?"

"I don't know. The horses think so." Aram pushed his plate away and spoke earnestly. "It doesn't matter, my lord, whether I am the man or not."

Lancer frowned. "I don't understand."

"Look—the horses think that the riddle is a prophecy of some kind. I don't. I think it is exactly what it is described as being—a riddle. No one can see the future, not even Kelven. No one can foresee the birth of a particular man thousands of years hence and say what that man is going to do. Only the Maker can foreknow such a thing—and that is because He can say what will be and then bring it to pass. But even He, I believe, does not manipulate time.

"Time moves in one direction only—forward. And no one, not even the gods, can visit the future. I don't think that Kelven was trying to foretell the future; I think that he was trying to impart information to the right sort of man, whenever that man came along." He tapped the table pointedly with a stiff forefinger. "My lord, I think Kelven left a weapon somewhere on the earth—one that can destroy Manon. I just need to solve the clues in the riddle and find it. And I'm going to."

Lancer nodded slowly and seemed to regain his composure. "That makes sense. But if it's true, the weapon must be found soon. And you believe that you can do it?"

"Yes." Aram answered. "I can."

"Will there be enough time?"

"My lord that is why we must raise and equip an army. We must draw a line upon the earth that we can defend until I find the answer to the riddle."

"Then do so with my blessing, lord Aram. All that I control is at your disposal." The old man reached across and touched his arm. "Please, protect my family."

"I will, my lord. Do not fear for them."

At that moment, footsteps sounded in the hall and the door swung wide. Findaen stepped inside the dining hall. Aram stood. Findaen glanced at his father and then addressed Aram. "The men are ready, my lord."

"I'm coming." He hesitated for just a moment. He wanted to ask about Ka'en and her plans for the day but then decided it wasn't the time. He bowed to Lancer. "Have a better afternoon, my lord."

Lancer stood and returned the courtesy. "Thank you, lord Aram, for everything."

Aram turned and followed Findaen out of the house and down through the town to the training grounds.

For a week, the men trained every day from early morning until supper with a break at lunch. During this time, Aram only saw Ka'en at the evening meal, and Kemul was invariably present, doing his best to monopolize her attention. Increasingly, two other young men who never showed up for weapons practice joined him at supper.

Every evening, at the end of the meal, Ka'en stood and pointedly smiled at Aram and rendered a pleasant, "Goodnight, my lord", but Aram, miserably, knew of nothing better to do than to stand himself and say, "Goodnight, my lady." His aching need to see her and speak with her— spend time with her—grew daily in intensity and was never met.

Finally, at the end of the week, when he'd scheduled a day of rest for the men on the next day, he followed her out into the corridor after the evening meal.

"Lady Ka'en."

She turned slightly and looked at him with an unreadable expression.

He spread his hands. "May I see you tomorrow?"

She smiled—tiredly, he thought—and nodded. "I would like that."

"We aren't working tomorrow—we have a strategy meeting in the morning but that's all that is planned. Perhaps we could have lunch together?"

She inclined her head again. "I'll cook for you." Her eyes looked past him and clouded. He turned. Kemul and his friends stood in the hall, preparing to depart. Kemul's eyes, like flat discs of cold steel, met Aram's for a moment, and then he looked at Ka'en standing beyond.

"Goodnight, Ka'en," he said. He used no title, just her name.

She nodded at him silently. He gave Aram another hard look and then he and his companions went out into the night. Aram looked back at Ka'en. She smiled.

"Tomorrow then, my lord."

"Tomorrow, my lady," he agreed, and he felt a frown descend over his brow as he watched her ascend the stairs. "Goodnight."

XXIV

Kemul came to the morning strategy session along with four other men, two of whom were his usual companions and two others who were unknown to Aram. Lancer was there as well but left the management of the meeting to Findaen and Aram. Findaen stood and looked around the table.

"I'm very pleased to report that all the men are becoming familiar with the use of a sword; there are about two hundred that show some measure of skill with a bow and a hundred and fifty, more or less, that show a propensity for the pike. Next week, lord Aram wants to start training the men to maneuver in units.

"Now, we need to start thinking about officers. Obviously, those of us here will serve in such capacity but we'll need men with leadership skills to serve as officers of the smaller groups. Watch for such men as they train. Lord Aram thinks we should begin drilling the men in units of tens—ten, fifty, one hundred, and so on. Any thoughts?"

Kemul leaned forward with a sneer on his broad face. "It seems to me that 'lord Aram' is doing an awful lot of thinking for all of us. Are the men of Derosa no more than sheep?"

He let the words fall like a challenge. There was a stunned silence that stretched out. Around the table, the others looked at each other and then at Aram. Aram said nothing. Kemul indicated him with his hand and went on.

"Before this man came—a man that none of us know anything about—there were no armies that came against us. How do we know that this man is our ally? He wanders in out of the wild and we place our fortunes in his hands. What kind of sense does that make? It seems to me that we should be negotiating with Manon instead of preparing to follow this 'lord' to our doom."

Aram looked at him. "You cannot negotiate with someone who is bent on your destruction, Kemul," he said reasonably. "It would be folly to try."

Kemul went red in the face. "Are you calling me a fool?"

"No," Aram shook his head. "I don't know you well enough. I'm simply telling you that Manon won't negotiate with those whom he thinks are rightfully his subjects."

"So you say," Kemul snarled. "But perhaps it would be better to be his subjects than yours."

Aram shook his head again. "I don't have—nor do I want—subjects. We're talking about freedom here. War with Manon will come to our part of the world whatever we do. War or slavery. We fight or we accept his chains. Those are our choices. There are no others."

Kemul leaned forward, his voice thick with bitter anger. "Again—so you say. We don't know the truth of any part of what you say. In fact, how do we know that you are not in league with him?"

Aram jumped to his feet in sudden fury, but Lancer intervened, waving him back to his chair. He turned to Kemul. "These are difficult times, Kemul. I understand your feelings. But we know lord Aram's qualities and we trust him. Let us all work together in this matter. You are a leader, yourself—lend your strengths to your people."

Kemul stared down at the table, his face dark with anger, but he went silent. Lancer's careful words seemed to have found a mark. After a few moments, Findaen got back to his feet. "Alright," he said, "today is a day of rest for everyone. Just remember—as we train, watch your men for signs of those qualities that might mark them as potential captains." He took a deep breath. "I'm buying drinks at the pub for anybody that wants one." He looked at Aram. "Are you coming, my lord?"

Aram nodded and got to his feet. He was not surprised by Kemul's dislike of him but he had been taken aback by its virility and openness. He glanced at the thickset man, who did not look at him, and then accompanied Findaen to the tavern. They got their customary table at the back and Findaen ordered drinks. He looked at Aram.

"I'm sure you know what that was really about, my lord. Do you want to talk about it?"

Aram glanced around at the men, Jonwood, Wamlak, Mallet, and Alred. He shrugged but shook his head and turned his attention to his drink. "Probably not right now."

He sat silently while the others discussed the qualities of the various soldiers under their training.

A little before noon, Findaen and Aram left the others and went back up the street toward Lancer's house. Aram was excited about the prospect of spending time with Ka'en and had put the earlier incident with Kemul from his mind but as they came into the broad courtyard before the main door, Kemul and his two companions stepped forward from beneath the trees at the side. Kemul had a long, broad sword in his hand. He stopped in front of Aram and pointed the weapon at his chest.

"I claim the right of duel," he said.

Seeing the murderous intent in the man's eyes, Aram reached instinctively for his sword.

Findaen stepped between them, his eyes wide in shock. "What is the meaning of this?"

Kemul glanced at him and then slid his gaze back to Aram. "Step aside, Findaen, this has nothing to do with you. I claim the right of duel with this man—it is my right under the ancient laws of our people."

Keeping his sword down but watching Kemul, Aram addressed Findaen. "What is this right of duel that he speaks of?"

Kemul stepped forward and roughly shoved Findaen to one side with the broad blade of his weapon. "I'll tell you what it is, usurper. It is my right under the laws of our land to remove any threat to my claims of ascension and of marriage."

Aram's eyes hardened. "So this has to do with the lady Ka'en."

"With Ka'en, yes," Kemul nodded and his sneer broadened. "But also with all Wallensia—and because I think you are a danger to us—an enemy."

Aram studied the man, trying to check his rising anger and at the same time find words that would turn the situation toward more reasonable discourse. "Your people have an enemy, Kemul—and so do I. It's Manon. We should be fighting him together, not fighting each other."

Kemul's face reddened and he took another step forward and shouted at Aram. "I don't want to hear any more of your lies, usurper. You don't belong here—we don't need you controlling the simpleminded among us and confusing Ka'en."

Aram raised the tip of his sword. "*The lady* Ka'en can make up her own mind about things. There is no point in my killing you, Kemul."

Kemul grinned savagely. "You don't want to kill me then, *my lord*?"

"No."

"Then I shall kill you." Kemul's steel slid suddenly forward in a flash. It was immediately obvious that the man was skilled in the use of a blade. Aram was just able to move aside at the last moment before the steel pierced his belly. Still, the blade caught him in the left side of his body, cutting a deep gash and careening off a rib. Aram stumbled and went to his knees.

"Die, you bastard." Kemul snarled. He raised his sword for a killing stroke.

There was an odd sound from above. Aram looked up. Ka'en was standing on the balcony of her father's house, looking down upon the scene. Her lovely brown eyes had gone very wide and her hands were over her mouth in an expression of shock and horror.

Kemul saw his chance in Aram's distraction. He swung his heavy sword in a high vicious arc, bringing it scything down toward Aram's head. Quickly, Aram brought his sword up to fend off the savage blow, but the man's arm was powerful. Kemul's blade clanged against Aram's, driving it downward.

The man was strong and skilled with a blade. At the end of its stroke, Kemul's sword ricocheted off the side of Aram's head and slashed into the top of his left shoulder. Intense bursts of light flashed behind Aram's eyes and there was an explosion of pain in his upper arm.

But, with the pain, came the old familiar eruption of cold fury. Everything vanished from Aram's mind but the intent to kill. As always, the inner fury focused him—made him quick and deadly despite the injury to his head and shoulder. Kemul did not recognize his peril. He swung his sword upward again, meaning to finish his rival in one tremendous down stroke. Before the stout man could bring his steel to bear, Aram rose from his knees, centered his blade, and stabbed upward with his might. The sharp point of his sword entered Kemul's body below the ribs and sawed upward, rending bone and sinew and turning his vital organs to mush.

Aram wrenched his sword from the man's body and stood up to strike again but Kemul was already finished. His broad, handsome face bore a look of overwhelming pain and shock. His arms automatically continued their swinging motion but the heavy sword fell away from his hands.

He went to his knees then as his arms fell limp at his sides and watched in dying fascination as his guts tumbled out of the open cavity that had suddenly appeared in his chest and abdomen. Blood gushed out in a savage flood and soaked the ground around him.

He looked up at Aram in surprise, his mouth hanging open. Then his eyes went flat and he crumpled backward over his legs in a heap. In his fury, Aram callously wiped the gore from his sword on the dead man's clothes. There was another sound from above. Remembering Ka'en, he looked up.

Ka'en was slumped against the railing of the balcony with her hands over her mouth and her eyes wide in horror and streaming tears. Aram's sudden fury subsided in a wave of sickening anguish as he stared up at her. The expression on her face as she looked from him to Kemul and back again made him go cold as death inside. It was as if she were gazing upon the vile business of hell being accomplished and Aram was its executor.

He looked down upon the ruin he'd made of Kemul and then focused his attention on the dead man's companions. They moved back in fear. He glanced at Findaen. Findaen seemed stunned and stared back at him open-mouthed and with rounded eyes. A terrible anger filled the cold emptiness in Aram. His hard gaze swept around at all of them. He did not dare to look up again at Ka'en and see the horror and revulsion registered there.

But then she made another small, odd sound and he heard her move. He looked up just as she turned away and fled into the house. The thought came that she could no longer bear to look upon him after what he had just done and that thought finished him.

His fierce, defensive anger erupted into words. "So instead of fighting Manon, we're killing each other. These are your laws?"

He slid his sword back into its scabbard and turned harshly to Findaen. "You called me a barbarian once, Findaen. Let me tell you something—with laws like this that allow for the killing of your own citizens—you people are the barbarians, not me. You're lucky that I am not lord of these lands. I would alter many things."

Findaen gazed back at him in stunned surprise. Aram glanced upward one more time. Ka'en was gone and had not returned. He realized then the terrible thing that had just been wrought in his life by the killing of this man. She could no longer bear to look upon him for she could see him for what he really was—a vicious killer. And there was another thought, one that brought him an even larger measure of agony—that maybe, in truth, she had really loved the man he'd just slain.

He took two steps backward, reeling from the horrible understanding that all his hopes had just died with the killing of one foolish man. He felt sick. He gazed with hardened eyes at the men surrounding him and the still-bleeding mess he'd made of Kemul and suddenly he despised them all. "But I am not lord of anything—only my valley. I am going back now. Let me never see any of you again."

He heard Findaen gasp at these words but he didn't look at him. Without another word, he turned and strode blindly down the street and out of the town, leaving behind him a shocked and stunned populace. No one followed.

The guard at the gate moved to open it for him but he kicked it open with his boot and went through and out into the hard sunshine of the open plain. A mile beyond, he turned off the river road and crashed up the hillside through the trees toward the top of the long ridge.

The pain and soreness in his head, side and shoulder increased throughout the afternoon but he went on, ignoring the possibility of infection and continued climbing up the long ridge in a blinding fog of heartache and anger. Sunset caught him near the camp he and the horses had used the year before, but still he went on, into the night.

He topped the ridge about noon on the second day and went down toward the river. His soul was filled with anguish and sickness. Night caught him before he came to the stream. When he reached the riverbank, he didn't go eastward to look for the crossing in the pale light of the moon but plunged directly into the dark, quick current. He no longer cared if he lived or died.

He crossed the second river in the same way and carelessly climbed the steep cliffs beyond in the waning depths of the night, coming above the rim just as the sky lightened in the east. The pain in his soul grew. There was no chance now that he and Ka'en would ever mean anything to each other. He'd slaughtered the man that, for all he knew, she'd intended to marry. He had cut him down like an animal as she watched.

Morning found him in the valley five miles from the city. His legs trembled from the unceasing exertion and his lungs burned with every shuddering gasp but he kept on. When he came into the orchard, he collapsed onto his face in the grass, exhausted and soul-sick. Darkness crept over him and he slept through most of the day.

When he awoke, the sun had dropped below the great mountain. He went up and sat on the bottom step of the south stairway. Only then did it occur to him that he'd not seen Borlus or Hilla. He gazed around the valley in the failing light but could see no sign of them anywhere. Neither

Willet nor Cree were visible in the sky but since he didn't want to talk to anyone anyway, he let it go.

That night, he slept in his room below the tower. He spent the next few days wandering the valley near the city, looking for Borlus and Hilla. But it was only for the purpose of distraction. Always, he could see Ka'en's lovely face before him, staring at him in horrified realization of the kind of man he was. He could not shake it. He tried to reason with himself but to no avail. The fear that he'd lost any chance with her forever pervaded all.

He needed to do something. He needed action that would distract his mind from its pain and harden his aching heart. Most of his crops were two or three weeks away from maturity and he was tired of farming anyway—and of farmers. He decided to make more weapons.

First, he used up his stock on hand, making seventeen pikes and forty-two lances, another bow and more than a hundred arrows, then he went into the foothills and collected more green stock and stacked it in the granary to dry. That process used up five days and still he was unbearably miserable. His thoughts turned then to the field from which he'd escaped all those years before.

There were lashers there that he could kill, or that could kill him—it didn't really matter to him now—and at least one overseer. He no longer cared about the slaves—they could do as they pleased once their masters were gone. And there was a practical side. Combined with the actions taken against the logging operation earlier in the year, Manon might be further convinced that he had troubles nearer to hand than Derosa.

It would buy Ka'en time. Though she would never love him, he still loved her—all the more desperately now that she was beyond his reach forever. He gathered his weapons, one pike, one lance, two swords, and a bow, with arrows, and provisions for several days. Then he went through the tunnel in the mountain below the tower, coming out into the jumbled foothills above the broad slope that looked down upon the distant fields of his servitude.

He camped that night beneath a tall jagged spire of rock in a cluster of pungent brush. During the afternoon's trek he'd encountered two of the serpents with the odd diamond markings like the one he'd killed below Cree's nest so he slept curled up on a rock above the level of the ground.

The next morning, he angled to the northwest as he went, intending to intersect the dike cutting into the slope from the west that eventually became the main ridge separating the fields where he once worked from his old sleeping quarters. It took two more days of picking his way around clumped piles of jumbled rock and through thick stands of the pungent, prickly brush to gain the dike.

There were lots of small, furry creatures that inhabited the rough tangles of the slope and snakes were plentiful. He was glad to reach the higher ground where there were fewer rocks and more soil, grasses, and trees. Once on the dike, he went quickly to the west throughout most of the third day, traveling more cautiously as it became the ridge that separated the broken hills above the fields on the left and the round valley containing the slaves' sleeping quarters on the right.

Late in the afternoon, he eased through a small stand of trees and out onto a brush-covered promontory where he could look down into the valley that contained the fields. It had been planted with a grain crop of some kind—wheat perhaps, or barley that was just beginning to ripen. There were no workers in the fields.

He slipped to the north and made his way across the top of the ridge and looked down into the round valley containing the habitations. Here, a surprise confronted him. During the time of his servitude there had been a single row of huts along the eastern side of the assembling ground. There was much more now.

Now, there was a walled village, with dozens of huts, a granary, and a main street leading diagonally out of a central square to a large double gate on the northwest corner. There were guard towers on two of the other corners—one over on the northeast by the stream that came out from the hills, flowed under a bridge near the main gate, and plunged into the canyon beyond. The other tower was on the southwest where the access road cut through the ridge toward the fields.

And there were women and children. It had become a sizeable village in his absence. Eight years had made a difference in Manon's commitment to this operation. In the center of the square stood a large house with a flat rooftop and high railing on all sides. A very fat man, probably an overseer, and a thin, bony woman lay naked on a bed in the middle of the rooftop.

Aram turned away in disgust from the sight of what they did there and examined the rest of the village. There was a lasher on each of the guard towers, though neither was overtly involved in keeping watch. One was leaning languidly over the railing of his tower, watching the villagers below. The other, nearest to Aram, sat in a corner of his tower gnawing on a pile of bones. This was another item of interest. During his time there had been three lashers; now, though he studied the village and its surrounding environs for some time, he could see only the two.

There were not many villagers in sight, only a few women cooking evening meals, a half dozen men sitting outside their huts, and three small children playing in a puddle of muddy water. Aram slipped down the ridge through the brush and trees until both lashers were in range of an accurate shot from his bow. Standing up and leaning against the trunk of a tree, he drew back his bow and targeted the nearest lasher.

One of the most basic of human urges stopped him. Curiosity. He released the pressure off the string and lowered his bow. There was time, and he could kill these monsters at will. He no longer feared a mere pair of lashers; especially when there was enough distance between them to allow him to deal with them one at a time.

But there were things he wanted to investigate first. How was this village managed? How many people inhabited it? Was there just the one overseer? And there was the surrounding countryside. He knew very little of this part of his world and it would be advantageous to explore it now before he raised a ruckus in the village below.

He watched the villagers until the sun rested on the hills to the west, then he went back up the ridge to the east until he found a spring. There was a large patch of sweetroot growing on the hillside above the spring, so, even though it was not the finest fare, he would not lack for food. He was tired, physically and mentally, so he curled up in a copse of trees east of the spring and slept.

The next morning, he went northward through the narrow valley, waded across a shallow place in the small river and entered the hills beyond. There was grass in abundance on these hills but very little vegetation of any other kind except for the pungent gray brush. The soil was soft and sandy and the outcroppings of rock that jutted up along the spines of the ridges crumbled under pressure from his fingers.

The deeply eroded, jumbled hills seemed to go on forever. Every time he crested a ridge, there was another one beyond, further but just a bit higher. And, as he gained altitude, there were scattered trees that grew thicker the deeper he penetrated the sandy hills. Short, stubby, and ravaged by an apparent lack of water, they were pungent like the brush that was interspersed among them.

Finally, several miles north of the village, he topped a ridge beyond which the sandy hills fell away toward a broad valley through which a wide shining river trended from northeast to southwest. It evidently had its origin in the distant mountains that lay to the north of his own valley. Keeping to the ridge tops, Aram descended throughout the morning and by the time the sun stood overhead, looked out across the wide valley from the vantage point of the lowest hilltop. As he gazed across the valley with its coiling, meandering river he saw that, running through its center, there was an ancient road.

To his right, the valley cut a broad swath between its surrounding hills as it went toward the northeast until eventually the distant mountains swallowed it up and the hills far off in that direction took on the green hue of timber. About a mile along, in a bend of the river, were strewn the ruins of an ancient town.

To the west, on his left, the valley broadened and its floor was deep in grass. Two or three miles away in that direction, Aram saw the telltale squares of yellowish green that indicated the ripening of summer wheat. Near those distant fields, tucked up against the flanks of the hills, was another village. The edge, at least for the moment, of Manon's empire. Even at that distance, Aram could tell that this village, also, was walled.

Out on the plains of his youth, there was never a need for walls. Except for the great marsh, which only the very foolish would enter, there had been no place to run. But here, on the border of the wild lands, Manon had to cage his slaves. Aram wondered idly if his own escape had engendered that result. More likely, as his empire grew and the frontiers expanded, Manon had simply found the need for more oppressive measures to control his subjects.

On Aram's right, far beyond the place where the valley merged with the hills north of his valley, tall, gray mountains marched away into the far northern reaches of the world, piling up to impressive heights. To the west, the valley broadened toward the distant plains. And to the north, far beyond the hills that tumbled up across the valley, away over the rim of the world, dark smoke rose up and blackened the distant sky.

He turned around and ascended to the south back up the sandy hills until he reached the top of the main ridge, then turned west, intending to come out on the road in the canyon below the village. Sunset caught him still on the ridge a half mile north of the village. He ate a cold supper of jerked deer meat, laid his weapons at his side and stretched out on his back in the grass, gazing up into the vault of the heavens as the sky deepened through all the hues of blue toward black. Tired from the many days of incessant travel, he slept.

In the morning, he went on to the west for about an hour, until he came out above the bridge over the stream where the dirt road that came up the south side of the long valley forked at the bottom of the canyon. One tangent went to his left—southeast up the steep-sided little canyon toward the village of his servitude—and the other angled away toward the village that lay on the opposite side of the broad valley. This long, wide valley, then, was the one that had lain at his back as he was trundled from the plains all those years before in the vile gloom of the wagon.

He went down to the road and turned southeast up the canyon toward the village, moving cautiously. There had not been any rain for some time so he couldn't be certain, but it appeared that there had recently been traffic on the road. At midmorning, he rounded the canyon's last bend and looked into the little round valley with its walled village. The river turned sharply and ran at right angles to the road beneath a bridge at the entrance to the valley. The gates of the village were just beyond the bridge.

The gates were closed and from his hiding place in the brush between the stream and the road he could see both guard towers. A lasher was on each. The fat overseer was outside the wall to the north, to his left, seated on a chair near the stream. He was watching a group of men from the village construct something of stone by the water's edge. The lasher on the northeastern tower was also watching this group.

He studied the situation. He did not care about the overseer—he could kill him easily—but he had to be sure of his plans for the lashers. There was a small tributary creek that angled into the larger stream just below the bridge. It flowed out of the south, from the ridge that separated this valley from the fields, and meandered northward across the west end of the little valley. Along the whole of its length, it was bordered by thick willows. It would bring him into the foothills of the ridge near where the road cut through it to the south.

He went down and waded the larger stream at the bottom of a long pool and then crept along the meandering creek under the cover of willows until he had passed the village and came to the base of the ridge. Then he moved eastward through the rocks and brush at the base of the slope until he could see the southwest tower with its lasher.

He decided to kill that lasher first, and then deal with the other as he either came out of the gates onto the level ground or crossed the village to check on his fellow guard. Moving cautiously, Aram found some high ground on level with the tower that had cover and was within arrow shot of the guard tower.

The lasher's back was to him. He counted the arrows in his quiver. There were fourteen. If he could get in a lucky shot with this first lasher, maybe hit something vital right away, he could finish him at a distance, using perhaps no more than three or four arrows. That would give him time to quickly deploy down the slope to level ground, lay his lances and swords to one side and by firing his missiles rapidly, kill the other lasher as he charged across the hundred yards or so of open ground.

He leaned against a small tree on the crest of a small corrugation in the slope and drew back his bow. The lasher was still facing away from him towards the interior of the village and Aram realized that this was problematic. He knew very little about the backside of a lasher's physique. If he struck shallow bone that kept his arrow from penetrating, it would be a lost shot. And he couldn't afford lost shots. There were no arrows to waste. He had to get the lasher to turn around.

He wedged a rock from the loose soil of the hillside and tossed it down toward the middle of the road that bisected the ridge to his right. It landed with a thump and rolled into the brush beyond the track, rustling the dried leaves there. Instantly, the lasher turned and came over to the low wall of the tower and peered down.

Aram drew back his bow to its limit and studied the lasher for the best shot. He knew from experience that the eye was a weak point for the great beasts, but the lasher was a good thirty yards from him. He could not risk having his first shot strike the broad forehead bones or one of the horns and risk accomplishing nothing more than raising the alarm. He had to do some serious damage with his first arrow.

He decided to aim for the upper torso just below the neck. He steadied himself while the lasher moved slowly along the wall of the turret until it reached the corner and paused. In that instant, Aram released his arrow and was pleased to hear, a moment later, the satisfying sound of the steel tip thunking deeply and solidly into prodigious flesh.

The lasher grunted, staggered slightly, and looked down at the slender cylinder of wood protruding suddenly and offensively from his chest.

Then, instinctively, he looked up at the slope from whence it came. Aram already had another flying toward him. The second arrow pierced the great chest just below the first.

The lasher howled in pain and leapt over the wall, charging toward the stand of small trees where Aram stood. There was no point in any further attempt at concealment. Aram stepped out with one arrow nocked and another at the ready in his bow hand and sent them quickly on their way. Both found their mark.

The lasher stumbled as it reached the base of the slope and gaped up at Aram as it tried to scrabble up toward him. The beast was close enough now and was slowed by pain and loss of blood. Aram nocked a fifth arrow, leaned forward and sent it into the lasher's left eye. The great beast made a low rumbling sound deep in its throat, pawed its face with one clawed hand, and collapsed.

Aram spun and slid down the slope to his left with all his weaponry to prepare for the second lasher's imminent attack. When he reached the level, he laid the pike and the lance down on the ground to his right and the swords and the quiver with the remaining arrows to his left. Then he nocked an arrow, holding another with two fingers of his bow hand, drew the string back with his right until the ironwood groaned, and waited.

There was a great commotion inside the village. Over by the stream, the overseer topped the rise, gazed quizzically at the gates, and then saw Aram standing in the meadow below the ridge and a little further on, the first lasher writhing in the throes of dying agony. He turned and sprinted clumsily toward the gates just as they crashed open.

Aram felt his blood freeze.

Two lashers—not one—came charging out of the enclosure and immediately made for the man standing alone out in the open. Aram had no idea where the third lasher had come from. For one moment, he considered running. But that idea collapsed beneath the weight of its own hopelessness and the raw force of the sudden fury that rose in him. All the bitterness and heartache of the last several days coalesced into a terrible anger.

He dropped to a knee and drew down on the lasher on the right, which was closer to him than the other by a step. He sent two arrows flying toward this lasher in quick succession, then, without waiting to see their effect, reached for two more. These he also sent into the lasher on the right, which by now had fallen behind the other. But the gap between them and Aram was closing dangerously.

He drew down on the lasher on the left, letting loose two more arrows in quick succession, only one of which found its mark. He was down to three arrows and both of the great beasts were still erect and still charging, though the one on the right had slowed and slipped further behind his companion.

Aram grabbed his remaining arrows and stood up, drawing back the bow with his might and sending them all into the leading lasher. The last arrow caught the beast in its throat and finally it stumbled, clawing at the offending shaft of wood. The second lasher—more slowly, but still determinedly—came on. And Aram was out of arrows.

As the great monster charged upon him, at the last instant, Aram dropped to his knee and raised the steel tip of the pike into the body of the beast. The force of the lasher's charge impaled its torso upon the pike but drove Aram backward to the ground. He rolled quickly to his left and gained his feet. The lasher was roaring with anger, but was badly injured by the steel-tipped pike stuck deeply into its body and had gone to its knees.

Careful to avoid its slashing claws, Aram retrieved one of his swords and slowly circled the beast. It was only then that he realized that, though the species was fierce and they were strong and fast runners, they were not particularly deft. This one was badly wounded, it was true, but at this close range, Aram observed that its movements were deliberate and somewhat clumsy.

The lasher was attempting two things at once. With one hand, it was pulling at the pike buried in its body while with the other it stabbed fiercely at its enemy with a short sword. Aram glanced over at its companion. The other lasher had regained its feet and though it was covered in black fluid streaming from the wound in its throat, its opaque eyes were fixed on Aram and it was approaching doggedly.

He had to make a decision.

Leaving the nearest lasher, which remained on its knees and was gradually focusing all its attention away from Aram and onto the pike grinding away at its insides with every attempt to dislodge it, he carefully approached the other. The lasher stopped a few feet away and set its legs wide apart. The sword it carried was longer than that of its companion and though the great beast was badly injured, it was still intent on killing and was still fully capable of accomplishing its intent.

The lasher's size and height made single combat a dangerous affair for Aram. He realized that his best chance of reducing the great beast would be by inflicting a series of small wounds to its legs and arms. He would, in effect, have to cause death—or at least debilitation—by a thousand cuts. And so began a long, cautious duel. The lasher was too badly wounded to simply risk rushing the man, but the beast was not wounded badly enough for that tactic to work for Aram.

They circled each other, looking for advantage, thrusting and parrying, both taking damage but not enough to decide the issue. The effort began to wear on Aram. If the other lasher had succeeded in rejoining the fray, he would have been overwhelmed. But when Aram glanced at the other great beast, it had ceased struggling and was kneeling with its head forward, breathing heavily. It was not yet dead, but the fight had gone out of it.

He had only to kill the one.

The lasher facing Aram was also breathing heavily but still seemed vital. At one point, it backed away and stood still for a moment, studying Aram.

"Who are you, little man?"

Aram stiffened. The deep, harsh voice was startlingly familiar, as was the inflections with which it spoke. Another lasher, long ago, had called Aram, "little man". Aram gazed at his opponent and slowly nodded.

"I know you." He said.

"Do you?" The lasher snorted with contempt. "And are you anyone that I should know?"

Aram stepped forward with cold deliberation, recommencing the duel. "I am the last man you will ever see." And he slid suddenly to his left but as he went, slashed through the thick muscles of his opponent's right thigh.

The lasher grunted and swung his heavy sword in reply, but his injuries were taking their toll and his movements were growing slower. As Aram circled again, he looked beyond the lasher and saw that the inhabitants of the village had gathered outside the gates and were watching the conflict. He attacked again, this time slashing across the beast's left thigh. Blackish blood poured from the deep lateral wounds and the great legs began to tremble.

Moving with renewed speed and strength Aram hacked and sawed at the coiled muscles of the beast's thighs and calves. Finally, the lasher dropped to its knees and Aram was able to attack its arms. Within minutes of going down, the beast was defenseless. Aram retrieved his lance and with deliberate aim, drove the steel point into the lasher's neck, feeling the tip grind to a stop against the spine. The lasher gazed at him a few moments as its life poured from the wound and then slowly toppled over.

Aram picked up his sword, looked at all three beasts a moment and then approached the villagers. There were about a hundred men, women, and children. He stopped ten yards away and studied them.

"How many overseers are here?"

A tall, thin, black-haired young man stepped out from the others. "There are two."

"Where are they?"

The man glanced around at the others, and then looked back at Aram. "They must be in the council house. I think they fear you."

Aram nodded savagely. "They have reason to fear me. Bring them."

"Sir?" The tall man stiffened in surprise.

Aram studied him a moment. "I asked you to bring them to me. Are you a man, or have you been a slave so long that you have ceased to be a man?"

The man's brow darkened in anger. "I may be in slavery at the moment, sir, but I am a man."

"Prove it." Aram growled. "Take a few others and bring me the overseers. Tell them if they don't come out to me, I will come in and kill them where they are."

The man stood motionless for a moment longer, then gathered four companions and went into the village. Aram waited quietly, watching the crowd. They were exactly as he remembered the villagers of his youth—ragged, thin, and frightened.

In a few minutes, two overseers, the fat one he'd seen earlier and a taller, thinner companion came marching importantly, if uncertainly, out of the gate in front of the five men who'd gone after them. They stopped at the front of the assembled villagers and glared insolently at Aram. The taller overseer spoke.

"Who are you, criminal, that you dare attack the servants of the great Lord Manon?" But even as he spoke these words, a bit too loudly, his eyes darted nervously toward the ruin Aram had made of the three lashers.

Aram ignored him and addressed the villagers as he paced back and forth near the overseers. "Look upon those that would oppress you. Look at what you fear."

He raised the point of his sword and approached the taller overseer. Men just like this man had taken his young sister, all those years earlier, into the horror of Manon's evil designs. Anger surged in him as he gazed at the man. The overseer stepped slightly back. Aram smiled grimly.

"And now watch how easily it is removed," he said, and he drove the sword suddenly into the man's belly, slashing to the side as he removed the blade from his victim's body, disemboweling him and severing the major arteries. The man collapsed in a startled, mangled heap, spewing a sudden dark flood of blood, dying as he hit the ground.

The fat overseer shrieked in fear and tried to run but the tall, black-haired villager tripped him. The overseer curled up on the ground, covered his eyes with his pudgy hands and sobbed like a child, begging for his life. Aram thought of his sister, taken by men like this into certain torment and probable death, and ended the man's life with a quick stroke.

Then, slowly and deliberately, he walked back across the meadow to the lasher that still lived, leaning heavily forward on the pike protruding from its body. Walking around behind him, Aram hacked at the broad neck until the head was severed. It took six heavy strokes before the great horned head came free and tumbled down upon the dry grass.

He went back to the assembled villagers. Driving his sword into the ground, he folded his arms across his chest and looked at them.

"I am Aram," he said, "son of Joktan. I am lord of all these lands. Your village stands upon earth that belongs to me. All the lands that you see are inside my borders. No servant of Manon will be allowed to live within those borders."

He waited for these words to have their impact, and then his eyes sought out the tall villager with the black hair. "Who are you?" He asked.

The man stepped forward. "My name is Nikolus Mathan." He hesitated, glancing around at his fellow villagers. Then he looked back at Aram. "What do you want of us, my lord?"

Aram shook his head. "Nothing. You are free."

The man's eyes widened at this stunning statement.

"All of you are free," Aram continued, "no slavery is permitted on my lands. You may live—or leave—as you wish." He settled his gaze back on Nikolus. "Where are you from?"

The tall man's eyes were wide with amazement. "Some of these people were already here, my lord, but most of us are from the city of Craun in the land of Aniza." He pointed roughly toward the southwest. "I think it is that way, hundreds of miles from here, near to the sea. Those of us here were enslaved by Manon's servants after a great battle in which the city was destroyed and then we were transported to this place." He frowned at Aram. "Do you also have armies, my lord?"

Aram thought briefly of the horses before answering. "Yes." He pointed deliberately to the north rather than east. "My capitol is beyond those hills, far to the north among the mountains, but these are my lands as well."

Nikolus gazed back at him, puzzled. "But we were told that Manon's capitol is in the north."

"So it is." Aram nodded. "But only until I destroy him," he added savagely. He pulled his sword from the earth and sheathed it. "Now—what will you do?"

Nikolus glanced at the others before answering. "What should we do my lord?"

"Why ask me?" Aram shrugged. "Whatever you want. You may return to Aniza if you like or you may remain here."

"Our homes in Aniza are gone and all that land is under Manon's heel." Nikolus shook his head sadly. "We have no place to go."

Aram's eyes narrowed. "Then stay here—work this land as your own."

"The servants of Manon will return, my lord."

"I will return as well, Nikolus. If there are lashers here when I return, I will destroy them. If they are too numerous, I will bring an army." He raised his voice so that all could hear. "I told you that these are my lands and I am lord of them. That is true and no one can change it. You may live here and better your lives. I will cede you the lands that you work as your own.

"If overseers and lashers return, and you do not wish to confront them, tell them what happened here and that you had no part in it. If you desire slavery over freedom—you may have it until I return. But know this—I will return, and no servant of Manon's may live on my lands."

Nikolus clenched his fists. "I will not be a slave if there is another way, my lord."

Aram looked at him coldly. "There is another way. Don't be a slave."

"But we have no weapons like yours with which to resist."

Aram indicated the sword lying on the earth near the lashers and the pikes and the arrows stuck in the bodies. "You have these and I will bring you more if you wish." He looked at Nikolus and around at the others. "Do you wish it?"

Nikolus did not consult the others. "Yes, my lord."

"Good. Then I will bring them within the week." He looked towards the river. "What is it that you build there?"

"It is a small dam. We do it that we may control the water and direct some of it into a supply of fresh water for the village." He smiled slightly. "I was an engineer before I was a slave, my lord."

Aram nodded. "Then you may want to find a way to isolate this village—destroy the bridge at the bottom of the canyon, or find a way to close the road completely."

Nikolus gazed down the road that wound out of sight down the canyon and nodded slowly. "You are right, my lord. We will see to that."

Aram turned and looked significantly toward the north. "I have business in other places. I will go now but I will return in six days with ten swords and enough steel points for twenty or thirty pikes and lances. I will show you how to make them." He glanced back at Nikolus. "Are you the head of these people?"

"There is no head of these people, my lord."

"There is now. I appoint you. Lead them. Decide together what way you will take—whether you will stay or go—and you will be their leader."

Nikolus nodded. "I understand, my lord."

"Where did the third lasher and the second overseer come from? They were not here two days ago."

Surprise at the extent of Aram's knowledge showed on the tall man's face. "They arrived last night, my lord. They came to oversee the harvest."

"As I thought." Aram nodded. "I will go now and return in six days."

He crossed the bridge and angled up into the sandy hills to the north of the village as if his path lay directly north. The people watched him go out of sight.

Once on top of the main ridge a couple of miles beyond the village, Aram turned to the east and when he came to the flanks of his mountain, went south to the cave and the passage to his city. He did not want anyone to know where he truly dwelt. The less reliable information Manon had about him the more difficult the task of finding him would be. And Aram intended that everything should be difficult for his enemy.

He gathered ten swords of varying lengths from his armory and tied them in a deerskin. Then he gathered twenty of the steel lance heads and an equal amount of arrow points and rolled them in a skin as well. Then he chose one of his lesser bows and went back through the tunnel.

Again, instead of crossing the snake-infested slope, he went to the north along the flanks of the mountain and turned west along the top of the sandy ridge, coming back to the village from the north.

In his absence, Nikolus and the men of the village had succeeded in causing landslides in the loose rock above the road, closing it in several places. Aram spent three days with the villagers, instructing them in the making of lances, pikes and arrows and the use of swords. The bow he gave to Nikolus. He hunted eastward along the narrow stream until he found a stand of ironwood and showed them how to harvest good straight shafts for their weapons. Then, with the summer nearly gone, he bade them farewell, leaving them to harvest their crops while he returned to his own.

XXV

Summer waned and he set about to harvest his crops but his heart was not in the effort. He would occasionally collect a basket of fruit or vegetables and carry it into the granary but most often he would just sit on the bottom step of the south stairway staring with unseeing eyes at the hills to the southeast. There was a pain in him that would not diminish, a wound that did not heal.

One evening, as he sat on the step, numb to the delights of the last hours of a late summer day, Cree came twisting down out of the sky.

"Wolves on the avenue, my lord." She said.

He stared up at her for a moment before comprehension pierced his brain. Then he gazed out along the broad avenue towards the east. "Wolves?"

"Two wolves, my lord. A large black wolf and a gray. They are coming toward the city."

"Are there any others?"

"No. The valley is clear except for the two wolves upon the road."

He drew his sword. "Thanks, Cree. Wait—have you seen Borlus?"

She sailed upward, calling her answer back to him as she flew away and there was a slight measure of disdain in her sharp voice. "The bears are in the foothills to the north. They are unmolested."

With his sword drawn, Aram sat back down and waited on the wolves. When they came into view, he immediately recognized the black wolf as Durlrang. He did not know the other. Durlrang approached and bent his forehead to the ground.

"I apologize, master, for coming unannounced," his harsh voice broke in upon Aram's mind. "But there is urgent news for your hearing. This is my nephew, Leorg. He would speak with you."

Aram studied the gray wolf that stood so easily before him. In places, his coat was tipped with silver and the fur on the underside of his throat was white. The handsome animal gazed back at Aram with clear eyes and a calm expression. Aram addressed Durlrang. "It is good to see you again, lord Durlrang. What is this urgent news?"

"Leorg will tell you, Master. It is he that brought the tidings to me."

Aram turned his attention again to the clear-eyed, gray and silver wolf. The wolf bowed his head slightly and when he spoke, his voice was confident and full.

"There are lashers, servants of the dark master, searching out of the mountain passes far to the north, near the great valley that lies beneath the mountains of Ferros. They search for you and for the horses."

"Lashers?" Aram stared at him. "How far away?"

"Far to the north, as I said. They have come through the passes to the northwest by the ruins of Firkesh. They search everywhere for you."

Aram shook his head. "I've never heard of these ruins."

"They are near the great passage through the mountains that goes toward the black tower of the enemy."

Aram looked at him sharply. "You think of Manon as the enemy?"

It was Durlrang that answered. "Leorg has always been different, master. His mother gave birth to him near to the region of Kelven, in the vast forests that lie to the south of the great mountain. His mother left his father before the birth. It is said that you slew his father out upon the avenue six years ago.

"When he heard of his father's death, Leorg came back to claim his place as lord of the western wolves. I met him and told him of you—the man who had come to change the world. Leorg said that his mother had spoken to him of such a man. He has always wanted to meet you."

Aram studied the gray wolf curiously. "Why did you and your mother not share in the troubles and confusion of your people?"

Leorg met his gaze. "My mother was from an eastern people, near to the mountain of Kelven. The actions of my father's people troubled her, so she went back to her own land for my birth. My father sought her but was unsuccessful. She is still there."

"Why have you come back?"

There was pride in Leorg's voice. "Because, like you, I am the rightful heir to a position of leadership. When Durlrang told me of your coming into the world, I knew the time had come to change the fortunes of my people."

Aram nodded, surprised at the clarity of the wolf's thoughts. "Alright. How many days will it take for the lashers to come southward into my valley, do you think?"

Leorg considered. "They are searching every old city, every ruined tower. They do not know where you are. They are still far to the north in the wide valley beyond the great pass. It will take many days."

"Good," Aram answered. "Then there is time to prepare to go out and meet them."

The wolves stared at him. Leorg glanced at Durlrang who remained silent. The gray wolf shifted uneasily. "Meet them, my lord? But there are very many. I thought to warn you that you might avoid them or get help."

Aram shook his head. "I will go to meet them. They must not come into this valley. How many are there?"

"Many. Perhaps as many as a hundred. Fifty or sixty, at least."

"Are they searching together, in one group?"

"No." Leorg answered. "They search the ruins, the forests, the valleys, and the hills in groups of five and six."

Aram considered. "Still formidable, but perhaps manageable."

"You're not going out to face them, master, surely?" Durlrang's eyes were troubled. "Not by yourself?"

Aram gazed back at him. "What else is there to do, my friend? I cannot let them harm the people of this valley. They must be faced in the wilderness before they can discover this place and bring their evil here."

Leorg glanced at Durlrang, and then looked back at Aram. "I will help you, master. And there are many among my people who will fight with us."

Aram considered that for a moment then shook his head emphatically. "No. Keep your people out of it. And you stay clear yourself. If you are leading your people into keeping the ways of Kelven then that is a bigger blow to the enemy than anything else that you could do."

"But how will you prevail against so many?" the gray wolf protested. "Nay, master, but we will help you. If you die all is lost."

For his part, Aram was tired of people telling him that his death would do irreparable damage to the world. And now, with Ka'en turned against him, there was very little reason to stay in the world, anyway. Still, he did not want to see the peace of his valley ruined by the presence of the vile servants of Manon. He looked at the wolves and smiled slightly but spoke firmly.

"Durlrang—you and your people stay out of it. If something happens to me, ally with the horses. Listen to Florm."

Durlrang bowed his head. "I will ever do as you command, master."

Aram turned to Leorg. "The lords of the air will aid me in knowing where the lashers are. Stay nearby with any of your people that you can trust. If you can make a difference when conflict comes, help me. If I am lost, continue on as you have and return your people to following the ways of Kelven."

Leorg bowed his head. "As you say, master."

"Good. Go—prepare your peoples. There is much I have to do."

The wolves bowed their foreheads to the ground and turned to go. Aram looked at Durlrang. "Durlrang."

The great black wolf looked back at him. "Yes, master?"

"How is your foot?"

"It is good, my lord. Thanks to you, it healed well." The wolf studied him for a long moment. "You remember such a small thing, master. It is not worth your trouble."

Aram spoke carefully. "But you are worth my trouble, lord Durlrang. Florm, the lord of horses, told me that you would matter more than any of us could know before all of this is over. Remember that, my friend. And you, Leorg. It may be that in the eyes of the Maker you are both more important than I."

The wolves looked at each other. Durlrang took a step toward Aram. "We will do our part, master. But please—stay alive."

After bowing again, the wolves turned away and trotted down the avenue. At the pyramids, they parted, with Leorg going north and Durlrang going down over the hill toward the river.

Aram sat back down on the step. In his soul, there was despair. He had been training an army for just such an occurrence as that which was now come upon him. But all that was lost in the killing of Kemul. Thinking about it now, even though the man was dead, Aram hated him.

In challenging Aram, Kemul had brought about the ruin of everything that Aram dreamed of. Now, he would go and face his doom alone and likely die. He'd already decided that he would not call upon the horses to help him. There was no point in multiplying death. At least, if he died far to the north, Manon would be temporarily satiated. Ka'en and her people—and the horses—would have more time, perhaps even years, of peace and freedom.

He was surprised at how little he cared about himself. Without the hope of a life with Ka'en, nothing much mattered. Still, he wanted to spare those that lived in the valley he'd come to love, the birds and the bears, wolves, and deer. So, he gathered his weapons, his best bow and all the arrows he could find, with his finest sword, and prepared to go north to meet his death.

He slept for the last time in his room below the tower and looked out over his valley at sunrise. He would have liked to speak again with Borlus but the bear was nowhere to be seen. As the morning mist lifted above the valley, he gathered his instruments of war, descended the steps, and turned his face north. Just then Cree came down out of the sky.

"My lord, there are horses on the avenue."

Aram turned in surprise and gazed eastward, into the sun. "Really? How many?"

"Two, my lord."

Aram glanced up at her. "Thank you, Cree, you are ever vigilant. I am in your debt."

She hovered for a moment, studying him with her shining, black eyes and seemed to want to say something, but then wheeled away without comment.

He placed his burden of weaponry down on the pavement and waited. In a few minutes, Florm and Thaniel came clattering up to him. Florm surveyed his pack and his pile of weaponry.

"It appears that you have travel plans, my friend. May I ask where you are going?"

Aram smiled slightly. "It is good to see you, my lords, but I cannot visit long. These are not the best of times."

"Indeed. What has happened since last I saw you?"

"Much." Aram glanced involuntarily toward the southeast, and then swung his gaze back to the north. "I am about to be invaded."

Florm studied him a moment. "That is an odd choice of words, my friend." The old horse stepped up and looked at him more closely. "There is something very different about you, my lord. Tell an old friend what it is that troubles you."

Aram had long felt the need to unburden himself, and these horses were his closest friends upon the earth, so he sat down and told Florm and Thaniel about the killing of Kemul and Ka'en's reaction to it. When he had finished he sat miserably silent and gazed unseeing out over the valley while the horses considered what he'd told them. At last Florm spoke.

"My friend," he said gently. "You tend to see the world and its people as monolithic things, but it is not true. Among those allied with evil there are some who have their doubts, just as among the allies of right there are some with a tendency to evil.

"This Kemul of which you speak had plans that your coming put at risk. He decided for himself that his plans were more important to him than the general welfare of his people. His motives and his actions were wrong. He challenged you. You destroyed him. What else could you have done?"

Aram looked up at him in sorrow. "I feel no particular grief for him but if you could have seen the lady Ka'en's face as she looked down upon what I'd done." He drew a shuddering breath and looked away. "She was horrified."

To his amazement, Florm chuckled quietly. "Of course she was horrified. Look, my friend." The ancient voice grew solemn. "Aram, look at me, and listen. You are a dangerous man, strong, confident, and skilled in the art of killing. She knew this but was nonetheless stunned to see it validated before her eyes.

"I doubt if she had any feelings towards the dead man other than the general sensitivity that a woman has about such things. You have faced death so often and dealt it out even more often that you have no particular sensitivity to its occurrence. To you, it's necessary work. But to her—someone who'd probably never seen a killing—it was horrifying.

"It does not mean that she admires you less. She just needs time to digest things. All will be well in the end, trust me. I have seen it before."

Aram looked up at him with new hope challenging the despair in his heart. Could it be true? Could Ka'en ever forget that she had been a witness to such a barbaric act? But then he thought about how he'd left things with the Derosans and hope faded. He described the parting fury of his words and the harshness of his behavior toward them to Florm and the old horse snorted dismissively.

"But I agree with you. Their law is a despicable one. It assumes that the woman has no ability to choose in the matter. They needed an upbraiding and you gave it. But tell me, Aram, how will they survive without you? They will not. They need you—your leadership and your strength.

Time will heal this wound. All will be well. Now, where are you going so heavily armed?"

Aram glanced northward. "There are several dozen lashers coming down out of the mountains looking for us—for Thaniel and me. I intend not to let them near my valley. I'm going to settle the matter before they get anywhere near here." He looked at Florm curiously. "And why are you here, my lord, so late in the year?"

Florm was gazing toward the north and ignored the question. "Who warned you of the lashers?"

"The wolves. Durlrang and a wolf named Leorg."

Florm looked at him in surprise. "That is an interesting thing, is it not?" He swung his head back to the north. "Well, we'll just have to find a way to get past them."

"What do you mean? Get past them? Why?"

"Kelven wants to see you."

Aram sat very still and felt his heart jump inside him. "Kelven?"

"Yes. He wants to see you. He wants to talk to you."

Aram's eyes narrowed. "The god—Kelven?"

"As I said."

"But he's dead."

"Who told you that, my friend?"

Aram hesitated. "I believe you did, my lord."

"No, I said that he disembodied himself in the last great battle and that he has not walked the earth since that time. I did not say that he had died."

"Durlrang stated it as an outright fact."

Florm snorted. "He is a wolf, you know."

"Meaning?"

Florm fidgeted in irritation. "Meaning that he and his people have not been on the right side of things for centuries. He believed what Manon told him but he was wrong. Kelven is alive—though trapped on his mountain—and he wants to see you. I come here under the most specific of orders to deliver you to him."

"And I would not be so impertinent as to ignore such a summons, but—" Aram waved a hand northward. "I have a situation here that demands my attention."

"Forget it, my friend. Kelven has sent for you and you will go to him. If you needed any further proof that you are the answer to his riddle, here it is. You must go."

"But what about the lashers? I do not want them coming into my valley and disturbing its peace."

Florm considered that for a moment. "The answer seems simple enough. It is highly unlikely that we can get past them entirely unnoticed. They will no doubt see us and pursue us and we will lead them away from this place. If we go now they will never find your valley."

"Where is Kelven?"

"Upon his mountain—to the east."

"East?"

Thaniel stepped forward. "Do you remember, lord Aram, asking me if there was something beyond the mountains to the northeast when we were near unto the sea?"

Aram nodded.

"Well, what you saw was Kelven's mountain. It is immense."

Aram stared at the horses in confusion. "If his mountain is to the east then why would we go north at all?"

"Because we cannot cross the sea and the mountains to the north of our land are impassable for horses." Florm answered. "From what I hear, even you would find it a difficult passage. No, we must go north along the great road and then over the pass of Camber and turn east through Vallenvale by the ruins of Tiras. We have to go past the lashers. We can't avoid them all but perhaps we can avoid a general engagement. Besides, you want them to go away from here, anyway, so it all works toward the same end."

Aram looked northward, trying in his mind's eye to see the distant and unknown places the horses described. Finally, he nodded. "Alright, I'll go see Kelven. I'll send Cree for the eagle, Alvern. Perhaps he will agree to be our eyes and make avoiding the lashers easier."

Florm snorted again. "A moment ago you were going to take them all on by yourself."

Aram grinned ruefully. "Before you came, my lord, I had no hope. Now, thanks to your wise counsel, I am not so anxious to die."

"I'm very glad to hear it." Florm stated caustically. "If you would, pack some apples for the road and I'll carry them. And you will need a vessel to carry water. You will ride Thaniel as always. No armor—we need to move fast—but perhaps you should use the saddle."

Aram agreed and within an hour they were ready to travel. Aram took his best lance and his best bow with all the arrows that he could secure to the saddle. He took his lightest and best sword as well. After sending Cree after Alvern, he climbed upon Thaniel's back and they went out the avenue to the intersection of the great roads and turned north.

XXVI

The horses moved briskly along and by early afternoon, they'd left the valley floor and were following the ruins of the road up through the timbered foothills where Aram had first found the material for his bowstring. A while later they passed the junction where the road from the west came down out of the foothills to the north of Aram's mountain. As they emerged out of the timber onto the crest of a long ridge and the road straightened out for a long run to the north, Aram heard a clear voice descend from the sky into his mind.

"I am here, lord Aram."

It was the eagle, Alvern. Aram looked skyward but could make nothing out in the blue depths of the sky. He answered with his mind.

"I am very grateful for your help, lord Alvern." He turned his head and squinted upward. "I cannot see you."

The eagle's laugh was sharp like crystal. "Never fear—I can see you well enough, my lord, and I am happy to be of service. Cree told me of your plans. There is nothing untoward in front of you for at least the rest of the day. I will go before you and watch with diligence."

"The Maker bless you, my friend."

"Oh, He has, my lord, I assure you. I will scout ahead and report back before nightfall."

"Thanks."

With Alvern's assurance of a clear road, they concentrated on making good time and by nightfall were in broken and rugged country, characterized by open, rocky ridges and steep, heavily timbered draws, that was unfamiliar to Aram. The ancient road, however, went straight on into the north, arching over massive stone bridges that traversed steep ravines with frothing streams and slicing through angled hillsides covered with dark-green, pungent brush. At sundown, they camped in a stand of enormous, ancient firs with broad, sweeping branches above a clear stream that tumbled down through rocky pools surrounded by stands of thick willows.

Alvern had reported that there was no sign of enemies for at least another day's journey. Aram decided to have a fire. It was late in the year

and they'd climbed ever higher throughout the day, and the night promised to be cool. The horses grazed on stray bits of grass that grew among
the patches of brush out on the open hillside. At dusk they joined Aram
beneath the trees.

After supper, Aram banked the fire and looked across at Florm. "How
far is Camber Pass, my lord?"

Florm considered. "Eight or maybe even ten days north of here. It's
been a long time since I came this way. The Pass is the only way through
these mountains to the lands beyond. That's why the road is here. Thousands of years ago this road was the main route for trade between the city
of Ram and the valleys and wooded lands to the north. It joins up with
the great valley road below the Pass on this side and ends beyond it at the
intersection of another great road that runs east and west through Vallenvale."

"And what is Vallenvale?"

"It is a great valley, more than four hundred miles long, lying east
and west between these mountains and the Forbidden Mountains further
north. Eastward, the road runs by the ruins of several ancient cities of men,
including Tiras, built by one of your ancestors. Westward, it angles around
to the north through the mountains and eventually comes to the tower of
Manon."

"Forbidden Mountains?"

"The mountains of Ferros. Many of them smoke and some weep fire
from their summits, even through the snow and ice. Men have never gone
there."

Aram shook his head in amazement. "I'm beginning to believe that I
have lived my whole life in one small corner of the world."

"The world is large, indeed," Florm agreed. "Kelven's mountain is in
the middle of it. That's why it is called the Mountain at the Middle of the
World."

"And that's where we're going?"

"That's where you are going." Florm corrected him. "Horses cannot
climb it. Rather, we cannot get to it in order to climb it. But you can and
we can get you close enough that you can reach it."

Aram lay back and stretched out on the ground by the fire, staring
up through the impenetrable darkness of the massive firs. "Why are the
mountains of Ferros forbidden?"

"I don't know that they are. Men have always called those mountains forbidden out of fear. I'm not certain that there is any official sanction against entering those regions." Florm answered. "They are too rough for horses anyway. But men fear Ferros—always have."

Aram frowned. "Like they fear Manon?"

"No. With Manon, they fear an evil they know—an evil with which you, yourself, are familiar—and horrors that they have seen. With Ferros, they fear what is unknown and what cannot be seen. He lives in the under-earth—that is all that men know. That, and the fact that he refused to help Kelven in the war against Manon." Florm lowered his head and closed his eyes. "We will take care to avoid his mountains as well on this journey."

Aram watched the sparks from the campfire rising like multi-colored, temporary jewels to vanish into the thin, dark air under the trees. "I won-der if Kelven will tell me where to find the weapon?" He said quietly.

Florm's head came up but it was Thaniel that spoke with sudden ur-gency. "What's that? What weapon?"

"The sword." Aram rolled over and looked across the fire at the hors-es. "The sword in the riddle. The Sword of Heaven."

"So you've been thinking about that, have you?" Florm asked.

Over in the darkness to Florm's right, Thaniel had moved closer and was listening intently, the light from the fire shining in the depths of his large eyes and illuminating the muscular outlines of his massive shoul-ders.

Aram sat up and looked at them both. "Yes, I have. I've thought about it often and long. The riddle states that 'he ascends the height to put his hand among the stars and wield the sword of heaven'. It must mean that there is a weapon that can be used effectively against Manon. Maybe he has it there—on the mountain. Maybe he will give it to me."

Florm gazed at him, the flames reflecting in his great black eyes. In the glow of the fire, the two horses looked otherworldly as they focused their attention intently on Aram. "So you no longer think that it is alle-gorical, or worse, rubbish."

"I never thought that it was rubbish, my lord. I've never thought that of anything you've told me. But what is the point of there being a riddle if it cannot be solved in such a way as to aid us in our war against evil?" Aram lay down and rolled onto his side, staring into the fire. "What other purpose could he have for summoning me?"

"Maybe he just wants to encourage you, my friend." The old horse suggested.

"Maybe." Aram agreed. "But I'd rather have the weapon than the encouragement."

Florm chuckled quietly and lowered his head. Thaniel continued to gaze at Aram a few moments longer then turned away and melded into the darkness.

There was frost on the ground in the morning and Aram awoke stiff, with aching in the wounds he'd received of Kemul and the fight with the lashers at the village of Nikolus Mathan. He stood slowly and looked about him. They were near the top of a long straight ridge that ran to the northwest but there were taller mountains on all sides, especially to the north and east. The sun would not rise high enough to shine upon them for some time. They ate and headed north. Aram looked up through the branches of the tall trees into the sky.

"Are you there, Alvern?"

"I am here, lord Aram."

"Where did you sleep, my friend?"

"On the high rocks. There are many lovely high rocks here. If the food was more plentiful in this part of the world, I could live here."

Aram smiled. "Are you hungry now? I could help you find food."

"No, I did not mean to suggest it. I am good for many days, thank you."

"What are your plans for today?"

"I am going all the way north to Camber Pass and search out the road and countryside for signs of the enemy. I will be back before nightfall."

"That is a long way. Will you not tire?"

"It is nothing to me, my lord. Kelven's winds will bear me."

As the morning passed away, and the ground became more rugged and the trees around them grew taller and thicker, Aram was increasingly troubled. Something in all of this seemed wrong to him the more he thought about it. He decided to mention it to Florm. "My lord, why is Manon searching this country for Thaniel and me so far from where we fought the battle?"

"I can see why it might puzzle you, my friend. This country is so vast and the distances great. It is time-consuming to search it. But Manon is not troubled by the passage of time. He is an immortal. And he is by nature thorough. It is true that he encountered you for the first time many miles south of this place." Florm stopped and stretched his muscles in the light of the sun that had just topped the mountains, luxuriating in its welcome warmth. Then he continued. "It is also true that he knows that you came from somewhere in the region to the north of the battlefield. It is a region he knows all too well. His troubles have always germinated in this part of the world."

"This part?"

"All of this land." Florm answered. "From these mountains south to your valley and eastward across the plains of the horse people all the way to the mountain of Kelven. Also Vallenvale to the north. It is the part of the world that was never fully under his control. It is this part of the world that has always produced the men that challenged him. Do not think it strange that he started where he did—he will begin here and move south and east. He does not care how long it takes. Unless we give him a reason to stop, he will search it all until he finds you."

They came just then out on the top of a long ridge running from the northeast to southwest where the road angled down through the timber into a broad, open valley. At the bottom of the valley there flowed a substantial river, running from their right to their left toward the southwest. Looking at it, Aram realized that it probably emerged from the mountains somewhere out on the plains of his youth. It might even be the river in the wide valley across the sand hills to the north of Nikolus' village.

The road upon which they traveled descended down around the timbered slopes to the valley floor and intersected with another on the near side of the river. This new road ran away to the southwest along the tangent of the river until it went out of sight around the edge of a mountain that jutted out into the valley. To the right the road ran along the grass-covered floor of the valley for several miles and then climbed ponderously up through a heavily timbered saddle that rose between high mountains from which the sources of the river bounded and fell.

"Camber Pass?" Aram asked.

"Yes." Florm answered.

"That will be a long climb."

"Indeed. It will take the better part of a week to gain that summit."

"You were explaining why Manon was looking for me here." Aram reminded him.

"In the great war," Florm continued, as they moved off the top of the ridge and down through the tall trees toward the valley floor far below, "Manon controlled the lands around his tower in the northwest and all the great plains to the south all the way to the ocean. Joktan ruled Vallenvale, as well as the valley where your city is, and the high plains where my people dwell.

"When Manon first encountered you, you were mounted. He knows where the horses live. And he knows that free men always lived in the vast lands between his tower and the high plains of the horse people. Since you were mounted, he knew that you were in alliance with my people, so he would assume—especially since you fought his army alone without any help from the people of the town—that the conflict near to Derosa only meant that you wished to show yourself there.

"I doubt that Manon would assume that you were from Derosa yourself and since he is ever methodical, he would send his minions into all the land between his tower and the mountain of Kelven to conduct a systematic search. And that's what he is doing. Besides, he needs to discover whether you are alone or if there are more like you."

"So he would have found my valley."

Florm looked at him. "He wouldn't have to find your valley—he knows that it is there. He just doesn't know where you are. He's not looking for a particular place; he is looking for you—and us."

The road wound downward at a gentle angle through vast, sweeping amphitheaters filled with conifers and around ridges punctuated by immense spires of rock as it fell toward the floor of the valley. Aram gazed up in awe at the ramparts of the mountains around him. They seemed to pierce the sky with their tall jagged peaks. He glanced at Florm.

"What do you think Kelven wants with me?"

Florm laughed quietly. "You assume that since I am old, I know so much. But compared to Kelven, I am an infant. How would I know what a god desires of you? He will tell you—he did not tell me."

It took two days more to descend to and negotiate the wide, open valley and five more to climb the broad, timbered slopes beneath Camber Pass. But at last they camped just below the summit of the pass by one of the clear, cold springs that fed the mighty river in the valley behind them. Alvern had reported that it was clear all the way to Vallenvale beyond but that there were lashers in the vale, searching the countryside and the ruins of the ancient towns. They would encounter them within two or three days.

That night, two wolves crept silently and suddenly into the firelight, startling the horses. They were Leorg and another wolf that he introduced as his cousin, Gorfang, a rangy black fellow that seemed to embody menace. Leorg stopped at the edge of the light and addressed Aram.

"We are gathered, my lord, at the base of the Pass, on the edge of the vale, if you wish us to fight. There are more than a hundred of us."

Aram glanced out into the darkness beneath the timber. It was unsettling to think of more than a hundred wolves gathered somewhere out in the gloom beyond the fire, but then he looked back into Leorg's clear eyes. This was a wolf, he realized, like Durlrang, who could be trusted. And unlike Durlrang, he already considered Manon an enemy, without any prompting from Aram. "Thank you, Leorg, but we are going to try and avoid fighting. With the help of the eagles we're going to try and slip past them to the east."

"East? But that way, beyond Vallenvale, lie the entrances to the mountain of Kelven."

Aram nodded. "The mountain of Kelven. That's where we are going."

The wolf sat on back his haunches and gazed at Aram in astonishment. "If I may ask, my lord, why do you go there? Lord Kelven has been gone from the earth for time out of mind."

Aram glanced at Florm, who said nothing. Beyond his father, Thaniel had turned his back to the fire and was gazing steadily out into the darkness. Aram looked back at the wolf. "We shall see, Leorg. It may be that Kelven's spirit survives. He may yet take an interest in the affairs of earth. Your mother suspected something of the sort, did she not? Why else would she have gone into that region to give birth to you, a prince of her husband's people?"

"I never thought of it in that way, my lord." The gray wolf stared into the fire. "It would be a blessing of the Maker if Kelven could yet help us."

"Well, we shall see." Aram said quietly. "I'm going there to see what can be discovered. It may be that I will find help beyond our imagining. That is why we cannot risk a general engagement with the lashers."

Leorg turned his nose up to the darkened sky and spoke almost in a whisper. "The Lord Kelven may yet live?"

"Yes, he may."

Leorg lowered his gaze to Aram's face and studied him silently, then the wolves stood up and at an unseen signal from Leorg, Gorfang bowed and left the light. "We will do whatever you need from us to aid you in escaping the lashers, my lord." Leorg said. "You only need instruct us."

Aram nodded his gratitude and the wolf turned and glided into the night. From beyond the fire, Florm studied Aram with his large, dark eyes for a long moment. He turned his head and gazed out into the darkness after the wolves and then glanced up into the deepening sky.

"Wolves answer to you, and eagles do your bidding. I declare, my young friend, if I didn't know better, I would think that you were Lord Kelven himself returned."

"I'm glad that you know better, my lord, for I am much less than that." Aram replied as he stretched out and gazed up through the trees at the stars. "Kelven wouldn't have knots in his stomach as he contemplated the next few days."

"Don't be so certain of it," the old horse answered. "There is not such a gap between his kind and yours as you would think. When the Maker made all His works, He created a hierarchy—it's true. But there is just a step, no more, between the ranks of most of His creatures. And the rank of men is just a step below that of the gods."

Aram sighed. "Would that that was true. I would take my best weapon and face Manon right now."

"It is true, and believe me; you will face Manon—when the time is right. But only when the time is right; Joktan's mistake must not be repeated." Florm cocked a leg and lowered his head, closing his eyes after one more furtive glance out into the gloom beyond the fire. After a few moments, he was asleep. In the darkness behind him, standing between his father and the night, Thaniel followed suit.

Aram lay awake for some time, thinking about many things. He thought of Ka'en and whether it might be true as Florm saw it concerning her consideration of the killing of Kemul—that she was horrified by the deed but not necessarily by the man that had done it. He thought of his harsh treatment of Findaen and his companions and regretted it deeply. Findaen was a friend and true, and Florm was right; their cause would undoubtedly be lost without him. For just a moment, he wondered if Ka'en might be lying in her bed even now, thinking of him.

Then his thoughts turned to the road ahead. Tomorrow they would cross the Camber Pass into the country beyond. If they could elude the lashers, they would then turn east toward the mountain of Kelven. He'd already seen a much larger portion of the world than he'd ever imagined had existed, a great expanse of it lying just to the north of his own valley. It made him feel small, poor, and inconsequential.

Pondering the imminence of contact with the lashers tied up his insides, and pushed necessary sleep far from him, so he sent his thoughts further ahead, to the meeting with Kelven on the mountain at the middle of the world. What would he find on that mountain? A god, alive and vibrant? A specter, like Joktan? Or something else? And was there, in fact, a weapon?

As he drifted toward sleep, his thoughts concentrated on Joktan. Where had the old spirit been during the past few weeks, he wondered? Joktan always showed up when Aram was in duress yet, when Aram was in torment over Ka'en, he'd been left alone. Perhaps the ghostly king only cared about those things that touched his own desires, like his ancient need for revenge upon Manon. Or maybe he had respect for Aram's privacy. Finally, as the fire decayed into a mass of cooling, darkening coals, his thoughts grew quiet and he slept.

There was a heavy mist in the morning, curling up the slope from the many collisions of the tumbling streams with the rocky hillsides. The mountains were hidden and they could see only a few yards along the road. The sun broke through an hour later just as they arrived at the summit of Camber Pass and looked down into the wide green land beyond. Aram gazed out upon it in stunned amazement.

Florm glanced sidelong at him. "Vallenvale." He said.

Aram's valley would fit inside the vast expanse of Vallenvale many times. It was a broad and long valley, green and lush, running east and west, bounded on the south by the mountains of which Camber Pass was a part. A wide river flowed from east to west along the vale's northern edge. Beyond that, mountains of massive size and stunning height rose up in great sheer walls of stone.

These mountains were majestic beyond imagining, with stupendously steep ramparts and massive flanks. Curiously, their summits were tinged with rust. Even the snow and ice clinging desperately to their peaks was touched with the peculiar hue. There were no foothills clustered at the bases of these mountains; their feet were planted securely in a broad band of heavy, dark woods on Vallenvale's northern border.

To the west, the vale was bounded by jumbled, thickly timbered hills, cut by a deep canyon through which the river made its exit. But back to the east the broad valley extended beyond the jutting mountainsides out of range of Aram's sight. Though the timbered slopes of the southern mountains extended their flanks in gentle intrusions of dark trees into the valley, most of the vale was open and carpeted with lush grass.

The great road on which they traveled wound down into the vale and met up with another broad thoroughfare that traversed the valley from east to west near to the distant river. As Aram's eye went along it, here and there, every twenty miles or so, it resolved large areas of piled stone ruins, the broken remains of ancient cities and towns. Once, long ago, thousands of people had lived in this lovely place.

There were indications of other roads and lanes as well, conduits that extended from the great main highway at right angles, and ran into the broad area of verdant green south of the river. Many of these ended at overgrown rectangles of crumbled stone. North of the river, at the base of the mountains of Ferros, dark and forbidding woods crowded to the edge of the water. In two places that Aram could see, bridges arched the great stream and roads went some way into those woods on the far shore and were swallowed from sight.

High in the air out over the valley, Alvern sailed on the currents. Aram could not see him but knew that he was there.

"What do you see, lord Alvern?" He asked.

"The lashers are below me, to the east," the eagle answered, "searching the meadows, the ruins, and the woods. There are many more than ten—in fact, there are many groups of three or four, or even ten. There may be as many as a hundred. They are thick on the valley floor from the river south to the mountains. I cannot easily see, lord Aram," the great bird stated matter-of-factly, "how you are going to pass them undiscovered."

"No," Aram agreed. "Nor do I."

He looked over at Florm. "What do you think, my lord?"

The old horse gazed out across the wide valley. "We could ease as close to them as we dare at the end of a day and then try to pass during the night, but I am certain they will post sentries and that might lead to a blunder on our part. I think we should try to make our run in the first light of morning—surprise them if possible. But it will be very dangerous if it can be accomplished at all."

Aram held up his bow. "For some of them as well, my lord. As long as we can avoid a general engagement, I can kill or seriously wound any that get too close, maybe enough to clear a path."

Florm nodded his great head. "I believe that Thaniel and I can escape them if we can get a clear road to the east. My only worry is about them wounding or killing one of us. I am the only one of us that knows the way to Kelven's mountain, Thaniel is the only one who can bear you across the high, barren plateau to the east of Vallenvale, and you are the one that Lord Kelven wants to see. Maybe we should take our time and let the eagle watch until there is an opening. Not rush things."

"If they give us an opening," Thaniel interjected, "surely we can out-run those clawed beasts. When the eagle tells us that there is a break in their lines big enough to run through, then our hooves will set the road on fire."

"Yes." Aram agreed. "We'll run for it. I'm certainly not anxious to fight three or four lashers at once, let alone an army. They may get careless and provide an opening. Until then, let's be circumspect, avoid a fight."

"If it comes to that," Thaniel said savagely, "we will take a fair amount of them into the next life with us."

Florm glanced at his son but said nothing.

For two days, they went slowly and cautiously up the great valley road toward the east with Alvern watching from his post high in the sky. At night, they took turns keeping watch. There was no thought of a fire and Aram slept fitfully with his weapons at the ready. Finally, on the morning of the third day, they heard Alvern's clear voice in their minds.

"My lords, a possibility has arisen. The lashers have broken their ranks into two scattered groups. The main group is examining the ruins of a large town near the south mountains, far from the road. The other group is farther to the east but they are also to the south of the road. At this moment, there are none near the river. If you can get past the first group undetected, perhaps you can outrun the second."

From Thaniel's back, Aram met Florm's eyes. "Now?"

The horse took a deep breath. "Let's go."

"Go." Grunted Thaniel.

The horses lunged forward. Thaniel's powerful legs began to eat up the pavement stones in great strides and Florm struggled to keep up with his son. Aram held his bow at the ready with three arrows clenched in his fist. The wind created by their speed stung his eyes as they rushed eastward along the worn but still smooth stones of the ancient road.

"The first group of lashers is to the south." Alvern's voice came again. "As yet, they do not see you. In another mile, you will be safely past. The second group is farther ahead, nearer the road. They will see you, but I think not in time to catch you."

"Thanks." Aram replied simply. He was lying low along the profile of Thaniel's neck, trying to reduce their resistance to the wind.

The mile that would move them safely past the lashers seemed never to end. The vale was so vast, green, and changeless that there was no sure marker to gauge their progress. As the horses thundered eastward, Aram kept his head flat against Thaniel's neck, watching the southern horizon, and Alvern was silent. The ruins of the ancient town to the south came even with them and began to fall behind. Then—

"They see you," Alvern said, his voice sharp and urgent. "They are coming."

Aram squinted hard and looked into the south. Pouring out of the distant ruins was a long dark line of lashers running at an angle to their flight in an attempt to intercept the horses and the rider. Even from that distance, Aram could hear their harsh, guttural shouts. The quarry they'd been sent to find had finally been flushed.

Then Alvern spoke again and he sounded frightened. "Lord Aram— they must have a means of communicating with each other over distance or their hearing is better than I thought. The group to your front is alerted and they are moving to close off your line of escape. What should I do?"

"Is there any way around that you can see? Any road that is clear?"

"No, my lord, I am sorry. They are forming a crescent to your east and southeast. You must retreat. To get through them you will have to fight." The eagle's voice had risen in alarm. "And there are very many."

"Is it a single line, Alvern? Can we punch through?"

"No, my lord." The eagle was in obvious distress. "They have learned from experience. Each line is four or five deep. I am afraid for you."

Aram loosened his sword and slipped his bow into position and wondered if they should turn around and run away. Even then, though, they would be pursued and the beasts would find his valley. That thought filled him with anguish. Thaniel and Florm had slackened their speed and raised their heads in indecision. He looked back toward the south. The dark line of lashers was closely rapidly, enveloping them in a sweeping crescent of deadly intent.

Fighting through that host would be a hopeless endeavor, but he despised the thought of turning back and guiding this bloodthirsty army of monsters into his homeland. Besides, very soon their line of retreat would be closed by the lashers charging from the south. Aram sat up in an agony of doubt as the horses slowed even further. The eager howls of their enemy rolled over them in fierce waves from across the sea of grass. He glanced to the north, into the deep, dark woods beyond the river, and he remembered the bridges he'd seen from the pass.

"Alvern, is there a bridge across the river nearby?"

"Yes, my lord. Less than a mile ahead on your left. But the lashers to your front are nearer it than you. The horses run faster—but they will have to run like the wind to reach the bridge before your enemies."

Florm heard him. "We can give the effort our all, if you wish. But lord Aram, do we want to go toward the mountains of Ferros?"

"It is that or fight, or run away, my lord. Perhaps, if we can get across the river, we can yet flee to the east, through the forest. It will be difficult but they will have no advantage, either. If all else fails, maybe we can defend the bridge."

"Well, we are in it, now." Florm sounded resigned but defiant. "I would rather race them through dense woods than face them on open ground. What is your word, Thaniel, my son?"

Thaniel responded as he surged suddenly forward. "Let's make for the bridge, my lord. I would not retreat in the face of these vile beasts. We will either reach the bridge before them or fight our way through."

Aram flattened himself against the horse's neck. Florm and Thaniel surged ahead, pounding along the pavement with their heads low, every muscle in their great bodies straining. Aram glanced southward and saw that, while the lashers had closed the gap, they were falling ever so slightly behind. But eastward, toward the morning, dark shapes came rushing at them in a long unbroken line curving out of sight to the south—dozens, perhaps nearly a hundred of eager lashers, closing in for the kill.

Then he saw the bridge, a narrow stone span arching over the broad, calm river, coming up on the left. It was ravaged by time but still intact, and they were going to get there first, if only by a moment. The lashers to their front seemed to suddenly understand their quarry's intent and made straight for the bridge, unloosing their weapons as they came.

The horses swung onto the bridge just as a volley of arrows from the massed crossbows plunked into the water, while a few of the missiles rebounded off the stonework on the upstream side. One whistled savagely past Aram's head. Then they were out over the current and charging for the far shore. Fifty yards behind them, the first of the lashers entered the span.

The broad, deep waters rolled solemnly and heavily beneath them as the horses raced over the ancient stones. Beyond the bridge, the road disappeared straight into the deep green wall of the tall dark trees, cutting a narrow swath into the gloom. They clattered off the bridge and were immediately swallowed up by the denseness of the forest. Aram stared to the right, looking for an entrance into the woods to the east but the road was sunken into the soft earth and above the steep, overgrown bank, the trees grew massive and thick. Florm and Thaniel also, even as they thundered forward along the deeply shadowed roadway, studied the thick trunks for egress to the east.

Then, suddenly, the trees were gone and they were racing northward between towering walls of stone, up through the narrow hall of a dark canyon. There was nothing else that they could do but go forward. On their left was a turbulent, tumbling stream bounded on its far shore by sheer canyon walls, to their right, a perpendicular mass of rock rose away toward the dim heights, and the howling mob of lashers shouted from the narrow road behind them.

"What now?" Gasped Florm.

"Keep going." Aram said. "Maybe we'll find a gap or another bridge, someplace defensible where we can turn and fight. Or maybe this road goes up and over the mountains somewhere."

But then the road turned sharply to the right and then left again toward a dark opening in the rock and they and the small stream entered into the mountain and utter darkness. Before the horses could slide to a halt, clinging strands of soft filament, like unseen spider's webbing, came out of the night and covered them. Aram had a moment of shock and surprise as he felt consciousness leaving him, and then the world went dark and silent, and he fell gently into a welcoming abyss.

XXVII

There was no pain, or any other sensation. Slowly, ever so slowly, Aram regained awareness but only of the fact that he existed in time and space. He seemed to have no body, no arms or legs, not even a head. And he could not see. As the scope of his awareness gradually grew in strength, he began a diligent hunt through the vaults of his memory but found them barren. He did not know where he was or even why he would be anywhere at all.

Then came nausea, sudden, painful and dizzying, but it gave him a sense of physicality and substance. The nausea was followed by a sensation of dense, uncomfortable heat. And though he could not remember opening his eyes, he was suddenly aware of the existence of sight and of the fact that there was light. Dim and diffused, reddish in color, but it was light.

Tingling and pricking pain far from his center of consciousness gradually brought his extremities back from the nether regions and incorporated them into his realm of sensibility. Fingers and toes, arms and legs, they were all there and evidently uninjured. After a few minutes, because of an increasing awareness of pressure against his shoulder blades and the rear of his skull, he realized that he was lying on his back on a hard, smooth surface.

Then, at last, came memory. He remembered the flight across the bridge, running from the lashers, and the dense woods and the canyon that led into the mountain. But there, memory ran out of ground. What had happened since, he did not know. At least he was whole and seemed to be unhurt.

And he was unrestrained. No ropes bound his limbs. He blinked his eyes and something very far away—or very far over his head—gradually came into focus. It seemed to him that he was looking into the deep recesses of a concave bowl of stone. It was, in fact, he finally realized, a ceiling, an exceedingly distant ceiling of smooth, curved rock.

When he could, he rolled his head to the left and saw above him an enormous dark object supported by columns of black. His head rolled further and there was a shiny black hoof, topped by a column of black hair.

Florm's leg—or perhaps Thaniel's. He lifted his head and tried to sit up but his muscles would not respond. He lay back, gasping in the heated air. He tried his voice.

"Lord Florm?" He croaked.

"Silence, Aram." Florm whispered urgently into his mind. "Do not speak in this place."

"But where—?"

"*Please*, my lord."

Hearing terror in a voice where he was unaccustomed to hearing it, he complied and lay silently on his back, gazing up at the remote stone. As his hearing improved, he became aware of a commotion occurring somewhere beyond the vicinity of his feet. Guttural and raucous voices rose up as if out of the depths of a well. Lashers. Now he understood the terror in Florm's voice. They had been captured.

And he was lying helpless, prone, with no strength in him. But as his vitality began to return he wondered—why was he not bound? Perhaps they were confined in a cage or a pen of some kind. He rolled his head to either side, searching beyond the columns of the horse's legs, but every architectural object in view seemed to reside at a great distance from him.

Finally, after several minutes, he felt his muscles responding. Quietly and slowly, with great effort, winded and quivering with weakness, he sat up and looked around. He tried to stand but could not. His legs would not yet respond to commands from his brain. He was seated on flat stone in a nook of the wall of an enormous chamber between Florm and Thaniel. The horses were standing but with their heads lowered. The three of them were on the upper level of what appeared to be a huge underground amphitheater carved completely from living stone. Below them, in concentric, descending levels, a seemingly unending series of steps curved down and away from them in enormous semicircles.

Over their heads, the ceiling rose away to an immense height. On their left, the chamber was bounded by smooth, vertical, gently curving walls of rock. On the other side, below and to their right, rose a series of simple columns, beyond which was the indication of a vast adjoining hall and the reddish glow of fire or flame. But it was that which was on the wall directly opposite and slightly below his position that drew Aram's unmitigated and somber attention.

A throne of stone was set high on a dais protruding from the opposite wall above a vast level floor. It had been fashioned with simple, powerful lines. On it sat a being. Tall and thin, with pale gray skin and a shaven—or perhaps naturally hairless—head, he was dressed in robes of gray. His face was long and gaunt with an imposing nose and a humorless mouth. His eyes, when they moved, appeared to flash fire. He was obviously a god.

"*Ferros.*" Florm whispered as quietly as possible.

Upon the vast, level floor below Ferros, penned in by swags of heavy iron chains and watched by severe guards who resembled their master on the throne, were collected at least a hundred lashers. Most of them jostled against one another in agitated confusion, clanging their shining black horns together in a terrific tumult, but a few leaders at the front of the pack, near the throne, were expressing themselves with loud words, and gestures of anger.

The being on the throne watched them calmly and listened without response. As he sat observing them, an unceasing flurry of activity occurred to his immediate left. Creatures similar to Ferros in appearance and stature would appear suddenly from the dark doorway behind and speak into his ear or to another being that was evidently a lieutenant, standing just behind his throne.

Each would receive answers or instructions, sometimes spoken by the lieutenant, at other times indicated with a slight movement of Ferros' head or brow. Then each would turn away and seem to accelerate quickly from the limits of visible sight as they vanished through the doorway. Ferros was conducting the business of his realm even as he contemplated his prisoners below.

The lashers were imprisoned a good distance away from Aram and far below the level where he sat but he turned his head and tried to catch what they were shouting. It soon became clear that they were arguing their case. Finally, one particularly large beast angrily silenced the others and spoke impudently to the god on the throne above him.

"You have no right, Lord Ferros. We are servants of the great Manon Carnarven. If you prevent us further, you risk his anger. We were chasing his enemy when we stumbled into your trap, but I make no excuses for that. We were within our rights. Free us and give us our quarry."

Ferros stirred slightly and flames seemed to sizzle about him. "You make no excuses to me, Worven Burlgar?"

The big lasher started. "How do you know my name?"

A look of contempt crossed Ferros' face; he waved his hand in disgust and the big lasher crumpled in a heap, howling in pain. "You do not question me. And, if you wish to live, you *will* make excuses to me. Believable and acceptable excuses—and reasonable requests. Now rise."

Two other lashers helped Burlgar to his feet. He gazed up at the throne with trembling, open-mouthed fury, seemingly unable to realize his peril. "If you harm me or any of us, you will answer to the wrath of Manon."

Ferros leaned forward slightly and smiled a thin, deadly smile. "I have not spoken to my brother in centuries and I answer to nothing from him or his. Is impudence all that you have to offer me?"

Burlgar raised a bulky fist. He was quivering with rage. "My master will destroy you."

Ferros sat back with a sigh. "I think not."

He gazed upon the mass of lashers gathered below him for a long moment longer and decided that his time was being wasted. He glanced at another slim, shaven-headed lieutenant standing on a protrusion of stone a few yards away on his left. He nodded slightly. The lieutenant moved and disappeared.

Suddenly, the floor beneath the lashers gave way, sliding apart into two sections, each one slipping to either side and tilting toward the center. Flames and smoke roared up out of the pit and in a moment, the mass of gnarled bodies went howling and screaming into the fiery abyss. The floor closed again.

Ferros looked up and indicated Aram and the two horses. "Bring them."

Instantly, the tall thin servants of Ferros appeared next to them and gestured for Aram to get up and move down to the front. Aram tried to rise but could not. There was still no pain, but his muscles remained stiff and unresponsive. After watching his efforts for a moment, one of the servants of Ferros touched him on the shoulder. Something like cold fire coursed through his body, making his muscles and joints twitch and jump with pain, but afterward his limbs responded more readily to the commands of his brain.

He got up stiffly, and then he and the horses made their way laboriously down across the seemingly unending courses of stone. The immensity of the chamber around them seemed to expand as they descended. At last they stood upon the broad, level floor below the throne. The view from below Ferros only served to increase Aram's sense of insignificance.

The vaulted hall rose above them to dizzying heights, yet everything was simple and plain, monochromatic, gray in color, even the robes of Ferros and his people. Aram looked up and found the god's gaze upon him. Close up, Ferros' eyes were like burning bronze, fierce and cold. Fear entered Aram's heart. This was a being that could kill without compunction and would do so at a whim.

Then Ferros moved his attention from Aram to Florm. "Who are you?" He asked quietly.

Florm bowed his head but spoke evenly. "By your leave, my lord, I am Florm, the lord of horses."

"No." Ferros disputed him. "I know Boram, the lord of all horses. You are not he."

"Boram was my grandfather, my lord. He has gone to his long home, along with my father, Armon. They were both of them struck down in the last battle of the great war between Manon and men."

"And I suppose that you blame my brother, Manon, for these tragedies?"

Aram could feel the terrible tension of fear emanating from the great horse as he struggled with his answer. But finally, Florm lifted his head and looked up into the eyes of the god. "It was his doing, my lord, the blame is his."

"I am certain that he would dispute such a contention." Ferros smiled a cold smile, seemingly unaffected by Florm's temerity, and moved his eyes to Aram. "And who are you?"

Aram gazed back at him with a horrible feeling of utter impotence. He had no power here; he could not even call upon the strength of his own arm. The god sitting on the throne above him could no doubt reduce him to dust with a gesture. But still he would not grovel, even before this great person.

"My name is Aram, son of Clif." He said. "I am lord of nothing."

"Indeed." Ferros answered him. "And what, then, is an insect like you doing here—entering my realm uninvited?"

Aram blinked before the severe power of the flashing eyes but kept his face turned upward. "I apologize for that, my lord, but I was only running for my life, trying to avoid conflict with the lashers. I did not mean to intrude."

"But you did intrude, nonetheless."

Aram did not know how to answer and so remained quiet. Ferros studied him in silence. The god seemed puzzled; a slight frown grew in the space above his brow and gradually sent creased lines across the gray smoothness of his features. The heat grew stifling. Finally, Ferros dismissed the frown and stirred.

"Tell me, why were you running from the lashers?"

"Because they are the servants of my enemy."

Ferros smiled. "Ah, but that cannot be so. They are the servants of your god, Manon. Are you an outlaw, then?"

Aram met his gaze. "Manon is not my god."

"Nonsense." Ferros' smile disappeared. "He is the lord of all humans."

"Nay, my lord, he is our oppressor. He has deprived my people of peace and freedom for time out of mind."

"There is no such thing as time out of mind, human. I have been on this world since the beginning of its time and all that has happened upon it is still in my mind. Do not deign to inform me of what has or has not happened. There is a thing that has been true from the beginning—the Maker Himself ordained it." Ferros leaned forward. "It is this: men must be governed."

"Yes, my lord. But not enslaved. Slavery is not governance."

Ferros' eyes flashed. "I suppose you think that is a clever answer. In my presence, foolish attempts at cleverness earn a quick exit from life." He let the words sink in and then leaned back. "But I care not." His slight smile returned and he shrugged. "It is Manon's affair."

Aram felt driven to speak. "Forgive me, my lord, I do not want to seem impudent. But my life is my own affair, none other's, certainly not Manon's. And I will live freely or die defending my freedom."

"Your death can be easily managed." Ferros replied softly.

"As I have witnessed, my lord." Aram admitted and he bowed his head for a moment before looking up again. "But before you kill me, pray allow me a question."

"I do not like being questioned." Ferros answered and his posture exuded sudden menace as he gazed down at Aram. Finally, however, he shrugged and moved his hand slightly. "Alright, one question. Ask what you will."

Aram looked up into the blazing eyes. "I understand your disdain for my kind, my lord. But why did you not help Kelven in the war with Manon?"

The god studied him a long time before answering. "I will tell you, human. It is because I care for nothing that happens on the surface of the world. My domain is here, in the deep. Besides, why would I fight against my own brother?"

"I have heard you state that Manon is your brother. But you are a child of the Maker, as is Kelven. Is not he your brother as well?"

"Not like Manon." The tenor of Ferros' voice had hardened. He was losing patience but still he answered. "Manon and I were made at the same time and we are much alike."

"I would hope not, my lord."

Anger flushed through the god's gray face. "You have seen how I reward insolence. I can make your death very unpleasant and enduring, if you like."

He raised his hand and looked to his left. At that moment, the air to either side of Aram erupted in stunning bursts of light that crackled and flashed like lightning, illuminating the entire chamber as if the sun had suddenly burst in upon them. The Guardians became visible. Ferros lowered his hand, jumped to his feet and stared.

"Why did you hide yourself from me?" He demanded.

"*Forshetha, Ferros, kindretha san.*" The voices of the Guardians roared like soft thunder through the vast hall. "*El zebetha carre un deves.*"

Ferros gazed at the Guardians in astonishment for a long moment, then sat back in his chair and looked at Aram. The expression of shock on his features was obvious but despite that he did not seem unduly dismayed and his anger was gone. He glanced back at Tiberion, on Aram's right.

"*Shethesh mor en senulthca?*"

"*Non.*"

"*Eren ish sekoya fincas donen?*"

"*Shuretha. El dantha.*"

Ferros nodded and his gaze came back to rest on Aram. The brilliant light of the Guardians slowly faded from the great hall, flickered and went out. The strange, otherworldly bodies of the Guardians dissolved from view. Ferros studied his prisoner curiously.

"You have powerful friends, human."

Aram returned his gaze. "If so, I am at a loss to explain it. I did not earn their friendship, my lord. I do not know why it has been granted."

"Do you not?"

"No."

"Your words have the ring of truth." Ferros mood had undergone a subtle but profound change. When he spoke there a hint of something that was almost respect in his voice. "I believe you. But the friendship of these people has been granted to you, nonetheless, whether you earned it or not." He frowned in remembrance. "You asked me a question, young man—would you still like an answer?"

"I asked why you refused to help Kelven in the war, my lord. It should be obvious to you that Manon has frustrated the will of the Maker."

"Many creatures frustrate His will, Aram. My brother is not alone in that."

"But he is a god. He should know better."

"Perhaps," Ferros agreed mildly. "But it is not my concern."

"So you did not help because Manon is your brother?"

Ferros irritation returned, as sharp as before. "Do you not listen? I did not engage myself in those affairs because they do not concern me."

"Pardon me, my lord, but we all share the same earth."

"No, we do not. Look around you." Ferros waved a hand about the vast chamber. "This is my realm—what your kind calls the underearth. The council gave the care of it to me alone. The deep engines of the world are my concern. I care not what happens above me. Because of my work in the deep places of the earth, life is possible on the skin of this planet. If my brother cannot keep his minions in tow, I care not."

Aram looked up at him. "It is the Maker's desire that all life be vibrant and constructive. If the world above is reduced to ruin and despair—pardon me, my lord—but what is the value of all that you do?"

A cynical smile crossed Ferros' face. "So now you propose to speak for the Maker?"

"No, my lord, of course not. But isn't His will obvious?"

"And how do you know that Manon's intent is ruin and despair? The fault of that could easily lie with those that oppose him."

"The loss of freedom is ever ruin and despair," Aram answered. "Any of the Maker's creatures will oppose all attempts to put it in a cage. Manon's idea of governance is to place my people in the chains of bondage. Many of us would rather die than be enslaved."

Ferros studied him in silence for several moments. "Tell me, what will you do if I let you go?"

Aram answered honestly. "I will continue to resist, by whatever means I can find and put to use, the forces of Manon."

"A straight answer—so be it." Ferros inclined his head slightly. "Well, you must do what you must do."

"Will you not aid us, my lord?"

The god stiffened. "You press most unwisely upon the boundaries of your good fortune, little man." Ferros voice was brittle with anger. "I will not."

Aram kept his voice calm. "I do not wish to anger you, my lord. But if you release me, I will fight Manon until he is destroyed or I am. I will not consider the fact that he is your brother. My people must be free as the Maker intended."

Ferros smiled cynically. "And when they are 'free'—then I suppose that you will rule them?"

"I have not tried to see beyond the end of the war with Manon."

Ferros' smile broadened. "Oh, there is a war? Does not war require armies? Where is your army, Aram?"

"You are looking upon the beginnings of it, my lord."

Surprisingly, Ferros did not laugh. He glanced at the horses standing silently to either side and then studied Aram for several minutes longer while he stroked his chin thoughtfully with his thumb and forefinger. Finally, he stood. "You may go. Before you do, I will grant you a thing."

Aram stared up at him in surprise. "My lord?"

"I said that I will grant you something." Ferros leaned forward with his hands on the railing before his throne. "If ever you are in great peril, Aram, get underground—in a cave or even under an overhanging rock. If you can get beneath the surface of the world, my power will protect you."

"Thank you, my lord." Aram answered in amazement.

Ferros waved his hand dismissively. "I do not do it for you alone, but for the will of the Maker, as well—something that I understand most clearly, despite what you think. Now, Bendan will escort you above the earth. Go in peace and bother me no more."

He turned and was gone. One of his thin, gray servants appeared beside them. He pointed back up the many courses of concentric curving levels carved into the stone with a long arm. "That way, if you please."

Bendan escorted them up and out of the great chamber, down a long corridor and into a square vault. A door slid shut, encasing them in a small room of stone. There was a floor but no ceiling. Looking up, Aram could see only darkness above. The floor began to move. It rose upward. After a long time, during which their rate of ascent grew to a sickening speed that pushed his body to the limits of its endurance, the floor slowed and stopped. A door opened into a broad, low-ceilinged, dimly lit corridor that ran away out of sight in either direction.

Bendan looked at Aram. "East or west, my lord?"

"We have a choice?"

Bendan nodded.

"East then. Does that mean we will come out of the mountain to the east of where we entered?"

"It does." Bendan turned and led the way left along the corridor. When they crossed over a bridge spanning a small stream, he stopped and indicated the water. "Drink, sirs, if you like."

They did so gratefully. After the oppressive heat of Ferros' hall, the water was marvelously cool and refreshing. Aram filled his hands with its healing coldness and let it wash down over his head and neck. As he waited on the horses to finish, Aram looked along the corridor. Everything in Ferros' domain seemed to be built for function rather than beauty. Aram decided that it suited the god. Despite his harshness and arrogance, Ferros did not seem to suffer from the sin of indulgent pride.

After leaving the stream, they traveled eastward through the marrow of the mountain for several hours; occasionally crossing other small streams flowing from left to right through conduits in the rock. Always the stifling heat drove them to revive themselves in the cool water.

On they went through the heart of the mountain along the narrow, smooth corridor lit by reddish light, the source of which Aram could not determine. Then, at last, they came to an intersection. To the right another corridor extended away from them toward a small distant point of white light. Bendan stretched out his arm and indicated the intersecting corridor with its distant glow.

"Your world is there." He said. "You have no further need of me."

Aram bowed. "Thank you, sir. And give our thanks to your great lord."

Bendan inclined his head and turned away. He strode quickly away from them in rapidly accelerating movements and faded suddenly from view. Aram looked at Florm.

"Are you alright, my lord?"

Florm gazed toward the distant light and chuckled. "There is a lovely sight for my old eyes." He glanced at Aram. "Life is ever interesting since you came along, my friend. Yes, I am fine."

"Thaniel?"

"Yes, but I want to get out of here."

Aram nodded. "Let's get back into the sunlight."

Two hours later, they stepped from the mountain onto another road like the one that had led them inside. There was no gate or any sign that the road was anything other than a conduit leading into a mine. The light at first seemed very bright, but the sun was angled down the sky to the west and after their eyes adjusted, the tall trees cast them once again into gloom. They moved southward through the dense forest toward the river.

When they reached the river's edge and came out from under the trees, they found another bridge like the other, weathered and ancient, but solid. Aram stepped onto it and looked westward down across Vallenvale. He estimated that they'd come out of the mountain at least a hundred miles east of the point where they had entered.

The valley was a bit narrower here than farther west and when Aram turned and looked east, he could see that the southern mountain range gradually bent northward toward the mountains of Ferros, effectively pinching off the vale. A hundred miles or so east of the bridge where they stood, the vale ended and the ground began to rise toward another broad, timbered summit between two high peaks. He remembered Alvern and looked up into the sky.

Bending his mind to the effort, he called to the eagle. "Lord Alvern, are you still there?"

"I am here, my lord." Came the immediate reply. The eagle sounded overjoyed. "You have come back from the dead."

"Not exactly," Aram replied, "but near enough. Where are you?"

"I see you now, my lord. You are standing on the bridge east of me."

"Where are our enemies?"

"Most of them followed you into the earth and have not emerged. The rest waited for two days and then went back through the mountains to the west out of Vallenvale."

"Two days? How long have we been gone?"

"This is the fourth day since you went into the underearth, my lord."

Aram glanced at the horses in surprise. "Did you realize that we were gone that long?"

The horses were as perplexed as he was.

"Perhaps," suggested Florm, "time moves differently in the realm of Ferros than it does on the surface of the world."

"Perhaps, or maybe we were unconscious for most of that time. It's no great matter now." Aram glanced westward at the sun's position. "We have some daylight left. Let's get across the bridge and move on to the east. Thaniel, are you strong enough to bear me?"

"I am, my lord. I will bear you as far as you wish to go."

Aram smiled. "Let's just get back across this bridge and into our own world a ways, my friend. That will suffice for today."

XXVIII

Alvern came down out of the sky before they reached the southern bank of the river, which Florm now informed Aram had once been called Secesh. The eagle swooped low. "I am happy to report that the valley is clear of lashers in all directions. But there is a great company of wolves coming from the west. I told them of your return, my lord. They would speak with you."

Aram nodded. "We'll camp a few miles to the east of the bridge tonight. You say the valley is clear of enemies?"

"I have searched it from one end to another looking for you, my lord." The eagle answered. "There is nothing but wild creatures about, anywhere."

Aram looked up at the great bird, hovering on the wind. "Thank you, Lord Alvern. I don't know how we will ever repay you. We owe you our lives."

"Forgive me, my lord." The eagle's golden eyes gazed back at him. There was an odd intensity in the rich honey-colored depths. "But nothing could be less so. Long have I traveled the highways of the air and with sadness watched as the world fell, land by land, and people by people, into the morass of madness and misery of the grim lord of the tower.

"It seemed to me that there was no hope—that the good things of the earth would ultimately fail from it completely and despair would hold sway forever. Then I looked down one day and I saw you, struggling into the wilderness through the long valley where the river bursts from the mountain. You went into the darkness of that mountain as well and emerged again alive, just as you did today.

"I observed you as you warred with the wolves and gained mastery over them. I watched you save the life of the king of horses. I know what you did for Willet and Cree, and for many others. And then I watched you, and this great fellow here, defeat the forces of the enemy and send them into ruin. My lord, the world has changed since you came into it. Hope has returned. I am at your service ever."

The great bird flexed his magnificent wings and the wind picked him up a few feet. He glanced toward the southern mountains. "But now, my lord, if there is no further need, I would like to go home."

Aram raised his hand. "Go in peace, my friend. Thank you."

The great eagle began to soar up into the sky but then immediately returned. "My lord?"

"Yes?"

"Return to us. Whatever you find upon the great mountain, return to us."

Aram nodded solemnly. "I will return."

"Farewell, my lord."

"Farewell, lord Alvern."

With great beats of his wings, the eagle rose and sailed high into the sky and went toward the southwest. Aram watched him go.

"Do you think he will fly over the very heights of those mountains?" He asked Florm.

The old horse chuckled. "It would not surprise me."

They exited the bridge and turned toward the east and moved along the ancient road in a steady walk. It was a pleasant evening, cool but not yet cold. Aram glanced over at Florm.

"My lord, what did the Guardians say to Ferros?"

"I can't say," the horse answered. "I don't speak or understand the high language."

"They did not seem to fear him."

"No," Florm agreed, "they did not."

"To whom do they answer then, if not the gods?"

"There is only One other. They must answer to Him."

Aram stared at him. "Why would servants of the Maker Himself become guardians of a device meant for communication between your people and mine?"

"I'm sorry, lord Aram," Florm answered. "But I don't know. It is a great mystery."

They camped that night near the tumbled stone ruins of a small village. Aram built a fire. The night promised to be cool. It was late in the year and they had traveled several hundred miles northward over the curve of the world from the more temperate regions around his valley.

There was mist in the valley in the morning, heavy and cold. Aram made kolfa while the horses grazed nearby, their noses deep in the heavy, damp grass. He decided to let them eat their fill while he waited for the arrival of the wolves. Always cautious, he set his bow discreetly to one side, but close to his hand, and kept his sword in its scabbard on his back.

When the mist lifted and the sun poured into the valley through the gap in the eastern mountains, Aram found the camp ringed with hundreds of wolves. These animals were generally smaller and more compact than Durlrang's people and their fur was thicker and longer. Leorg was in the midst of them sitting on his haunches, with Gorfang at his side.

Aram stood and raised his hand, palm out. "Good morning, Leorg."

Leorg bowed his forehead to the ground. "Good morning, master."

About a third of the wolves mimicked Leorg's act of obeisance but the rest watched silently and did nothing. Aram looked around at them. They stared back at him appraisingly and the air was thick with doubt and suspicion. Leorg raised his head and spoke.

"You have come back alive from the underearth, master. Is there nothing you cannot do?"

Aram realized instantly that this was spoken for the benefit of the others. He replied evenly and without emotion.

"I came back because Ferros and I reached an understanding, Leorg."

"And your enemies?"

"They will not return."

Leorg nodded with satisfaction and glanced furtively at his companions. "Is there anything further we may do for you, lord Aram?"

Aram shook his head. "Thank you, Leorg. But there is nothing. Now we will go on to the mountain of Kelven."

Leorg let this information sink in to those around him. Then he indicated a small, black wolf seated on his left by the rangy Gorfang. "This is my cousin, Kolgar. He is lord of the wolves of this valley. My people and I will lodge with him this winter. We'll wait here for your return, master."

Aram acknowledged the new wolf with a slight nod of his head and thought that he saw something akin to shrewd calculation in Kolgar's dark brown eyes. Turning back to Leorg, he squatted down so that his head was on the same level as that of the gray wolf. "Leorg, is it true that I slew your father?"

The question surprised Leorg. Aram could see in the wolf's clever eyes that he was not certain of the turn in the conversation. But Leorg had long since decided to trust this man and he nodded. "As I heard it told, my lord, it was out on the great avenue before your city."

"So your father and his people originally inhabited my valley?"

"His people, yes—but not all of those here. Kolgar's people have always dwelt in Vallenvale. But your valley was the home of my father's tribe."

"And you are now lord of that tribe."

The wolf gazed back at him evenly. "I am."

"Then go home."

The wolf cocked his head slightly. "Master?"

"Go home, Leorg. You and your people. Go home to the lands of your fathers."

Leorg straightened his head and stared directly into Aram's face. "But that is your valley, my lord, and you drove us from there."

"Because at the time your people did not keep to the laws of Kelven. But this has changed, has it not?"

"Because of you, master, yes."

Aram stood up and looked around at the assembled wolves before he spoke. "And also because of you, lord Leorg. While most of your people fell under the evil of Manon, you did not. You always honored the laws of Kelven. Kolgar is gracious to extend to you an invitation. But it is time. There are plenty of deer for all in my valley if their populations are respected. And I know that you will respect them. Take your people and go home."

Astounded by this, Leorg stared for a moment then bent his head to the ground. One by one, slowly but surely as the meaning of Aram's words sank in, all the others did the same. "Thank you, master." Leorg answered, and his voice was thick with emotion. "You are kind. We will obey all that you have taught us."

"Good, my friend. Travel well—get home before winter." Aram turned to leave but then hesitated. "Leorg?"

"Yes, master?"

"There is a bear there. He lived in the grotto near the city wall but now has sought a new home in the hills to the north of the city. He and his family are not to be molested."

"Yes, master, we know of Borlus. We are all aware of your regard for him." Leorg's quiet laugh was quick but sincere. "We will guard him and his family."

"Good." Aram looked around again. "Watch, all of you. Watch to the west. Tell me of anything that occurs when I return. And hold always to the laws of Kelven. Farewell."

"Farewell, master." After bowing to him again, the wolves turned and glided away in small groups.

Aram broke camp, retrieved his weaponry, secured the saddle upon Thaniel's back and climbed into it, and he and the horses turned eastward into the rising sun. The broad green swath of Vallenvale stretched before and behind them. To the north rose the immense sheer wall of the mountains of Ferros. To the south were the northern ranges of the high mountains that Aram could see from the tower in his city, not as formidable as those to the north but tall and rugged nonetheless.

Two days later, they came to where the road ended in the ruins of an ancient town and began the climb up through tangled and timbered wilderness toward the saddle between the peaks. The ground rose gradually and though rocky and timbered and cut by many small tumbling streams that fed the headwaters of the Secesh, was not as difficult to negotiate as it had appeared from the valley.

For two days they climbed while behind them Vallenvale fell into the mists. On the second night they camped just below the summit of the saddle. It was cold and the clouds sagged heavily down, hiding the peaks, and gathered close to the ground. Aram started a fire in a stand of firs where the ground was flat enough that the horses could pass a reasonably comfortable night.

It snowed during the night, just a skiff, but the morning dawned clear and crisp. Aram sat close to the fire, cupping a hot mug of Findaen's kolfa in his hands. Florm came out of the trees and cast a critical eye over his clothing.

"We will pass over the summit today, lord Aram, and we will face the wind. A wind more fierce than any you have likely experienced before. Do you think that you are dressed warmly enough?"

"These are all I have, my lord, whether they are suitable or not. I am committed to climb a mountain in winter in these clothes. They will have to withstand the wind."

Florm chuckled ruefully. "To be honest, I am more worried about myself. I've been here before and I remember the wind. I was much younger then. I fully expect to be miserable and misery seems to be less if it is shared."

"I'll be as miserable as you like, my lord, if it will help. I can even complain from time to time."

"Good, because I can expect nothing in the way of commiseration from a young buck like Thaniel."

"How many sons do you have, my lord?"

"Just Thaniel." Florm answered. "Just one fine son."

Aram looked over at the younger horse. Thaniel had wandered over to the stream and lowered his nose into the clear, cold water. "He is that. As well as a good friend and a great warrior. He is a person of superior quality—your son."

"It is kind of you to say it."

"It was not kindness that prompted me, my lord," Aram answered evenly, "but honesty."

An hour later, they crossed through the saddle and came out of the trees upon a broad high plateau covered with clumps of short grasses and punctuated with spires of barren rock. The morning sun shone in cold, clear sky. They had gained several thousand feet of altitude and the mountains that bent away to the south and those that continued on along the northern border of the plateau appeared less formidable from this vantage than they had from the valley. Their frosted peaks, however, viewed at closer range, appeared, if anything, more rugged. The bitter wind blew strong in their faces and felt as though it had originated somewhere upon ice.

Aram gazed out across the plateau. The pale ground, barren between widely scattered bunches of yellow grass, was rocky, covered with broken slabs of thin, flat stone. Punching up through this bleak aspect, spires of darker rock rose up like bent and broken daggers all about the rolling country, fading beyond sight into the distance. There were no trees. If there had ever been trees on this high wild ground, Aram thought, the fierce wind would have long since blown them into wreckage and thrown them over the pass into Vallenvale.

The tops of the mountains to the north were white with snow—snow that looked as if it never left those barren peaks and slopes. The mountains to the south were also snow-covered, but Aram couldn't be certain that this wasn't the result of a recent storm. Those peaks were steep-sided and point-ed, like wolves' teeth. Thaniel had been right to call them impassable.

As they trended eastward, both ranges of mountains veered away from the broad, cold, rocky plateau and went beyond the line of sight. The plateau itself seemed to go on until it vanished over the edge of the world, until it and the mountains that angled away on both sides, and even the horizon, were at last swallowed up by the thin, icy sky.

Aram pulled at the collar of his coat and looked over at Florm. "It's a bit late in the year to be making a journey through country such as this, is it not?"

Florm chuckled even as he bent his great head and half closed his eyes against the gale. "Do not worry, my friend, there is no winter on Kelven's mountain."

"Why? Is it that much farther to the south?"

"No." Florm answered and he halted, swinging his head around to-ward the southeast. "It is because Kelven controls its weather. It is there."

Aram looked toward the southeast. Far away across the world, beyond the pale brown and yellow vastness of the plateau, a great mass, slightly darker than the pale sky behind it, rose up into the heavens. It was still so distant and so vast that it seemed almost to be a part of the sky itself.

"The mountain of Kelven." Florm said. "The mountain at the middle of the world."

Aram narrowed his eyes against the force of the wind and stared at the enormity of the thing that rose above the southeastern horizon. The mountain was so massive that his eye could not reveal it all. It was a clear morning but even so the top of the mountain extended so far into the sky that details of its summit could not begin to be resolved.

"And you want me to climb that?" He asked incredulously.

The horse looked at him. "More importantly, Kelven does. Whether you will or will not, of course, is up to you."

Aram grinned ruefully and tugged his collar higher. "Do you think I will live long enough to complete such a task?"

"It's not that high."

Aram turned to gaze once more into the southeast. He nodded slowly. "Yes, it is."

Florm laughed. "There is a road that encircles it to its summit. Oth-ers have climbed it."

"But not you."

"No, nor any horse that I am aware of. A few other men and an army of lashers have been to its summit. But your feet will be the first to scale it in more than ten millennia."

"And Kelven is up there."

"He is."

Aram pulled his gaze away from the mountain and turned to look straight into Florm's black eyes. "You told me once that he was disembodied in the last battle of the great war."

"I did." Florm agreed.

"And yet he lives?"

Florm looked at him patiently. "You must understand, Aram. The force that binds the spirit to the body, thereby keeping the body alive, is a strong and potent force, the most powerful force in the universe. It is much stronger in some than in others. In your people, for instance, it has grown very weak over the centuries. That is why your people do not live very long lives and are so easily slain.

"It was not always so. In ancient times your people lived rich and full lives encompassing hundreds of years. Many of your ancestors lived for more than a thousand. Joktan ruled for more than seventeen hundred. But Manon broke the will of your people and the life force has grown small inside you. It is not so with horses. I, myself, as you know, am almost twelve thousand years old." He chuckled as he blinked his large eyes in the face of the viciously cold wind. "And today, by the way, I feel it."

"With the gods, the force is unbreakable by any will other than their own or that of the Maker Himself. Kelven knew this when he went to war with Manon. He also knew that the only way to stop Manon was to break the force within him. Therefore, Kelven devised a plan. He intended to sacrifice himself for the good of humankind and the world.

"He thought that if he could engage Manon and his armies in close combat, he could violently disembody himself, ripping his soul from its bodily moorings in such a detonation that the resulting blast would slay Manon's army and sever Manon from his body as well. Then neither of them could be physically active in the affairs of the world. Kelven would lose his power and influence but so would Manon.

"No one knows whether rumor of Kelven's plan had reached Manon's ears or if he was simply fortunate in the fact that his own designs counteracted those of Kelven. But Manon had learned a dark skill that no one knew of or thought possible. By expending just some of his life force, he could project his image to great distances. During the wars, he often employed this dark art, seeming to appear suddenly in the midst of battles, demoralizing his enemies.

"You saw this yourself. In the battle before the walls of Derosa, such a thing almost killed you and Thaniel. And that was the result of only a small effort on his part. In times past, by immense effort, he was able to appear to be in several places at once and this helped his cause greatly.

"When it came time to confront Kelven during the siege of the Mountain, Manon put an enormous amount of himself into one singular projection, so that Kelven would see him and believe him to be present. It was a dangerous gambit. Manon had to put enough of his force into his projection that Kelven would take the bait, and yet keep enough back so that he could survive the confrontation.

"Kelven saw Manon's projection and believed it to be him, and when the battle lines closed, he destroyed himself, slaughtering every soldier in Manon's army and slaying his enemy, or so he thought. But Manon did indeed survive though he was so battered that it took him nearly a hundred centuries to recover. And after he regained much of his strength, of course, he had to rebuild his armies before he could resume his quest to dominate the world.

"Even though Kelven failed, this blow to Manon was the only reason any free peoples survived, especially those out upon the fringes. Now though, he has rebuilt a good portion of his strength and is seeking by dark means to enlarge it. Once he has brought the world to heel, he will use it to gain access to the stars. If he succeeds, the world will succumb to complete darkness and the stars themselves may go out. Hope will be forever lost for all of us."

Florm's great frame shivered from the force of the biting wind, or perhaps because of the significance of his own utterances. He looked earnestly over at Aram. "We must not let him succeed."

Aram stared up the massive slopes of the distant mountain. "I told you that I thought the riddle meant that there was a weapon to aid us in this fight. I still believe that. But if, in fact, it doesn't mean that there is a weapon—then what is to be gained by me going up to see Kelven, if indeed he is still there?"

"I don't have all the answers," Florm answered. "In truth I know very little. I only know that Kelven *is* still there for I have talked to him, and that he wants to see you. It is up to him to answer the rest of your questions."

Aram gazed at the ancient horse and slowly nodded. "Alright. Then I will go to him. Let's move on."

It took four more days of grueling travel to reach the mountain; all the time fighting the fierce wind that slashed obliquely out of the north and never once relented. There was no wood for fires and they were reduced to huddling together at night in low places of the plateau or behind the tall spires of rock. There were no trees and very little grass for the horses.

The wind, though bitterly cold, drove the moisture from their bodies. The water in Aram's canteen gave out quickly and they were forced to find and break through the frozen surfaces of ice-covered pools scattered here and there about the high plateau. And the supply of food in Aram's pack shrank alarmingly.

The mountain grew before them, day by day, until it was immensely broad and terrifyingly high. About noon of the fourth day, they came at last to the end of the plateau, arriving suddenly at the rim of an enormous crater, the walls of which fell away from their feet in a nearly sheer precipice. Here, the wind sweeping across the plateau was challenged by an equally violent rush of bitter cold that roared up and over the crater's rim.

"You can see," said Florm, gazing down the perpendicular slopes, "why we cannot accompany you. No horse can descend this."

"Indeed," Aram answered. "I don't know how I will do it."

He studied the rocky crags descending to the plain far below. Looking down slopes that angled just a few points off vertical, he wasn't sure how a descent could be accomplished. Here and there, though, there were places where the walls of rock had slid away, creating chimneys filled with loose rubble that might allow a very deliberate man to descend hand over hand, foot by careful foot, to the floor of the crater far below.

And far below, where the walls of the crater merged with the plain, the flat, arid land stretched away for fifty miles or more until it touched the base of the mountain. The plain was everywhere desolate, dry, and rocky. Here and there, plumes of smoke rose from fissures in the cracked and broken earth.

From the very center of the crater the mountain arose in an enormous mass, fifty miles at least across its base, towering into the firmament. As he stared at it, Aram could see that here and there upon its broad slopes, there were hints of dark green, as if there were trees. His eye traveled upward to where the summit seemed to merge with the distant sky.

"Winter will catch me long before I scale that." He said as he dismounted from Thaniel's back.

"I told you, Aram." Florm answered. "There is no winter on Kelven's mountain." He stepped back from the rim of the crater, out of the cold wind rising from the plains far below. "Although it will soon be upon us here in force. It is time to part, my friend."

Aram met the horse's gaze for a long moment without speaking. Then he looked quickly away as his eyes suddenly filled and his heart threatened to burst with emotion. He drew in several deep breaths of the frigid air, lifted his pack to his shoulders and slipped his bow and one quiver of arrows over his head. He studied the rocky slope below him for the best way down. Then he looked back at Florm.

"Will you be here when I return?"

"No." Florm shook his great black head. "We cannot winter in this high country. We must return to the shelter of your valley at the very least—and if there is time and the passes are not closed, to our own lands. But you have the Call, Aram. Use it when you descend the mountain and Thaniel and I will hurry to meet you here or out upon the plateau. Don't delay your return beyond the spring. Every day the world slips further into peril."

Aram nodded and adjusted his pack. "Perhaps, my lord, I will return with something that can turn the tide of all our fortunes."

He stood for a moment with one hand on the arched neck of his ancient friend, and the other on the muscular shoulder of Thaniel. Then he slipped over the rim of the crater and began his descent down the rocky slope toward the wide, arid plain and the vast bulk of the mountain rising beyond.

End Book One

1116621

Made in the USA